JOSH

"ALL I CAN THINK ABOUT IS THIS."

Josh fought to keep the kiss soft as he felt Sierra sink into it with a sigh, wrapping her arms around his waist and leaning into him. But the taste of her, as fresh and clean as a mountain stream, had him wanting more. So much more.

On a moan of pleasure he took the kiss deeper, and his hands began moving up her sides until his thumbs encountered the soft swell of her breasts.

He heard her little gasp of shock as her body reacted in a purely sensual way, pressing against him until he could feel the imprint of every line and curve inside his own body.

Dear heaven, she felt so good here in his arms...

Raves for R. C. Ryan's Novels

Quinn

"Ryan takes readers to Big Sky country in a big way with her vivid visual dialogue as she gives us a touching love story with a mystery subplot. The characters, some good and one evil, will stay with you long after the book is closed." —*RT Book Reviews*

"*Quinn* is a satisfying read. R. C. Ryan is an accomplished and experienced storyteller. And if you enjoy contemporary cowboys in a similar vein to Linda Lael Miller, you'll enjoy this." —GoodReads.com

"Engaging... Ryan paints a picturesque image of the rugged landscape and the boisterous, loving, close-knit Conway family."   —*Publishers Weekly*

"I thoroughly enjoyed reading about the Conway family and their ranch. Each of the brothers was interesting in different ways and it will be fun to read their stories... a wonderful introduction to a new trilogy that looks to be unique and full of surprises."

—NightOwlReviews.com

Montana Glory

"The child adds a lovely emotional element to the story, the secondary romance is enjoyable, and all loose ends are nicely tied up."   —*RT Book Reviews*

"[The Montana Trilogy] is a good series of hunky cowboys and nail-biting mystery. Zane and Riley have great chemistry and are a read that you can't put down."

—*Parkersburg News and Sentinel* (WV)

"These not-to-be-missed books are guaranteed to warm your heart!"   —FreshFiction.com

"Ms. Ryan did an amazing job keeping the story line at a perfect pace... A standalone novel, but I would definitely recommend you grab the other two... because I promise you will love them, too!"

—TheRomanceReadersConnection.com

"Wonderful romantic suspense tale starring a courageous heroine who is a lioness protecting her cub and a reluctant knight in shining armor…a terrific taut thriller."

—GenreGoRoundReviews.blogspot.com

Montana Destiny

"5 Stars! Watching this wild rebel and independent woman attempt to coexist was so much fun…The author, R. C. Ryan, delivers an ongoing, tantalizing mystery suspense with heartwarming romance. Sinfully yummy!"

—HuntressReviews.com

"Ryan's amazing genius at creating characters with heartfelt emotions, wit, and passion is awe-inspiring. I can't wait until *Montana Glory* comes out…so that I can revisit the McCord family!"

—TheRomanceReadersConnection.com

"The series continues to intrigue, and each page brings you closer to finding the treasure. Another terrific story from R. C. Ryan."

—SingleTitles.com

"[A] wonderful series…I couldn't put this book down. I can't wait until Zane's story comes out."

—NightOwlReviews.com

Montana Legacy

A *Cosmopolitan* "Red Hot Read"

"A captivating start to a new series."   —*BookPage*

"Heart-melting sensuality...this engaging story skill-fully refreshes a classic trilogy pattern and sets the stage for the stories to come."   —*Library Journal*

"Fabulous...a well-written story with fully developed characters that I easily came to care for."
                                        —HuntressReviews.com

"Delightful...Jesse and Amy are a breath of fresh air, and R. C. Ryan beautifully translates the intense feelings they stir in one another."   —SingleTitles.com

"A fresh, entertaining tale that will keep you wanting to read more...We only get tantalizing hints of Wyatt and Zane, but I can't wait to read their stories."
                                        —RomRevToday.com

JOSH

R.C. RYAN

FOREVER

NEW YORK   BOSTON

Copyright © 2012 by Ruth Ryan Langan
Excerpt from *Quinn* Copyright © 2011 by Ruth Ryan Langan
Excerpt from *Jake* Copyright © 2012 by Ruth Ryan Langan

Forever
Hachette Book Group
237 Park Avenue
New York, NY 10017

www.HachetteBookGroup.com

Printed in the United States of America

First Edition: September 2012
10 9 8 7 6 5 4 3 2 1

OPM

Forever is an imprint of Grand Central Publishing.
The Forever name and logo are trademarks of Hachette Book Group, Inc.

The Hachette Speakers Bureau provides a wide range of authors for speaking events. To find out more, go to www.hachettespeakersbureau.com or call (866) 376-6591.

The publisher is not responsible for websites (or their content) that are not owned by the publisher.

For my beautiful daughter-in-law Patty Langan,
whose tales of hiking the Grand Canyon enchant
those of us who remain earthbound.

And for Tom, who makes my heart soar with the eagles.

JOSH

PROLOGUE

Conway ranch—Wyoming—1990

Quinn." Cole Conway, weary from a day of unrelenting ranch chores, paused in the mudroom to roll his plaid shirt to the elbows before scrubbing the grime from his hands. "Go fetch your brothers for supper."

"Yes, sir." As the oldest of Cole's three sons, twelve-year-old Quinn was accustomed to running and fetching. He saw it as part of his responsibility to his younger brothers, especially since the mysterious disappearance of their mother, Seraphine.

He hurried to the barn, where he found seven-year-old Jake struggling to unsaddle his pony. While he helped, Quinn glanced around the cavernous building. "Where's Josh?"

Jake shrugged. "Don't know. Haven't seen him."

Quinn tossed the saddle over the side of the stall. "Better get inside. Pa's ready to eat."

When Jake hurried away, Quinn searched the barn, then made his way to the house, where he climbed the stairs to Josh's bedroom.

Standing in the open doorway he called, "Josh. Better hurry downstairs. Pa's hungry."

His words were greeted by an ominous silence.

He started across the room toward the bathroom, when a scrap of notepaper in the middle of the bed caught his eye. He picked it up, scanned the words, then raced down the stairs and into the kitchen, where the rest of his family was gathered.

Old Ela, a member of the Arapaho nation, who had been with the family for nearly forty years, was cutting warm corn bread into squares. Phoebe Hogan, their newly hired housekeeper, was placing a platter of steaming roast beef, potatoes, and gravy in the center of the big trestle table. Cole and his father, Big Jim, stood on the far side of the room, before a roaring fire, sharing a beer and an animated conversation.

Cole looked up. "Quinn, I told you to fetch—"

"He's gone." Quinn paused to catch his breath.

Cole looked annoyed at this disruption of their routine. "What's that supposed to mean?"

"Josh is gone, Pa." Quinn held up the scrap of paper. "I found this note on his bed."

Cole crossed the room in quick strides and snatched the paper from his son's hand. After reading it, he passed it to Big Jim.

As he read the words, the older man's eyes narrowed in concentration.

Cole turned away, muttering every rich, ripe oath he could think of. "When I get hold of that boy, he won't be able to sit down for a—"

"Hold on." Big Jim put a hand on his son's arm. "You stay here. I'll go after him."

"That note says only that he's gone to the mountain." Cole glanced out the window at the Teton mountains towering in the distance. "He could be anywhere."

"He can't be too far ahead. He was mucking stalls less than an hour ago. You stay with your boys. I'll find him."

Before Cole could argue, Big Jim snagged a handful of corn bread and some slices of roast beef, which he stuffed into a plastic bag before striding out the door.

Along the way he grabbed his parka and one for Josh. Though the spring days were shirtsleeve weather, the nights, especially in the mountains, grew downright frigid after sundown.

Though he would have preferred the comfort of his truck, he saddled the big bay, knowing a vehicle would never make it where he was headed.

He pulled himself into the saddle and prayed that the light would last another couple of hours. Just until he could find one ten-year-old boy who'd taken himself off to the mountains to brood.

There weren't many things left in this world that frightened Big Jim Conway. He'd been little more than a boy when he'd left Ireland to seek a life in this brave new land. He'd buried a wife and five sons, and had raised his only surviving son on his own. He'd faced the fierce whims of Wyoming weather, had turned extreme poverty into extreme wealth, taming this wilderness and making his ranch one of the finest in the country. And he'd done it all his way, by the sweat of his own brow. But the words scribbled on the scrap of paper by his middle grandson had him running scared.

I've gone off to the mountain.

It was so like Josh. The boy had always been the rebel of the family. The rule breaker. The independent thinker. The loner.

Big Jim had no idea why the Tetons, towering over their land, called to the boy. But they seemed to hold some sort of power over him. Whenever Josh could manage to slip away, his family knew they could find him somewhere in those hills, climbing. Always climbing. And each time he climbed, he went higher than the time before, without regard to the perils that lurked.

That was what had Big Jim so afraid. The boy had no fear. Not of the cougars that roamed the higher elevations, nor the storms that often blew in without warning, covering the mountains with wind and sleet and snow. A boy of ten wouldn't give a thought to the fact that a single misstep could cause him to fall hundreds of feet into an abyss where he might never be found, or leave him with crippling injuries that could cause him to be paralyzed for life.

All these fears played through Big Jim's mind as he tethered his horse and began making his way along the steep trail, picking up an occasional thread or torn scrap of fabric that told him Josh had passed this way.

He looked up at the spectacular sunset, unable to appreciate its beauty. To Big Jim it meant only that dusk would soon be upon the land, making his task even more perilous.

He rounded a bend and spotted a lone figure sitting on a shelf of rock overlooking the land to the west.

The sight of his grandson left him weak with relief, and he took a moment to study the boy, his knees drawn up, arms around them, a pensive look on his face.

Big Jim took a deep, calming breath before striding closer and sitting down beside him.

Josh barely spared him a sideways glance.

"Your pa was worried, boyo."

"No need. I'm fine."

"It's late. A lot can happen on this mountain."

"I know how to take care of myself."

"Yes, you do." Big Jim leaned his back against a rock and turned his head to study the boy beside him. "Feel like talking?"

Josh shrugged. "Why bother? Nobody ever listens."

"I'm here. I'm listening."

The silence stretched out for so long, the old man began to think he'd made a mistake intruding on his grandson's solitude.

Then, haltingly at first, the words began to tumble out of Josh's mouth.

"Nobody ever talks about Mom."

"It's painful to talk about her. Ever since she went missing, your pa's heart's been broken. To cover it up, he turns to work, hoping if he pushes himself far enough and hard enough, it won't hurt so much."

"What about my heart? And Quinn's? And Jake's? How're we supposed to keep on going without ever seeing her again?"

And there it was. Out in the open. All the nerves exposed and raw.

Big Jim prayed for the right words.

"I know your hearts are all broken, boyo. I know a thing or two about a broken heart. I learned a long time ago that it's the price we have to pay for loving someone. When the time comes to let them go, we're never ready. But it isn't our choice. It's up to the Almighty."

"Are you saying God took my mom? 'Cause if that's

so, why can't we find her body? Or is God really some evil spirit, like Ela's Arapaho spirits?"

Dangerous territory, Big Jim thought. But he had no choice now but to plow ahead.

"As far as I know, Ela's native spirits don't do harm. As for the Almighty, I've always thought of him like a father. Tough, but fair. Loving, but always expecting us to do the right thing."

"And if we don't? What if we do something bad? Is that why Mom is gone?"

Big Jim lay a hand over his grandson's. "Don't ever think that. Bad things don't happen to us as punishment for something we did or didn't do. They just happen. They're part of life. They happen to good people and bad. As for your mom, we don't know if she's dead or just missing. The fact that she disappeared without a trace left more questions than answers. I wish I could make you a promise, but I can't. We may never know what happened. But we're trying, boyo. Your pa's hired a team of private investigators, and the police chief has the state police working on it. Chief Fletcher said that if they believe your mom crossed out of Wyoming, we can count on the FBI to lend a hand. But for now, we have to carry on with our lives. You know that's what your mom would want for all of us. To get up every morning, put one foot in front of the other, and do the best we can."

"But it's like she was never in our lives now. Pa never talks about her."

"He can't, son. He's tried, but every time he does, he breaks down. He doesn't want you boys to see him cry. That's why he takes himself out to the barns, or up to the hills, to work off his grief." Big Jim cleared the lump from his throat. "But she'll always be in our lives. Your daddy only has to look at you and he sees her. In your eyes. In the shape of your face, the tilt of your head, the jut of your chin. And know this, boyo. I give you my solemn promise. From now on, whenever you or your brothers want to talk, I'll be here to listen." In the silence that followed he closed his hand over his grandson's shoulder and squeezed. "You hear me?"

"Yes, sir."

"Good. Good." The old man let out a long, slow breath and realized that it was the most he'd ever said about the terrible loss that had them all reeling. And though he'd been forced into it, it had been good to finally get it out. Like cutting open a festering wound and letting the poison seep out.

He leaned his back against the stone and allowed himself to admire the sky streaked with deep red and pink and purple, and to relish the silence that had settled over the land as darkness descended.

"This is a good place, boyo. You come here a lot?"

The boy remained pensive, but some of the tension had slipped from his hunched shoulders.

He nodded. "It's my thinking place. Sometimes, when I'm up here, I swear I can hear Mom telling me what to do."

"You'll make her proud, I'm thinking. You've got some very special talents, boyo."

Josh's head swiveled. "I do?"

"Yeah. There aren't many lads who can climb this mountain the way you do. Not many, I'd wager, with your fearlessness. You have the sort of pioneer spirit that built this great land. You just keep on honing your skills, and your future is going to be bright."

He could see that his words touched the boy's heart and seemed to settle deep in his soul.

Seeing the boy relax, Big Jim pulled on his parka, and handed one to his grandson. Then he withdrew the plastic bag from his pocket and shared the corn bread and beef, wishing he had a tumbler of good Irish whiskey to wash it down.

At last, warm, replete, content, the smile came to Josh's face. That same wide slice of mouth that was so like Seraphine's, crinkling the eyes, putting a light in them. A smile that could brighten the darkest hour. "Thanks, Big Jim."

The old man knew Josh wasn't thanking him for the food, but for something much deeper. A chance to be heard. A chance to share a real conversation. A chance to know that he mattered. That he was valued.

"You're welcome, boyo."

The old man and the boy remained there for what seemed like hours before they began the slow descent.

When they reached the tethered horse, Big Jim pulled himself into the saddle and his grandson climbed up behind him, wrapping his arms around the old man's waist and pressing his cheek against his broad back.

They never again spoke about the incident, but a very special bond was formed between the old man and his middle grandson during that time shared on the mountain.

CHAPTER ONE

Conway ranch—Present Day

Hoo boy." Josh Conway, fresh from morning chores in the barn, shook the rain from his dark, shaggy hair before hanging a sodden rain slicker on a hook in the mudroom. He bent to wash his hands at the big sink, and stepped into the kitchen of the family ranch. "Rain's coming down out there like the storm of the century."

"That's what it looks like to me, boyo." Big Jim was standing by the window sipping coffee and watching dark clouds boiling around the peaks of the Tetons in the distance. Jagged slices of lightning illuminated the ever-darkening sky and turned the leaves of the cottonwoods to burnished gold.

Though it was early autumn in Wyoming, there was a bite to the air, hinting at what was to come.

"Do I smell corn bread? Now that ought to brighten my day." Josh made a beeline for the counter beside the oven, where Ela was cutting a pan of her corn bread into squares.

"Wait for the others." The old Arapaho woman rapped his knuckles with her wooden spoon, but she couldn't help grinning as he stuffed a huge slice in his mouth before turning away to snag a glass of orange juice from a tray.

Cole, who had been going over financial papers in his office, paused in the doorway just as Quinn and his new bride, Cheyenne, came striding in, arm in arm.

"Good," Quinn said in a loud stage whisper. "They haven't finished breakfast yet."

"Haven't even started." Phoebe, the family's longtime housekeeper, hurried across the room to hug them both.

After the disappearance of their mother, she had been hired to help Ela with the household and to help raise the three boys. A young widow herself, she'd sold her hardscrabble ranch and moved in to become their trusted friend and confidante, and their biggest supporter as they'd made the difficult journey through childhood and adolescence. Now, looking at the grown men she'd helped raise, she was as proud as a mother hen.

"And you just happened to be in the neighborhood," Josh deadpanned.

"That's right." Quinn helped himself to a cup of steaming coffee. "After morning chores at Cheyenne's ranch, we figured we'd amble over here and see if you needed any help."

"Amble? Bro, you had to drive a hundred miles an hour to get here in time for breakfast." Jake, their youngest brother, and the family prankster, stepped in from the mudroom, his sleeves rolled to the elbows, his hair wet and slick from the downpour.

Cheyenne shared a smile with her husband. "I told you

they wouldn't buy the story that we just happened to be in the neighborhood."

"The only thing that happens to be in this neighborhood is Conway cattle," Big Jim said with a chuckle. "And maybe a few of Quinn's wolves and Cheyenne's mustangs."

"I'm betting they'd start a stampede for some of Ela's corn bread."

At Quinn's remark, they all laughed louder.

"That's one of the reasons we're here." Quinn turned to Ela. "Cheyenne and I have used your recipe, but it never turns out like yours."

Josh winked at his new sister-in-law. "I bet she left out a key ingredient, just so you'd always have to come back here to get the best."

"You see, Ela?" Jake was grinning from ear to ear. "I told you it would work."

They all joined in the laughter.

"Sit down, everybody."

At Phoebe's invitation they gathered around the big wooden trestle table and began passing platters of ham and eggs, potatoes fried with onions and peppers, and Ela's corn bread, as well as an ample supply of wild strawberry preserves, a favorite of Big Jim's.

Phoebe circled the table, topping off their cups of coffee.

Jake filled his plate before handing the platter to Josh. "Big Jim and I are heading up to the hills after breakfast."

"You're heading right into the storm," Josh remarked.

"Yeah. I've been watching those clouds." Jake nodded toward the window, where the sky had been growing murkier by the hour. "Want to come along, bro?"

Josh helped himself to eggs. "Sure. A little rain doesn't bother me. I can lend a hand. You doctoring some cattle, Doc Conway?"

Jake nodded. "Pretty routine stuff. But the work goes a lot faster with an extra pair of hands."

When Josh's cell phone rang, he idly glanced at the caller ID. His voice took on a businesslike tone as he answered. "Josh Conway." He listened in silence before saying, "Okay. I'm on it."

As he tucked his phone into his shirt pocket, he turned to Jake with a grin. "Guess I'll have to take a pass on going along with you and Big Jim. I'm needed on the mountain."

Cole shook his head. "I wouldn't want to climb those peaks in this storm. How come they never call on you to climb on a sunny day?"

"I guess because no fool hiker ever gets himself lost in good weather, Pa." Josh drained his cup and pushed away from the table. "I think it's some kind of rule of the universe that every careless hiker in the world decides to climb the Tetons just before the biggest storm of the century blows through."

He left the room to fetch his gear, which he always kept packed and ready for emergency calls. Through the years Josh Conway had built a reputation as a fearless, dependable climber who could be counted on to locate lost hikers who couldn't be found by the rangers.

When he returned to the kitchen, Phoebe handed him a zippered, insulated bag.

At his arched brow she merely smiled. "Something to eat on the drive to your mountain."

"Thanks, Phoebe." He brushed a kiss over her cheek

before giving a salute to the rest of his family. "See you soon."

"Take care, boyo," Big Jim said gruffly as Josh turned to leave the room.

Big Jim listened as his grandson's footsteps echoed through the mudroom and out the back door and then glanced at his family gathered around the table. Though their conversation had resumed, it was muted. And though they never spoke of it, every one of them knew that there was no such thing as a routine climb. Not when the one doing the climbing was there because the professionals had already tried, without success, to find a missing hiker.

Josh was their last resort. The strong, capable loner who would never give up until the one who was lost was found.

See you soon.

Josh's parting words played through Big Jim's mind.

Funny, he thought, that ever since Seraphine disappeared all those years ago, none of them could ever bring themselves to say good-bye.

Maybe it was just as well.

Good-bye seemed so final.

"The missing hiker's named Sierra Moore." Mitch Carver, a ranger who had been working the Teton Range for over twenty years, tipped back his chair and idly tapped a pen against the desktop, the only sign of his agitation. "A professional photographer and veteran hiker. When she filled out the required backcountry use permit, she was warned of possible storms in the area, and she said she was hoping to capture them on film. I didn't think much of it until she failed to check in with our station. I tried her contact number, and she never responded. It could mean that she simply forgot to power up her cell. Or the storm may have knocked out any chance of a signal. But her lack of response could mean she's in trouble. And since she didn't fill out the names of any friends or family to contact, I decided to send Lee to track her. But she wasn't found in the area where she'd said she was heading." He glanced at the papers she'd filled out. "Midlevel, possibly climbing as high as the western ridge."

"Lee knows his stuff." Josh had worked with rangers Mitch Carver and Lee Haddon for years, and was comfortable that neither of them would ask his help unless they were convinced that they'd chased every lead they could.

Mitch returned to his pen tapping. "Lee found no trace of her. None of the rangers spotted her. So far she hasn't taken advantage of any of the rest areas or campsites, though they're all on alert to watch for her. It's like she just vanished."

Vanished.

Josh felt the quick little shiver that passed through him and resented the fact that even now, all these years later, the word could have this effect on him.

"Okay." He forced himself to relax. "We know she's somewhere on the mountain. And with the storm, she's probably hunkered down somewhere until it blows over. Mark all the places that Lee hiked, and I'll chart a different route."

Mitch handed over the map with a highlighted overlay.

Seeing Josh's arched brow, he grinned. "After all these years, I'm pretty good at anticipating what you'll ask for."

Josh studied the trail taken by Lee Haddon. It was the logical path to the area the missing hiker had indicated. That meant that she'd been sidetracked along the way, or had chosen to climb higher than she'd first planned. The latter seemed unlikely, considering the fierce storms she must be dealing with. But he had to consider every possibility.

He began making a mental trail of his own. Though most hikers came to these mountains once or twice in their lives, this was Josh's home turf. He didn't need a physical map to tell him where every peak, every dangerous dip, curve, and valley lay.

The storm changed everything, though. Here at ground level, he had to contend with only thunder, lightning, and heavy rain. If forced to climb to the higher elevations, that would change to snow and sleet and tremendous winds.

Josh picked up his gear and strode to the door of the ranger's office. "I'll be in contact."

"I know you will." Mitch Carver lifted his hand in a salute as the door closed.

Josh had been climbing steadily for hours. And though he'd found no trail, not even a trace of another human being, he continued on.

As he'd suspected, the rain had turned to sleet in the higher elevations and now had turned to a bitter snow driven by an even more furious, blinding wind. It whistled up the side of the mountain, flinging a sudden spray of ice and snow in his eyes, like a slap in the face.

He needed to stop for the day and make camp. His muscles were beginning to protest the extra effort it took to climb over slick, ice-covered rock. His fingers had long ago lost all feeling. Despite the protective glasses, his eyes burned from the constant buffeting of wind and snow.

When he arrived at a flat stretch of space between two towering peaks, he lowered his pack and used it as a seat while he fumbled with his cell phone.

Hearing Mitch's voice, he said, "Good. At least I have service here. I was afraid I was too high to get through."

"You're fading. I'll probably lose you any second now. Any sign of our hiker?"

"Not yet. I'm at the North Ridge."

"That high? You've been doing some serious climbing, my friend."

Josh laughed. "I'm going to call it a day. Make camp here, then start a horizontal tomorrow before deciding if I want to go any higher."

"Okay. Stay in touch."

"You do the same."

He tucked away his cell phone and began looking around for a spot to set up his small tent.

The wind had picked up to nearly gale force, kicking up snow in little funnels that were nearly blinding.

He blinked, wondering if his eyes were playing tricks on him. When he looked a second time, he knew that what he was seeing was real. A small white bubble tent was snugged up against a snow-covered peak, making it almost invisible. Had it not been for the extreme wind, causing it to shimmer with each sudden blast, it would have been impossible to see. Almost, he thought, as though it had been deliberately set up that way to deceive the eye.

At the same moment, a strange thought leapt unbidden into his mind.

Was this how his mother had been able to leave without a trace? Had she yearned for a new life, far from the demands of a husband and sons and the loneliness of ranching, using camouflage to make her escape across the mountains?

Almost as soon as the thought formed, he banished it from his mind. His memories of his mother, though distant and scattered, were happy ones. Seraphine had been a loving, though unconventional, mother. She neither cooked nor cleaned, but she had happily read to her sons, and played classical music, and directed them in plays and musicals for hours on end. When her boys grew weary and insisted on doing the things boys loved, playing outside or riding their ponies, she would simply take her books and music outdoors and watch them from a nearby hill.

Though she was athletic, with a lithe, sinewy dancer's body, she never took part in any of their outdoor activities that Josh could recall. That told him that she would have never resorted to climbing these mountains.

Josh had never seen her unhappy or moody or less than exuberant about life. She would often tell her boys that while she missed the thrill of dancing onstage and the adulation of the audience, she didn't miss the gypsy lifestyle, living in dingy hotel rooms, traveling from town to town. She seemed to genuinely love being a rancher's wife and their mother, and she had treasured being anchored by their big, comfortable home and the sprawling land around it.

But there had never been an explanation for the fact that she vanished without a trace. There had been only theories.

The code of silence that had descended upon the

family prevented any of them from knowing just what Cole Conway believed to be true. Did he suspect desertion by an unfaithful wife? Foul play? An alien abduction?

Josh pulled himself back from the thoughts that had plagued him for a lifetime. He forced himself back to the present and the job at hand.

If, as he suspected, this was the tent of Sierra Moore, his task had just become a lot simpler than he'd imagined.

Hopefully the saga of the missing climber would have a happy conclusion, and by this time tomorrow he would be enjoying another helping of Ela's corn bread.

CHAPTER TWO

———◆———

Josh got to his feet and hefted his pack before facing into the storm. At this elevation, it was much worse than it had been below. Wind whipped about, causing him to bend almost double as he crossed to the snow-covered wall of rock.

Outside the small tent he dropped his gear and cupped his hands to his mouth.

"Hello in the tent."

He paused a beat, hoping to hear a voice above the sound of the roaring wind. Hearing nothing, he unzipped the flap and stepped inside, bracing for the sight of a frightened and possibly injured female, cowering from the wrath of such a fierce storm howling around her.

With his first step he felt something shoved roughly between his shoulder blades, and a sultry voice that was barely a whisper above the roar of the wind.

"State your business. If you make any sudden moves, I'll shoot you where you stand."

"Hold on now." He lifted his hands, while his gaze swept the tiny space. There was a bedroll and a portable cookstove casting an eerie, flickering light. "I'm searching for Sierra Moore."

"Why? Who sent you?"

"Mitch Carver, chief ranger."

"Why would the ranger—"

He moved so quickly, the words she'd been about to speak were cut off as his fingers closed like a vise around her hand and he took her down in the same instant, sending her weapon flying through the air.

"Damn you…" Her muffled comments were lost in the sound of their fierce scuffle.

Josh gave a hiss of pain when she sank her teeth into his hand and another as her knee landed in his groin. Despite her furious attempts to fight him, she was no match for his size and physical strength.

He quickly subdued her, straddling her and locking her arms above her head in an iron grip.

"Now, as I see it, you have two choices." He was breathing hard. "You can keep fighting me, in which case you'll wear yourself out and I'll eventually subdue you anyway, or you can promise to hear me out without any more attempts at violence. After which, if you're not satisfied with my explanation, I'll be more than happy to leave." He stared down into her eyes, which were narrowed on him with utter contempt. "Your call."

From between clenched teeth she said, "I'll listen. But only after you let me go."

He eased his grip on her hands, and got carefully to his feet. When he offered her a hand up, she ignored it, and got to her knees, before standing and facing him.

She was dressed all in black, from her skintight leggings to the black turtleneck, revealing a reed-slender body and long, long legs. Straight, waist-length blond hair fell in disarray around a face that would have looked right at home in a toothpaste commercial, with high cheekbones, porcelain skin, and dark lashes outlining golden-flecked blue eyes that were, at the moment, staring daggers at him.

He saw the way she darted a glance downward, as though searching for her weapon. "Don't even think about going for it. I'm not here to hurt you."

She crossed her arms over her heaving chest and fixed him with a hateful look. Her voice was soft and breathy from their skirmish.

"If that's true, say your piece and leave me alone."

"Happy to." He indicated the tiny cooker. "That throws a lot of heat." He was sweating, and he wasn't sure whether it was because of the exertion from the fight, the heat of the tent, or the heat generated by this female.

She wasn't at all what he'd been expecting. She was the exact opposite of a timid, frightened female. Because of the rugged location, he'd assumed she would be athletic, and she was. Everything else was just a bonus, especially those eyes. Right now they were narrowed on him with such fury, he could imagine them shooting bullets through his heart.

"Whenever a storm hits, it's the job of the rangers to make certain that all the hikers in their district are safe."

He waited for her to say something.

Instead, she held her silence until he added sarcastically, "In case you haven't noticed, the mountains have been hit with a hell of a storm. Mitch Carver tried unsuccessfully to reach you by phone before asking his rangers to fan out to search for you. But as you know, you weren't where you said you'd be, and that caused alarm bells to ring in the mind of every ranger on this mountain."

She said nothing in her own defense, though her eyes had turned to pale icy chips.

"Mitch and his rangers take great pride in their work, even when careless climbers don't do their share. So he called on me to find you."

"You're a ranger?"

"I'm a rancher. I live in the area, and know these mountains."

"You must know them pretty well to be out hiking in this storm."

He arched a brow. "I see you noticed that it's storming. That's the reason I'm here."

She flushed slightly. "I told the ranger that I intended to get some good shots of the mountains covered in snow. When the storm started raging, I figured it was heaven-sent. The perfect opportunity to capture something that is rarely seen." She pointed to her camera. "I was just going over the shots I took, and some of them are really amazing. I could have never found these images anywhere else but here, right in the middle of it."

Josh could hear the thread of excitement and pride in her voice, a far cry from the tone she'd used with him moments earlier.

"I'm glad you got what you came here for. But that doesn't excuse the fact that you neglected to contact the ranger station to let them know you were safe. They've been trying to phone you since the storm first broke."

She glanced toward the phone lying on her bedroll. "I

never thought to check in. Sorry. If they tried calling me, I have to guess my phone isn't working."

"Mine's working just fine." Josh's patience was wearing thin as he turned slightly and retrieved his phone from his pocket. "If you didn't want to be disturbed, all you had to do was file a report with the park rangers letting them know that you wanted to be left alone, no matter what the circumstances."

Feeling something under his boot, he bent down to retrieve the weapon he'd forgotten about until this moment.

He looked up at her with a quizzical grin. "A plastic spoon?"

A sly smile teased her lips. "It was all I had time to grab before you stepped in."

He managed to swallow his laughter as he touched the speed dial for the ranger station. "Mitch? Josh Conway here. I've located Sierra Moore. Yeah. She's safe. She's also a very resourceful woman. I'll let you speak with her."

He handed over his phone.

She kept her gaze fixed on him while she spoke into his phone in that same breathy voice. "Ranger Carver? This is Sierra Moore. Yes, thank you. I'm fine. I'm sorry you felt obligated to send someone to find me. I've been so involved in my photography, I guess I neglected to check in." She listened in silence, then added, "Of course. That works for me. I can be ready to leave here in the morning. I'll tell him. And again, I'm sorry for causing you any concern."

She handed Josh his phone. "I owe you an apology, too. I'm sorry you had to be dragged out in this weather. It never occurred to me that the rangers would be searching for me. I can't say I'm sorry for my"—she couldn't stop the grin from touching the corners of her lips—"unorthodox greeting. Since I'm alone and unarmed, I needed to take precautions with a stranger invading my space. But I had no right to treat you so badly." She took in a deep breath. "Ranger Carver suggested that if I have all the photos I need, and I'm ready to leave in the morning, he would feel better if I would make the descent with you. That works for me. That is," she added, "if you have no objections to having me along."

Josh gave a grudging nod of his head. He had to admit that she'd been resourceful when faced with an intruder. The fact that she'd been so quick to apologize to both him and Mitch Carver scored points as well. Without her apology, he'd have written her off as an ungrateful diva.

"That's fine. I'd like to leave at first light."

As he opened the flap, Sierra felt the sting of the frigid night air. "It'll be a tight squeeze, but if you'd like, you can share my tent."

He gave her a long look. "I have my own gear."

"Even so..." She gave a dry laugh. "Mine's already assembled and warm as toast. I don't think I'd sleep very well knowing that I was the reason for you assembling a tent in this weather, in the dark of night. Please feel free to share mine."

Josh shrugged. "Thanks. I'll take you up on it. I'll get my gear."

Minutes later he returned and zipped the tent against the bitter cold.

He removed his parka before opening his backpack and retrieving a bedroll and an instant cooker. When he pulled out a packet of freeze-dried food, Sierra smiled.

"Like minds, I see." She held up her own packet.

"Chicken or beef?" Josh asked.

"Beef stew. Why don't I use mine? There's enough for two."

"Okay. I'll try it."

He used his bedroll for a seat and watched as she dropped the packet into the instant cooker. Within minutes the tent was filled with the wonderful aroma of beef stew, which she divided between her bowl and his.

He opened a pouch containing squares of Ela's corn bread and offered some to her.

While coffee bubbled in his instant cooker, he sat back and enjoyed his first hot meal since taking to the trail.

Sierra relaxed, displaying a radiant smile. "I really needed some hot food. And that corn bread was an added bonus. Did your wife bake it?"

"Our cook, Ela." He returned her smile. "Ela is probably as old as these mountains. She's been baking corn bread since my grandfather first came to Wyoming. She's been with us since before I was born."

"Us?"

"My father, grandfather, and two brothers."

She looked startled. "You all live together?"

"Yeah. Except for my older brother, Quinn. He recently married, and he and his bride are spending time at both her ranch and ours. I guess sooner or later they'll figure out where they intend to plant roots."

"How about you?" She glanced at his ring finger. "Are you married?"

He arched a brow. "No. You?"

She shook her head. "No, thank you. I'm married to my career."

He nodded toward her camera. "Do you photograph weddings and fancy occasions?"

"That's not at all what I'm interested in capturing. I want to use my photography as art. I hope someday to see my photographs hanging in galleries and on people's walls." She chuckled. "I think that's a look of skepticism on your face."

"Sorry if that's what you think. I guess I'm just surprised that anyone would pay good money to view a photograph of a storm in the Tetons."

"That's because you live here and can see the real thing whenever you want. You'd be surprised what people would pay good money for." She grinned. "But to answer the question you're too polite to ask... I'm not a starving artist. I make enough to get by, and that's all I need."

He laughed. "Now that's what I call fancy mind reading."

"Oh, how I wish I had such a gift. I'm not a mind reader, but I've seen that look of skepticism before. There are a lot of people who don't consider photography art."

"Sierra Moore." He spoke her name aloud and searched his memory. "I'm embarrassed to admit that I'm not familiar with your work."

"Not many people are... yet. Actually, my photographs sell better in Europe than they do here in the States. But my agent hopes to change that, starting with the pictures I'm taking on this trip."

"Then I'm glad the weather cooperated and gave you such a photogenic storm."

They shared an easy laugh.

Sierra topped off his cup and then her own before sitting back on her bedroll. With so little space between them, they were barely able to stretch out their legs without touching.

"How often are you called on to find lost climbers?"

He shrugged. "Whenever there's a real emergency. Most of the time, the rangers can handle it. But whenever they need a hand, they know I'm available."

She studied him more closely. "What do you bring to the climb that they don't have?"

Again that negligent shrug of shoulders. "I've been climbing here since I was a kid. It's my playground. I was homeschooled until high school, and whenever I had any free time, I was climbing. How about you? Where did you go to school?"

"Boarding schools in England."

"That explains the accent. How do you go from boarding school in England to climbing the Tetons? And why now?"

"School was quite some time ago. As for the timing, it seemed right. I don't have any commitments. I wanted to catch the flavor of autumn in the Tetons and, hopefully, some fierce storms. My agent is hoping to get some American galleries to take a look at my work. If the images I captured today are as good as I suspect, his job just got a lot easier."

Josh lifted his cup in a toast. "Then here's to some great pictures and a big, fat contract."

She touched the rim of her cup to his. "Thanks. I'll drink to that."

He stretched out on his bedroll, enjoying the warmth, the coffee, and the company. "How does your family feel about you climbing mountains alone?"

Her smile dissolved. "I'm a big girl now. I live my life

as I please." She stared into her cup and forced a yawn. "Sorry. I think I'm ready for lights-out. How about you?"

Josh stretched out his long legs. "Yeah. More than ready."

She reached over and turned off the battery-operated torch.

In the darkness, the only sound was the slight shuffling as they each sought a comfortable position in their sleeping bag.

And then, with the wind howling outside their tent, they were soon fast asleep.

CHAPTER THREE

———◆———

Josh awoke in the predawn darkness.

The howling winds had stilled, replaced by a silence that was as soothing as the soft breathing coming from the bedroll beside his.

Sierra Moore.

What a surprise she'd been. Gritty enough to catch him without warning when he'd first entered her tent. He'd broken his first rule, to always expect the unexpected. But who would suspect a missing hiker of threatening her rescuer with a weapon? Even if the weapon had turned out to be a useless piece of plastic.

She was a mystery. A fascinating mystery.

First of all, there was this tent, and its location, huddled against a white mountain peak, making it practically invisible. Though she claimed to be here only to photograph the mountains during a storm, he couldn't shake the suspicion that she'd been hiding out here.

Then there was her secrecy. The moment he'd mentioned her family, she'd shut down completely, leaving him to wonder just who she was and what sort of childhood she'd experienced.

Could her family be searching for her?

He quickly discarded that notion. He hadn't seen anger so much as pain in her eyes when he'd asked about her family. Still, she'd gone to great lengths to find the perfect spot to be invisible.

From the little she'd revealed, she seemed to be the complete opposite of him in every way. Where he still lived as an adult with his large and loving family, she was completely on her own.

That would explain her survival skills. She'd used whatever was handy to attack when she'd felt threatened by his unorthodox arrival at her tent.

Where he'd been homeschooled until he was old enough to drive himself to high school, Sierra had grown up in structured, demanding boarding schools, no doubt forced to abide by strict rules not of her making, living with people who weren't her family.

What would it be like, he wondered, to have no one to count on when the world came crashing down, as it often did during childhood and adolescence?

He thought about Phoebe, who had been surrogate mother to him and his brothers after their mother had disappeared. Though they thought of themselves as rugged, independent men, in truth they'd spent a lot of years turning to Phoebe when their father and Big Jim were too busy with ranch chores to listen to their problems.

It had been Phoebe who had gone with him to buy his first suit, for the prom. Phoebe who had painstakingly taught him the rudiments of leading a girl through the dance.

Who did a girl turn to at boarding school? Her friends, most probably. Friends who were probably just as young and inexperienced in the ways of the world.

Maybe that was why she seemed to be such an enigma. One minute she was the tough little warrior, the next she became the very civilized, proper lady, apologizing for causing any concern.

Despite her flippant comments, Josh had the sense that there was a lot she was concealing.

When he'd first found her snug and warm in her tent, he'd wanted to throttle her for being the cause of this wild-goose chase. He had every right to resent the fact that her carelessness had cost him a day on the trail. A day that he could have spent with Jake up in the hills, tending the herd. But his anger and resentment had faded when she'd expressed genuine sorrow that she'd been the cause of concern to the rangers, and regret that he'd had to leave his ranch to chase after her.

Once again he found himself thinking how mysterious and fascinating Sierra Moore really was. She had not only survived the storm but also had used it to her advantage.

Not all his climbs had such happy endings.

He was curious to see the photographs she'd taken, but decided that he had no right to ask to view them. Like any artist, she probably chose to guard her work until she'd had time to edit it and make it perfect.

He rolled to one side, determined to remain as quiet as possible, to allow her to sleep until first light.

Sierra lay in the quiet darkness and listened to the soft rustling of the man in the bedroll beside hers.

She'd been absolutely furious when Josh Conway had stepped into her tent. The thought of having her precious space invaded had her reacting like a cartoon character. What had possessed her to grab that plastic spoon? And when he'd managed to overpower her and take away her only means of defense, she'd had a moment of real panic until he'd explained his reason for being here.

The panic had been because of Sebastian. For that one brief moment she'd thought that he'd managed to track her down here. Impossible. She'd gone to great lengths to see that nobody but her best friend even knew where she was. That part of her life was behind her now. She was starting fresh.

Still, she couldn't deny that the white tent against a snow-covered wall of rock had added to her feeling of safety and invisibility.

Until Josh Conway, intrepid hero, had discovered her refuge.

Thank heavens he'd proven to be an honorable man. So honorable that she'd actually been able to sleep for a few hours, even though he was mere inches away.

Of course, it didn't hurt that he was easy on the eyes, she thought with a quick grin.

Easy on the eyes didn't come close to describing her intruder. The man was gorgeous. With all those muscles and that sexy smile, along with piercing dark eyes that had a way of making her want to blush, he could easily be mistaken for a Hollywood hunk.

But what mattered more to Sierra was the fact that he'd been easy to talk to. She'd sensed no pretense in him. Apparently he was exactly what he appeared to be: a busy rancher who was an experienced climber called in to find a lost hiker.

She'd had her fill of good-looking guys with egos. She'd take an unassuming rancher any time, thank you very much. Not that she had any romantic ideas. The last thing she needed was a romance. Even if the guy was a Greek god.

His all-too-brief mention of his life had been fascinating. She tried to imagine three generations living and working together. A grandfather, father, and sons, all sharing one house and working a ranch together.

It was so far from the life she lived, it was impossible to imagine. But this much she knew: Josh Conway was the epitome of every wild Western fantasy she'd ever enjoyed. The strong, silent, and thoroughly capable cowboy who rides up to save a damsel in distress.

Even if said damsel didn't want to be saved.

She actually chuckled at the thought.

"Something wrong?"

Josh's voice in the darkness had her head turning. "What?"

He sat up. "I thought I heard crying."

"Sorry. I was laughing."

"Ah. I misunderstood. Nobody should ever apologize for laughing. Care to share?"

Her mind raced. How could she possibly explain? "No. Just a silly thought. Did I wake you?"

"I was already awake, and trying to be quiet so you could sleep."

She was touched by his thoughtfulness and suitably impressed. She slipped out of her sleeping bag and sat up in the darkness. "Well then, we may as well enjoy some coffee and trail mix before heading out."

"Trail mix?" Josh flicked on the battery-operated torch and reached into his pack to retrieve a pouch of egg mixture and another of beef, made especially for an instant cooker. "Step aside, woman. We're going to have steak and eggs before tackling the trail."

To Sierra's delight, he was as good as his word, producing a breakfast that would fortify the hungriest mountain climber.

"Careful. Let me go first and test that ice shelf." Josh stepped around Sierra and probed the snow-frosted ice in front of them. Because of the icy trail, they'd attached cleats to their boots for traction.

Satisfied that it would take their weight, he nodded. "Okay. It's good."

With Josh leading, she carefully followed in his tracks.

The descent had been slow and treacherous, since the temperature had begun to climb, making the snow wet and the ice soft. Already they could see depressions in the snow where the runoff had begun, forming little streams and rivulets that would, when they reached the lower elevations, turn into gushing rivers.

Hearing her breathing, Josh paused and turned. "Do you need to rest?"

"Thanks. Just for a minute." Sierra dropped onto a rock and released her backpack, which weighed nearly half her body weight.

Josh eyed it warily. "That's a lot of supplies for a simple photo shoot."

She managed a smile. "There's nothing simple about hiking a mountain. I wanted to be prepared for anything. Of course, if you hadn't come along when you did, I may have stayed up here for a week or more."

"I hope you're not leaving on my account."

"Oh, but I am." She grinned. "Ranger Carver 'strongly suggested' that I accompany you down the mountain."

Josh threw back his head and laughed. "Yeah. Mitch has a way of giving suggestions that most folks wouldn't dream of ignoring."

He turned and studied the trail ahead of them, but his mind was on Sierra. She was such a contradiction. Strong enough to hike the mountain with a pack that would stagger most hikers, male or female. Yet there was an air of fragility about her, as though she would blow away in a strong wind. It wasn't a physical thing, but rather an emotional fragility. And layered over both her strength and her fragile nature was a sadness that appeared occasionally in her eyes, and a sweet, easygoing attitude that made her a joy to be around.

So far on their difficult descent, he hadn't heard her utter a single complaint.

"Oh, look." She pointed to a pool where the swiftly running water formed frothy caps on the boulders that rimmed the shore. The water reflected a mirror image of the fiery foliage above.

Moving quickly she pulled her camera from her pack and began snapping pictures.

Josh paused to enjoy the beauty of the scene, and realized that though he'd seen such a thing hundreds of times before, he'd rarely taken the time to appreciate it the way he was now, thanks to Sierra's unbridled joy at the beauty of nature all around them. She was, he thought, the perfect hiking companion. Independent enough to carry her own weight, and so fresh and exuberant her attitude was contagious. Though he'd always preferred to travel alone, he found himself enjoying her company far more than he'd expected to.

Keeping the camera dangling around her neck, Sierra adjusted her backpack. "Okay. I'm ready to move on."

He led the way, pausing often to make certain that every step of the trail was safe and secure before allowing her to follow. The last thing she needed, with all that extra weight, was to take a nasty fall that resulted in an injury.

Each time Josh paused, Sierra used the moment to snap off yet more pictures of the fiery autumn foliage that lined the trail.

Sierra trailed slowly behind Josh, grateful that he was being so thorough. The weighty pack was affecting her balance, though only minimally. If forced to move faster, she knew she could do it. She was an accomplished hiker and in excellent physical shape. Still, she was more than willing to make a slow, methodical descent. Though she told herself it was all about safety, the truth was she was in no hurry to reach the ranger station and get back to reality.

Reality. The thought was jarring. Especially after the past week.

She'd loved her time on the mountain. Appreciated the pristine beauty, the silence, the aloneness of the place. There, in her little cocoon of ice and snow, she'd felt completely insulated from the real world.

She had intended to remain for at least another week. Possibly more, if her supplies held out. The only thing she hadn't counted on was being discovered. And so, here she was, descending the mountain a week or more ahead of her timetable.

Not that it mattered. As she trailed Josh, she was convinced that the time she'd spent on the mountain had been enough to get the pictures she'd wanted, and to let the dizzying pace of her life prior to arriving here slip away.

Dizzying pace. It was too mild a term. Her life the past few months had been chaos. But there was no looking back now. She refused to think about the fact that she had left everything familiar behind. This was her clean slate. A whole new world that she was about to explore, to see whether or not it suited her.

"You okay?"

At Josh's words she put aside the disquieting thoughts and forced her mind back to the task at hand.

She adjusted her heavy pack and stepped up her pace. "I'm keeping up. Don't worry. I'm fine."

"Yes, you are." He surprised her by waiting until she was beside him. "I have to admit, when I first saw the size and weight of your backpack, I was pretty sure I'd be recruited to carry it before we were halfway down."

She shot him an offended look. "Oh, please. You're not going to pull that me-Tarzan-you-Jane nonsense, are you?"

He pretended to take an arrow to his heart. "Ouch. Great aim. You just shot me down."

She grinned at his humor. "I'll have you know I've carried packs heavier than this, and I've never resorted to asking a guy for help."

"Uh-huh. I get it. I am woman, hear me roar?"

That had her laughing out loud. "Now you're getting the message."

"Loud and clear."

As they rounded a bend in the trail, he pointed. "The ranger station is down that path. We should be there in half an hour." He shot her a sideways glance. "If you think you can hold out for that long."

"Careful, Conway. I might dare you to a race."

He threw back his head and roared. "I'm thinking with your attitude you just might beat me."

"Count on it."

She moved past him and, to prove her point, led the way for the rest of the trek.

CHAPTER FOUR

Mitch Carver looked Sierra up and down as she and Josh stepped inside his office. "Well, Miss Moore. You don't look any the worse for your time in the storm."

"I'm sorry I caused so much concern. I never felt that I was in any trouble."

"That's good. We like our guests to feel safe, and stay safe on the mountain. But when you didn't check in, we got nervous. Especially since you were climbing alone, you weren't where you said you'd be, and my rangers couldn't locate you anywhere in that area. When those things happen, Josh Conway is our go-to guy. He's even been known to find needles in haystacks." The ranger glanced at Josh. "You made good time."

"Sierra's a good hiker."

She flushed. "Thanks. I was determined not to take up any more of your time than I already have." She unhooked her backpack and realized what a relief it was to be free of it. Then she flexed her neck and shoulders. "After all this, I think a good soak in a hot tub will be just what the doctor ordered."

"Sounds like a good prescription, Miss Moore." Mitch Carver steepled his fingers on the desktop. "Are you staying at a nearby dude ranch?"

"I wish I'd thought about making reservations. But I plan on driving to Casper before catching a flight."

"Casper? That's a killer drive from here. Why not just drive to Jackson Hole?"

She evaded his look. "I'm not in any hurry. I thought I'd see some more of the state before I have to leave. The autumn color is fabulous, and I want to capture as many photos as possible."

"I see." Mitch Carver glanced at his watch. "The day's half over. You might want to think about staying some place nearby, and heading out tomorrow."

Josh nodded. "I agree with Mitch. You'd be wise to take the rest of the day to bunk somewhere and start out in the morning when you're fresh. If you'd like, you could follow me to my ranch. We've got plenty of room."

Mitch turned to her. "I can vouch for the Conways. They're good people, and they'll make you feel like one of the family."

"Thanks." Sierra shrugged. "I don't mind long drives. I'm feeling really energized. I'll just drive until I'm tired, and find a place to crash for the night. Besides, a good, long drive will make that soak in the hot tub even more wonderful when I finally get to enjoy it."

"Suit yourself. I'll warn you, though. You're going to drive through a lot of desolate land, with very few places to stay. The scenery may be breathtaking, but the solitude could be a problem." Mitch glanced at a notation on his desk. "I almost forgot. Somebody phoned here asking about you."

Her head came up sharply, her eyes narrowed. "When?"

"This morning."

"Did you"—she paused to take in a quick breath —"get a name or a message?"

"Neither. I told him you were up on the mountain somewhere shooting pictures, and planned on hiking down today."

Him.

Sierra's smile was forced. "Thanks, Ranger Carver."

She turned away and heaved into the straps of her backpack, sagging under the extreme weight of it.

Josh and Mitch exchanged handshakes.

"Thanks again, Josh."

"Anytime, Mitch. I'll see you around."

Josh followed Sierra out to the public parking area, where a few employees' cars were scattered here and there.

She paused at the shiny silver SUV. "This rental is mine."

When Sierra stopped, Josh halted beside her. "Why don't I give you a hand with this gear?"

"Thanks."

He opened the back hatch and, with a great deal of effort, managed to shove the enormous backpack inside the storage section.

When he'd finished, she offered her hand. "Thanks again, Josh, for everything. I'm really sorry to have caused you so much time away from your work." Without warning, she stood on tiptoe to brush a quick kiss on his cheek.

It had been meant merely as a friendly gesture, the sort

of thing she'd often done with friends in Paris. But the moment she was touching him, she felt a rush of heat that left her sweating, and a quick, sexual jolt that raced all the way to her toes.

She pulled back as quickly as she had stepped forward.

She saw his eyes narrow fractionally on her, and she wondered if he'd felt it, too. Or was he merely annoyed at such intimacy?

"No apology needed, ma'am. The pleasure was all mine. If you change your mind, feel free to take me up on my offer of a room for the night."

His lips curved into that sexy smile that had her heart doing somersaults, before he turned away.

He was heading toward his truck when he heard a cry of alarm.

He turned. The driver's door of Sierra's vehicle was open. She was standing outside the car, holding a slip of paper, her eyes wide with emotion, all the color drained from her face.

He hurried to her side. "Hey. What's wrong?"

She fisted her hand at her side, crushing the paper into a ball and stowing it in her pocket.

Her action wasn't lost on Josh, who watched in silence.

It took her several seconds before she found her voice. "If you don't mind, I...I believe I'll take you up on your generous offer of a room for the night."

He studied her face, so pale, her eyes looking too big and much too bright. "Sure thing. Would you like to follow me?"

She gave a quick shake of her head. "I believe I'll just leave my rental car here and have the agency pick it up. Maybe they could deliver something a bit smaller to your ranch."

He arched a brow. "I'm sure they'll do it, as long as they have your credit card on file. But it'll cost you an arm and a leg for the extra service."

"I don't mind. I'd prefer something smaller and less... showy, anyhow."

"Well then..." He nodded toward her vehicle. "Let's unload your gear. I have plenty of room in the back of my truck."

She walked to the rear of the SUV and removed everything. With Josh's help, she loaded it into his truck before climbing into the passenger side.

As they drove away, she watched in silence as her rental car receded in the side-view mirror.

Leaving it behind was definitely safer.

She dropped her head back and pressed a hand over her eyes. And prayed that the rest of her troubles were as easy to dispose of as the rental vehicle.

From his vantage point on a snow-covered hill, the man lowered his high-powered binoculars and gave a chilling smile. So, she thought to throw him off her trail by begging a ride with one of the hikers. He noted the license plate, committing the numbers to memory. In a place as sparsely populated as this, it would be no trouble to find out who the driver was and where he'd taken her.

He'd seen her reaction to his note. Had watched through narrowed eyes as she'd crumpled that paper and stuffed it into her pocket. A clear sign that she'd been caught by surprise.

Good. Let her stew awhile and think about what she'd done to him. Hadn't he offered to use his family connections to nurture her career? Hadn't he taken her under his wing, introducing her to all the right people in Paris? He'd had every right to expect some gratitude on her part. She couldn't possibly be naive enough to think he had done all of this out of the goodness of his heart, without expecting payback.

She had not only refused him but had also run off like a thief in the night, without a word, thinking she could hide away on some mountaintop.

He was a generous man. He would forgive her. But only after she apologized and recognized him for what he truly was. Without him, she was nothing. And one day soon, she would come to her senses.

Until then he would watch and wait. For he was not only generous but also patient. Especially when the object of his obsession was so tantalizingly near.

Josh drove in silence as they followed the long highway leading away from the mountains. Though he craved answers to all the questions playing through his mind, he knew this wasn't the time.

From the little he knew of her, Sierra Moore appeared to be a series of contradictions. Open as a book about her career, but more than a little secretive about her private life. Completely independent but willing to take him up on the offer of a place to sleep. Or to hide.

She'd had a scare. Of that he was certain. And though she'd been quick to pocket something, he'd have bet good money that whatever she'd found in her car had her running like a rabbit.

An old debt? An old enemy?

The fact that she'd agreed to let him drive her and leave her rental car behind meant that she was feeling more than a little overwhelmed.

She would talk when she was ready. Until then, he'd give her what she needed. Time to sort through whatever was going on in her life and figure out how to deal with it.

They drove for hours in silence through some of the most spectacular scenery imaginable. Despite whatever was weighing on her mind, the beauty of the countryside in all its autumn glory didn't seem to be lost on Josh's passenger, who was watching with avid interest.

When they reached the town, Josh slowed his pace and turned to Sierra. "Welcome to Paintbrush, Wyoming."

She lifted her head and glanced around the sleepy little place. "Do you live here?"

"My ranch is about a hundred miles from here. But this is the closest town, and the closest thing to civilization in these parts."

He watched her reaction as they drove down the main street, past the row of old buildings that housed the courthouse and jail, with the police chief's office in front, and beyond that Thibalt Baxter's Paint and Hardware. A newer cluster of buildings announced Dr. April Walton's Family Practice and the medical clinic next door, which shared office space with a dental clinic, and next door to that a barber and beauty shop. The last building in the row was the rainbow-colored Odds N Ends Shop.

He saw Sierra's spirits lift considerably as she read aloud the sign above it:

"If we don't have it, you don't need it."

Seeing her smile, he winked. "If you like that, you're going to love Flora's Diner." He pointed to the gaudy wooden building painted pink and bright lavender, with shocking pink letters spelling out the name.

"Flora's been a fixture in this town since my grandfather came here. And her daughter, Dora, is older than my dad. The two of them know everybody for miles around and can tell you anything you want to know about anyone's business. Believe me, there are no secrets in a town this small."

"That must be a comfort."

He chuckled. "Unless you're the one with the secrets they're all sharing with your neighbors."

She lifted a brow. "I hadn't thought of that."

"We like to say that the good thing about living in a small town is knowing everything about your neighbors. And the bad thing about living in a small town is having all your neighbors know everything about you."

She shared a laugh, and Josh was relieved to see that her wonderful smile had returned.

At the end of the street he pointed to the Paintbrush Church, with its gleaming white steeple pointed heavenward, and the Paintbrush Elementary School next to the Paintbrush High School, with its new football field and modern track. "Just beyond town is the fairground. During rodeo days, the town swells to about five times its normal population."

"Do you take part in the rodeo?"

He shook his head. "I leave that to my brother Jake. He's always been crazy enough to try his luck with a bucking bronc or an angry bull. Quinn and I are more than willing to stand back and cheer him on."

"Is Jake a rancher, too?"

"Yeah. It's the family business. And now he's our veterinarian as well. We never say it aloud, but we're pretty proud of him."

"Why?"

He shrugged. "It takes guts for the youngest of the family to travel a thousand miles away from home to chase a dream. But as I said, if you're looking for a crazy, gutsy guy, Jake's your man."

"Are you saying it doesn't take a crazy, gutsy guy to climb the Tetons during a storm to locate lost hikers?"

Josh grinned. "Just doing my job, ma'am."

After making a slow tour of the town, Josh brought his truck to a halt in front of the diner. "I don't know about you, but right about now I could use a good, hot meal."

She nodded. "Sounds wonderful. That's not to say that your steak-and-egg breakfast wasn't really good. But my stomach is telling me that it hasn't been filled for hours."

She climbed from the truck and followed Josh inside the ancient diner. Arranged on one side were a couple of old metal tables and scarred wooden chairs, and all of them were filled by people who called out greetings to Josh as he led her toward the gleaming counter lined with a row of old-fashioned stools.

The minute they were seated a plump woman hurried over to greet them.

"Josh Conway. Haven't seen you in weeks. Busy time up at the ranch?"

"You bet." Seeing the way she was studying Sierra, he said, "Dora, this is Sierra Moore."

Dora stuck out a hand. "Nice to meet you, Sierra. Coffee?"

Sierra accepted her handshake. "Yes, please."

"Make that two," Josh called as she started away.

"You don't need to tell me that," the woman said with a laugh. "The day you come in and order tea, I'll know you're not feeling like yourself."

While she poured two cups of coffee, a white-haired woman peered at them from the pass-through to the kitchen. "Josh Conway. How're you, honey?"

"Great, Flora."

She stared at the woman beside him. "Don't tell me you finally got yourself a serious girlfriend."

"Just a friend, Flora."

"Tell that to someone else. A female that pretty is never just a friend."

Josh ignored her little jibe. "Flora, this is Sierra Moore."

The older woman gave her a bright smile. "Any friend of Josh Conway's is more than welcome here."

"Thank you."

Flora's daughter, Dora, set down two hot cups of coffee and indicated the faded, plastic-coated menus. "You decided what you want?"

Before they could say a word her mother called out from the kitchen, "The special today is chicken and dumplings. You don't want to order anything else."

Josh winked at Sierra. "That settles it for me. Make mine chicken and dumplings."

Sierra couldn't help laughing. "Make that two."

Dora nodded and shouted out the order to her mother, even though the old woman had obviously heard every word. Then Dora proceeded to place two premade salads in front of them before turning away.

The rest of the meal was delivered on steaming plates, along with homemade rolls and Flora's special honey butter.

Both Josh and Sierra cleaned their plates before sitting back to sip their coffee.

Sierra turned to him. "I can't remember the last time

I had a real home-cooked meal in a diner. This was amazing."

Having overheard her, Dora stepped closer. "If you liked Ma's chicken, you're going to love her coconut cream pie. It's the best in the West."

"I'm sold." Sierra smiled. "I have to try it."

"Me too." Josh winked. "I'm not about to pass up a piece of Flora's homemade pie."

They were still grinning as they dug into the mile-high confection, and both were sighing with pleasure by the time they'd finished.

Dora picked up their empty plates. "It's nice to see a pretty young thing like you enjoying Ma's pie without worrying about your figure."

"Why, thank you," Josh deadpanned, causing both women to roar with laughter.

"Be sure to tell your mother that I've never tasted coconut cream pie that good," Sierra said.

"I will." Dora studied her a minute, then asked, "You wouldn't happen to be a photographer, would you?"

Both Josh and Sierra shot her puzzling glances.

Josh arched a brow. "Have you taken up mind reading, Dora?"

The woman laughed. "Don't I wish? It just dawned on me. There was a man in here asking if anybody knew a beautiful photographer who was supposed to be in the area." She puffed up with importance. "Someone in town told him that if he wanted to know anything about anybody in these parts, he ought to ask at Flora's Diner. But Ma and I told him we'd never heard of her." She turned to Sierra. "Since you're the prettiest woman who's been in our place in a long time, I just now put two and two together."

"How long ago was the man here?" Sierra asked softly.

"Yesterday. Handsome devil," Dora muttered. "And oh, such fancy clothes. I'm betting he paid more for his watch than I did for that new truck I bought. Ma and I thought about locking him up in the cooler and keeping him for ourselves, but we resisted temptation."

She turned away, laughing uproariously at her little joke.

Seeing the stricken look of Sierra's face, Josh dropped some money on the counter. "Thanks, Dora. Bye, Flora," he called to the older woman in the kitchen.

At once the white-haired figure popped up at the pass-through. "Bye, you sweet, sexy thing. Bye, pretty woman. Hope you'll both hurry back."

Sierra managed a weak smile before turning away.

Josh led the way to his truck. Once inside he turned to her. "Okay. Either something you ate doesn't agree with you, or the news Dora delivered just added to your misery. I'm betting it's the news."

She nodded, staring hard at her hands.

"Want to talk about it? I'm a good listener."

She shook her head. "No. But thanks for the offer to listen."

"Anytime."

She shrugged. "Maybe...later."

"Okay. Would you care to pay a visit to the chief of police?"

As his words sank in, she seemed to shrink back against the seat. She lifted her gaze to his. "I don't think that's a good idea."

"I do. Especially if the good-looking guy asking about you at Flora's happens to be an ex-husband."

"I've never been married."

"And the guy?"

When she remained silent, Josh shrugged. "Okay. Suit yourself."

As he turned the key in the ignition and began to drive along Main Street, he watched her out of the corner of his eye. She'd gone somewhere else in her mind.

A dark place, from the looks of her. And not one she cared to share with him or with anyone.

At least not yet.

Sierra Moore looked as though she desperately needed someone to trust. And though he barely knew her, he knew that at least for tonight, he and his family would make her feel not only welcome but also safe.

Chapter Five

———◆◆◆———

W e've been on the road a long time." Sierra had grown silent, content to drink in the sight of the spectacular scenery, which seemed so foreign to her. Aspen and cottonwood trees and foliage lined the road in every shade of red and orange and gold imaginable. "When do we get to your ranch?"

"We've been on it for the past ten miles. You'll be seeing the house pretty soon now."

"This beautiful land is all yours?"

He nodded, and found himself seeing it through her eyes. "I guess the vastness of it can be pretty overwhelming if you're not prepared."

"So much land. And all of it so breathtaking. Do you wake up every morning and pinch yourself?"

That had him laughing. "Actually, most mornings there's no time for anything except chores. And believe me, when you're mucking stalls, you're not thinking about how grand and glorious all those cows are."

That had her laughing. "Sorry. Shoveling cow manure is just not an image I wanted to carry in my mind."

"I know. You want to see grand mountain peaks covered with snow and cowboys on horses herding cows beneath a spectacular sunrise."

"Exactly. And if you'll find such a scene, I'll snap it and make a fortune selling it in galleries."

"I'd be happy to be one of those cowboys. Right after I finish shoveling the manure. Which reminds me. I'd better warn you." Josh looked over with a mock-serious frown. "Here in Wyoming, we have an awful lot of cow manure to shovel."

"Is that the price I'll have to pay for room and board?"

"Absolutely. All our guests are expected to lend a hand with ranch chores." That sexy grin was back on his lips. "I should also warn you that our ranch doesn't have a hot tub. But it does have a jet tub in the guest suite. I hope that'll be enough to ease your aching muscles."

She returned his grin. "I guess, after shoveling manure, I'll be happy to have the jet tub."

They were still laughing as they rounded a curve and caught their first glimpse of the ranch house in the distance.

"Oh." The word slipped from Sierra's lips and was drawn out in a long sigh of pleasure. "Talk about spectacular."

"Yeah." He couldn't help smiling. "Big Jim built the original structure, and it's been added on to a number of times through the years."

"Big Jim?"

"My grandfather. Everybody calls him Big Jim."

"And your dad? Is he Big Something-or-Other?"

Josh was enjoying her zany sense of humor. She was unlike any woman he'd ever met. He'd watched her interaction with Mitch Carver and noticed her obvious concern when she'd realized that he and his rangers had spent a great deal of time and energy searching for her on the mountain. That kind of genuine interest in someone she'd just met was rare and wonderful.

"Cole Conway is just 'Pa.'"

"I'll probably call him Big Pa. Or else Big Cole. To distinguish from Big Jim, of course."

"Then there's Ela."

"Who bakes that wonderful corn bread," Sierra put in.

"Right. She's Arapaho, and has been with us forever."

"Arapaho. How fascinating. I can't wait to ask her all sorts of questions about her people."

He was grinning. "I'll just bet you can't. And then there's Phoebe, who came to live with us shortly after our mother disappeared and—"

"Wait." Sierra held up a hand. "Your mother disappeared? How? Where? When?"

He shook his head. "When I was ten. And that's all I know. She disappeared one day without a trace, and there's been no information uncovered since. My father hired private detectives, and the state police and Chief Fletcher did all they could, but in the end we have no more information now than we did when it first happened. We don't know if she's dead or alive, if she was kidnapped or if she abandoned us. All we know is that she disappeared without a trace."

"That's horrible." She looked over at him. "And here I am, barging in on your life without offering a thing in return."

He lay a hand over hers and was caught once again by that quick rush of heat. "It happened a long time ago. By now it's old news."

"Not to you and your family."

He saw the flare of heat in her eyes and found it oddly touching. Though she was hearing this news for the first time, she understood without question the depth of his pain and was able to relate to it.

She had, it seemed, that rare gift of empathy. She was doing to him exactly what she'd done to Mitch Carver. In just minutes she'd managed to win over his respect and his friendship.

The truck slowed and came to a stop at the rear of the house, where several vehicles were parked.

As he stepped out and hurried around to open the passenger door, he offered a hand. "Come on and meet the family."

He'd expected some hesitation on her part as she accepted his assistance from the truck. Meeting new people was always disconcerting, of course. At least for most people. But Sierra sailed toward the back steps as though she were coming home.

Josh held the door for Sierra. "We call this our mudroom."

She looked around, noting the concrete floor sloped toward a drain in the middle, where beads of water were all that remained of the recent spray of a hose. "Where's the mud?"

Josh chuckled. "Down the drain. But believe me, this room sees lots of it."

Boots of every size and shape stood in orderly rows on a low shelf. Wide-brimmed hats and parkas and rain gear were hung on pegs along a wall. A large sink anchored one wall, and a soap dispenser hung over it. Beside it sat a pile of fluffy towels. For a working ranch, this room seemed uncommonly neat.

This room led to a large, open kitchen, with a cooking area, an eating area, and a gathering area. Four men, two of them about Josh's age and two older, stood in the gathering space, talking and drinking longnecks in front of a blazing fire. Three women, one of them young, one middle-aged, and one who appeared to be ancient, moved about the cooking area, removing dishes from the oven, stirring something on the stove.

Everyone, it seemed, was talking, laughing, creating a chorus of sound that rolled over her in waves. Could all these people be Josh's family?

"Well." A handsome, white-haired man was the first to catch sight of them, and called out a greeting. "Back so soon, boyo? We figured with all this weather, you'd be days up on the mountain searching for that latest crazy hiker."

Josh grinned and, because Ela was closest to him, dropped a kiss on the old woman's cheek. "I was in a hurry to get back to Ela's corn bread."

"Oh, you." She blushed like a schoolgirl and pretended to slap away his hand.

"Everybody," Josh called, "I'd like you to meet Sierra Moore."

"The crazy hiker," she put in with a smile.

For a moment the room went deadly silent. Then there was a burst of raucous laughter.

"Sierra, this is my family, some of whom obviously enjoy putting their feet squarely in their mouths."

"Careful, boyo," his grandfather called. "I can still outmuscle you."

"Uh-huh." Ignoring Big Jim, Josh dropped his arm around the old woman. "This is Ela, whose corn bread you enjoyed last night."

"It was the best." Sierra smiled and the old woman did the same, showing a gap where one of her teeth used to be.

"Josh tells me you're Arapaho. I'd love to hear all about the Arapaho nation."

"Few people have even heard of us." Ela smiled broadly.

"And this is Phoebe Hogan. Our second mother."

"Welcome, Sierra." Phoebe hurried across the room, wiping her hands on her apron before extending a handshake.

"Josh sang your praises," Sierra said, taking her hand between both of hers.

Phoebe flushed with pleasure.

"My new sister, Cheyenne." Josh chuckled. "You know, the more I say that, the easier it becomes. I think I like having a sister in the family. Even if she is one of us by marriage."

"Hi, Sierra." Cheyenne held out a tray of glasses. "We have beer, lemonade, milk, and water."

"Nothing yet, thank you."

Josh led Sierra across the room to the fireplace. "This is my father, Cole."

Sierra and Cole shook hands.

"My grandfather, Big Jim."

"The one with his foot in his mouth," Big Jim said without apology.

Sierra couldn't help the smile that split her lips. "Big

Jim." She emphasized each word as she tilted her head upward toward his handsome Irish face. "You're a tall one. I see how you got your name. It's a pleasure to meet you."

"And my brothers, Jake and Quinn." As Sierra shook their hands, Josh added dryly, "Quinn's the one who did us all a favor by marrying Cheyenne."

That had everyone laughing.

"Will you stay for dinner, Sierra?"

At Phoebe's question, Josh turned. "I'm sorry I forgot to call ahead. Not only have I invited Sierra to stay for dinner, but I've also invited her to stay overnight."

"I hope that's not a problem," Sierra put in quickly.

"Not at all. It's grand. We have plenty of room for company." Phoebe began adding another setting to the big trestle table. "Dinner will be ready in just a few minutes, but there's time to show Sierra the guest suite and take her things up, if you'd like."

"Thanks. We'll deal with our gear later." Josh plucked a longneck from the tray and held it out to Sierra. "Sure you wouldn't like one before we eat?"

"All right. Thanks." She accepted the bottle.

He snagged a second one for himself.

"Where are you from, Sierra?" Big Jim asked affably.

"Here and there. My last place of residence was Paris."

"Is that where you were born?"

"I'm told I was born on a bus traveling to New Orleans. My father was playing a gig there."

"He's a musician?" Jake was suddenly interested. "Anybody we'd know?"

Sierra laughed. "He never made it to the big time. But that's never stopped him from trying. He's currently playing with a band in Germany."

"How does your mother like that?" Quinn asked.

"She isn't with him. She's a sculptor, currently working at a studio in Italy."

"Sounds like a fascinating family." Big Jim glanced at Josh, who was standing quietly beside her. "Do you have any brothers or sisters?"

"Not that I know of." At their raised eyebrows she added, "But I've always thought it would be fun to have a house full of siblings." She swept a hand to encompass all of them.

"I'm sure an evening with all of us can change your mind about that." Josh winked at her, and she felt a rush of heat stain her cheeks.

Cole set aside his beer. "How'd you happen to get lost on the mountain, Sierra?"

"I wasn't lost, exactly. I was just so busy working, I didn't realize that the rangers were worried about me until Josh came along."

Cole shot her a look of surprise. "You weren't in any trouble?"

She gave a lopsided grin that was endearing. "The storm threw a lot of snow and ice at me, but I never felt threatened by it. In fact, when Josh found me, I was feeling quite warm and snug in my tent." She didn't bother to add that she'd found the isolation gratifying, after the turmoil of the past weeks.

Cole glanced at Josh for confirmation. "So you made the climb for nothing?"

Josh shrugged. "I wouldn't call it nothing. I got a good workout."

"And, as a bonus, we now have a pretty guest for dinner, boyo." Big Jim turned to Phoebe. "Something smells wonderful."

"Pot roast. And it's ready. Come sit down."

At her invitation, the family made their way to the table, with Josh and Sierra following.

Josh held a chair for Sierra, then took the seat beside her. The rest of the family slid effortlessly into their familiar places, with Big Jim at the head of the table, Cole at the other end, his sons and new daughter-in-law on opposite sides, and anchored at each end by Ela and Phoebe.

While platters of beef and potatoes and late-garden vegetables were passed, the conversation moved just as easily. From weather—uppermost in their minds—to the herds and ranch chores. Through it all, Sierra was content to sit back and soak up every word.

Big Jim glanced out the window at the storm clouds hovering over the peaks of the Tetons. "There's more snow coming. I'm thinking we may get an early taste of winter. It may be time to start bringing the herds down."

Cole nodded. "I agree. Last year we waited too long and got caught up in the hills." He turned to Jake. "Want to take a crew up tomorrow?"

His youngest son gave a negligent shrug of his powerful shoulders, honed by years of routinely handling hundred-pound calves with the same ease as sacks of grain. "I'll have to check my calendar and see if I've got any important patients scheduled."

"Patients?" Quinn shot him a look. "Since when did you start scheduling regular patients?"

"Since old Doc Hunger decided to hang it up and spend this winter in Phoenix with a grandson."

"Phoenix?" Big Jim spat the word like an oath. "What's the old geezer planning on doing there?"

"I hear he took up golf." Jake helped himself to a

mound of mashed potatoes and poured a river of rich brown gravy over it.

"What about his ranch?"

Another shrug before Jake said, "He has plenty of family. Maybe one of them is going to take over. He called me out of the blue and asked if he could add my name and number to his phone message, and refer his regular patients to me while he's gone this winter. That's all I know, but I'm hoping to meet with him later in the week. When I see him, I'll try to get more information for all these inquiring minds."

Phoebe laughed. "See that you do. Because if you're remiss, we'll have to pay a call on Flora and Dora."

Cole joined in the laughter. "I'd say their information will be much more reliable than anything Jake gleans from old Doc Hunger."

That had the others laughing, while Josh leaned close to Sierra to explain.

"Old Doc Hunger has a reputation for being tight-lipped. His usual conversation is *hello* and *good-bye*, with an occasional *yep* or *nope* thrown in for good measure."

Big Jim nodded. "Josh isn't exaggerating. I once spent half an hour telling Doc about the problems I was having with my best mare. She was listless. Off her feed. I'd been planning on breeding her with—"

"Doc Hunger?" Jake asked with a gleam in his eye.

Around the table the family roared.

Big Jim shot him a hairy-eyed look for daring to interrupt. "So old Doc listens to my litany of complaints, while he's running his hands around and around the saddle hanging over the side of the stall. He asks if the saddle is new."

At the far end of the table, Cole was already grinning from ear to ear, having heard the story a dozen times.

Big Jim glanced around at his captive audience. "I say, 'Yes, it's a new saddle, but I'd rather talk about my mare.' And old Doc says, 'This is about the mare. What did you pay for this big, fancy, oversized saddle?' I tell him, 'Six hundred dollars.' And he says, 'You wasted your money.' And he points out a ridge of hand-tooled leather that had been the reason for the high price, before touching a spot on the mare's back bearing the same marks. And old Doc says, 'Toss the new saddle that's rubbing her raw and your mare will be good as before.' Then he sticks out his hand and says, 'That'll be fifty bucks.'"

While the others laughed, Jake gave a nod of his head. "And that, ladies and gentlemen, is why I became a veterinarian. I can't wait to collect fifty bucks from all my friends and neighbors for pointing out the obvious."

"You try that, son, and you may not have many friends and neighbors left," Cole said, while still wiping tears of laughter from his eyes.

"And if you try it with us"—Quinn winked at Josh—"we'll do what we used to do when we were kids and you got too full of yourself. You'll find yourself cooling off in the river."

There was more laughter.

Jake gave a mock-pained expression. "At least now I can swim."

"Again, thanks to us." Quinn turned to his wife. "Whenever our little bro got to be too much to handle, we'd just toss him in a creek to cool off."

"And then they'd walk away," Jake added, "without even bothering to see if I was swimming or sinking. For all they cared I could have drowned."

"That was our big mistake." Josh couldn't keep the

laughter from his voice. "We should have tied a rock to your feet, just to be sure."

"Now you tell me," Quinn added.

"It's never too late to try." Josh helped himself to another square of corn bread.

Sierra sat back, enjoying the sound of their laughter. This was a new concept. It had never occurred to her that family members could have as much fun together as friends did. There was no denying that this family, all three generations of them, actually enjoyed one another's company.

Phoebe circled the table, topping off cups of coffee. "Would you like your dessert here, or in the great room?"

"The great room's fine with me." Cole pushed away from the table, and the others followed suit.

Josh led Sierra into a room with comfortable sofas arranged around a massive, four-sided fireplace. A log blazed, filling the air with the wonderful fragrance of evergreen and woodsmoke. Large floor-to-ceiling windows revealed a spectacular sun setting over the peaks of the Tetons.

The older family members lounged on the sofas, while the younger ones settled on cushions on the floor, keeping their backs to the warmth of the fire.

Phoebe carried in a tray of brownies smothered in ice cream and drizzled with raspberries. While the others helped themselves and made little sounds of appreciation, Phoebe handed Cole a dish of plain raspberries.

"What's this?" He shot her a thunderous look.

"Your dessert." She set a steaming cup on the side table.

"And I suppose that's some kind of unleaded, decaffeinated, and tasteless swill that you're trying to pass off as coffee, too?"

Phoebe merely smiled. "The doctor said you're allowed one cup of coffee a day."

"And the rest of the day?"

"This," she said simply.

Jake interrupted. "Drink your poison, Pa. And stop whining."

The others enjoyed his joke.

"Whining, am I?" Cole studied the chocolate square on his son's plate, mounded with ice cream and fruit, and then looked down at the measly dish of raspberries in his own hand. "You're all going to be sorry when you're bloated and lazy, and I'm fit and trim and running circles around all of you."

"That's right, Pa." Quinn raised his own dish in a salute. "I know I'd much rather be eating your dessert than mine."

Cole brightened. "You'll trade?"

"Sorry." Quinn nudged his wife, and the two of them laughed together. "But since Cheyenne went to all the trouble of baking these brownies, I'm honor bound to do my part just so all her hard work isn't in vain."

"A hero and a martyr," Josh deadpanned. "See what marriage does to a man?"

Jake snorted. "That's just pitiful."

Quinn shot his brothers a quick smile. "Yeah, but it earns me plenty of points with Cheyenne. And she has the nicest way of rewarding my heroic behavior."

"A very sweet reward," Cheyenne said with a purr.

"More information than we wanted." Jake pressed his hands to his ears before glancing at Josh. "If this is what marriage does to a man, I'm going on record right now and declare to one and all that I intend to remain a bachelor forever. How about it, Josh? You willing to join me?"

Josh chuckled. "You don't see me settling down, do you?"

Jake crossed the room to high-five him. "Way to go, bro. And now, I'm heading off to bed." He turned to his father. "I'll be hitting the trail at dawn with a crew of wranglers."

Cole looked surprised. "I thought you had to check your schedule."

Jake pointed to his cell phone. "I did. My day is clear."

Cole shook his head as his youngest son started toward the stairs. "What's the world coming to? Fancy phones that act as secretaries, calendars, even weather maps. Pretty soon we'll just program our phones to herd the cattle back down from the hills."

Jake paused to turn and grin. "I'm betting there's an app for that. And if not, some clever nerd will come up with it soon." He lifted a hand. "'Night, all. And, Sierra?"

As she glanced over, he winked. "It was nice meeting you. Since I'll be on the trail before you're awake, I'll say good-bye now."

"Good-bye, Jake. It was nice meeting you, too."

And it was, she realized. Josh's family had been a most pleasant surprise. Fun and funny, and as relaxed and comfortable as though she'd known them for a lifetime.

CHAPTER SIX

———◆◆◆———

Cole turned to his oldest son. "You and Cheyenne staying the night, or do you have to get back to her place?"

"We thought we'd sleep here and then head back after breakfast."

"Smart move." Josh exchanged grins with Quinn. "That way you get to enjoy more of Ela's corn bread before you face morning chores."

"That's the plan. And Cheyenne thought of it first." Quinn lifted his wife's hand to his lips for an easy kiss. "If you don't mind, we'll say good night now. We put in a full day on her ranch before coming here."

The rest of the family deposited their dessert plates and empty cups on a wheeled cart near the door of the kitchen before heading toward the stairs.

Josh turned to Sierra. "I'll just get our gear and be right back." A minute later he returned with both their backpacks.

Sierra hesitated and called to his family's retreating backs, "Will I see all of you in the morning, or should I say my good-byes now?"

"Don't worry, sweetheart." Big Jim winked at her. "The one thing you can count on in this family is finding everybody around the table for breakfast. It's the most important meal of the day."

"Then I'll save my good-byes for the morning."

After calling good night to the others, Sierra followed Josh up the stairs and along a hallway.

When he opened a door and stood aside, she stepped past him into a room as large and welcoming as the rooms she'd seen downstairs. While Josh deposited her gear in the walk-in closet, she took the time to study her surroundings.

A king-sized bed was mounded with pillows and a down comforter. One wall was dominated by a stone fireplace, where logs and kindling were already in place on the hearth. Across the room was a desk and chair tucked under a wide window affording a glorious view of the Tetons standing tall and majestic against a red-tinged sky.

An open door revealed a luxurious bathroom that resembled a spa, with a rainforest shower, jet tub, and a pile of fluffy towels.

Josh stepped up beside her. "As I said, no hot tub, but I hope this will do."

"Oh, Josh." She turned to him with a dreamy smile. "I can't wait to climb into that tub."

"I don't blame you." He ran a hand over the beard stubble that added to his rugged good looks. "I wish I could join you."

She started to laugh until she caught sight of the smoldering look in his eyes.

"Usually I prefer to take my baths alone. Especially until I get to know my bath partner a lot better than I know you. Sorry."

"Not nearly as sorry as I am." He grinned, softening the look.

He started to turn away when Sierra stopped him with a hand on his arm. Only a touch, but the intense expression on his face had her backing up.

"Changed your mind about sharing the bath?"

"No, I . . ." Her hand went to her throat. "I just wanted to say thank you for bringing me here."

He gave her a slow, appraising look. "You do have a way of making a guy want to do nice things for you."

"I know you're only teasing, but you don't know how grateful I am, Josh."

His tone gentled. "You're welcome."

"I really enjoyed meeting your family. They're all so warm and welcoming. They made me feel like it was the most natural thing in the world to have an overnight guest barge in without warning."

"They've always been that way with our friends. Knowing that you were my guest made you theirs as well." He arched a brow. "Now, about that bath. I could stay and scrub your back."

She managed a laugh. "Nice try, Conway."

He shot her a dangerous smile, causing her heart to tumble. "Can't blame a guy for trying."

As he started to turn away, she dropped a hand on his shoulder. "You've been a real lifesaver. Thanks, Josh."

Without warning she stood on tiptoe and, as she had outside her car, brushed a quick kiss over his cheek.

At her kiss he went as still as a statue. His voice was unusually gruff. "Do you always thank people with a kiss?"

She flushed. "It's just a reflex action, I guess. In Paris, everyone kissed on the cheek. But even before that, my parents believed that all of life should be spontaneous, without a thought to the consequences. The headmistress at my first boarding school was absolutely horrified when I kissed my ancient professor on his withered old cheek in front of the entire class."

He chuckled. "I just bet she was. Did you get a detention?"

"I said it was my first boarding school. Actually, it was the first of many."

"Are you telling me that you kissed all your professors?"

Now it was her turn to chuckle. "Not at all. I've made a lot of mistakes in my life, but I'm proud to say I rarely make the same mistake twice. Still, I seem to mess up more than most of my friends. At any rate, you can trust me when I say that little kiss was just a friendly gesture."

"I think I really like the way you express friendship."

She took a quick step back. "Does that offend you?"

"Is that what you think?" He closed a hand over her upper arm, sending a sudden rush of heat along her spine. "That I'm offended by a kiss?"

She flushed. "I don't know what to think. When I kissed you, you didn't try to kiss me back. Most men I know usually return my kiss on the cheek with one of their own."

"And that's what you'd like?"

She found herself mesmerized by the cool, appraising look in his eyes. "I...certainly wouldn't refuse you. It's considered quite proper in Paris."

"Well then." His lips curved, and the look in his eyes went from cool to blazing in the space of a heartbeat before he blinked, veiling his feelings from her. "This isn't easy for me to say. But I don't think either of us is ready for that yet."

"For a simple kiss?"

He gave her a smoldering look, and she felt the heat all the way to her toes. "Trust me. If and when I choose to kiss you, it won't be a simple peck on the cheek." He touched his index finger to her lower lip, causing it to tremble. "But I have to admit, I'm sorely tempted to taste your lips."

He turned away then and in quick steps, walked to the door. Over his shoulder he called, "Good night, Sierra. Sleep well."

He closed the door with a quiet click.

She stood perfectly still, wondering at the fact that the mere touch of his fingertip to her lips had sent the most amazing shock waves through her system.

Even after his footsteps receded along the hallway, she remained where she was, telling herself to breathe in and out, until her heart rate returned to normal.

When she felt in control, she sank down on the edge of the bed, wondering what had just happened. A fall from a high, sheer peak of the Tetons would have been less shocking than what she had just experienced at the hands of Josh Conway.

And he hadn't even kissed her.

It had all happened in less than a second.

She couldn't help wondering what he could do to her in an hour.

Outside Sierra's door Josh picked up his gear and made his way to his room. Once inside he stashed his backpack in the closet and kicked off his boots while unbuttoning his shirt, which he balled into a heap and tossed on the bed. Barefoot and naked to the waist, he stalked to the window and leaned a hip against the sill to stare at the Tetons, silhouetted against the rosy sky. Though he was looking at the mountains, they weren't what had his attention. His mind was on the woman in the room down the hall.

There was no denying the attraction. From the first moment he'd seen her, dressed in body-hugging leggings and a turtleneck, that mane of honey hair spilling around the face of an angel, he'd been hooked.

He couldn't say exactly why he was so reluctant to kiss her.

It wasn't for lack of wanting to. But he'd forced himself to resist.

That first time, outside her car, he'd been caught unaware by the hot flare of lust that had slammed into him. The feelings had caught him completely by surprise. He'd been hungry to touch and taste and feel that lithe, willowy body pressed against his.

It wasn't just her looks that had snagged his interest. Sierra might be beautiful, but she was also smart and funny and ambitious. All the things he admired in a woman. But she was different from any other woman he'd known. Maybe it was her very different background. He was intrigued by the idea that she'd been on her own in boarding schools since her earliest years.

He thought about their first meeting, when he'd found her in that tent, not hurt or afraid as he'd expected, but angry as a spitting cat and armed with nothing more than a piece of plastic. What a display of bravado.

She was very guarded about her life. Except for Paris, and a childhood of boarding schools, he knew next to nothing about her. She appeared to be a woman completely on her own as she made her way through the maze of life's challenges. And yet, life hadn't made her bitter or brittle or angry as might have been expected. Instead, she was a breath of fresh air. Like one of those beautiful circus high-wire creatures who danced high above the audience without a safety net.

The moment he'd met her, he found himself intrigued. There was just something in his nature that made him eager to protect her.

He'd told her that he'd brought her here to spend a night in comfort before moving on. And it was true, as far as it went. But now that he'd had a chance to spend some time with her and to observe her interaction with his family, he wanted to know more about her. He wanted to know the woman behind the expressive eyes and gorgeous face.

He marveled at the ease with which she met total strangers and found out as much as she could about them without any effort whatever. He'd been touched by that little laugh when she'd called his grandfather Big Jim. As though it were a private joke that only the two of them shared. The expression on her face as she'd watched and listened to his family at the dinner table, and later in the great room, had been priceless. As though she were privy to some secret Stone Age society that she had just come upon in some remote part of a strange new world, and she was eager to know more about them.

What surprised him the most about Sierra was the rush of absolute desire unleashed each time she touched him. It was as though he'd been waiting for her for all his life so that they could unlock all the secrets of the universe together.

Together.

He gave a rough shake of his head to dispel such thoughts. He'd obviously been spending way too much time on a frozen mountaintop. He was a loner by choice. He liked it that way. And yet, what he was feeling was something so new, so puzzling, he kept turning it around and around in his mind, looking for answers, or at least a few sensible questions.

This wasn't like him at all. He'd always been the calm, deliberate one in the family. He might love climbing, but he'd never felt afraid or vulnerable. He always knew exactly where he was going. But suddenly, he wasn't as sure of his life as he'd been just days ago.

Sierra wasn't just another pretty woman. There had been plenty of those in his life. There was something different, something special, about her. He was forced to admit that, whether he liked it or not, he was, quite simply, hooked.

Dangerous, he cautioned himself. He knew almost nothing about her except that she was married to her career. She was ambitious, uninhibited, and, as far as he could determine, not interested in being in a relationship, brief or otherwise.

This was a puzzle. One he couldn't seem to put together neatly.

He swore and turned away from the window.

She was like a pretty little hummingbird, flitting from flower to flower, yet never landing. And tomorrow, she would be gone from his life, as quickly as she'd come.

Tomorrow he would drive Sierra to Paintbrush to rent different car for the drive to Casper, after which he'd have a lifetime to contemplate all the mysteries of the universe and whether or not he should have followed up her innocent kiss with one of his own.

The truth was, he wasn't at all certain how to behave around an irrepressible free spirit who happened to have the face of an angel and the body of a temptress. And that was why he'd backed away from what she seemed to be freely offering. Whether it was a kiss, or much more, it went against his code of honor to take from someone who wasn't in complete control of her situation.

She had just come off a tough climb from the Tetons during a savage storm. And something she'd found in her rental car had frightened her. What she needed was a haven. A good night's sleep, and then she could get on with her freewheeling lifestyle.

It was a waste of time thinking about what might be. In the morning she'd be gone, never to be seen again.

What he needed was to put her out of his mind, and the best way he could think of would be to engage in some good, old-fashioned ranch chores first thing in the morning.

There was nothing quite like mucking out a few dozen stalls and loading a mountain of dung into a honey wagon to bring him back down to earth with a thud.

He shucked his jeans and showered before climbing into bed, hoping to find some peace of mind in sleep.

Instead he spent a long, miserable night thinking about the beautiful angel with a broken wing who'd fallen from the sky and landed smack in the middle of his orderly life.

CHAPTER SEVEN

———◆◆◆———

Sierra dragged her heavy gear down the stairs and left it beside the closed kitchen door.

She tried to ignore the sinking feeling at having to leave so soon. It would have been interesting to witness the day-to-day operation of a real working ranch and to spend more time getting to know this fascinating family.

This life couldn't have seemed more alien to her if she'd just landed here from another planet. The people, the countryside, the lifestyle, were so different from anything she'd ever experienced. She itched to capture them through the lens of her camera.

Especially Josh. He was, in her mind, the epitome of a real Western cowboy, with that tall, lanky frame, that rugged, handsome face, and those piercing dark eyes that could frost over with a single look or, in a blink, crinkle with laughter.

Who was she kidding? He was the reason she was so

reluctant to leave. She wanted to get to know him better. Not just the fearless hiker who had appeared on the mountainside in a snowstorm, but the real Josh Conway, the mysterious, enigmatic rancher who could make her heart trip over itself with nothing more than a smile.

From the kitchen came a chorus of voices, male and female, old and young. She found herself amused at the snippets of conversation she could make out.

An early storm somewhere.

A road washed out in the vicinity.

A leak in the barn roof.

An entire herd of cattle stranded in snow up in the hills.

It was enough to make her glad she wasn't responsible for running things around here. Wasn't there any good news to share?

She pushed open the door and the voices went silent for just a moment, as though they'd all forgotten about the stranger in their home. Then, just as quickly, they were all speaking at once.

"'Morning, sweetheart."

This from Josh's grandfather.

She shot him a dazzling smile. "'Morning, Big Jim." As soon as she spoke his name, her gaze flew to Josh's face, and she could see the laughter lurking in his eyes. Just seeing that sexy grin at their private little joke had her heart rate speeding up.

"How'd you sleep, honey?"

This from the woman Josh had described as a surrogate mother.

"Like a baby, Phoebe, thanks to your warm hospitality."

"I'm glad."

"Coffee?" Josh indicated a tray of mugs on the kitchen counter.

"Thanks." She helped herself to a mug of hot coffee and breathed it in before taking a sip. "Mmm. That's heavenly."

"Fresh-ground." Cole's voice rang with pride. "Half the pleasure's in the smell of those beans grinding."

"I agree." Sierra smiled up at him. "That's the first thing I noticed when I walked in. That and the wonderful smell of corn bread baking."

That had old Ela grinning. "I'll save you an extra slice."

"How're those aching muscles?" Josh asked. "Did you use the jet tub?"

"I was in it for so long last night I practically slept there. But it was worth every minute. I feel good as new this morning. How about you?"

Before Josh could respond, Quinn walked in from the mudroom and greeted everyone. "Hey, bro. I thought I was an early bird." He turned to his wife, who was just helping herself to a mug of coffee. "I'm usually the first one up, but this morning Josh beat me to it. Did you sleep at all last night, bro?"

"Some." Josh snagged a square of corn bread as Ela carried a tray of it to the table.

"I left the barn chores for you while I tended to the horses out in the corral."

"I noticed." Josh took his time polishing off the last bite. "You looked like you were having fun in the slush."

Sierra glanced out the window and was surprised to see sun reflected off a layer of fresh snow.

"Some fun. After we eat, I get to do it all again at Cheyenne's place."

"That's the price you pay for having two ranches. Have you two given any thought to consolidating?"

Cheyenne and Quinn shared a secret smile.

Quinn dropped an arm around her shoulders. "We've been talking about it. But it's Cheyenne's legacy, and the decision has to be hers."

"Come and eat," Phoebe called.

As Sierra took her place beside Josh, she shot him a sideways glance. "Isn't it a bit early for snow?"

"Not in Wyoming." He accepted a tray of eggs scrambled with onions and red-and-green peppers, and he held it while she spooned some onto her plate. "We've been known to have blizzards as late as May or June, and as early as September."

Sierra arched a brow. "I guess that means you soak up as much summer as possible while you can."

That had the others smiling.

Big Jim helped himself to a sizzling steak before passing the platter to Quinn. "This storm wasn't that much of a surprise. We could see those storm clouds blowing in across the Tetons. That usually spells some severe weather."

"How severe?" Sierra looked across the table.

"I'm afraid you won't be heading to town anytime soon, sweetheart." Big Jim smiled at Ela as she handed him a tall glass of milk. "We've got enough equipment to clear the roads here on the ranch. And the county will clear the main highways as soon as the snow stops falling. But they may not get to the outlying roads for a couple of days. There are a heap of miles between here and Paintbrush."

She ducked her head to hide the little jolt of pleasure that shot through her as his words sank in.

"So." Cole lifted his cup to his lips and drank before

adding, "It looks like you're stuck here with us for a while. I hope this won't spoil any plans."

"I have no plans." She looked around at the others. "I'm happy to stay. I just hope I won't be in the way."

"Oh, trust me, you won't be." Phoebe gave a dry laugh. "We always welcome an extra pair of hands to help with the chores."

"Have you ever mucked a stall?" Cheyenne asked.

Sierra laughed. "The only time I've ever seen a stall is when I've had to lead a horse from the stable to be saddled before riding. That was in Spain, when I was staying with a school chum whose family owned a vineyard."

Cheyenne's eyes lit. "So you ride?"

"Yes. Do you?"

That had all of them laughing.

"If you grow up on a ranch in Wyoming, you know how to sit a horse by the time you can walk. And you can drive a tractor by the time you're eight or nine years old."

"You can drive at eight?"

Cheyenne chuckled. "You can't get a license, but when you're the only available laborer, you do what you have to."

Sierra studied her. "Is driving a tractor different from driving a car?"

Cheyenne shrugged. "Not that much. Are you thinking of taking a tractor to town?"

There was another round of laughter.

"I'm not in any hurry to get to town. But if you need someone to lend a hand, I'd like to try."

"Good girl." Big Jim polished off the last of his steak and eggs and sat back with a sigh. "I think I've got enough fuel now to go full steam ahead for a few hours."

As he pushed away from the table, the others followed suit.

Josh turned to Sierra. "If you'd like to give us a hand in the barn, you can help yourself to boots, gloves, and a parka from the mudroom."

"Thanks. I'd like that."

He shot her a dangerous smile. "I wonder if you'll feel the same way an hour from now."

"Careful, cowboy." She opened the kitchen door and retrieved her camera from her gear before trailing him to the mudroom, where she located a pair of oversized boots, a warm, hooded parka, and a pair of leather gloves. "I'll remind you that I managed to keep up with you on our hike down the mountain."

"So you're not about to wimp out on me now?"

"I'm thinking I ought to be able to handle a few ranch chores without breaking a sweat."

Josh threw back his head and roared. "Oh, I think I'm going to enjoy this." He held open the door and followed her onto the back porch. "Come along, Ms. Moore." He led the way toward the first of several barns and outbuildings. "Something tells me it's going to be fun introducing you to the real world of ranching."

Sierra and Josh had opted to muck stalls, while Cheyenne and Quinn led the horses from each stall to a fenced pasture out back, where they were turned loose to run.

Afterward Cheyenne and Quinn returned to the barn to fill feed and water troughs.

Through it all they continued trading jokes and teasing insults.

"I think Jake was smart to head out early this morning." Quinn lugged a hose across the floor and began filling a water trough.

"Did he take one of the trucks, or one of the ATVs?"

"What's an ATV?" Sierra asked.

"All-terrain vehicle. They come in handy when we're heading up into the hills in snow." Josh paused to lift his wide-brimmed hat and wipe sweat from his forehead.

"That's what I heard around dawn." She smiled. "It sounded like someone using a power saw."

"That's what you heard." Josh grinned. "And knowing Jake, he probably circled the house once or twice, just to rouse the household before he headed up into the hills. According to Jake, anyone who isn't out of bed by five or six in the morning is lazy."

Sierra laughed out loud. "Lazy? At dawn?"

"Ah, the life of a rancher." Cheyenne looped an arm through Quinn's and looked up at him with an intimate smile. "If we ever decide to blow off our chores, I'd be more than happy to sleep until noon."

"You?" Quinn dropped a kiss on the tip of his wife's nose. "If you ever sleep that late, I'll rush you into Paintbrush to have Dr. Walton check to see if you have a fever."

"Or a pulse," Josh added.

That had all of them laughing.

Quinn looked at Josh. "Remember the time Phoebe and Pa rushed you to town and had old Doc Walton check you after that fall?"

"From a horse?" Sierra asked.

"From the mountain," Quinn said matter-of-factly. "With Josh, it was always the mountain."

Sierra put a hand to her throat. "How far did you fall?"

"I don't know. It was pretty high." Josh frowned. "The

fall was bad enough. The hardest part was after I landed. I had to get myself home."

"Did you drive yourself?"

He laughed. "I was only thirteen. I had to drag myself into the saddle of old Blue and hope he'd get me back before I passed out."

Quinn took up the narrative. "Phoebe was looking out the kitchen window and saw the horse coming slowly toward the barn. At first she thought it was riderless, because the reins were dangling, but then she caught sight of Josh lying forward in the saddle, holding on to old Blue's mane. She went flying outside, hollering for Pa to come help. The two of them threw Josh, who was all bloody and not making a whole lot of sense, into a truck and started driving to town. Phoebe still refers to it as the longest drive of her life."

Josh saw the look of shock on Sierra's face and tried to keep things light. "According to Phoebe, I was carrying on a very long and confusing conversation with my mother. Old Doc Walton was training his daughter, our current Dr. April Walton, in the intricacies of small-town medicine, and figured she needed to see for herself just how crazy ranchers could be. Together they mopped up a river of blood and managed to stitch me up before they set my broken bones and sent me home, with instructions to Pa and Phoebe to wake me every hour or so because of the concussion I'd suffered."

Sierra gave a shake of her head. "That would be enough to cure most people of climbing alone."

"Most people," Quinn said with a laugh. "But not my crazy brother. Just weeks after Doc removed the cast from his arm, Josh was missing for hours, and returned to say he'd conquered a new peak of the Tetons."

When Sierra sent him a surprised look, Josh grinned.

"I guess it's like falling off a horse. All you can do is climb back in the saddle and give it another try."

"Falling off a mountain isn't quite the same as falling off a horse."

Josh tugged on a lock of her hair. "That depends on where you land."

"And my brother landed on his head, which is why he's still crazy after all these years." Quinn dropped an arm around his wife's shoulders. "Come on. Let's get the last of these troughs filled."

Sierra paused in her work to snap off a couple of quick shots of Josh as he pitched a load of straw and dung into the wagon.

He glanced over. "Quitting on me?"

"Not on your life. Just taking a short break." She grinned. "I figured I'd take advantage of the opportunity to record the life of a real working cowboy."

He winked. "I doubt you could sell many copies. Mucking stalls just isn't pretty."

"I'll be the judge of that." She leaned her hands on the top rail of a stall and studied him. "Do you do this every morning?"

He shrugged. "Somebody has to do it. If I'm busy somewhere else, one of my brothers has to take up the slack. Or one of the wranglers."

"How many do you employ?"

"Depends. We have the biggest crew in springtime, during calving. And again in fall, for roundup."

"You actually round up your cattle?"

He laughed. "How else would we bring them down from the high country?"

"I don't know. I never thought about it." She suddenly became animated. "Will that happen soon?"

"You bet. With this early snow, we'll be looking at bringing the herds down to the lower pastures right away. That's why Jake was on the trail so early this morning."

"So I might see some of the herds coming down from the hills before I leave?"

"Count on it."

She touched a hand to the camera around her neck. "Oh, I can't wait to get some shots of it."

Josh couldn't resist laughing at the look of ecstasy on her face. "The real West and the Old West coming together in your mind?"

She nodded. "Something like that." She lay a hand on his. "Oh, Josh, I can't wait to see them."

She caught the sudden narrowing of his eyes and lifted her hand away before returning to her chore.

As she worked, she wondered at the heat she'd felt at that quick touch.

What would it be like to have those big, work-worn hands on her, touching her everywhere? To have that sexy, smiling mouth moving over hers?

The thought had her glancing sideways at the rugged man who was working beside her. At that very moment he looked up and caught her staring.

He smiled and winked, and she actually felt her heart do a somersault.

Damn him. He was too sexy for his own good. Or hers.

CHAPTER EIGHT

———————◆◆◆———————

Cole hauled a saddle into the barn and tossed it over the side of one of the stalls before turning to his son. "Phoebe's got lunch ready."

"Thanks, Pa. It's about time." Josh hung his pitchfork on a peg along the wall. "I've worked up a powerful appetite." He turned to Sierra, who was spreading fresh straw. Other than to take photos, she hadn't stopped working since they'd first entered the barn. "Had enough of ranch chores?"

She straightened. "I wouldn't mind a break."

He shot her a teasing grin. "Admit it. You're ready for a long rest on a white sandy beach."

"Oh. Doesn't that sound grand?" She pressed her hands to the small of her back and leaned to the left, then to the right, stretching her aching muscles, before walking toward him. "Which would you choose? Hawaii or the Virgin Islands?"

He led the way from the barn. "Right about now, I'd settle for any place where the sun was shining, and my only chore was choosing whether to have a cold beer or a hot babe."

As he held open the door to the mudroom, she brushed past him and felt her body strain toward his. "I'm sure you could have both."

He leaned close enough to whisper, "Since I've already got the hot babe right here, I don't have any need for that beer."

Her eyes went wide and she turned to find his mouth inches from hers, curved into that sexy smile she found so appealing.

It would have been so easy to lean in and touch her lips to his. With anyone else, she would have followed the urge without giving it a thought. But she wouldn't let herself do that with Josh. He was different. So very different from any man she'd ever met. Cool. Reserved. Even though the temptation was great, she went perfectly still, hoping this time he would make the first move.

She saw the way his gaze was drawn to her lips. Her heartbeat started to race in anticipation.

Just then Quinn and Cheyenne burst into the room, laughing together in the way of two lovers completely comfortable with each other.

Their two heads came up sharply, and Sierra and Josh stepped apart, taking great pains to look busy removing their boots, hanging their parkas, and washing their hands at the big sink.

When they walked into the kitchen, Quinn and Cheyenne followed.

Sierra stopped in her tracks and breathed in the heavenly scents that filled the room. "What do I smell?"

Phoebe looked up from the oven. "Bread baking."

"Not corn bread. This smells like hot crusty bread."

"That's it," Phoebe said with a laugh.

"You actually bake your own bread?"

Phoebe exchanged a smile with Ela.

"Bread. Rolls." Ela stirred a pot of chili simmering on the stove. "If our men like eating it, we enjoy making it."

"I think you spoil them." Sierra couldn't help smiling as she watched Josh reach over Phoebe's shoulder to break off a steaming hunk of bread.

"You bet they do." Josh popped the hot morsel in his mouth. "And we wouldn't have it any other way."

Phoebe set the warm, sliced loaf on a platter in the center of the big table, while Ela ladled chili into bowls. Within minutes Big Jim and Cole came sauntering in from the mudroom, their sleeves rolled to the elbows, their hair wet and slicked back.

Big Jim gave a deep sigh. "Nothing quite like bread hot from the oven, and even hotter chili."

Josh settled himself at the table beside Sierra. "A certain guest of ours, who shall remain nameless, thinks we're all spoiled."

"You're absolutely right about that." Big Jim winked at Sierra as Ela set a bowl in front of him. "This woman's been spoiling us since Cole was a pup." He tucked into his meal. "How about you, Sierra? Did you have a grandma who loved to spoil you?"

Sierra shook her head and saw Ela turn to watch and listen. "Neither of my parents had family. Maybe that explains why they had no desire to settle down and have a real home."

"Did your mom ever bake bread?" Phoebe asked.

"Cooking, baking, homemaking aren't even on my mother's radar," Sierra said with a laugh. "I don't recall ever eating a home-cooked meal. We ate in fast-food places traveling from one town to the next. The closest thing I ever had to a normal home life was in boarding school, where there were rules, like when to eat and when to turn out the lights."

Big Jim arched a brow. "I'm curious about your life in a boarding school in England. It had to be a shock after a life with no rules whatever. Tell us what it was like."

Sierra tasted the chili and gave a sigh of pleasure. "Well, I can tell you that the food was never like this."

That had everyone laughing.

"Did you have a private room?" Cheyenne was clearly intrigued. "Or did you have roommates?"

"There's no such thing as a private room in an English boarding school. We shared everything. Dorm rooms. Bathrooms. Study rooms. Dining halls. There was absolutely no privacy in my growing-up years."

"Sounds like growing up on this ranch." Quinn stared pointedly at Josh. "Everywhere I looked, I had a younger brother shadowing me."

"Me, too," Josh said dryly. "Which is why I took to climbing mountains. I figured out early on that nobody wanted to shadow me a few thousand feet straight up."

"You got that right, bro." Quinn nudged his wife beside him. "And none of us wanted to shadow you when you took those thousand-foot falls."

Everyone joined in the laughter.

Cheyenne turned to her husband. "Is that why you started following your wolf pack? To get away from the others?"

"Quinn never had to worry about that," Josh said with a laugh. "We were all too smart to spend our winters sleeping out in the wilderness just to record the life cycle of a wolf."

"You slept in the wilderness?" Sierra's lunch was forgotten as she studied Quinn across the table. "To follow a wolf pack?"

"Not *a* wolf pack. *My* wolf pack," Quinn corrected.

Cheyenne added proudly, "Quinn is considered one of the leading authorities on wolves in Wyoming. He's made a name for himself studying their life cycle in their natural habitat."

Quinn closed a hand over Cheyenne's and smiled into her eyes. "I'm afraid my wife tends to brag about me."

"I'd say she has a right to." Sierra glanced at Josh. "You never told me."

He gave a quick laugh. "I figured Cheyenne would get around to bragging about it sooner or later."

Sierra turned to Quinn. "That's impressive. While you're studying your wolves, how long are you usually gone from home?"

Quinn shrugged. "It could be weeks. Could be months."

"Months?" She couldn't hide her surprise. She turned to Cheyenne. "I guess my parents aren't the only ones who are footloose. Don't you get lonely?"

"Hardly. Since I get to go along." Cheyenne shared a long, simmering look with her husband. "We just recently got back from weeks in the wilderness."

"Oh." Sierra sat back with a smile. "Now that's more like it. I guess as long as the two of you are together, it could be fun."

"Fun?" Josh cast her a sideways glance. "We're talking

about moving out every time Quinn's wolf pack decides to go hunting for food. And sleeping in snowdrifts in the high country if the pack decides to take shelter during a blizzard."

Sierra chuckled. "How is that different from climbing a mountain during a snowstorm, just because some careless hiker doesn't report in to the rangers' station when she's supposed to?"

Big Jim winked. "I think she's got you there, boyo."

Josh gave a grudging nod. "Yeah. I guess you do have a point. Still, I'd much rather climb a mountain and gaze down on some magnificent views than trudge through waist-high snow just to watch a wolf pack take down some poor unsuspecting deer."

"That's just a small part of what we saw." Quinn smiled at his bride. "How about that litter of pups?"

"The cutest things I ever saw," Cheyenne said with a sigh.

Cole helped himself to a thick slice of bread slathered with melting butter. "I'm glad to know my sons have found some noble ambitions, but personally, I'll take good old bone-jarring ranch chores any day, as long as I can be rewarded with a meal like this."

Big Jim nodded in agreement. "There's nothing quite as satisfying as mentally crossing off a list of ranch chores, and knowing at the end of the day that everything's done."

Sierra gave a shake of her head. "I think that's called being obsessive-compulsive."

"That would describe my entire family," Josh said with a smile. "We're never happier than when we're knee-deep in work."

"Or manure," Cole added.

Big Jim joined in the laughter. "We've all been there a million times or more."

"Speaking of which…" Big Jim turned to Sierra. "How'd you do with those barn chores?"

"She held her own," Josh remarked.

"Wrong. I believe what I was holding belonged to the horses." She wrinkled her nose. "And it wasn't pretty."

That had everyone around the table howling.

"I guess the first thing every tenderfoot notices on a ranch is the smell." Cole winked at Sierra. "If you stayed here long enough, you wouldn't even notice it."

"Just how long does that take?" She helped herself to another slice of warm-from-the-oven bread.

"Oh, I guess a couple of years," Cole remarked.

"Don't let him kid you." Cheyenne sipped a tall glass of lemonade. "I've spent my entire life on a ranch, and there are times, especially in the heat of summer, when the last place I want to be is in the barn, mucking stalls."

"See," Josh said, pointing a finger at his brother, "this is the problem with bringing a woman into our family. Women stick together. The minute we tell a little white lie, even though one of them"—he wiggled his brows at Cheyenne like a mock villain—"is supposed to be a member of our family now, she just can't help spoiling our fun by telling the truth."

"You call that the truth?" Quinn nudged his wife with his elbow. "Are you saying the barns actually smell in summer?"

"If it's possible for them to smell worse than now," Sierra said with a straight face, "then I have to believe that all of you have lost your senses. Or at least your sense of smell."

"Speaking of smell…" Big Jim set aside his spoon and looked around the table. "Cole, do you remember the time Quinn and Josh came running in to tell us that Jake was missing?"

Cole looked up. "The time they were playing hide-and-seek and he bet them a dollar that they'd never find him?"

Big Jim nodded and turned to Sierra. "Jake was about six. His brothers had said he could hide anywhere inside the barn, and they'd find him within minutes, or give him a dollar. But after an hour of searching every inch of it, they'd been forced to give up. Then they got to worrying that something bad had happened to their little brother, so they figured they'd better ask for some help."

Sierra was hooked. "Where did you finally find him?"

"Hiding in the honey wagon."

"The honey wagon?" She arched a brow. "I've never heard of that."

"That's what we call the wagon you were tossing the smelly hay into," Josh said with a wicked grin.

When the realization dawned, she gave a shudder. "Jake was hiding in a load of manure?"

"Burrowed deep inside, where no one would ever think of looking. From the time he was a kid, that boyo would do anything to win money from his brothers. Anything," Big Jim said with a chuckle. "He was still bragging about having found the perfect hiding place when Phoebe got a whiff of him, and ordered him to strip and get upstairs to a shower before she took a hose to him right there in the mudroom."

Around the table, the others roared at the image that came to their minds.

"It took about half a dozen showers and a long soak in

the tub," Phoebe added, "before I would allow Jake to join us at the dinner table that night."

Sierra wiped tears from her eyes. "It sounds like Jake was a handful, Phoebe."

Phoebe circled the table, topping off their coffees. "No more than his older brothers. I swear the three of them used to stay awake nights thinking of ways to test my patience."

Sierra caught the look in Phoebe's eyes as she spoke. Though her humor was biting, there was so much warmth and tenderness there, it did something strange to her heart.

This woman, brought in to help with three motherless boys, showed a depth of love for them that Sierra could only envy.

It brought home once again the pieces that were missing from her own life. She knew her parents loved her, but their love was abstract. They seemed capable of loving her only from a distance. Whenever they came together, there was a kind of disconnect, as though they were a family of strangers.

A family of strangers. The words were a knife in her heart. Especially here, seeing the deep and affectionate bond this family shared.

"Well?" Josh's voice beside her brought her out of her reverie. "What do you say?"

"Sorry." She blinked and felt her face flush. "I was distracted."

He'd noticed. And had seen the quick little frown that told him wherever she'd gone, it hadn't been a pleasant place.

"I said I'm going to head out to the equipment barn and take the backhoe. While Big Jim plows the roads,

I'll move the snow off to one side. Would you like to stay warm in the house, or join me in the barn?"

"Since I've never seen a backhoe or, for that matter, a snowplow up close, I guess I'll tag along to the barn."

Josh pushed away from the table, calling to Phoebe and Ela, "Great lunch, as always. I'll see you at dinnertime. I figure, after a few hours playing in the snow, I'll be packing an appetite."

Sierra followed Josh from the room, while the others hurried off to their own chores.

CHAPTER NINE

———◆◆◆———

This is our equipment barn." Josh rolled open the huge doors to the building and snapped on lights, revealing row after row of vehicles. Tractors. Earth movers. Giant trucks.

Sierra looked around in amazement. "Your family actually owns all these? They're"—it seemed she couldn't take it all in—"so big. Like something I'd expect to see on a construction site, or in the fleet of some big city."

"In a way, I guess we're like a city. We've got thousands of acres of land that we have to maintain."

Josh could see her digesting this information, and trying to imagine thousands of acres.

"We're responsible for keeping all the roads and trails clear if we want to keep things operating efficiently." He moved along a wall of keys, each one clearly marked, until he found the one he was looking for. "Come on. I'll introduce you to Big Bertha."

Sierra trailed him between hulking vehicles until he slapped his hand against the tire of a giant yellow monster.

"Do you give all these things a name?"

He laughed. "Only those I love. And I'm crazy about this one. She's a front-end loader, with a backhoe."

He pointed, and Sierra could see the giant scoop on one end, the big claw on the other. "How do you know which way to drive it?"

"Inside the cab, the seat swivels 180 degrees. Want to come aboard?"

He climbed up, reached a hand down to Sierra, and pulled her up beside him. The two of them could just fit inside the small glass cab.

Josh patted the seat. "Come on. There's room for two."

She sat beside him as he inserted the key, and the big rig rumbled to life. Once the cab door was closed, the sound of the engine was muffled. While she watched in amazement, Josh maneuvered the vehicle past the others and out into the snow-covered yard.

Behind them, Big Jim rumbled by, at the wheel of a snowplow, leaving in its wake mounds of snow pushed to one side.

Josh pressed a button, and the cab grew warm enough that he could shed his parka. Sierra followed suit.

With a shift of gears they were crawling along at a snail's pace, with Josh handling the controls that had the giant front end scraping up the mounds of snow. When the scoop was filled to overflowing, he drove Big Bertha to a spot at the rear of the barn, where he deposited the load.

Within a couple of hours, a mountain of snow had formed behind the equipment barn.

As they deposited yet another load, Josh sat back with a contented sigh that had Sierra laughing.

He looked over. "What's so funny?"

"You. You're so happy doing this. It's obvious that you love it."

"What's not to love? It has wheels and big jaws and all this power."

"That's what I mean. It's such..." She shook her head. "It's such a guy thing. Driving a big old machine, and moving a mountain of snow. And all the while you manage to look so sexy, as though..."

She saw the flare of heat in his eyes and stopped. "What's wrong?"

"I look sexy?"

"Is that what I said? I meant to say goofy."

"Uh-huh." He managed a smooth, easy grin. "If you think this is sexy, you should see me dig ditches during an ice jam."

She touched a hand to her heart. "I'm not sure I could take it."

He gave her a long, slow look, and she could almost see the wheels turning in his mind. "Now what?"

"It's your turn." In one smooth motion he managed to lift her up, slide over into her spot while holding her on his lap, and then deposit her ever so gently in the middle of the driver's seat.

"Pretty smooth, cowboy."

He winked. "Didn't you notice? I'm a smooth operator." He pointed. "Push that lever."

She did as he told her and the big machine began lumbering forward. As they rounded the barn and headed along the long, curving driveway, he said, "Now lower that lever."

She did, and the scoop lowered until it was scraping the snow.

"Oh, Josh. Look." Her eyes were wide with excitement as they rolled along, scraping snow until the massive scoop was filled.

"Now pull back on that lever," Josh instructed.

She did, and the scoop lifted smoothly until it was at eye level.

"Now press that lever to turn around."

She did, and executed a perfect circle before heading behind the barn.

Once there Josh showed her how to lift the scoop high before tipping it to spill the contents. When the scoop was emptied, she turned to him with a look of absolute delight.

"Oh, that was wonderful. Can I do it again?"

He was staring at her with the strangest look. And then, without a word his arms came around her and he dragged her against him.

And kissed her.

It was the most amazing kiss. His lips warm and firm and seductive, moving on hers with all the skill of a very capable lover. While his mouth worked its magic, his hands at her back had a skill of their own, moving along her spine, across her shoulders, sending heat radiating all the way to her toes.

"Mmm," he muttered against her lips. "You tasted just as sweet as I'd thought you would."

"And you taste..." She sighed. "Delicious."

His hands were in her hair, his mouth moving seductively along her throat to nestle in the sensitive little hollow between her neck and shoulder, sending the most amazing shivers along her spine.

After her initial shock, it occurred to her that this had been worth waiting for. Here was a man who knew exactly what he was doing. And what he was doing to her was magic. She couldn't seem to form a single coherent thought except one: she never wanted this to end.

He nuzzled his way back to her lips. The kiss spun on and on, until her breath backed up in her throat and she could see stars behind her closed lids.

When at last he lifted his head, she actually moaned, wishing he would do it again.

She strove to keep things light. "So this is what it takes to get you to kiss me. All I have to do is drive some manly equipment."

He gave her that dangerous smile she'd come to love. "In truth, I've been wanting to do that since I first saw you on the mountain."

"Then why did you wait so long? Were you afraid I'd think you were easy?"

At her joke his smile grew. "Yeah. That's it. I was playing hard to get."

"You want to kiss me again?"

His gaze burned over her mouth. "Oh yeah. But I think I'd better wait."

"All part of your hard-to-get game?"

He shook his head. "Big Jim. About to come aboard."

She turned just in time to see the white-haired man climbing up to their machine.

Josh leaned close. "I hope we can continue this another time."

His grin nearly stopped her heart. "Count on it."

Josh's grandfather opened the cab door and poked his head inside. "Good job, boyo. I think we've cleared

enough snow to get ourselves out to the main highway now."

Sierra felt her heart tumble. How easy it had been to
forget that she was leaving. Now reality was slapping her
in the face.

She didn't want to go. Especially now. She wanted
more than anything to stay here with this fascinating family, and get to know them better.

Who was she kidding? She wanted to stay here with
Josh. He was just beginning to warm to her.

Warm? It was too mild a term. If that kiss was any
indication, he was hotter than chili peppers. And she
wanted more.

Big Jim indicated the barn, where he'd already parked
the snowplow. "Drive us around, boyo." He remained
standing on a metal runner and clung to the door.

Josh easily lifted Sierra and slid into the driver's seat
before setting her down beside him. With a flick of the
controls, he drove them into the barn and parked neatly.

"Come on, lass." Big Jim climbed down and held out
his hand.

Sierra took hold of it and jumped down beside him.

"How did you like riding in Big Bertha?"

Josh stepped down beside them and handed Sierra her
parka before saying, "She didn't just ride in her, Big Jim;
she drove her."

The old man gave her a long look. "You handled the
controls?"

"I did. With Josh coaching me."

"Well, doesn't that beat all." The old man paused to
hang his keys on a hook while shaking his head from side
to side. "City girl, I didn't think you had it in you."

"Neither did I," Sierra said with a laugh. "I guess if I stayed here long enough, I'd turn into a real manure-shoveling, truck-driving cowboy."

Josh tugged on a lock of her hair. "You might get the first part of it down, but I doubt you'll ever be a cowboy. And believe me," he added with a simmering look, "that's just fine with me."

"You don't like kissing cowboys?" Sierra asked with mock innocence.

"I've just discovered that I prefer kissing city girls with long, long legs and hair the color of a wheat field and a body like sin."

His words, spoken in that gruff tone, sent a little thrill coursing along her spine.

"Come on, boyo." Big Jim stepped between them and dropped an arm around each of their shoulders. "Let's see what Phoebe and Ela cooked up for our supper."

The two of them matched their strides to Big Jim's loose, easy gait as they headed toward the back door. Once inside they hung their parkas and shed their boots before washing up at the sink.

Quinn and Cheyenne came in, windblown and apple-cheeked, as they laughed together over a private joke.

When they trooped into the kitchen, Phoebe and Ela looked up from the stove.

"There's beer and soda on the counter, and cheese on a tray by the fire," Phoebe called.

The family gathered around a blazing fire and caught up on the day's events.

Quinn sipped a longneck. "Cheyenne talked to Micah." In an aside he said to Sierra, "Micah Horn's been with Cheyenne's family since she was a baby. He and her wranglers make it easy for us to go back and forth between the ranches without worrying. Anyway," he said to all of them, "Micah said they got over a foot of snow at their place. So the higher elevations took a hit last night."

Cole nodded. "I talked to Jake. He made it up to the high country, and said they hoped to bring the herd down by tomorrow. It all depends on how much more snow falls."

Big Jim glanced at the clouds hovering over the peaks of the Tetons in the distance. "There's more of it coming. But I think he'll get a break tomorrow."

"All he needs is a day to get them down. Then it can snow all it wants." Cole nibbled a slice of cheese. "Crazy weather. Shirtsleeves one day, parkas the next."

"Hey, you're in Wyoming, son." Big Jim laughed. "Like I always say, if you don't like the weather, stick around. It's bound to change by morning."

They all smiled in agreement.

"Dinner's ready," Phoebe called.

They made their way to the table, which was groaning under a feast of thick steaks, mounds of whipped potatoes, fresh beans from the garden, and a salad of tomatoes and red onions in a dressing of olive oil and balsamic vinegar.

As they took their places and began passing platters, Sierra turned to Josh. "This feels like a holiday."

He glanced over. "Why?"

She blushed when she realized that everyone was listening. "The only time my family ever ate together was for a special occasion."

Big Jim glanced at his son at the far end of the table. Cole was studying the girl seated beside his son. When he looked up and caught his father's eye, the two men smiled knowingly at each other.

"I guess we sometimes forget how lucky we are." Big Jim helped himself to a thick steak before passing the platter to Quinn. "As long as we have our family, every day's special here."

"It's been special for me, too." Sierra held the bowl while Josh spooned mashed potatoes onto his plate. "I got to muck stalls and handle the controls on Big Bertha."

Across the table Cheyenne's jaw dropped. "Josh actually let you drive his special rig?"

"He did. And I didn't knock over any barns or outbuildings, either."

That had everyone laughing.

Cheyenne looked at her brother-in-law. "When I asked if I could try the controls last week, you said girls weren't allowed."

Quinn lay a hand over hers. "That's only because Josh knew I wanted to be the one to teach you."

She smiled into her husband's eyes. "Will you?"

"Right after dinner, if you'd like."

She gave a mock shiver. "I think I can wait until morning."

He gave a careless shrug of his shoulders. "Don't say I didn't offer."

Josh was grinning. "If I know my brother, he'll want you to sit on his lap while he teaches you the controls."

Cheyenne quickly tossed it back at Josh. "Is that what you did with Sierra?"

Before he could answer, Sierra said, "Darn. Why didn't you think of that?"

"What makes you think I didn't?" At the laughter around

the table he added, "But I figured I'd better behave and stick to teaching you how to drive it."

"Good thinking, son." Cole drained his longneck. "You get tangled up with a female in one of those rigs, you could level half the barns before you know what's happening."

They were still laughing as Phoebe suggested they take their coffee and dessert in the great room.

They were just stepping away from the table when they heard the sound of a truck.

Cole glanced out the window. "One of those delivery trucks. I guess the roads from town are cleared."

He walked to the back door before the driver could knock. A moment later he called, "Sierra. You have to sign for this delivery."

Puzzled, she hurried to the door and scrawled her name for the driver, before accepting a package with a typed label, addressed to her in care of the Conway ranch. There was no return address.

"Aren't you going to open it?" Cheyenne stepped up beside her, looking as eager as a girl at Christmas, while the others gathered around.

"I guess I should." Sierra tore open the brown paper wrapping, to find a jeweler's box inside, bearing the name of a Paris jewelry shop.

For the longest time she merely stared at it.

From his vantage point Josh studied her face and could see the anxiety in her eyes.

Beside her Cheyenne was fidgeting. "Is it your birthday?"

"No."

"Well? Aren't you the least bit curious to see what's inside?" Cheyenne was twitching with nervous energy.

Sierra lifted the lid to reveal a dazzling diamond and ruby bracelet and matching earrings.

"Oh." Cheyenne gave a gasp, while the others merely watched in silence as Sierra opened a small note card.

Reading over her shoulder, Cheyenne said the words aloud. " 'All is forgiven, darling. Call this number. A car will pick you up and bring you to me.' "

CHAPTER TEN

———◆◆◆———

Darling?" Cheyenne turned to Sierra, whose face had lost all its color. "I don't understand. Who is this from? There's no signature."

Before Cheyenne could press further, Josh crossed the room and dropped an arm around Sierra's shoulders. His words were low, for her ears alone. "Sorry. I know you value your privacy, but my family and I have a right to know what's going on."

"I agree." She drew in a long, deep breath. "It's only fair that all of you should know. I should have told you sooner."

"Told us what?" Big Jim demanded.

Josh was already steering Sierra through the doorway. "Let's talk in the great room. You look like you need to sit down."

The others followed, eager to hear everything.

Ela pushed a trolley loaded with coffee, mugs, cream

and sugar, and plates for apple pie and ice cream. Phoebe trailed her, carrying a bowl of spiced apple slices and skim milk for Cole.

Seeing it, he made a face and bit down hard on the oath that sprang to his lips.

When they'd gathered around the fireplace, Josh said, "When Sierra and I were ready to leave the park, she found something unsettling in her car. I could see that she was upset, and I offered to bring her here to spend the night before she started on her way to Casper. Now I wish I'd been more forceful when I suggested she pay a call on Chief Fletcher."

"Everett Fletcher?" Cole's voice was sharper than usual. "What's all this about?"

Sierra took a long, deep breath. "There's a man who befriended me in Paris—we went out on a few dates. I wanted to keep things light and casual."

Big Jim glanced at the jeweler's box, held stiffly in Sierra's hand. "From the size of those diamonds, this guy doesn't think of your relationship as casual."

He turned an icy stare at his grandson. "You suggested that Sierra talk to Everett Fletcher, but you didn't think you ought to share this with your family, boyo?"

Josh felt the sting of his grandfather's look. "I should have. But I thought I owed Sierra the right to her privacy, especially since she'd only planned on staying the night, before driving on to Casper. And now..."

His words trailed off.

"Mind if I see that note?" Cole held out his hand, and Sierra passed it to him.

He read it in silence before passing it to Big Jim, who did the same.

The older man's head came up sharply. "'All is forgiven'? What did you do to him?"

"I left him without a word. Actually, I told my friend, Janine, to tell him I'd left after I was safely out of the country."

"Safely?" Big Jim zeroed in on that single word. "You wanted to be safely away before he knew you were gone?"

Sierra swallowed. "I... was afraid."

"Of him?" Big Jim demanded.

Sierra nodded.

"And he forgives you. He even calls you 'darling.'" The older man stared at her. "That sounds pretty intimate. Did he have a right to be offended?"

She shook her head, afraid to meet his stern gaze. "It was never more than very casual dating, like glorified friendship, at least on my part. When I realized that he wanted more, I left. But by that time I was afraid of him."

Josh's eyes narrowed. "Why? What did he do?"

"It's what he implied. I found his behavior alarming. But then, after some time on the mountain, with a lot of distance between us, I decided that I'd probably just magnified everything in my mind. You know. A mountain out of a molehill. That's why, when you suggested that I talk to the police chief, I refused."

"At the time, I didn't know what you'd found in your car that had you so upset. Do you care to share?"

"It was a note."

"That must have been a hell of a note." Josh studied her. "A note in a parked car is one thing. But this..." He swept a hand toward the jewelry box. "How does he know you're staying at our ranch?"

"Maybe he stopped in at Flora's," Quinn said. "Isn't that how everyone in Paintbrush gets their news?"

"We never told Flora that Sierra was coming here," Josh said patiently.

"But you said that you two stopped at Flora's place on your way through Paintbrush. You think you were followed?" Cole's tone was grim.

Josh shook his head. "It never occurred to me to keep an eye out, but the road was practically deserted. I'd have spotted a vehicle behind us all the way from town. Still, he could have seen us leaving Flora's together and made a calculated guess. And now there's no need for him to guess. Sierra just signed for that package."

Around the room heads nodded in understanding.

Big Jim turned to Sierra. "You said you weren't afraid enough to talk to Chief Fletcher. How're you feeling now?"

She looked up, then away. "I'm afraid all over again. I thought—that is, I'd hoped—that he would just give up and go home and leave me alone. But now..." She forced herself to meet their eyes. "I think, now that the roads are clear, I should make arrangements to rent a car and fly out of Casper to New York."

"Do you have family there who can watch out for you?"

She shook her head. "There's an old classmate. A girl I knew in school. I have a standing invitation to bunk with her whenever I'm in the city."

"As long as you don't have family there, I don't think that would be a wise thing to do right now." Big Jim's voice remained stern as he took Sierra's hand. "If this guy followed you from Paris to Wyoming, he can just as easily follow you to New York. You need to be somewhere safe. With people you can trust."

"I don't have any—"

"You have us. You're here. Why not stay?"

"You don't understand. I don't want all of you involved in this. This isn't your fight—"

The old man held a finger to her lips to silence her protest. Though his words were gruff, there was a softness in his eyes when she looked up at him. "You'd better get used to the fact that the Conway family never backs away from a fight. And as long as you're here, you're with family. You got that?"

"I . . ." Her lips trembled, and she was afraid that she might embarrass herself by weeping. "Yes. Thank you, Big Jim."

"You're welcome. Now I want you to remember something else, while we're at it. Family doesn't hold back. If you find yourself worried about something while you're here, you need to share it. Will you do that?"

"All right. I promise." She stared hard at the toe of her shoe. "You'll never know what this means to me."

"I think I do. Now . . ." He glanced around at the others, letting his fierce gaze linger a moment on his grandson before his smile returned. "I think it's time we enjoyed our dessert and coffee while you consider your options."

While Phoebe and Ela passed around cups of coffee and slices of apple pie, each with a dollop of ice cream, the conversation was stilted, as the various family members began to tread carefully through Sierra's past as though maneuvering through a minefield.

"This man . . ." Cheyenne paused. "How long have you known him?"

"A few weeks."

"Weeks?" Cole's head came up sharply. "He only

knew you for weeks and he's chasing you halfway around the world?"

"He..." Sierra searched for an explanation. Here among these good people, she realized it made no sense. But while in Paris, among the assorted wealthy and quirky people who surrounded young artists, she had been persuaded that it was perfectly normal. "He was smooth and sophisticated, and he made me feel special. And my friends there told me I'd be a fool to refuse the friendship of a man whose family could make or break my career."

"How do you feel now?" Cole set aside the hated apple slices and glowered at his sons enjoying their pie and ice cream. "Was your career worth the worry this man has caused you?"

"Now that I've put some distance between us, I realize that it was all an illusion. My career will stand or fall on its own merits, and that's the way I want it."

"Good girl." Big Jim, who'd been watching his grandson's face all this time, turned to Sierra. "About the police chief. Don't you think you ought to consider it now that this fellow has made it clear that he knows where you are?"

Sierra turned to Josh, who was staring at her with a look of intense concentration.

She looked at the jewelry box, which she'd dropped on a nearby table. The expensive jewels winking in the firelight mocked her.

"Yes. I'm sorry I didn't do it when Josh first suggested it."

"It isn't too late." Big Jim motioned to his grandson. "Why don't you call Everett and ask him to stop by for some pie and ice cream, Josh?"

Josh nodded. "As long as that's what Sierra wants."

"I do. But do you want to bother the police chief now? After hours?"

"Everett doesn't have hours. He does his job around the clock." Josh plucked his cell phone from his pocket and dialed.

Minutes later he said, "Chief Fletcher said that he'd even drive to Casper and back as long as he was promised a slice of Phoebe's apple pie. He'll be here in an hour."

While the others enjoyed their dessert, Josh noted that Sierra's lay forgotten while she sipped her coffee, allowing the others to carry on the conversation that swirled around them.

Chief Everett Fletcher was as good as his word. He stepped into the Conway family's great room, greeting the family warmly before being introduced to Sierra. Afterward he cheerfully accepted a huge slice of apple pie smothered in vanilla ice cream.

"Thank you, Phoebe." He stretched out his long legs toward the warmth of the fire and dug in to the heavenly confection. "My mouth watered all the way here just thinking about this."

Sierra had been expecting a stern, businesslike lawman, and was pleasantly surprised to find him welcomed with affection like a member of the family.

Big Jim's voice warmed. "This big, tall athlete was the pride of Paintbrush High. When he played for the football team, he led Paintbrush to a state championship."

He slapped the chief on the back.

Everett smiled. "It was an experience I'll never forget. My best season ever, until an injury in college ended my chance to turn pro."

"Oh. I'm sorry." Sierra shot him a look of sympathy.

He smiled broadly at her obvious concern. "After college I poured all that energy and athletic aptitude into a career with the state police."

"I bet you were good at your job."

He nodded. "I became a sharpshooter before returning to Paintbrush when they offered me the position of chief."

"Six feet of pure muscle," Big Jim said proudly. "And from the looks of you, I'll bet you could still fit into your old state police uniform."

Everett laughed. "Probably. Though now I deal mainly with drunks and petty criminals."

"The chief knows everyone in town and most of the outlying ranchers by name. In turn they know him to be a good man, fair and honest, who takes pride in his work."

"Don't we all love our work?" When the chief had devoured his pie, and washed it down with two cups of steaming coffee, he set aside his cup and turned his attention to Sierra. "Now, Ms. Moore, why don't you tell me why you asked to see me."

"I guess I should begin with this." She dug out the crumpled note that she'd been carrying in her pocket and handed it to the chief. "After hiking the Tetons, I found this note in my rental car."

He read it aloud. " 'Did you think you could just walk away from me?' "

Around the room, the others simply stared at her in silence. It was another bit of mystery that she hadn't, until now, shared with them.

Chief Fletcher tapped a finger on the wrinkled paper. "Do you know who wrote this?"

Sierra nodded. "His name is Sebastian Delray. And

tonight, he had this delivered here at the Conway ranch for my signature."

She handed over the jeweler's box and the note that had been inside the wrapped package.

Everett whistled as he lifted the jeweled bracelet and very carefully placed the two earrings in his big palm. "Expensive taste." He dropped them into the box and read the note before looking up. "He forgives you? For what?"

Sierra shrugged. "There's nothing to forgive, except for the fact that I left him without saying good-bye or telling him where I was going."

"Sebastian Delray." The chief peered at her. "I've been running that name through my memory bank." He tapped a finger to his temple. "It sounds vaguely familiar. Who is he?"

"An international financier. His family owns blocks of valuable real estate in London, Paris, and Rome, including several art galleries."

Everett shook his head. "I don't follow international finance or art. What else does he do?"

"He gets his photograph in newspapers and magazines." Sierra sighed. "You've probably seen pictures of him escorting rich and famous women to important events like royal weddings and worldwide movie premieres."

Cheyenne gasped. "Oh, my gosh! I've seen that name." Her eyes rounded as the light dawned. "A royal wedding in Monaco. He was there with an Italian actress."

Sierra nodded. "Sebastian enjoys the spotlight."

"Which shines on him as long as he's dating beautiful women." The chief frowned. "In other words, using them to enhance his own image." He looked over. "Who introduced the two of you?"

"He introduced himself. At a showing of my work in one of his family's galleries. He's very brash. I guess, at first, that's what I liked about him. But I didn't understand why he bothered with me. I don't travel in his circle. I'm not royalty, or a celebrity. I don't live a glamorous lifestyle. I'm a working woman just trying to carve out a career."

"So you're a starving artist?" the chief asked with a smile.

"Not starving, by any means. But I'm certainly not famous."

The police chief crossed his hands over his midsection and leaned back. "You say you met him in Paris, Ms. Moore. You don't sound like a Frenchwoman."

"I'm an American. But educated in England."

The chief nodded. "That would explain the accent. I couldn't place it."

"In England I was teased for sounding too American. Here at home, I'm teased for sounding too British."

Everett gave her an encouraging smile. "And now you're here by way of Paris. Which you left rather quickly after ending a relationship with Sebastian Delray."

Sierra shook her head vehemently. "I told him I wasn't interested in any kind of a real romantic relationship. You see, I have this career—"

"But he tried to persuade you otherwise, isn't that right?"

Sierra flushed. "He was persistent. He had an uncanny way of showing up at places where I happened to be with friends."

"Could he have had some inside information?"

She raised an eyebrow.

Patiently, Everett said, "Didn't it ever occur to you that

he may have befriended people who knew you, just so he could learn more about you?"

It was clear from her look of surprise that she hadn't thought about that possibility. "I don't see why he would go to all that trouble. I let him know that I wasn't going to change my mind."

"So you became a challenge he couldn't resist?"

She stared hard at the floor, mulling his words. "I hadn't thought of it that way. I suppose so."

"Who won the debate?"

"Debate?"

"About whether or not you'd see him."

Another flush stole over her cheeks. "In the beginning, I guess he did. At first, I agreed to dinner. But only dinner. And then he took me to an old classmate's wedding. There were a few gallery showings. And just like that, he decided that we were a couple, and he became"—she shrugged, searching for a word—"controlling and possessive."

The chief's tone sharpened. "In what way?"

"He started complaining about the time I spent with my friends. He started insinuating himself into every aspect of my life. I was feeling smothered."

"Did you ask him to stop?"

She nodded. "He excused his behavior by saying that he couldn't bear to be away from me for even a few hours. But I told him I needed my space."

"Did he back off?"

"No. It got worse."

"How much worse?"

"He started calling me dozens of times a day. When I wouldn't answer his calls, he started showing up at my apartment. The final straw was when he persuaded my apartment manager to let him in while I was out with friends. I arrived home to find him sitting there in the dark, my apartment filled with dozens of flowers. On the coffee table was a jeweler's box. Inside was a…" Her gaze flew to the jewels spilling out of the box on the table. "A diamond necklace."

Everett Fletcher turned to study the jewels. "I guess that would turn a girl's head."

"That's what my friend Janine said. She told me I was crazy to pass up a catch like Sebastian Delray. But all I could see was a man who thought he could buy me, and I ordered him to leave. After the apartment manager escorted him out, I called Janine and asked if I could stay the night at her place, because I was afraid he would come back." She took a deep breath. "I loved that apartment, but I couldn't go back."

"You moved out?"

She nodded. "I went to Janine's. The next day I contacted the leasing agent and terminated my lease." She chewed her lower lip. "It cost me a fortune to pay the balance in full, along with the closing and cleaning fee because of the short notice."

"You were that afraid of him?"

She mulled that for several moments before saying, "Looking back, it sounds like a bad melodrama. But at the time, when I realized how obsessive he'd become, and had a taste of his anger…"

"Wait a minute. I think you glossed over something." Chief Fletcher held up a hand to stop her. "Tell me about this anger."

"It was the reason why the apartment manager showed up. The neighbors heard the breaking of glass when

Sebastian put a fist through the door after I refused to allow him to stay the night." She swallowed. "At the time, I was afraid of his black mood. I was afraid that he would... force himself on me."

"Did he threaten to?"

She shook her head. "No. It was just a feeling I had. He was in a full-blown, out-of-control fury."

"Did you see him again?"

"No. I stayed with my friend Janine until I made arrangements to end my lease and purchase a one-way ticket out of Paris. I asked Janine to contact Sebastian after I was safely gone, letting him know that I had left the country and wouldn't be seeing him again. I was certain that would be the end of it. He would cool off, get used to the fact that I'd left, and move on with his life, and I could do the same."

"This note was the first you'd heard from him since then?" The chief stared down at the handwritten words on the paper.

"Yes. It was in my car. A rental, which I'd parked at the ranger's station at the Tetons before I started my climb."

"Why the Tetons?"

For the first time she smiled, and a light came into her eyes that caused her to glow. "I love climbing and hiking. I did a lot of it in Europe. I've always wanted to climb the Tetons. And since I'd had enough of big cities, and because I was craving some solitude, I thought the time was right. Besides, I'm an American. I wanted to come home." She shrugged. "And like I said, I was confident that Sebastian would accept that I was gone for good and move on with his life."

"Did you tell Sebastian Delray you were coming to Wyoming?"

Sierra shook her head. "I didn't tell a soul except my best friend—"

The chief interrupted. "A best friend who may have been persuaded to reveal your whereabouts?"

When he could see that she was about to disagree, he held up a hand. "Think about this. An abject boyfriend comes to your best friend and says he really needs to apologize for his behavior. Would she think she was doing you both a favor by giving him one last chance to redeem himself?"

Sierra took a long, deep breath. "I can see Janine doing exactly that, and believing it was the right thing to do. She kept calling me a fool." Her eyes grew stormy. "And I thought I could trust her with my secret."

"So now he's found you here and left his calling card so that you'd know that he knows where you are," the chief added.

"That still doesn't explain why he's doing this. Why has he targeted me?"

"In case you haven't noticed, Ms. Moore, you're easy on the eyes. Along with that, you're open and friendly and trusting, something that is extremely attractive to a man who likes to be in control. If that isn't reason enough, I'd guess that part of this man's obsession has to do with the fact that he can't have you. You walked away from him, and he can't accept that from a woman."

"But he can have any woman he wants." She shook her head. "He has the money, the connections—"

Everett Fletcher interrupted. "Not to mention the ego, to believe that he can pretty much do whatever he wants, without consequences. That sort of man can be dangerous." The chief nodded slowly as he put his thoughts into words. "Ego and obsession and anger can be a deadly combination, especially in someone with extreme wealth who feels entitled to live by his own rules."

The chief leaned back in the comfortable chair. "I'm no psychologist, but my years as a police officer have taught me to read people. I think this speaks of a certain arrogance on Delray's part. He needs to prove to himself that the relationship wasn't fractured by anything he did, but rather by some failure on your part. So he's generously offering to forgive you. And if that isn't enough, he's offering a reward as well. A carrot, if you will, instead of a stick. Thus, those very flashy jewels. There are a lot of young, vulnerable women who would take him at his word, put the past aside, and begin again. Is that what you would like to do?"

Sierra's eyes flashed. "I'd like to do whatever I can to see that he isn't allowed to contact me again."

"You're talking about signing a restraining order." The chief gave her a stern look. "I need to know that you aren't being coerced in any way. Are you requesting this of your own volition?"

"I am."

"I'll be right back." He got to his feet and walked outside to his car. When he returned, he was carrying a sheaf of documents.

With a click of the pen he filled out the top lines before handing them to Sierra to be completed.

When she handed them back, he read them carefully, then signed and dated them.

He looked up. "I'm obliged to tell you the following. What you have filed is a restraining order, or an order of protection, which is recognized by the State of Wyoming

as a form of legal injunction requiring the party named
herein to refrain from coming near you, or contacting
you, or asking a third party to contact you in his name.
If this party refuses to comply with the order, he faces
criminal or civil penalties that could result in arrest and
possible jail time." He looked up. "Do you have a business card or phone number of a legal representative of Mr.
Delray's, who can be notified of this legal action?"

Sierra gave him the name of the gallery in Paris. "It's
a family-owned business, so I'm sure they can put you in
touch with Sebastian or his lawyer."

"Thank you." The chief made a notation, then folded
the documents into his pocket and pointed to the jeweler's
box and notes. "I'd like you to keep everything. The two
notes, the box, the wrapping, for evidence."

Sierra didn't make any move to touch them. "Why
don't you take them? I don't want to even look at them."

"I'm not authorized to take them. But see that they're
kept in a safe place." He got to his feet. "I'll record these
documents tonight. I have to stop by my office anyway.
I'll scan them and send a copy via e-mail to Mr. Delray's
counsel, and ask him to contact Delray, since I have no
idea where he's staying. I hope once Delray realizes that
you have the law on your side, he'll be willing to let this
thing go."

Sierra managed a weak smile. "Thank you, Chief
Fletcher."

"You're welcome. But I must warn you, Ms. Moore,
that these legal documents can't guarantee your safety.
They may not be a deterrent if someone is hell-bent on
taking the law into his own hands. But at least it offers a
paper trail, stating that you have cause for concern. It's a

reason for me to keep my eyes and ears open around town to see if the guy is hanging around, and to keep track of where he goes and who he sees. Once these documents are recorded, he can be found in contempt of the law if he tries to contact you. If this man chooses to ignore the warning, you'll have the power of the law on your side."

"That's a relief."

"Are you planning on staying in Wyoming?"

Before she could respond, Big Jim spoke. "I think we agreed that Sierra will stay here for a while longer. Right, sweetheart? At least until the chief can file these documents and settle this matter."

Sierra glanced at Josh, then away. "Yes, thank you, Big Jim. I certainly feel a lot safer here than I would anywhere else."

Chief Fletcher held up a beefy hand. "I should warn all of you to be careful. A person who is obsessed enough to travel halfway around the world may not be deterred by a few documents. If he's exhibited violent behavior in the past, there's no telling what he might be capable of now."

Sierra blanched. "You think this is all going to get worse?"

"Sorry." The chief put a hand on her arm. "It's not my job to sugarcoat the facts. My job is to present them as I see them. This man isn't behaving in a normal, rational manner. Therefore, I have to consider him a threat to your safety and to the safety of those who offer you refuge. As soon as I leave here, I'll be in contact with the state police, checking out both you and Sebastian Delray."

Josh shot her a smile meant to comfort her. "Everett's not kidding. When the state police are finished with their investigation, they'll know more about you and Delray than your mothers do."

The chief's eyes danced with laughter. "Josh is right on that point. So a word of warning, young lady. I consider myself the guardian of Paintbrush, Wyoming. I take my job seriously. If you're hiding anything, now's the time to spill it."

Sierra sighed. "It wasn't easy telling you such personal business. But now that I have, I'm feeling so much lighter. As though a huge weight has been lifted from my shoulders."

"I'm glad." The chief started toward the door. "Thanks again for the apple pie, Phoebe. Ms. Moore, you'll be hearing from me as soon as I have any information."

Big Jim followed the police chief from the room. In the kitchen their muted voices could be heard through the closed door.

When the lights of the chief's truck faded, Big Jim returned to the great room.

Seeing the concern etched on the faces of his family, he dropped an arm around Sierra's shoulders. "I'm glad you're staying, sweetheart."

"I'm grateful for the sanctuary. But after hearing what the chief said, I'm afraid that my being here could cause all of you trouble."

"We'll deal with trouble the way we deal with everything here in the Devil's Wilderness." He looked around, hoping his words would lift all their spirits. "Head-on, full steam, and all of us together."

At the vehemence of his words, Sierra felt her eyes fill.

"Thank you, Big Jim." Without thinking, she threw her arms around his neck and pressed a kiss to his cheek.

He held her for several seconds before releasing her.

She took a long, deep breath before saying, "But I should warn you. I wasn't completely honest with Chief Fletcher."

She saw the way she had everyone's sudden, complete attention.

"I don't mean about Sebastian. But I haven't been honest about my family."

She glanced at Josh, wondering how he and the others would feel about her when she had finished baring her soul.

CHAPTER ELEVEN

———◆◆◆———

I told you that my father is currently playing with a band in Germany, and that my mother, a sculptor, has a studio in Italy." Sierra stared down at her hands, aware that Josh and his entire family were listening in rapt silence.

They were entirely too silent, their attention riveted on her.

She could feel herself beginning to sweat. Hadn't she revealed enough already? It was actually painful to have to bare her family secrets like this.

Though she kept her tone light, she couldn't hide the hint of sadness in her eyes. "I guess you'd call my parents the poster children for the term 'free spirits.'"

To ease her tension Cole said, "I believe you told us you had no brothers or sisters."

Sierra tossed her head. "My parents were barely together long enough for me. There was no time for any others."

Despite the flip comment, there was an underlying note of something deeper.

Big Jim kept his tone gentle. "All right. Go on, sweetheart."

She gave a dry laugh to cover her pain. "My mother likes to say that I was born on a bus heading to a gig in New Orleans. That night my dad performed with his band and my mother wrapped me in one of his T-shirts and watched from backstage." Her voice lowered. "That was pretty much their lifestyle in their early days together, before they split up and moved abroad."

Josh decided to let that pass without comment, since their breakup was obviously still painful to Sierra. "Where they sent you to England to boarding school?"

She nodded. "A number of schools, in fact. By then my parents had decided that I needed some stability. You could say I was a bit of a wild child until I discovered photography. That came later, of course. I pursued art at the university, fell in love with the spontaneity of capturing images in photos, and I've been earning my own way since graduating."

Josh glanced around at his family, wondering if they were as fascinated as he was, not only by what she'd revealed but by that sweet, breathless tone of voice, and the edgy nerves she seemed to exude with each sentence. It was as though she needed to say it all as quickly as possible, so it wouldn't hurt quite so much.

He felt an instant and overwhelming desire to put his arms around her. To hold her and tell her that it didn't matter. That her past was just her past, and that she ought to be proud of the fine person she'd become.

Instead, he held his silence, watching and listening along with the rest of his family.

"I think I ought to warn you." Sierra was staring straight ahead, refusing to look at Josh or his family. "Since your police chief is going to delve into my background, you deserve to know everything about me. For openers, my parents never married."

"And you're telling us this because...?" Josh bit back the grin that threatened.

She gave a toss of her head. "I just thought you deserved to hear the truth from me, before you heard it from another source. My parents don't believe in the need for vows, or for a legal document that would bind them forever. And when they decided to go their separate ways"—she spread her hands—"they just split. Right now my father is living with the lead singer in his band. A girl who's younger than me. And my mother's partner in the studio used to be her nude model."

Josh fought to keep his tone level, though a grin tickled the corners of his mouth. "Is there anything else Chief Fletcher might find in your deep, dark past?"

She looked over. "Are you laughing at me?"

"Maybe just a little." He couldn't hold back the laughter any longer. "Sierra, as far as I know, we don't ask for any kind of legal proof of your birth before offering you a room and a bed."

She looked around at the others, who were now breaking into wide grins.

"Okay. I just didn't want you to think I was keeping secrets, especially since all of you seem so..." She struggled to explain. "You're all so good and decent and... traditional. You're this large, loving family that does everything by the book. I figured you'd be a little shocked. I know most of my teachers and the parents of my friends found my background...strange." She ended with a shrug, as though too embarrassed to go on.

"We appreciate your honesty, sweetheart, but your family history is your business." Big Jim wrapped a beefy arm around her and squeezed.

He was smiling when he turned to the others. "We'd better get some sleep if we're going to join Jake and the wranglers on the tail end of that cattle drive."

"Think they'll make it through this snow?" Quinn asked.

"According to Jake, the afternoon sun melted enough snow to make passage possible. Unless it snows overnight, they're planning on getting started at first light."

One by one the men began heading for the stairs as they called out their good nights.

Cheyenne caught Sierra's hand in hers. "It had to be awkward, telling us so much about your private business. I'm sorry you felt obliged to talk of it before Chief Fletcher learned it. I hope you understand that it doesn't change the way we feel about you."

Sierra looked at their joined hands, then up into Cheyenne's eyes. "I guess it wasn't so bad, spilling family secrets."

"Every family has them. Good night, Sierra." Cheyenne surprised her by giving her a hard hug before turning toward the stairs.

Phoebe walked closer and wrapped her arms around Sierra's shoulders. "I hope you can feel safe here, Sierra. Safe and...appreciated."

Sierra swallowed. "Thank you, Phoebe. I do. Really. Thanks to all of you."

"Good night, dear." Phoebe pressed a kiss to her cheek before turning away.

Sierra touched a finger to her cheek, wondering at the warm feeling around her heart.

Ela paused in front of her.

With those blackbird eyes staring intently into Sierra's, the old woman said, "My people believe that it is good to free the soul of all that burdens it. Honor those who gave you life, but choose your own path. Remember this: There is no one else quite like you. So, as you journey, make wise choices, for each road leads you closer to your goal."

"Those are beautiful words, Ela. But what if I don't know what my goal is?"

Ela smiled. "As we begin our journey, we do not know where it will end. That is why we have spirits to guide us."

"I think my spirits must be sleeping."

The old woman smiled, softening those shrewd eyes. "Trust them. They will show themselves when you most need them."

She touched a hand to Sierra's fair hair, brushing it from crown to the very ends. "Believe in your own goodness."

Still smiling, she turned away.

When she slipped from the room, only Josh and Sierra remained.

Sierra studied Josh's hooded eyes, wishing she could read the secrets he hid in those depths.

"I'm sorry about all this trouble, Josh. I really didn't mean to dump my messy childhood on you, on top of my problems with Sebastian. I can still be ready to leave in the morning, if you say the word."

"Why would I want you to leave?"

"Because of what Chief Fletcher said. The danger that could come to your family because of me."

"Is that what you think? That I'm worried about us?"

"Aren't you?"

"Sierra, *you're* the one being stalked. This guy is a loose cannon that could explode at any time."

"But now that I've filed an order of protection—"

"—he's going to be as mad as a nest of hornets and looking for vengeance."

She fell silent for a moment before looking up at him. "Then I guess I'd better be careful where I step."

He couldn't help smiling as he looked into her eyes. Despite that air of sophistication, there was so much innocence in this woman's soul.

He dropped an arm around her shoulders and steered her toward the stairs. "Yeah. Be careful where you step. Especially in the barns."

"Now I don't think you're talking about hornets."

"You got that right." He paused outside the door to her room to draw her close. "I'm not thinking clearly about a lot of things right now." With his lips on hers he whispered, "All I've been thinking about for the past hour or more is this."

He fought to keep the kiss soft as he felt Sierra sink into it with a sigh, wrapping her arms around his waist and leaning into him. But the taste of her, as fresh and clean as a mountain stream, had him wanting more. So much more.

He thought about driving her back against the wall and devouring her. Instead, with great care, he held her as carefully as though she were made of spun glass, as his mouth moved over hers with a hunger that caught him by surprise.

On a moan of pleasure he took the kiss deeper, and his hands began moving up her sides until his thumbs encountered the soft swell of her breasts.

He heard her little gasp of shock as her body reacted in a purely sensual way, pressing against him until he could feel the imprint of every line and curve inside his own body.

Dear heaven, she felt so good here in his arms. And just beyond this doorway was a private space that was calling to him, offering him a taste of heaven.

He indulged himself as long as he dared before coming up for air.

His tone was low and nearly as stern as his grandfather's. "I'm heading off to bed now. When you go inside, lock your door."

She looked startled. "You think Sebastian will come here tonight?"

"It's not Sebastian you need to fear." He dragged her close and kissed her again until the need for her was so tangled up inside him, his head was spinning. "Right now, I'd like very much to stay here with you. Except then you wouldn't be safe . . . from me."

She looked up to see his dark eyes burning into hers.

When she hesitated, he put his hands on her shoulders and urged her inside, before turning and walking quickly away.

As he made his way to his own room, Josh's hands were fisted at his side, another sign that he was fighting for control.

One kiss and he was a smoldering fire about to explode into flame.

How had this happened? What was it about this woman that had him losing all his control?

He knew he was playing with fire if they continued along this path. She'd made it very plain that this was just a brief stop on the way to her real love—her career. And yet he couldn't seem to stop himself. There was just something about this independent little female that tugged at him.

He'd have to see that they kept things cool and impersonal. Otherwise, he was apt to get burned.

Sebastian Delray checked the caller identification on his cell phone, noting idly that it was his family's solicitor. Though it wasn't yet dawn, he'd been awake for hours. His body and mind, it seemed, were still on French time.

"Yes, Jacques. How are things in Paris?"

He listened quietly, noting the harsh edge to the lawyer's voice. Though he kept his tone level, his eyes narrowed to slits. "She did what?"

He fell silent until the lawyer had finished his tirade. Forcing a bored tone into his voice, he said, "She's a woman. That's reason enough for the hysterics. They're all the same. I've broken no laws."

There was a burst of staccato French words peppered with expletives. In the silence that followed he said very deliberately, "Yes, I can imagine that my family would not welcome such publicity. Nor would I. As I said, I've broken no laws. Of course I'll present myself to this local gendarme so that he can give me a copy of whatever documents the little gold digger has filed. And I shall be suitably respectful, as you suggest. Now, what else would you like to say?"

He listened, before adding, "I'll be home soon enough. Though I may ask you to prepare the secluded villa at Cannes. I'll phone you from my plane with more details. After all this snow and cold, I have a sudden yearning for sun-drenched beaches."

He rang off and stood staring into space.

That smug little witch had actually filled out papers with some small-town lawman. Papers that stated that he was forbidden to come near her, or to contact her, or to even have an intermediary contact her on his behalf.

Sierra Moore had gone too far. Dragging his name— his eyes narrowed fractionally as he thought—*his family's name*, into the glare of public scrutiny.

Did she know who he was? Really know? Did she have any idea just how much power he wielded?

A slow smile touched the corners of his lips, though it never reached his eyes.

She was about to find out.

And when he was finished with her, the high-and-mighty Sierra Moore, the ice princess who teased and tormented but failed to deliver, would be begging his forgiveness. Even while she pleaded for her very life.

CHAPTER TWELVE

————◆◆◆————

Sierra awoke to the sound of voices in the hallway outside her room, and the steady tattoo of boots on the stairs.

Earlier, she'd lain awake for hours, going over in her mind all the secrets she'd revealed to the Conway family. It had been really awkward telling them about her parents, her childhood, and her major error in judgment with Sebastian. And yet there had also been a sense of relief that it was all out in the open. When she'd finally given in to sleep, she'd felt a childlike peace that had been absent from her life for too long. Despite the police chief's words of warning, she felt safe here on their ranch. Safe and protected.

She touched a finger to her lips and thought of Josh, and that kiss. He'd warned her to be afraid of him.

A dreamy smile softened all her features. It wasn't fear she felt whenever she was alone with Josh. Oh no.

It was something far different. In his arms she felt alive. With him she felt free to be herself. And now, with all her secrets no longer a burden, that sense of freedom was heightened.

She crossed the room to peer out the window.

When these ranchers said dawn, they meant it. There was only the faintest pale pink light on the horizon, and yet it sounded as though the entire household was up and moving.

She hurriedly dressed, unwilling to miss even a minute of the coming day.

In the kitchen doorway she paused. Phoebe and Ela were bustling about stirring, mixing, preparing a hearty meal guaranteed to sustain hard-working cowboys. From the looks of them, they'd been up for hours.

While they carried platters of steak and eggs and potatoes to the table, the entire household was bursting with energy. The family was loudly arguing over who would ride up to the hills to meet the herd, and who would remain below to guide the cattle into the holding pens when they arrived.

"Quiet!" Big Jim's voice instantly quieted the others.

He turned to Quinn. "Between our two ranches, you and Cheyenne have been doing double duty since you got here a couple of days ago. You two will stay here and wait for the herd." He turned to Josh and Cole. "The three of us will head to the high meadow."

"Do you mind if I ride along?"

At the sound of Sierra's voice, the entire family turned to where she stood. She wore faded denims and a plaid shirt, her long hair tied back in a ponytail. Around her neck was her camera.

Big Jim didn't mince words. "Suit yourself, sweetheart. But be warned. We've got no time to look out for you. I don't care if your horse gets spooked and tosses you, or you take a wrong trail and get yourself lost up in the woods, we can't spare anyone to lend a hand."

"I promise I won't be any trouble."

"I'll hold you to that." He turned when Phoebe announced that breakfast was ready.

Few words were spoken as they all sat and began passing the platters, filling their plates, and eating quickly. It was clear that their minds were on the job they were about to do.

Their excitement was contagious. Sierra looked around the table and wished she could capture their faces on film. The anticipation. The determination. The thrill of what they were about to do was etched in the set of their jaws, the light in their eyes.

As she lifted her coffee cup, her hand was trembling, and she knew it was nerves. The very best kind of nerves. She would actually witness a cattle drive. A roundup. Something so typically alien to her lifestyle, something she'd seen only in movies.

A short time later the family shoved away from the table and trooped out to the mudroom to don parkas, scarred leather chaps, and wide-brimmed hats. In the barn they spoke softly to their horses as they saddled them and led them outside, breath pluming in the frosty air.

Josh led two horses out of the barn, a big bay gelding and a roan mare. "I saddled Lady for you."

"Thanks." Sierra pulled herself into the saddle of the roan and took the reins from him.

He mounted and moved his big bay beside her. "I'll try

to keep an eye out for you, but once we reach the herd, it won't be easy."

"Josh." She lay a hand over his and wondered at the rush of heat that she felt all the way to her toes. From the look in his eyes, he felt it, too. "You have a job to do. I don't want to be a distraction."

He shot her a wicked grin. "Now that's going to be a problem. You see, you've already become a very big distraction."

He turned his mount and caught up with his father and grandfather, leaving her to follow at a slower pace while she mulled his words.

She'd really meant it when she'd said that she didn't want to distract him from his job. She wouldn't be able to bear knowing that her presence caused him to do something careless. Still, his words had caused the strangest little hitch around her heart. She couldn't deny that she was flattered. He had a way of saying something in that short, staccato way that was so unexpected and sweet it caught her by complete surprise.

Feeling on top of the world, she passed the corral and waved to Quinn and Cheyenne, who were standing quietly, their arms around each other, their matching smiles revealing a sweet contentment.

What must it be like, she wondered as she clicked off a series of photos, to know in your heart of hearts that you'd found the one with whom you wanted to spend the rest of your life?

And why, she wondered, did some people search a lifetime and never find that pot of gold at the end of their rainbow?

So many questions. And no time to search for answers

as she followed Josh and his father and grandfather up a steep, high path.

The low, rumbling sound of the herd alerted all of them to the approaching cattle long before they actually came into sight.

There was a deep, rolling roar like thunder. A pounding rhythm so loud, so fevered, it reverberated inside their chests like the beat of a huge drum.

"They're coming." Big Jim stood in his stirrups and peered in the distance.

Suddenly he lifted his hat and waved it. "Get ready."

The first of the cattle appeared over a ridge, moving in an undulating wave, their hooves sending up sprays of snow and grass in their wake.

At the spectacular sight, Sierra felt an unexpected lump in her throat. It actually looked like something out of a movie. But this was real. For Josh and his family, this was their life, their livelihood.

The horsemen began to fan out, ready to join the wranglers who rode in a loose formation on the fringes of the thundering herd.

Sierra reined in her mount at the top of a rise, which gave her a panoramic view of the scene below. She focused her camera on the great black sea of cattle, snapping off shot after shot.

Gradually her attention was caught by the individual wranglers. From a distance they were merely men astride horses, occasionally waving a rope or hat to keep a stray cow in line. But as she zoomed in on their faces, she could see the shaggy hair beneath the wide-brimmed hat; the rough growth of beard on a man who had been living in the high country for endless nights; the body, lean and muscled from years spent in hard, manual labor; and even the eyes, alert to the job at hand, catching sight of an errant cow almost from the moment it began to stray.

As the herd thundered past, she saw Josh take up a position near the rear. Even as she focused her camera on him, his rope snaked out, neatly dropping over the neck of a cow that had veered away from the others. While the cow thrashed about, Josh's horse drew back until the rope was taut. Horse and rider worked as a perfect team until the cow settled down, then, with the rope still around its neck, meekly followed along behind until they rejoined the rest of the herd. Josh slid from the saddle and his horse moved just enough to loosen the taut rope. When the noose was removed, the cow was swallowed up in a sea of cattle. Josh climbed back into the saddle, and horse and rider moved to the far side of the herd to do it all again and again.

Through it all, Sierra snapped off photo after photo, recording every moment.

She heard a yell and watched as Big Jim spotted a line of cattle breaking away from the herd and heading for a narrow canyon. Because of the tremendous noise, none of the other wranglers heard his warning or took notice. Big Jim's horse broke into a furious gallop as it raced to get ahead of the runaways.

Using her zoom, Sierra captured every moment of the heart-stopping teamwork between man and mount as they inched forward over rocky terrain until they were able to head off the mutinous action and return the line of cows to the herd.

Instead of remaining at her vantage point behind the herd, Sierra was suddenly eager to return to the corrals, so that she could record just how such a large number of cattle would be contained when they finally reached their final destination. Urging her horse up a hill and over the other side, she managed to get there well ahead of the herd.

Quinn and Cheyenne were quickly joined by Cole and Big Jim. Astride their horses, they shouted and whistled and waved coiled ropes and hats to keep the cattle moving through the open gates of the corral. When one corral was filled, they opened the gates of a second and directed the rest of the herd inside.

Josh and Jake arrived at the rear of the cattle, making certain that the last of the cows followed the others into the holding pens.

Once inside, the cows milled about, churning the snow and dirt into a sea of mud. Outside the corrals the lathered horses blew and snorted from the effort, their breath pluming in the air.

The wranglers dismounted and led their weary horses toward the barn, where feed and water and a good rubdown awaited them as a reward at the end of their long journey from the high country.

Sierra recorded all of it, pausing to frame a lanky wrangler as he shook Big Jim's hand, and catching a stunning moment when Quinn lifted Cheyenne from her horse, then continued holding her in his arms as he took the time to slowly lower her to the ground while thoroughly kissing her.

The two were laughing as they walked toward the house, arm in arm.

When Sierra lowered her camera and turned, she found Josh beside her. "Why were you photographing them? I thought you were looking for shots of the real West."

"They're not real?"

Jake strode up behind his brother. "Real mushy, if you ask me."

Josh touched a hand to her camera. "Did you get some good pictures?"

"Yes." She felt almost breathless, and blamed it on the excitement of the roundup. It couldn't possibly be because he was standing so close while she was feeling so emotional. "I can't wait to see every frame."

Jake peered over his brother's shoulder. "You going to share them with all of us?"

She nodded. "You bet. As soon as I sort through them and see just what I've got."

"Good." Josh turned toward the house. "It's not over yet."

"What do you mean?"

"I'll show you." Instead of heading toward the mudroom, he led her around to the front of the house, with its wide front porch that ran the entire width of the building, offering a sweeping view of grassy meadows and towering mountains for miles in every direction.

Tables and benches had been set up on the sheltered front porch. The tables were covered in lengths of festive red-and-white-checked plaid, and groaned under mountains of roast beef and ham and chicken and barbecued ribs. There were bowls of whipped potatoes, corn on the cob and baked beans, and baskets of hot buttered rolls. There were gallons of foamy milk, as well as a side table holding coffee, and a tub of ice filled with beer and soda.

Josh leaned close. "I hope you brought your appetite. Because, believe me, our wranglers have been thinking about this feast for weeks now."

Jake, trailing behind them, added, "Phoebe and Ela are our secret weapons."

Josh laughed. "He's not kidding. This is the bonus we offer every year to persuade cowboys to spend endless days in the high country with nothing but cows and coyotes for company. By this time every year, all they can think about is a real home-cooked meal."

"Well," Jake added with a laugh, "this feast might be number one on their list of favorite things, but heading into town with fat paychecks is a close second." He punched Josh on the shoulder. "Hell, after so many nights of seeing nothing but cows, no woman will be safe. Even old Flora and Dora will look good to them tonight."

Josh joined in the laughter and winked at Sierra. "Too bad we can't be flies on the wall tonight at Flora's Diner. I'm betting Flora's been baking dozens of apple pies all day, just to satisfy everyone's sweet tooth."

"You know what they say." Sierra couldn't help getting into the spirit of the moment. "The way to a man's heart..."

Jake gave a shake of his head. "These cowboys don't need any bait. But that won't stop Flora's daughter, Dora, from practically bathing in enough cheap perfume to clog their lungs."

"And dull their brains," Josh added.

Jake chuckled. "They don't need brains for what Flora and Dora have in mind for them tonight."

"In fact," Josh said, "they'd be better off leaving their brains home. Thinking will just get in the way."

The two brothers were still laughing as they climbed the steps of the front porch and dipped into the tub of ice to help themselves to cold, frosty longnecks.

CHAPTER THIRTEEN

———◆◆◆———

Sierra hurried upstairs to shower and change into fresh clothes. After a long day in the saddle, she'd expected to feel bone-weary. Instead, she was feeling surprisingly agile, and for that she was thankful for the years of conditioning her muscles got from her hiking and climbing.

She slipped into clean denims and a turtleneck sweater the color of ripe raspberries before reaching for her ever-present camera. She couldn't wait to record the feast.

Downstairs the wranglers streamed from the bunkhouse, their faces clean-shaven, their shaggy hair slicked back from their showers. All were wearing fresh denims and flannel shirts, their once-filthy, trail-dusted boots polished to a high shine as they made their way to the banquet awaiting them on the front porch.

When Sierra approached, Josh looked up from the corner of the porch, where he was deep in conversation with

Jake and Cole. He stepped away from them to hurry to her side.

As he led her toward the others, he looked her up and down approvingly. "Well, don't you look pretty."

She dimpled. Why was it that a simple compliment from this man meant more to her than a dozen flattering comments from anyone else?

"Want to take our picture?" Jake dropped an arm around his brother's shoulder, and the two of them stepped up beside Cole.

"I'd love to." Sierra lifted her camera, framed the shot, and snapped.

"That's it?" Jake looked puzzled. "Usually we have to stand here wearing silly grins for a minute or more."

"That's for amateurs." Josh nudged him with his elbow. "You're looking at a pro here."

"I wouldn't know about that." Jake winked at his father. "So far, we haven't seen a single picture to back up that claim."

"All in good time." Sierra turned and snapped off several shots of the tables laden with food.

"Want a beer?" Josh held up a cold bottle.

"Thanks." She sipped, then set it aside when she caught sight of Big Jim stepping up to the center of the porch and calling for silence.

In a whisper she added, "For now, if you don't mind, I'd like to capture this for posterity."

As she quietly moved about, snapping off shot after shot, Josh stood to one side, keeping her in his line of vision.

He couldn't take his eyes off her. He was clearly captivated by this woman.

That fact wasn't lost on his father and brother, who exchanged knowing looks.

After Big Jim's words of thanks to the wranglers for their hard work, they filled their plates and settled around the tables. The good food, the abundance of beer, and the friendly atmosphere loosened them up until they were regaling one another with stories of their time spent in the hills.

As Sierra moved among them, snapping off pictures, she overheard snatches of conversation that were as revealing as any photo.

"...was glad when Josh joined us." The speaker was a stick-thin cowboy with skin the texture of aged leather and dark hair threaded with gray.

"Yeah." The stocky young wrangler beside him nodded. "Funny thing. He's never pushy or loud. But he has a way of taking charge. I swear those old cows know when he's around."

A sandy-haired, freckled cowboy overheard and added, "If I didn't know he was one of the owners, I'd think he was just another hired hand. He works harder than any of us."

"That's how you get to be the owner of one of the biggest spreads in the state," another said with a laugh. "Just ask his grandfather. Big Jim has always been able to outwork, outplay, and outthink every man in Wyoming."

That had the entire table of cowboys laughing and nodding.

Sierra glanced over to where Josh and his brothers stood, tipping up longnecks and talking in low tones.

It was reassuring to hear such nice things being said

about Josh and his family. But, she thought with a smile, they were wrong about one thing. That loose, easy style couldn't hide the fact that Josh Conway knew exactly who he was and what he was doing. He wasn't just the go-to guy on the slopes of the Tetons. He carried his share of responsibility every day here on the ranch.

She watched as Josh, Quinn, Jake, Cole, and Big Jim moved among the men, shaking hands, listening, smiling. They couldn't fake the appreciation they felt for every man here and for the job they all did so well. That was evident in the way the men responded to them. Not as employee to boss, but man to man.

She continued to snap photos until Cheyenne touched a hand to her arm. "You haven't eaten a thing."

Sierra turned to her with a look of surprise. "You're right. I guess I got so caught up in trying to capture every single moment of this day, I forgot about food."

"That would explain that tiny waistline."

Sierra laughed. "I could say the same about you. If you'd like to borrow my clothes, be my guest. I'm betting they'd fit you like they were your own."

"Thanks. I may have to take you up on that if Quinn and I stay here a few more days. I didn't bring much with me, thinking we'd be back at my ranch yesterday."

"How far is your ranch from here?"

"About an hour." She pointed. "It's just over those foothills."

"I wish I could have seen it while I was here."

"Maybe you could extend your visit?"

Sierra shrugged. "I've already been here longer than I'd planned. I'd hate to overstay my welcome."

"You could never do that with the Conway family.

They're the most welcoming people I've ever known. Someday I'll tell you about how long I was here while my ranch was being rebuilt after a fire, and how welcome they all made me feel. Besides," she added with a laugh, "I know one Conway who wouldn't object if you stayed longer."

When Sierra shot her a questioning look, she said, "Don't pretend you haven't noticed the way Josh hovers over you."

The two young women laughed as they moved along the food-laden tables, filling their plates before finding an empty spot to sit and eat.

"Okay." Sierra turned to Cheyenne. "Tell me about the fire you mentioned, and the amount of time you spent here."

She listened in wide-eyed amazement as Cheyenne described the house fire that swept through her place while she slept, and how Quinn's heroics managed to save them both.

"Is that when you knew you loved Quinn?" Sierra asked.

Cheyenne laughed. "I barely knew him then. But I will admit that I was very intrigued. And by the time I'd been here a few weeks and got to know Quinn's family, I knew that what I was feeling was something very special."

"Were you afraid?"

"Of my feelings?"

Sierra shook her head. "Of making a lifelong commitment."

"Oh." Cheyenne smiled. "I guess everyone has some concerns about making promises for a lifetime. But with Quinn, it was so easy."

"Why?"

Cheyenne touched a hand to Sierra's. "I can't explain it. I just knew he was the one I'd been waiting for." She pointed to Sierra's plate. "You haven't eaten a thing."

"You're right." With a laugh Sierra sampled a little of everything, from chicken to steak to ribs and baked beans, and gave a sigh of pleasure. "With food like this, how do you keep from weighing a ton?"

Cheyenne laughed. "Discipline and hard work."

Sierra nodded. "I've had a sample of the hard work today. How do you and Quinn manage two ranches?"

Cheyenne sighed. "We're finding out that it isn't easy. When he's here helping his family, he feels guilty that he isn't at my place helping me. When I'm here with him, the chores at my ranch suffer. That's why we know that we have to make some decisions soon."

"What about your family?"

Cheyenne's face clouded for a moment, and Sierra wished she could take back her question.

Then Cheyenne managed a smile. "My family is all gone now. My father, mother, and brother."

"Oh, Cheyenne." Sierra touched her hand. "I'm so sorry."

"Thanks." The young woman sighed. "Having Quinn's family around me has softened the loss. I love all the teasing that goes on among his brothers."

"Yeah. They're fun to be around. I never thought that families could enjoy one another's company so much."

"I guess you haven't had a lot of experience with family, have you?"

Sierra shook her head. "It's so much better than anything I could have imagined. The private jokes. The shared history." She looked at Cheyenne. "You must miss that with your family gone."

"I do. But with every day that passes, Quinn's family becomes mine as well." Cheyenne polished off a biscuit. "Quinn and I plan to meet with Big Jim and Cole soon, to talk about whether or not we could merge the two ranches."

"How will you ever decide which one to live on?"

"That's easy. Quinn built a cabin on the property Big Jim gave him. It's nestled in high country, near his current wolf pack, between this ranch and mine." Her smile became dreamy. "It's a place we both love. We spend as much time as possible there, until we can make it our permanent home. As for merging the two ranches, and the crew of wranglers, it will take some planning, but we think we can make it work."

"I hope so." Sierra gave her a gentle smile. "I'll hold a good thought for you."

"Thanks. That's sweet of you. I appreciate it."

They looked up when Quinn and Josh walked over to join them.

"About time you ate something." Josh sat down beside Sierra. "I was hoping I wouldn't have to hog-tie you and force you to eat."

"With food this good, no force-feeding's necessary. I just got busy and forgot for a while. Now I don't need any reminder to eat."

He nodded toward the dessert table, laden with slices of gooey chocolate cake and apple pie. "You don't want to miss that."

Sierra shook her head. "Believe me, I intend to sample

a little of everything. But not just yet." She sat back. "This has been the most amazing day."

Josh nodded. "And it isn't over yet." He leaned close, causing a shiver to race down her spine. "Maybe, if we're lucky, it'll be an even more amazing night."

Her eyes went wide, and she turned to him with a look of surprise. Before she could respond, Cole tapped him on the shoulder.

"The light's starting to fade, son, and these cowboys are getting eager to head to town. I need a hand passing out the paychecks and bonuses."

"Right." Josh stood, then bent low to whisper to Sierra, "When I get back, remind me where we left off."

Before turning away he touched a finger to her cheek. Just a touch, but she absorbed the pleasure of it all the way to her toes.

She watched as he sauntered away.

And wondered at the lightness around her heart.

Sierra and Cheyenne loaded trays with dirty dishes and hauled them to the kitchen, where Phoebe and Ela had already begun to wash and dry.

Cheyenne set down her tray and gently nudged Phoebe from the sink. "You've done enough. I'll wash."

Following her lead, Sierra reached for Ela's towel. "You join Phoebe at the table and eat, while I dry."

"I ate," the old woman said in protest.

"Then have some of that fantastic pie," Sierra said with a laugh. "Before Cheyenne and I eat the whole thing."

Laughing, Phoebe set the kettle on the stove and began slicing the pie, setting the slices on pretty plates.

While the two younger women worked their way

through a mountain of dishes, Phoebe and Ela sipped hot tea and sampled the desserts.

Sierra dried a platter. "I can't believe the amount of food the two of you managed to prepare today."

"We do it every year at roundup," Phoebe remarked.

Ela nodded. "It is as natural as breathing. Spring calving, fall roundup, we cook all day so the wranglers can keep up their strength."

"When is it your turn to get pampered?" Sierra asked.

The two women looked at her with matching arched brows.

"Now why would we need pampering?" Phoebe topped off Ela's cup, and then her own.

Sierra set the platter in a cupboard and turned. "Everybody needs a little pampering now and then."

Phoebe shrugged. "I wouldn't know what to do if I had a day off. I'm much more comfortable with hard work."

Sierra nudged Cheyenne. "I think, when things settle down here, we ought to take Phoebe and Ela into town and show them how to relax."

"What would we do to fill an entire day away from here?" Phoebe, clearly intrigued, shot a smile at Ela.

"We could start with lunch at Flora's Diner," Cheyenne said. "And get all the latest gossip."

Phoebe and Ela chuckled.

"And we could find a salon and get our hair done. And maybe a manicure and pedicure, while we're there."

"Paint our toes?" Ela laughed right out loud.

"You wouldn't have to get them painted, if you didn't want to. But once you had your feet soaked in warm, scented water, and then maybe a foot massage, you'd find out how much you can love being pampered."

At Sierra's words, both Phoebe and Ela put their hands to their mouths to cover their laughter.

Cheyenne drained the water from the sink and turned. "That settles it. I believe it's our duty to take the two of you into town and treat you to a day off."

Sierra nodded. "And since you spent all day on your feet, I think we should do it tomorrow."

She looked from Phoebe to Ela, and could see that, though they were offering mild protests, their eyes were sparkling. She turned to Cheyenne. "Do you have a number for a salon in Paintbrush?"

"I do." Cheyenne dropped an arm around Sierra's shoulders. "I'll call right now and see what time they can take us tomorrow."

When Cheyenne and Sierra turned to the two older women for confirmation, they were pleased to see both of them nodding in agreement.

"Done," Sierra said.

She and Cheyenne shook hands, then burst into fits of laughter.

"Oh," Cheyenne said as she poured herself a cup of tea. "This is going to be such fun."

Sierra walked through the mudroom and stepped out onto the back porch to stare at the spectacular sunset. Ribbons of red and mauve and pink streaked high above the peaks of the Tetons, where the sun, now a ball of fire, hovered.

Working with Cheyenne and Phoebe and Ela in the kitchen had been as satisfying as the hard, physical work she'd shared in the barns with Josh and his brothers.

These women were so easy to be around. Phoebe was

fun and funny, with a surprising sense of humor. Old Ela's
sharp eye and even sharper mind was a delight. It was
easy to see why the Conway men were able to concentrate
on the many demands of a ranch of this size, when they
had such wise and capable women working behind the
scenes to make their lives as easy and uncomplicated as
possible.

She had once remarked that the Conway men were
spoiled by such good help in their home. Now their
women would get their opportunity to be equally spoiled.
She couldn't wait to spend tomorrow with Phoebe, Ela,
and Cheyenne.

The wranglers had pocketed their paychecks and had
left for town in a caravan of vehicles. Trucks, cars, vans,
and even a motorcycle had roared away, leaving the house
and the land strangely silent.

Eager to see as much as she could, Sierra wandered
past the corrals where the cattle, fed and watered, were
now quiet, except for the occasional lowing. Moving on,
with no particular destination in mind, she climbed the
hill behind the horse barns, her mind whirling with all the
wonderful things she'd witnessed this day.

As she came up over the ridge, she caught sight of Big
Jim, standing with his hand on a tall stone. In the stillness
of evening she could hear his voice, and wondered who he
was talking to.

She moved closer. Not wanting to disturb him, she
paused and peered around.

Forming a semicircle around the tall stone were five
smaller stones.

Headstones.

As the knowledge struck, Sierra's heart nearly stopped.

"...was roundup, Clemmy. You'd have loved it. Those grandsons of ours make me so damned proud. They can work circles around the best wranglers on this ranch."

As Big Jim's words washed over her, she looked around helplessly, wishing she could leave him to his privacy. She had no right to be here, intruding on such an intimate scene. But it was too late. She would die before she would disturb him now. So, rather than draw attention to herself, she remained in the shadows and hoped he wouldn't realize that she was here eavesdropping.

Big Jim laid a big, calloused hand on the headstone, as though stroking it. "You know how I used to complain about there being no females around here? At least none since Cole's Seraphine went missing. Oh, I know that Phoebe and Ela help balance it some, but we're in need of more. There they are, those three handsome sons of Cole, who'd rather chase wolves or climb mountains than settle down. Well, just when Quinn got Cupid's arrow through his heart and fell hard for Cheyenne, now I'm seeing Josh wearing his heart on his sleeve over a certain young lady he brought back from the mountain." He gave a low, throaty chuckle. "I like her. A lot. So would you. She reminds me of you, Clemmy darlin'. She's honest and direct. A free spirit with a mind all her own."

Sierra's eyes widened in the lengthening shadows. Big Jim liked her?

A wild thrill of pleasure shot like an arrow through her heart.

The old man set a plate on the ground, beside the headstone. "I brought you a slice of Phoebe's apple pie. I know this just invites the wild critters to swarm all over here when I leave you these things, but I can't help it. It makes me smile just thinking about the way you and I always loved sharing our favorite foods. You know what I miss? The way you always took the first taste of my dessert and then you'd tell me whether or not I'd like it. I don't recall a single time when you were wrong. You knew my taste better'n I knew it myself."

He straightened and touched a big hand to the headstone. His voice softened. "'Night, darlin'. I'll be seeing you tomorrow."

He turned and strode quickly away, without a backward glance.

When he was gone, Sierra walked closer to read the names and dates on the headstone and then on the smaller stones.

Big Jim's wife and five sons. All buried here on this lovely rise overlooking their land. All these years later, he still came around to talk over his day with his beloved wife.

What would it be like to love someone that much? To be loved that completely?

Even her parents, who proclaimed their love for her, had never displayed that sort of devotion. She doubted they were capable of such deep, honest emotions. She had always come in second behind her parents' relentless pursuit of their own pleasures.

A sob caught in Sierra's throat, and she slumped to her knees on the ground.

Moments later she heard footsteps. Before she could compose herself, Josh loomed out of the darkness and dropped to his knees beside her.

"Hey. What's wrong? What happened?" His voice

lowered with anger. "Did you get another message from that bastard?"

She looked at him, tears welling up to spill over and run in little rivers down her cheeks. It was a struggle to find her voice. "No. I'm not crying over Sebastian."

"Who then?" He cupped her chin in his hand and stared angrily at the tears she couldn't hide. "Whoever made you cry will answer to me."

"It's..." She lifted a hand to swipe at the tears. "I didn't mean to be here. I didn't realize..." She spread her hands to indicate the headstones. "I overheard your grandfather talking..." She sucked in a breath to stifle the sobs that threatened.

"Ah." Josh said the word in one long, low sigh as the truth dawned. "Clemmy. My grandmother. Big Jim's sweet darlin' Clementine. She was the great love of his life. His one and only. He stops by whenever he can to share his day with her."

"That's just so..." Her lips quivered and she knew she was going to embarrass herself by starting to weep again. "Oh, Josh. That's just so sweet. And so heartbreaking."

"Yeah." With great tenderness he stood and drew her up and into his arms, holding her close while she wept against his chest, dampening the front of his shirt.

When at last the tears had run their course, she pushed a little away. Josh offered her his handkerchief.

"Thanks." She blew her nose and wiped away the tears before gripping it tightly in her hand while she looked at the headstones. "I've never known a love like that. I didn't even know such a love was possible. It's...a little overwhelming."

"Yeah. It's special. I guess, growing up with it, I some-times take it for granted."

They stood together for long, silent minutes, letting the peace of the night wash over them.

Seeing how deeply touched she was, Josh turned away, drawing her with him. "Come on."

"Where are we going?"

Keeping his arm around her shoulders he leaned close to whisper, "I don't know. But we need to get away from here. I don't know about you, but it's got me in a strange mood."

She sniffed. "Me, too."

"Where would you like to go?"

She shrugged. "I don't care. Anywhere, I guess. Your choice."

"Now that's living dangerously, woman. Maybe I'll take you to the barn"—he wiggled his brows like a car-toon villain—"and have my way with you."

She started laughing. It felt so good to be able to laugh again after that heart-tugging scene she'd just witnessed.

Josh was right. She was in a strange mood. Strange and solemn, as though she'd witnessed something almost religious.

And now, with Josh beside her, her heart felt as light as air.

Feeling reckless, she leaned into him, her head dip-ping to his shoulder, her arms wrapping around his waist as they meandered through the tall grass. "Maybe I'll just let you have your way with me."

She was still laughing as she tilted her head and looked up at him.

What she saw there had the laughter dying in her

throat. His eyes, hot and fierce, told her, as plainly as any words, that what had started out as a joke had suddenly become something much more.

His tone was gruff. "I hope you mean what you just said."

She fell silent before whispering, "I do." It was all she could manage from a throat that suddenly felt as dry as dust.

"Well, then..."

His steps were no longer aimless but purposeful as he led her toward the barn looming in the distance.

CHAPTER FOURTEEN

———◆———

Josh kept his arm firmly around Sierra's shoulders as he made his way unerringly toward the barn. Once there he led her through the open doorway and paused just inside the cavernous building, waiting for his eyes to adjust to the dim light.

He drew her into his arms and pressed his lips to her temple. "That was the longest walk of my life."

Laughing, she lifted her face to his, brushing her mouth over his. "It was the same for me."

"That's a relief. I'm glad these feelings aren't one-sided. Now let me..." His big hands were just framing her face when he heard his father's voice from a nearby stall.

"Well, you two. Just in time. I was thinking about looking for you." He gave a final pat to his horse and stepped out of the stall, closing the door behind him.

"What for?" Josh lifted his face. A face that was now as dark as a thundercloud.

Sierra's look was equally frustrated.

"Thought I'd head into town and have a couple of beers with the boys at the Watering Hole. No sense letting them have all the fun."

"You go ahead, Pa. Enjoy the night."

Cole wasn't about to be dismissed so lightly. "Now, son, I was hoping you'd agree to be my designated driver."

Josh gave a sigh of disgust. How could he possibly refuse such a request? His father asked so little of his sons. And though Cole wasn't much of a drinking man, he was wise enough to take along a driver if he thought he'd need one.

Josh looked down into Sierra's face and thought about refusing. This wasn't just an inconvenience; it was a real sacrifice. "I guess, if you really need me..."

"I'll go, too." Sierra squeezed his hand.

"You don't have to," Cole warned. "This could prove to be a long, rowdy night."

"Really?" She gave a delighted laugh. "Well then, that settles it. I have to go along, just so the two of you don't have all the fun."

"Good girl." Cole stepped between Josh and Sierra, looping his arms through theirs. "We'll have us some kind of fun, all right."

As he led them from the barn, Josh nearly groaned aloud.

He'd been this close to heaven. And now, instead of a night to remember, he'd been suckered into babysitting his dear old dad.

The little town of Paintbrush was hopping. Cars, trucks, and vans were parked up and down the main street, and spilled over into the public parking area behind the courthouse and even into the Paintbrush church's parking area.

To take advantage of all the potential customers, Flora had added tables and chairs on a little patch of concrete outside the door of her diner. Inside and out, every table and chair was filled, and Dora was being assisted in serving by two of her nieces, who were flirting shamelessly with the customers.

Farther down the street, the Watering Hole, the ancient Paintbrush saloon, was nearly bursting at the seams with thirsty cowboys.

Josh pulled up at the curb and deposited his father and Sierra, before driving on to find a parking space behind Dr. April Walton's clinic.

When he stepped into the saloon a few minutes later, the twang of country music had been amped up so it could be heard above the chorus of voices. The familiar chest-thumping, heart-stomping sound rolled over him in waves.

He looked around and found Cole and Sierra seated at a table in the middle of the room. As he attempted to thread his way between clusters of cowboys talking, laughing, and swearing, he was forced to stop and exchange greetings with all of them. He edged between tables big enough for four but now filled with six, eight, or more, all frisky cowboys with eager young women from town seated on their laps or draped around them. Judging by the beers that littered the tabletops, none of them would go home thirsty. And he doubted that any of them would go home alone.

"About time you got here." Cole shoved a longneck toward Josh as he took a seat beside Sierra.

"I'm driving, remember?" Josh slid the bottle toward Sierra and signaled the waitress over. After ordering a tall iced tea, he sat back and took in the crowd.

"Looks like a lot of happy people here," Sierra remarked.

"They won't be so happy in the morning." Josh winked at her. "Let me rephrase that. Some of them will be very happy, especially all those wives waiting for their long-absent husbands."

"Not to mention their husbands' paychecks," Cole muttered.

Josh nodded. "But a lot more of these customers will be nursing hangovers for the next week."

"Ouch." Sierra laughed and sipped her longneck. "I guess I'll switch to what you're drinking after this one."

"Speaking of which . . ." Cole signaled the waitress and ordered another beer.

When he looked at Sierra, she shook her head. "One's my limit."

He smiled. "Me, too. Except for tonight. We're celebrating." He accepted another beer from the waitress and drank nearly half the bottle in one long chug before turning to Sierra. "What did you think of your first roundup?"

"I loved it. It was everything I'd ever thought it would be. The sea of cattle. The wranglers keeping the strays in line. The horses working with their riders like a team." In her excitement she placed a hand over Cole's. "I still can't believe I got to witness it up close. And all thanks to you."

He closed his other hand over hers. "I can see that it really meant a lot to you."

"It was like a dream come true. Like something out of a movie. I couldn't believe I was really there, experiencing it in the flesh."

He glanced over at Josh. "You know who Sierra reminds me of?"

Josh arched a brow.

"Your mother." He turned to Sierra. "You would have loved my Seraphine."

"I'm sure I would. Tell me about her."

That was all the encouragement Cole needed. That, and the beer he'd already consumed.

He sat back, long legs stretched out, his eyes warm with memories. "She was tall, slim, with this fantastic long hair that would be blond one day, black the next, and red a day later. I loved being surprised by her. No matter what color she dyed it, she was a real knockout." Cole shook his head. "Of course, Big Jim warned me that we were all wrong for each other, and he was right. I was a cowboy, all rough edges, fresh off the range. She was city born and bred, touring with a dance troupe. I took one look at her and I was a goner. I mean head-over-heels gone. And I guess I caught her in a weak moment. She was sick and tired of touring from town to town, living like a gypsy, she called it, and the thought of settling down on a big Wyoming ranch, far away from people, sounded like her idea of heaven." He laughed. "Until she got a taste of the isolation."

"She didn't like living on your ranch?"

"On the one hand, she loved it. And once Quinn was born, she seemed to settle in well enough. After two more sons, I was the happiest man on earth, but there she was, surrounded by all those men. She was this gorgeous, prissy girly-girl who loved expensive perfume and fancy cocktails. She never seemed to know just where she fit into the rough-and-tumble lifestyle of a rancher's wife. I suggested that she learn to drive, so she could go into town and make some friends. She refused. So I tried to persuade her to join me and the boys in the barn, or go riding with us up into the hills, but she wanted no part of it. And no part of homemaking chores either. She left them to Ela."

"Really? What did she do all day?"

That had Cole glancing at his son before throwing back his head and roaring with laughter. "What didn't she do? She put on plays and dances for her sons. Read them endless books, and played her classical records for them, day and night. I don't think my boys ever fell asleep to anything but Beethoven and Bach when they were little buckaroos. When they were really little, she colored with them. Later she switched them to paint and canvas. If it was highbrow, my Seraphine loved it. If it was plain old country, she just didn't relate."

"It doesn't sound as though you were unhappy with that."

"Girl, I was so damned happy with my Seraphine. She didn't need to muck stalls or ride horses to own my heart. If she wanted to wear a tutu and dance across the hills, that was fine with me. No matter how different our worlds were, when we came together at the end of the day, we both knew without question that we were meant to be together for all time. For all time..."

His voice trailed off. He fell silent and stared hard at the table, lost in thought.

Sierra thought about how startled she'd been when

Josh told her that his mother had just disappeared one day, never to be seen again.

"It must be a terrible jolt whenever you realize she's really gone."

When Cole made no response, she glanced at Josh, wishing she could take back her words. Now they lay between them, adding to Cole's burden.

She could see the pain mirrored in Josh's eyes. Not only for himself and his loss, but for the father he adored and the loss that could never be explained or eased.

It was the sort of pain and loss that Sierra couldn't even imagine.

She knew, in that moment, that her own troubles with her parents, and the pain they inflicted on their only child by their careless choices, were nothing compared with the loss the Conway family had suffered and continued to suffer every day. A loss that couldn't be explained. A pain that was endless.

If only she knew how to distract them from their dark thoughts.

Just then a big hand clamped over Cole's shoulder. He looked up to see a grizzled old cowboy grinning down at him.

"Hey, Chester." With an effort, Cole pulled himself back from his painful memories, forcing a smile. "Where've you been keeping yourself?"

"Got a job at the Randall ranch. Sorry I couldn't lend a hand with the roundup this year."

"That's okay." Cole nodded toward Sierra. "Chester, this young lady is a guest of ours. Sierra Moore, Chester Coggins."

"Hi, Chester."

The old man snatched his hat from his head and blushed to the tips of his ears before offering a handshake. "Ma'am."

"Come on, Chester." Cole indicated a chair. "Join us for a beer."

"I will if you're buying."

"I am."

As the old cowboy pulled out a chair, Cole looked over at his son. "Why don't you and Sierra go out there and dance while we reminisce over old times?"

Josh grinned and held out his hand to Sierra. "What Pa's saying is that he and Chester want to be free to enjoy their man talk and cuss without apology. Come on. We'll give them some space."

As they walked toward the small wooden dance floor crowded with swaying couples, the two men lifted their beers and bent close so they could hear each other over the throb of twanging guitars.

The music had switched to something slow and bluesy.

Josh gathered Sierra close and found, because of the crush of bodies around them, that he could do little more than sway to the rhythm.

He pressed his lips to her temple. "I think I like this better than dancing."

She lifted her face to his and smiled.

Though their lips weren't touching, he could almost taste her. "I'm sorry Pa came along and spoiled the great seduction I'd planned."

"I'm sorry, too. If you hadn't planned a seduction, I planned on seducing you."

"Yeah?" A slow grin touched his lips.

"Oh yeah, cowboy. But it's hard to be offended when your dad's such a sweet man."

Josh grinned. "Now that's a word I haven't heard anybody else use to describe Cole Conway. Tough, rowdy, hard-nosed. Those are words usually reserved for Pa. But not sweet."

"Then they just don't see him the way I do. He almost had me in tears."

"Yeah. I think you should know something. Pa never talks about his loss. Not to us. Not to anybody. The only way he's managed to cope all these years is by holding it all inside. So when he started telling you that you reminded him of his Seraphine, I couldn't believe my ears."

"Really?" Sierra's brows drew together in a frown. "I was feeling so terrible because I'd opened up his obviously painful wound."

"Yeah. The pain is real." Josh swallowed. "For all of us."

"I'm so sorry, Josh." Sierra lifted a hand to his cheek.

He closed a hand over hers and looked into her eyes. "Watching the two of you"—he shook his head in disbelief—"I could see just how comfortable Pa is with you. You got him to open up in a way I've never seen before. If Chester hadn't come along, there's no way of knowing what else he might have told you."

She lifted a finger to still his words. "Maybe Chester's arrival was a blessing in disguise. I saw your eyes when he was describing your mother. You were feeling the pain as deeply as he was."

At the press of her finger to his mouth he felt his body react. It was the sweetest torture to hold her like this, swaying softly to the music, knowing that if they'd only waited a few minutes longer, or refused Cole's invitation to come to town, they could be lying in the soft hay right now, indulging all their fantasies.

He wanted her. Wanted her with every fiber of his being.

To lighten the mood he said, "There must be something in the air here. First Big Jim, and now my father. I think they've both been bitten by the same kind of love bug that—"

Josh stopped swaying and went very still. He could feel a tingling at the nape of his neck and between his shoulder blades, as though someone were staring daggers through him.

He deftly turned Sierra so that he could have a better view of the entire room. He studied the faces of the men at the bar and swept the crowded tables, but he couldn't see anyone staring directly at him.

Still, the feeling persisted. It was time to head back to the ranch.

"What's wrong with you?" Sierra shot him a puzzled frown. "Josh, where did you go just then?"

He shrugged. "Just a feeling." He smiled down at her. "Sorry. Now about that love bug…" He lowered his face to hers and brushed his mouth over hers. "I just felt something bite me. Quick. Let's get back to the table and see if Pa's ready to go."

They were both laughing with delight as they returned to where Cole was seated.

Sebastian sat on the bar stool, a wide-brimmed hat pulled low on his forehead. In faded denims and plaid shirt, he managed to look like just another cowboy celebrating roundup.

While the voices, low with curses or high-pitched with laughter, swirled around him, his complete focus was fixed on the couple on the dance floor.

He'd seen Sierra walk in with the gray-haired cowboy and knew, from his detailed research, that her escort was Colby Conway.

It hadn't taken her long to find a rich, powerful champion, Sebastian thought with a wave of fury. By all accounts, the Conway ranch was one of the largest and most successful in the country. Not that it mattered. An American rancher couldn't hold a candle to his family's empire. As for power, the Delray family had wielded both power and influence for generations, long before the Conways had ever even planted a foot in Wyoming.

Wyoming. The very name annoyed him. This was the last place he wanted to be. He hated these coarse clothes he was forced to wear in order to blend in. Loathed the crude saloon that smelled of horses and leather and sweat. Couldn't abide the rough voices with an accent that grated on his nerves.

He had envisioned himself at the villa by now, lazing in the azure Mediterranean, with Sierra at his side. He wanted to dress in a tuxedo and head over to Monte Carlo for an evening of dinner and gambling.

He wanted, desperately, to get away from this disgusting place and these people who were so beneath him that he could barely tolerate being in the same room with them.

And all because of Sierra Moore.

Sebastian watched as she swayed in the arms of the

Conway son. Josh, the one who found lost hikers in the mountains.

His eyes narrowed as he watched the way the two of them gazed into one another's eyes, like lovestruck teens. Was this why Sierra hadn't come to him?

Hadn't he given her every opportunity to repent? He'd let her know that he was here, and that he was willing to forgive her. The diamonds had cost a king's ransom, but they couldn't hold a candle to her beauty. Yet, she'd ignored his offer of a truce. She hadn't even responded to his offer to send a car and leave this primitive place in her dust. And then she'd done the unforgivable. She had named him in a document ordering him to keep his distance from her.

That slut had ordered him to stay away.

And now she was here, looking at some rough cowboy the way she ought to be looking at him.

His fingers tightened on the longneck the way he wanted to tighten them around Sierra's neck, until she begged for forgiveness.

Sebastian couldn't recall the last time he'd ever wanted for a thing that he didn't instantly receive. And right now what he wanted, more than anything in the world, was to exact revenge.

Did this ungrateful little bitch really believe she could just walk away from him and go on her merry way, cozying up to other men, without any consequences?

She would pay. Oh, she would pay dearly.

Someone tapped him on the shoulder. A man's voice, slurred from alcohol, said, "Hey, Bremmer."

Sebastian glowered at him. "You have the wrong man."

"Oh. Sorry. My mistake."

The cowboy moved on until he paused beside a tall, dark-haired cowboy just walking into the saloon with some friends.

Watching him, the germ of an idea began playing through Sebastian's mind.

And as the loud country music blared from speakers, and the revelers around him added to the din, he retreated into his mind, turning the plan over and over, looking for flaws, until he was satisfied that it would work.

Though he yearned for champagne, he ordered another beer and slowly drained it while he watched the woman who consumed his every waking moment.

Josh led the way from the saloon. Behind him Cole had his arm around Sierra's shoulders and moved along beside her, swaying slightly.

Josh breathed deeply, grateful to clear his lungs in the sting of cold air. "Come on, Pa. I'm parked behind the medical clinic. The walk will do you good."

When they were settled in the truck, Josh turned the key in the ignition, eager to get home. If he played his cards right, he and Sierra could still find some time alone.

As they started along the street, Cole tapped his son on the shoulder. "There's a parking space right in front of Flora's Diner. Grab it. I have a powerful urge for a couple of her greasy sliders with grilled onions."

"Pa—"

"Don't argue with me, Josh. Pull over here."

Josh turned the truck into the empty space and turned to glare at his father. "You know what the doctor said. If Phoebe hears—"

"You've seen the rabbit food I've been eating since

the heart attack. Are you going to begrudge me this one simple pleasure?"

Josh sighed and saw the smile on Sierra's face.

"Now how could I deny you anything, Pa? Come on. Let's load up on calories and cholesterol."

"That's my boy."

Cole was humming a little tune as he followed Josh and Sierra into the diner.

Josh quickly studied the faces of everyone. The crowd had thinned to a couple of tables, and Josh was relieved to see that he knew them all.

Cole nodded a greeting to everyone before making his way to the counter. Josh and Sierra took up places beside him.

Flora looked up from the grill and called a greeting at the open pass-through: "Well, Cole, honey, how're you doing?"

"Doing just fine, Flora. Especially now that I'm here."

"You hoping for some of my banana cream pie?"

"Maybe a sliver or two. But first I've got a powerful hankering for a couple of your sliders."

"You got 'em. With grilled onions, just the way you like 'em."

She turned to Josh and Sierra. "How about you two?"

They shook their heads.

"I see. Living on love, are you?" The old woman cackled at her joke, and the folks in the diner did the same.

Flora's daughter, Dora, made her way to the back room, carrying a tray of dirty dishes from the tables outside. After depositing them she stepped behind the counter and began filling three cups with coffee.

She set them down with a grin. "I don't know if you ordered coffee, but tonight I'm handing it out to anyone who comes in. Hits the spot after a night of drinking at the saloon."

"Thanks, Dora." Cole gulped the coffee, then broke into a wide smile as Dora set a plate of greasy hamburgers in front of him. "Now this is what I've been craving."

While he dug into his food Dora glanced at Sierra. "That great-looking guy was in asking about you again."

Very deliberately Sierra set her coffee down and carefully schooled her features. "When?"

"This morning. He had lots of questions about the Conway ranch. How to get there, how big it is, how many people work there. What was this roundup he'd heard about. And he asked if you were still there."

"What did you tell him, Dora?" Josh fought to keep his tone disinterested.

She tucked a stray strand of hair behind her ear while she considered. "I hope you don't mind, but I may have bragged a bit. After all, the Conway ranch is the biggest in the state, and that gives us bragging rights. And I told him that, as far as I knew, the pretty blonde was still there."

"Anything else?" Josh stared into his coffee to hide the flash of temper he knew she would see if he looked at her. Beside him, he could actually feel Sierra's body vibrating with the nerves she was struggling to conceal.

"I told him if I had to put my money on the reason she was staying, it was because of you, Josh honey."

She caught the flush on Sierra's face and turned to her mother. "What'd I tell you? Women just can't resist our hunky cowboys, can they, Ma?"

"And why should they?" Flora's laughter filled the room.

"We surely do love our cowboys." Dora was still wiping away tears of laughter a half hour later when she picked up Cole's empty plate, bearing a trace of the giant slice of banana cream pie he'd indulged in after devouring three sliders.

CHAPTER FIFTEEN

As the truck left the little town of Paintbrush behind, Cole leaned back, feeling mellow.

"Now that was worth driving into town for."

His words brought Sierra out of the somber mood that had come over her since Dora's words back in the diner. "The beer with Chester Coggins, or the food at Flora's Diner?"

"Both. Chester's an old buddy. He helped Big Jim out when I was just a kid, and I'll never forget that. I owe him big-time. As for Flora, that woman can cook."

Josh glanced across Sierra. "She sure can. Just don't eat there too often, Pa, or your arteries will be over-loaded."

At Josh's word of caution, Cole frowned. "I'd appreciate it if you wouldn't mention our little visit to Phoebe. She worries."

"Worries, hell. If she knew, she'd have your hide, Pa."

Cole threw back his head and laughed. "That's why it has to be our little secret."

Josh's smile faded as he glanced in the rearview mirror. As far as he could see, there wasn't another pair of headlights in view. Yet he couldn't shake the feeling that they were being followed.

What in hell was happening to him? First at the saloon, and now along a completely deserted stretch of highway.

He'd definitely been alarmed when Dora told them "that handsome guy" had been back, asking questions about their ranch and whether or not Sierra was still there. It told him in no uncertain terms that Sebastian was still in town, and still trying to get information, despite the order of protection.

There was no law that prohibited asking questions. As long as Delray didn't violate the rules of the restraining order, there was nothing Josh could do except to remain vigilant.

Still, the knowledge that Sierra's stalker was out there somewhere left him feeling on edge. Maybe that was why he couldn't shake this feeling that something about tonight just wasn't right.

He kept glancing in the rearview mirror. He would feel a whole lot better if Chief Fletcher could call them with a report that Sebastian Delray had left the country. For good.

Until then, he'd have to keep up his guard and keep Sierra close.

Not that he minded the second part of that. Keeping her close was exactly what he had in mind.

As the truck's taillights faded around a bend, a sleek car with tinted windows, its headlights turned off, came to a stop under the arched entrance to the Conway ranch.

Above the vehicle, the old sign blew back and forth, creaking ominously in the wind.

Sebastian Delray stepped out and looked up, studying the letter C that was burned into the wood, along with the words DEVIL'S WILDERNESS.

His lips were twisted into a snarl of fury as he pounded a fist into his palm, and kicked at the tire of his rental car.

This land was uncivilized. Now that he'd actually traveled over it, he knew it to be much more primitive than he'd imagined.

He was out of his element here. If Sierra had fled to London, or Lisbon, or even Italy, he would have the advantage over her. He had connections all over Europe. But here, in this wasteland, he had a need to come up with a very detailed plan.

Today he'd managed to ride undetected across these hills, but only because the land was crawling with cattle and cowboys driving them toward pens. He'd never get away with it a second time. And he couldn't simply drive in and carry Sierra away without being caught. The ranch house where she'd taken refuge was a fortress. It would be impossible to approach it without being spotted. Before he was halfway there, he would no doubt find himself surrounded by enough family members and wranglers to stop an army of invaders.

Not that he needed an army. He had no doubt that if he could persuade Sierra to listen to him, to really listen, she would choose to be with him again. Couldn't she see that they were the perfect couple? Her rejection made no sense. He was wealthy, educated, and had access to every luxury imaginable. His life had been one of endless ease and comfort. As he had patiently explained to her, she could have everything she'd ever dreamed of, as long as she continued to please him.

Was that so difficult? Was he being unreasonable?

He had generously offered her a life that most women would die for.

Die.

His eyes narrowed on the lights in the distance.

If Sierra Moore wasn't careful, she just might blow her only chance at living the good life.

He thought about all the beautiful, glamorous women he'd had and then discarded, some of whom had thrown themselves at him shamelessly as soon as they'd learned his name. And yet this little nobody, whose background and talent couldn't hold a candle to any of them, had walked away.

No, he corrected himself. She'd run away. Run from the best thing that had ever happened in her life. Little fool. Didn't she understand just how much power he could wield?

He'd done his research. Her father was a small-time musician who would never become the superstar he hoped to be. Unless, that is, he happened to acquire a "benefactor" who could arrange for him to open concerts for some of the biggest musical acts in the world. As for Sierra's mother, she had a certain amount of talent as a sculptor, but she squandered the bulk of her energy on her partner, who was spending their money like a drunken sailor in a nearby town in the Italian Alps, where his mistress lived. A collector with enough influence in the world of art could provide the exposure that would guarantee that even a mediocre talent like hers would earn her a comfortable living.

But none of these things would happen unless Sierra agreed to come back to him.

His hands fisted at his sides, flexing and unflexing with an almost uncontrollable urge to lash out.

The longer she made him wait, the more he would have to punish her. He would have to cleanse her, purify her, before letting her bask in the glow of his forgiveness. There was nothing quite like a little suffering to drive home the benefits of love. And he did love her. A love that was all-consuming.

The more he burned for her, the more he hated her for spurning that love.

He loved her. And he hated her.

He thought about the angry phone call from Jacques. There had been an angry exchange between him and his father hours later, with a reminder that their good name not be dragged through the mud again. Not that Sierra was anything like that other time. Katia had been the daughter of one of the richest men in Europe. A man almost as powerful as his own father and grandfather. He wouldn't make that mistake again. Katia had nearly cost him his inheritance. Sierra Moore, on the other hand, was a nobody.

If Sierra couldn't be swayed by intimidating notes or fabulously expensive diamonds, perhaps she needed to see just how all-powerful he could be when angered. The thought that had come to him at the saloon continued to grow in his mind.

Once Sierra believed she was safe, he knew exactly where she would go. To the place that held her heart. The place she had talked about with her friend, Janine. Poor, foolish Janine. Thank heaven for her childlike trust and loose tongue. It had been Janine who had steered him here. To Sierra's dream destination. The Tetons.

While his devious mind began working through the

knotty issues, Sebastian remained standing under the arched sign for what seemed hours until, far in the distance, lights that had been flickering in the ranch house were finally extinguished.

With the mountains, the ranch house, and the surrounding countryside all in darkness, he climbed back into the car and sat scrolling through the missed messages on his cell phone.

The illumination of the phone cast his face in an eerie light, giving him the look of a tortured demon.

The ranch house and outbuildings lay in darkness. Apparently everyone had retired for the night.

As Josh brought the truck to a stop in the barn, Cole stepped out.

Minutes later he began frantically checking his pockets.

"What's wrong?" Josh paused beside him.

"I can't find my keys." Cole looked clearly annoyed as the thought struck. "Hell. I bet I left them on the table in the saloon."

"Or maybe on the counter at Flora's." Josh touched a hand to his father's arm to still his frantic movements. "Do you remember if you had them in the diner?"

Cole shook his head. "The only thing on my mind in that diner was Flora's sliders and a great big slice of her banana cream pie."

"Maybe your keys fell on the floor of the truck." Sierra opened the truck door and the light went on as she and Josh scrambled around, moving the seats, checking under the floor mats.

After a thorough search yielded nothing, Josh reluctantly reached for his cell phone. "I'll call the saloon first, and then the diner. If you left them there, they've probably already found them and set them aside for you."

"I sure hope so." Cole was shaking his head. "I have just about every key to this place on that key ring. I'd be lost without them."

"Don't worry, Pa. We have spares."

"That's not the point. I just hate losing something so important."

Josh felt a rush of anger, mixed with fear. Those keys in the wrong hands could spell danger for all of them.

Just then Sierra, who'd been circling the truck, felt something under her foot. "What's this?"

She paused and peered down. "Look what I found." She reached into the fresh straw and lifted a ring of keys.

"Little lady, you're a life saver." Cole pocketed the keys and gave her a hard, quick hug.

Josh paused beside her to mutter, "In more ways than one. I wasn't looking forward to driving all the way back to Paintbrush tonight. I had . . . other things in mind."

"Now that sounds interesting, cowboy." With a laugh, she caught Josh's hand.

It was as hot as hers, the palm sweating, the pulsebeat rocketing. She released her hold on him, hoping to quiet her own unsteady heart.

The three of them left the barn and walked to the house.

As they drew near, they could see Phoebe sitting on the porch glider, wrapped in a warm robe.

"What're you doing up at this hour?" Cole took in the look of her, hair brushed soft and loose, eyes twinkled in that wonderful, relaxed smile she always managed, even during the most stressful times.

"Enjoying the silence. After the noise of the roundup and cooking for all those wranglers, it's the most amazing thing to hear the gentle lowing of a cow or the sweet cooing of a dove."

"Yeah." Cole dropped down beside her and set the glider into motion with his foot. "It's been a long while since I've had the time to just sit and listen, but now that you mention it, this quiet time used to be a favorite of mine, too."

Phoebe looked up at Josh and Sierra, standing close together, but not touching or even looking at each other. "Would you two like to join us? There's plenty of room." She patted the cushioned seat beside her.

Josh shook his head. "No thanks. I..." He seemed lost for an explanation until he suddenly blurted, "I promised Sierra a tour of the place."

"In the dark?" Cole's tone was incredulous.

Phoebe merely smiled and squeezed Cole's hand to silence him. To Sierra she said, "Well then. It's the perfect night for it. Cool, but not freezing. And not a snowflake in sight. Enjoy your tour."

"Thanks." Sierra shot her a grateful smile. "Good night, Phoebe. Cole."

"Yeah." Josh took hold of her hand. "'Night, Phoebe. Pa."

The two turned away and headed toward the horse barn, which was closer to the house than the vehicle barn they'd just left.

The farther they got from the porch, the more hurried their steps became, until they were practically sprinting away.

"What in hell is that fool thinking, giving her a tour in the dark? I have half a mind to—" Cole started to rise, but Phoebe caught his hand and drew him back down.

"Oh, Cole." She gave a girlish laugh. "Have you forgotten what it feels like to be young and want to get away from everyone else?"

"Of course I haven't forgotten. But it's the middle of the night."

"Exactly. As I recall, it's the very best time for young people to make love."

"Make love?" Cole turned to her with a look of absolute astonishment. "Now where did you come up with that?"

"It's there in their eyes. All you need to do is look. You can't tell me you haven't seen this coming."

Cole's mouth opened, then closed, but no words came out. After a long, silent minute his expression changed from one of questioning to one of dawning acceptance.

"I guess I have, but I just wasn't paying enough attention. Too much going on around here to think about something like that. You think they've already...?" His voice trailed off. This was, after all, his son they were discussing. And though Josh was well into manhood, Cole could still see the distant, tough, independent face his son had been presenting to the world since losing his mother at the age of ten.

This wouldn't be something Josh would confide to his father.

There had been women in his son's life. Too many to count. But until now, Cole would have bet a fortune that none of them had meant a thing.

Until now.

Phoebe laughed again. A clear, sweet sound of pure joy. "I'm thinking those two looked a bit too uneasy to be lovers yet. There was way too much tension between them."

"Yeah." Cole thought over the past few hours that he'd spent with them. "Now that you mention it, Josh was cranky. Edgy. Like he had a burr under his saddle."

"Don't you remember that itchy feeling, Cole?"

He looked over at her, and a smile split his lips and crinkled his eyes. "I surely do. That first time I saw Seraphine I took a hot poker straight through my heart. I remember thinking that if I couldn't have her, my world would never be the same again."

He fell silent for a moment before asking, "You think they're headed down that path right now? Tonight?"

Phoebe shrugged. "Hard to say. But Josh looked like a tiger about to pounce."

"He did." Cole shook his head. "Were we ever that young?"

"I don't know about you, but I was." She smiled, remembering. "And madly, wildly in love."

He was oddly touched that she would share this with him. It was a portion of her life that Phoebe had always kept to herself. Some pain, he knew from firsthand experience, was just too intimate to bring out into the light.

"Your Tim died much too young. How old was he?"

"Twenty-five. And I was just twenty-three."

"I remember that fiery truck crash. It was the talk of the county." Cole took her hand and noted idly that it was cold. "I don't know how you kept that ranch going all alone."

"It was rough, but no harder than you, trying to care for three motherless little boys while running this spread with Big Jim."

"But we both did it, Phoebe." He kept her hand in his. But only, he told himself, because it was cold.

He'd spent so many years trying to remain faithful to the memory of his beloved Seraphine, his strict code of honor had become second nature. But surely a man ought to warm the hand of a friend, even if it brought him the kind of pleasure he hadn't felt since before Seraphine went missing. "I remember the first time you walked into the chaos of our household, all calm and serene, and started setting things in order. The kids, the house, even Big Jim and me." He chuckled. "And old Ela. Especially Ela. Befriending her had to be one hell of a mountain to climb."

Phoebe joined in the laughter. "She was a tough one. She wanted nothing to do with the intruder who was encroaching on 'her menfolk,' as she referred to all of you."

"But you handled her just right. And you gradually won her over. Just the way you won all of us. You saved us all, Phoebe."

She shivered and he wrapped his arm around her shoulders and drew her close. It was the neighborly thing to do. Though at the moment, he wasn't feeling as much neighborly as he was feeling young, and alive, and frisky as a colt.

"And having all of you depending on me saved my sanity and my life, Cole. You'll never know how desperately lonely and unhappy I was. One day I was a blissful bride, planning the rest of my life with Tim, and the next I was all alone in the world. No husband. No family. Struggling to run a failing ranch with no way to pay off a mountain of debt. And then suddenly I had these three little boys who needed me."

"Not just my boys, Phoebe. Big Jim needed you." He cleared his throat. "I needed you. Still do, if truth be told."

Phoebe looked away.

Cole tilted his head and watched the path of a shooting star as it streaked across the sky. "Quick. Make a wish."

He closed his eyes.

Beside him, Phoebe did the same, before suddenly getting to her feet.

Cole's eyes snapped open. "What's wrong?"

"Nothing. Time I headed up to bed." She stepped back, hands clasped tightly at her waist. "'Night, Cole."

"'Night, Phoebe. Would you like me to walk you upstairs?"

"No. I'm...I'm fine."

"Okay then. Guess I'll just sit here a while and watch the stars."

But when she disappeared inside the house, he realized the night had gone flat.

Phoebe managed to reach her room and close the door before the tears started.

The rush of emotions had caught her completely by surprise. One minute she'd been enjoying Cole's quiet presence beside her. The next she'd been so overcome with emotion, she'd almost embarrassed herself right there in front of him.

She'd come to expect his declarations of love for his Seraphine. It was as much a part of Cole Conway as his handsome Irish face, his booming laugh, or his rare outbursts of temper that were quickly forgotten. What she hadn't expected was her reaction to the touch of his hand on hers. Or the warm tingle along her spine when he'd dropped his arm around her shoulders.

But when he'd made that grudging admission that he'd needed her in those early days and needed her now, his words had warmed her heart as nothing else could. Though, in truth, there was but one thing Cole needed: Seraphine. Didn't the entire family know it?

Still, when he'd invited her to make a wish, a thought had sprung, unbidden, into her mind, that had shattered all her composure.

Pure foolishness, she knew. It was useless to wish for things that were completely out of her reach.

She pressed a hand to her heaving bosom. She'd had a lifetime to practice firm self-discipline. Why was her silly, childish heart betraying her now?

It had to be that glimpse of Josh and Sierra, thinking they were so clever, when all their heartfelt emotions were there in their eyes for the whole world to see.

Whatever the trigger, she needed to push it aside and get back to the careful discipline that had ruled her life for the past twenty years. She was content to be a cook and housekeeper, and a surrogate mother to three grown men who made her proud of whatever meager influence she'd had in their lives.

What she would never tolerate—what her pride would never permit—was being a surrogate wife.

CHAPTER SIXTEEN

I thought we'd never get away." Laughing, Josh led Sierra to the barn. He paused just inside the doorway and turned to her, keeping his eyes steady on hers as his hands moved across the tops of her shoulders and down her arms. "You're making this awfully easy."

"You mean because I don't play games about wanting what you want?"

His grin was quick and disarming. "Yeah. But I have to warn you. I—"

She pressed her hand over his mouth to still his words. "I know. You can't make me any promises. Isn't that imprinted in a guy's DNA? Don't worry. I'm not asking for any. As my parents have told me time and again, sex is not a good reason to commit for a lifetime."

"That isn't at all what I was going to say." His smile remained, but his eyes narrowed slightly as he gripped her wrist and pressed a kiss to her hand before closing her fingers over the kiss.

That small, romantic gesture sent heat spiraling through her until her eyes widened. "All right. What were you...?"

"Maybe I'll tell you another time. But right this minute, it doesn't matter. Nothing matters except this."

With an urgency that caught them both by surprise he pressed her back against the rough wood and covered her mouth with his in a hot, hungry kiss that had sparks flying instantly between them. There was nothing soft or easy or tender as they came together in a storm of need.

His tongue found hers, his hot breath filling her mouth as he framed her face with his big hands and continued kissing her until they were both breathless.

For a moment he lifted his head and simply stared at her in a way that had her heart thundering in her chest. He looked like something wild and primitive and completely untamed. She lifted a hand to his chest to hold him at bay when he started to lower his head.

He put a hand over hers. "Afraid?"

"Should I be?"

"Yeah." He gave her a smoldering look that had her pulse jerking. "If you want to play, you have to be in the game all the way. I won't take less." He dipped his head. "You in?"

She never even hesitated. "Oh yeah. I'm in."

She gave herself up fully to his kiss.

This time, as his lips moved over hers, the grip on her shoulders loosened, softened, as did the kiss. Almost as if he'd reminded himself that she was small and female and deserved to be treated with tenderness.

"You taste so damned good." His lips moved over her face, softly, like a snowflake, nibbling her cheek, her lobe, along her jaw, before returning to tease her lips until they opened for him.

The kiss slowly began heating again, draining him, then filling him.

He loved the fact that she gave as eagerly as she took.

"Josh." Her fingers curled into the front of his shirt, drawing him closer.

At that simple movement his hands tangled in her hair, drawing her head back, while his mouth continued to plunder hers.

At the urgency of his kiss she couldn't seem to catch her breath. She absorbed the quick jittery charge to her system, and the sudden rush of pure adrenaline as his hard, muscled body imprinted itself on hers.

"Wait." She lifted a hand to his face just as he changed the angle of the kiss.

"Can't." It was all he could manage before taking the kiss deeper.

She could feel her blood heating, pulsing through her veins, throbbing in her temples. Her heartbeat sped up until her breathing was strained and ragged. Her hands gripped his head, her fingers digging into his scalp until she came up for air.

"I didn't mean 'wait.' I just meant...give me a minute to breathe."

"No time. I'm through waiting. I'll leave the breathing to you." His eyes were hot and fierce when they met hers. "I need to see you, Sierra. All of you."

His strong fingers clutched the hem of her sweater and he tore it from her before tossing it aside. Beneath it he found nude lace that revealed more than it covered. The sight of her nearly staggered him.

The look in his eyes had her throat going dry as he dipped a finger beneath one slim strap and drew it slowly off her shoulder and down her arm.

He moved to the other strap and did the same in slow motion, as though tempting himself with the first glimpse of a rare and glorious treasure.

"Do you know how much I want you?"

She shivered at the look in his eyes.

Without a word he unclasped the front hook and released the scrap of lace, tossing it to the floor.

Moonlight spilled through a crack in the door, bathing her in golden light. She looked like some kind of mythical goddess, with all that blond hair and pale, flawless skin.

"You're even more beautiful than I'd imagined."

With his hands gently cupping her breasts he brought his lips down her throat.

She arched her neck, loving the feel of his mouth on her flesh.

His mouth moved lower, across her collarbone, then lower still, until his tongue circled one taut nipple.

She heard a moan, and realized it was her own voice. Low, sultry, and throaty with passion.

His clever mouth moved from one breast to the other until she clutched blindly at his waist to anchor herself and keep from falling.

She absorbed the most exquisite pleasure and wondered how much longer her legs could continue to support her before her knees buckled.

As if reading her mind, he lifted her in his arms and

carried her into an empty stall, before shrugging out of his clothes.

All she could do was gaze at that amazing, perfectly sculpted body, the muscles honed by a lifetime of ranch chores. He was so beautiful, he left her breathless.

Before she could reach a hand to the snap of her denims he moved her hand away.

There was that sexy smile again, doing strange and wonderful things to her heart.

"I want to do that."

Without another word he knelt and tugged off her boots, then drew off her jeans and the lace bikini underneath.

When he stood, his narrowed gaze moved over her until his eyes met hers. "*Beautiful* doesn't even begin to describe you, Sierra. You're absolutely stunning."

"And you're—"

Before she could get the word out, his mouth covered hers in a kiss so searing, she could feel the heat from her toes to her scalp. A heat so intense, it had her struggling for breath.

She wrapped her arms around his neck and offered him everything.

And he took, with a greediness that caught them both by surprise.

His hands moved over her, stroking, gently caressing, and she responded with soft sighs and hot, wet kisses across his shoulder, his neck, the little hollow of his throat.

"You're making me too hot." He caught her hands, stilling their movements, and began nibbling his way down her body, taking her on a hard, fast ride before she reached the first shocking crest.

His name was torn from her lips, but he gave her no time to recover as he continued touching her, teasing her, until she could do nothing more than hold on and let him have his way.

"This is how I dreamed of seeing you. Just this."

Without warning he suddenly cupped her hips and dragged her roughly against him. With a growl that was more animal than human he lifted her and drove her back against the side of the stall.

His mouth covered hers in a savage kiss that spoke of hunger, of need, of blinding, desperate passion. She responded, her hands clutching his shoulders, her nails digging into his flesh as she gave all and urged him to take more.

"You know there's no going back now."

This dark side of him excited her, causing her voice to catch in her throat. "I'll go anywhere you lead, Josh. Anywhere."

He heard the desire in her voice and it thrilled him.

And though he'd hoped to take more care with her, there was no way to stop the firestorm of passion that had them in its grip. It was like a long-caged beast struggling to be free.

He thrust into her and felt her open to him, taking him into all that velvet warmth.

"Josh. Josh."

His name on her lips was the sweetest sound. A part of him wanted to slow down and savor each moment of this glorious journey. But his body refused to obey. He'd already stepped over the line, and there was no denying the needs that were ripping him apart.

He would have her now. All of her.

They began to move together, climb together.

Their breathing was labored, their flesh pearled with sweat as they continued the climb.

He whispered her name. Or thought he did as he moved with her, straining toward release.

Now they were beyond words. Beyond thought. Beyond everything of this world until they broke free and soared.

As they reached the crest, they exploded into millions of glittering pieces before drifting slowly down to earth.

"Oh, baby." Josh pressed his forehead to Sierra's and continued holding her in his arms while his heartbeat slowed and his world gradually settled. "That was—"

"—earth-shattering," she finished for him.

"More than that. Maybe universe-shattering." He looked down at her. "You okay?"

"Umm. Fine." She managed to lift a hand to his cheek before letting it drop weakly along his arm.

After a minute she managed to say, "Am I getting heavy?"

"Hmmm? Oh." With a grin he lowered her until her feet touched the floor.

He took hold of a saddle blanket tossed over the rail of the stall. He dropped it onto the clean straw and took her hand before kneeling on the blanket and pulling her down with him.

"Are you cold?" He ran his hands up and down her arms.

"You must be kidding." She looked over at him with a sly smile. "After what we just shared, I'm as hot as the Fourth of July."

"Yes, you are." He chuckled and stretched out on his

back before drawing her down beside him. "I thought for a minute we'd both burned to cinders."

She lay on her side, her hand on his chest. She could feel the uneven pumping of his heartbeat. It matched her own. "That was...pretty amazing."

"You're amazing." His fingers played with the ends of her hair. He lifted a strand and watched through narrowed eyes as it sifted like silk before drifting around her face and shoulders.

At his touch she felt tiny splinters of fire and ice curl along her spine. "Do we have to go back to the house now?"

"You in a hurry?"

She heard the warmth of a smile in his voice and looked up at him. "Of course not. But won't your dad and Phoebe wonder about us if we don't come back?"

"Do you think, because I live on my family ranch, that I have to account for my comings and goings?"

She flushed. "I don't know. I don't know what it's like to live at home, to be surrounded by family. That's not part of my experience. But when I was at boarding school, there were rules."

"When you lived in a boarding school, you were a kid. You're a grown woman now. And in case you haven't noticed, I'm a grown man."

"Oh, I've noticed."

He chuckled, low and deep in his throat. "The rules here are work, eat, play. I haven't been tucked in by anyone since I was seven. And if I want to spend my nights in the barn, or in the guest room with you, no one is going to make either of us feel uncomfortable about the arrangement."

"So, you're telling me that there's no bed check."

"Exactly." He laughed. "Now"—he gathered her into his arms and kissed her soundly—"if you don't mind, I'd like to go for seconds. And this time I'd like to take it slow and easy. I'm afraid the first time was more frantic than I'd planned, but a certain sexy little female had me so hot, I nearly burned down the barn."

She felt the rumble of his laughter against her throat and thought it the most wonderful feeling in the world. "I didn't mind that frantic rush, especially since I was as hot as you. But I'd be more than happy to slow things down a bit. And then, if you're up for it, we could even go for thirds."

"Glutton." He spoke the word inside her mouth as he took the kiss deeper.

And then there was no need for words as they took each other on a very slow, lazy journey back to paradise.

CHAPTER SEVENTEEN

———◆◆◆———

Sometime during the night Sierra and Josh climbed up to the hayloft. Josh had promised that it was the very best place in the world to listen to the sound of rain, and he couldn't have been more right. So they lay there for hours, talking, laughing, as the soft, warm rain fell from the night sky, washing away the last of the snow.

Now, after a night of loving, they lay in a lazy tangle of arms and legs, feeling completely sated.

Cushioned in the straw by the saddle blanket, they were as comfortable as they would have been in a soft feather bed.

Outside the open door of the hayloft, millions of stars twinkled in the sky. The full moon was a huge golden disk.

Sierra sat up, playing with the hair on Josh's chest. "You were right about the rain. It was wonderful to hear.

But I'm glad it's gone now. Look at those stars. They look close enough to touch."

Josh lifted a hand to her cheek. "If you'd like some, just say the word. I'd be happy to climb up there and fetch them for you."

"That's so sweet."

"Not as sweet as you, Sierra." He gathered her against his chest and wrapped her in his arms. "This night was special for me."

"Me, too."

He studied the way she looked, all soft and sleepy, and completely comfortable in her nakedness. "You're such a contradiction."

She arched a brow. "How?"

"So generous with your love. So relaxed and easy about sex. And yet, you seem surprised that a man might want more from you."

"More?" She sat up, her hand going still. "I thought I gave you all you wanted."

"You did. Even more than I expected. I'm not talking about sex. I'm talking about feelings."

"I told you. I don't equate sex with commitment."

He smiled. "There's that word again. You seem fixated on commitment."

She folded her arms in front of her. "I'm not fixated. But I'm well aware that men don't—"

He touched a finger to her lips. "I'm not men. I'm one man."

"All right." She pushed a little away, so that they weren't touching. "Then let me say this clearly. I don't expect you to feel you owe me anything because of what we shared tonight. It was lovely."

"Lovely? Is that the best you can come up with? I'd say it was much better than lovely. It was"—he grinned—"memorable."

"All right. I'll admit. It was memorable. But it was sex between two consenting adults—"

"Two adults who consented again and again, as I recall."

She heard the thread of laughter in his voice and couldn't help smiling, though she was trying very hard to remain serious while she made her point. "Yes, we did. But I'm not foolish enough to think it was anything more."

"Oh, it was a hell of a lot more. And I mean to show you just how much more it was, woman."

With a growl of pleasure he made a grab for her and dragged her into his arms, then proceeded to run hot, wet kisses down the length of her body until she was giggling like a child.

Suddenly the giggles turned into sighs, and the sighs into breathless little moans of pleasure. And then there was only ragged breathing, and whispered words of endearment, as they lost themselves once more in that magical place where only lovers can go.

Sierra yawned and stretched, then went very still when she realized that Josh was watching her.

"'Morning." She sat up and peered out the window of the hayloft. "Look at that sunrise. It's beautiful. I wish I had my camera."

"There will be other sunrises." He lay with his arms beneath his head, studying the way she looked all sleepy-eyed and glowing from their night of lovemaking.

"But not here, just as the sun climbs over the horizon.

Look at the way it reaches out to touch all the foothills
with that wonderful light."

"That's exactly how I'd describe my family around
you."

She turned to stare at him with a puzzled expression.
"Now what's that supposed to mean?"

"All you have to do is smile that open, sunny smile of
yours, and they all seem to reflect your light. Big Jim. Pa.
My brothers. Even Phoebe and Ela, the toughest, shrewd-
est women I know, aren't able to resist your charm." He
gave a short laugh at the look on her face. "You don't have
any idea what kind of power you wield, do you?"

"Josh . . ."

Laughing, he dragged her down into his arms and said
against her throat, "Woman, the most incredible thing
about you is that it's not an act. It's all so honest and innocent. *You're* so honest and innocent. And real. No wonder
Big Jim is crazy about you." He pressed kisses down her
neck until she wriggled and sighed. "And so am I."

At his words she went very still.

Josh took no notice as he continued raining kisses
until she began to respond.

As she wrapped her arms around his waist and gave in
to his tender ministrations, she tried to cling to the reason
that she'd been brought up short by his words. She considered herself a sharp cookie. She'd heard every empty,
meaningless line a man could use. And she'd vowed that
she would never again be swayed by such foolishness. If
she was going to guard her heart, she needed to be strong
and careful. After all, she'd been able to witness firsthand
what happened to a man and woman who based their
entire relationship on sexual attraction.

But Josh's words, spoken so innocently, had caused a little hitch around her heart.

Was he—and his entire family—really crazy about her? What a sneaky way to break through all her defenses. Of all her fantasies, this was by far the most tantalizing. To be loved, to be cherished, to "belong." To be part of a large and loving family...

Careful, she cautioned. But even while she struggled to remain vigilant, her mind began to empty. All she could think about was the pleasure this man gave her. Every kiss, every touch took her higher than the time before.

And then all thought fled as she was lost in the wonder of this newfound joy.

Sierra and Josh walked arm in arm from the barn and into the mudroom. After depositing their boots they greeted Ela and Phoebe, who were dashing about the kitchen as usual, stirring, slicing, baking, and all the while chatting happily.

If the two women took notice of their early arrival, they gave not a clue as they greeted them warmly and continued working.

With matching smiles Sierra and Josh climbed the stairs to their rooms, to shower and dress.

An hour later they joined the family for breakfast.

In Sierra's hand was a big manila folder.

Cole looked up from where he stood holding a mug of coffee. "What's that?"

"Some pictures." Sierra opened the folder and began laying out the photos she'd taken during roundup. "Some of these are grainy. I'll play with them on my computer until they're more polished."

Everyone gathered around to study and make comments.

"Look at you, Pa." Jake held up a picture of Cole astride his big gelding, turning a stray cow back to the herd.

The photo showed the strain and sweat on Cole's face as he leaned far down in the saddle, coaxing the errant cow along.

"And look at this." Josh pointed to the flecks of snow and grass flying around the hooves of the running cattle. "How did you manage this?"

"It took a little time to get the focus just right." Sierra couldn't hide the pleasure and pride she felt in knowing that he'd recognized the skill required for that shot.

With picture after picture they laughed or exclaimed or nodded approval at the images she'd captured on film.

"Here you are, Big Jim." Cole held up a photo of his father steering a line of cattle back to the main herd after they'd bolted. "When did this happen?"

"When you were busy with the rest of the herd," the older man said. "Old Blue and I had to push hard to get ahead of those ornery critters, but we did it."

He took the photo from Cole's hand and studied it in the clear morning light, before shaking his head from side to side. "I've got to hand it to you, sweetheart. These are amazing photographs. All these details. Clear as a bell. These look like something I'd see in one of those glossy nature magazines."

"Why, thank you, Big Jim." Sierra shot him a dazzling smile. "That's the highest compliment you could give me."

He peered at a speck on the ridge above him and his horse. "What's this?"

Sierra studied it and gave a shrug. "It looks like a man kneeling in the snow. But I don't recall any of the wranglers on foot."

The others gathered around to study it and comment.

Quinn pointed to the herd. "It could be one of the cows that broke free."

Jake chuckled. "To me it looks like a guy taking pictures of you taking pictures, Sierra."

She lifted the photo to the light and felt her heart stop. "That's what it looks like to me, too. But instead of a camera, it looks like he's holding binoculars to his eyes."

Josh took it from her hand and turned toward the window. After studying it in the light he nodded. Was it Sierra's stalker? Watching from Conway land? Had that bastard dared to trespass on their property?

"Can you enlarge it on your computer?"

Sierra nodded. "I'll see what I can do later."

"If it turns out to be important, we'll save it for the chief."

Everyone felt the sudden hum of uneasiness.

To soothe the tension, Jake pointed to a photo of his brother roping a cow, and then another showing the teamwork between Josh and his mount, and yet a third photo as Josh returned the cow to the herd.

He exchanged a knowing look with Quinn. "There are an awful lot of pictures of Josh in here." He shot a grin at Sierra. "You sure you aren't looking to land him a job on Madison Avenue selling manly cologne?"

That had everyone roaring with laughter.

Josh took the photos from his hand and looked at them before arching a brow. "I'm certainly looking like one damned fine cowboy in these pictures. Maybe, when I get sick and tired of ranching, I'll take that job as a pitchman."

"And give up your mountains?" Big Jim shot a glance out the window at the Tetons, their peaks ringed with clouds. "I'd give you less than a week in New York before you'd be so lonesome for home you'd be asking me to fly in and save your hide from extreme boredom."

Josh nodded his head. "Maybe. But that would be one hell of a memorable week in the big city."

"A legend in his own mind," Jake muttered just as Phoebe called them to eat.

At the table they passed around platters of steaming sausage and ham, as well as omelets and toast, before digging into their meal.

"The snow may be gone," Cole remarked, "but there's more coming. Look at those clouds over the Tetons."

Big Jim nodded. "Even if I didn't see those clouds, I'd know it in my bones. We're going to be hit with a big one."

Sierra's eyes widened. "Are you sure?"

At the older man's nod she ducked her head.

He put a hand over hers. "What're you thinking?"

She shrugged. "That I'd love to go hiking again during a really big storm. The time I spent on the mountain was surreal. I've never seen anything like it. I took some of my best photos ever."

Sierra heard the ping announcing a text and removed her phone from her pocket to read it.

Her appetite suddenly faded. She pushed aside her plate and looked up. "It's my agent, saying that he's leaving for the West Coast. He'll be there for the better part of the month."

Big Jim shot a meaningful glance at Josh. "What about your contract?"

She shrugged. "He said he needs something tangible to show the gallery owners."

"Why not send him the pictures you took of the roundup?" Jake asked from across the table.

"I'm . . . not ready to let go of them."

Was that the truth? she wondered. Or was that all she was prepared to admit to? In truth, her life was in such turmoil, she needed some time here, where she felt safe. Safe from Sebastian. Safe from the constant moving that had become so much a part of her life.

Or maybe that was another less-than-truthful admission. Maybe what she was really craving was more time with Josh. More time to lie with him, laugh with him, make wild, crazy, passionate love with him.

She sat in silence a moment, considering what to type in response, before her fingers flew over the keys. "I told him that he can take all the time he wants. I'll be delayed here for a while longer."

"Good girl." Big Jim lay a hand over hers. "We certainly don't want to stand in the way of your career, but . . ."

He heard the announcement of another text and watched as she read the words before relaxing into a smile.

"Good news?"

"Not exactly. But my agent said he'll be meeting with some gallery operators on the Coast, and when I'm ready to send him a sample of my latest work, he'll have a few more contacts who may be willing to showcase my photographs."

She glanced at Josh and felt her cheeks color at the way he was looking at her.

Could he read her expression? Was he as happy as she was to know that she was free to stay on, without any pressure from her agent?

She could hardly contain her relief that she could now relax and simply enjoy her time here, safe and happy and...

She refused to even think the word *loved*. But at least here she was accepted and, for now, treated with so much care. That was more than she'd ever dared hope for.

Big Jim clapped a hand on her shoulder. "I'm thinking, when your agent sees these latest photos you took, he's going to be negotiating a fat, new contract. Judging from just these few pictures I've seen, you're one damned fine photographer, sweetheart."

"Thank you, Big Jim. That's just so sweet of you." She leaned over and kissed his cheek.

As the others continued their meal, Josh watched as his grandfather touched a finger to his cheek. The old man was practically blushing.

Sierra was sipping coffee and chatting across the table with Cheyenne, looking for all the world as though she didn't have a clue that she'd just made Big Jim's day sweeter.

It was a very special gift she had, Josh realized. She gave her affection spontaneously, without expecting anything in return. And that generosity of spirit made everyone on whom she bestowed her attention want to shower her with love.

Including him.

He was hooked, and had been since he'd first come upon her in that damnable tent in the middle of a blizzard. Even when she'd conned him into believing she had a gun. And after just one night with her, he'd been half in love with her.

Half in love.

And now?

Now he didn't want to probe his feelings too deeply. He'd grown up with the realization that happiness was fleeting, and that life could change forever in the blink of an eye.

For now, he would accept the fact that Sierra had agreed to stay on a while longer. And he intended to savor every moment of whatever time they had together.

He couldn't wait to get through this day so he could get her alone and explore even more ways to show her all the new and wonderful things he was feeling.

CHAPTER EIGHTEEN

I made the reservations." Cheyenne got Sierra aside after breakfast.

"Good. When do we need to leave?"

"In the next hour. I've already managed to persuade Phoebe and Ela. But there's just one thing." She grimaced. "Quinn said he's phoning Chief Fletcher to let him know we're coming to town. That way, he can decide if it's safe for you to be there."

"That's the right thing to do. If Quinn hadn't taken it on himself, I would have called the chief myself. I'll be sure to thank him."

"Don't be so quick to show your gratitude yet. Quinn also insists that he and Josh are driving us to Paintbrush and following us around like bodyguards."

Sierra's eyes widened. "Tell me you're kidding."

"I'm serious."

Sierra put her hands on her hips. "But this was supposed to be our girls' day."

Cheyenne shrugged. "I don't see that we have a choice if we want to treat Phoebe and Ela to a special day."

The two young women hurried off to their rooms to get ready for the day in town. A short time later, when they walked outside, they found Quinn and Josh standing beside one of the ranch trucks.

When Josh opened the door, Sierra shot him a smile, before holding up a set of keys. "Sorry, gentlemen. I talked to your father and explained that this was a day for ladies only, and he agreed that you'd follow along at your own peril."

Josh and Quinn shared a conspiratorial smile before Josh explained, "We talked to Pa, too. The only reason he agreed to let you drive yourselves is because the chief gave his blessing for you to come to town and go anywhere you please."

It was Sierra's turn to be surprised. "Did he say why?"

"He said he was following up on something, and when he was sure of it he'd call. In the meantime, as long as he says it's okay to go to town, we won't stop you. But we'll be close behind."

Sierra handed Josh a manila envelope. "As long as you're coming to town, you can leave this photo with the police chief."

Josh opened the envelope and studied the computer-enlarged photo, showing a man on a hill, clearly watching through binoculars. He looked up. "Do you recognize him?"

Sierra nodded. "It's Sebastian."

Josh's eyes narrowed. "I'll leave it up to Chief Fletcher to determine if he's in violation of the terms."

Sierra touched a hand to his arm. "Either way, as long as the chief is aware of this, he'll know how to deal with it." He saw the worry etched in her eyes. "I hope this won't put a cloud on your plans."

"I won't let it." She tossed her head, determined not to allow Sebastian to ruin yet another day.

As Phoebe and Ela climbed into the backseat, Sierra tossed the keys to Cheyenne. "You drive, since you know these roads."

Josh slapped his brother on the back. "I'll get another truck and we'll follow behind."

Minutes later two trucks rolled down the long, curving driveway toward the highway. An hour later, they parked in front of the Paintbrush Salon, where the owner, Mary Lou Healy, a pretty, little, round dumpling of a woman, threw open the door to greet them warmly.

"Why, Phoebe and Ela. In all the years I've known you two, this is the first time you've ever been in my shop."

"And it'll probably be the last," Phoebe said, eyeing the two chairs, where Mary Lou's daughter, Mary Alice, and niece, Justine, stood at attention. A fourth woman, brought in just for the occasion, was introduced as Mary Lou's younger sister, Beth.

On the far side of the room, two leather chairs positioned in front of footbaths were already humming, the scented water swirling, emitting clouds of steam.

"Where would you ladies like to begin?" the dumpling asked.

"I think their hair first." Cheyenne took charge when she realized that both Phoebe and Ela were feeling overwhelmed and ready to run out the door. "And then we'll want manicures and pedicures."

Before either Phoebe or Ela could protest, they were being led to the shampoo chairs and draped in pink smocks bearing the name of the salon.

As Beth began unpinning Ela's long, intricate braids, the old woman gave her a word of warning. "Don't even think about cutting my hair."

"I wouldn't dream of it." The young woman let out a gasp as the thick, gray braids began unraveling to reveal hair that fell below Ela's waist.

Sierra watched as Beth began running a brush through Ela's hair. "Oh, Ela. What amazing hair. Has it ever been cut?"

The older woman smiled. "I snip a few strands here and there, if they're sticking out of my braids. But I've never had a real haircut. I've never even been in a place like this before."

"I hope you can relax," Beth told her, as she began running warm water into a basin. "I promise to be gentle and to massage your head for as long as you like."

Minutes later, when Quinn and Josh poked their heads inside, Cheyenne shooed them away. "I warned you. This place is off-limits to the two of you."

"We wouldn't dream of setting foot inside. We just wanted to ask if you need anything at Thibault's place."

"Not today. Go," Cheyenne said firmly.

They turned away. But not before they caught sight of their cook and housekeeper wearing pale pink smocks and sighing contentedly while having their scalps gently massaged.

"How did you like your shampoo?" Sierra asked, as Beth began drying Ela's hair.

"I can't believe how relaxing it felt."

Sierra and Cheyenne exchanged smiles as Beth began braiding the long strands.

"I've been doing that all my life," Ela told the girl. "I can do it in half the time."

"I'm sure you can. But today, I've been ordered to pamper you. So, unless you object, I'd like you to just close your eyes and let me do this."

The older woman shrugged. "I just thought I could save you some time."

"You have all the time in the world," Phoebe called to her. "At least that's what Sierra just reminded me."

Ela sat back, eyes closed, humming softly to herself while her hair was secured in a perfect braided crown atop her head.

Minutes later her feet were immersed in warm, scented water, and her hands were being gently massaged by Mary Alice.

"How about a little color?" Justine held up a bottle of pearl nail polish for Phoebe's approval.

Before Phoebe could refuse, Sierra suggested, "Why don't you dab a bit on her nail and see if she likes it?"

When the girl did as she'd asked, Phoebe held out her finger, turning it this way and that before smiling. "All right. I guess it isn't too shocking."

"Shocking?" Cheyenne laughed. "Phoebe, bloodred might be a bit of a shock to those fingernails. But pale pearl nail polish is as sedate as that old denim shirt that you favor."

That had all of them laughing.

"What about me?" Getting into the spirit of things, Ela lifted her hands. "Should I go for green or neon pink?"

"Definitely the neon," Cheyenne said.

"Don't listen to them," Ela told Beth. "Whether it's fingers or toes, I'm not having my nails polished."

"Yes, ma'am."

Cheyenne and Sierra, already finished with their own manicures and footbaths, were now in the shampoo chairs.

Cheyenne leaned close to Sierra to whisper, "Look at the two of them. I know they were feeling anxious about all this when the day began, but now that they've let go of their fear, they're having a grand time."

Sierra couldn't hold back the laughter that bubbled up inside her at the sight of those two sweet, hardworking women being fussed over. Without a word she lifted her ever-present camera and captured the images for posterity.

Two hours of giggling and teasing later, feeling thoroughly pampered, the four women were ready to leave the salon.

Sierra walked to the counter and opened her wallet.

Mary Lou shook her head. "Sorry. Cole Conway already phoned me to say that your money is no good here."

Sierra stared at her in complete surprise. "What are you talking about?"

"Cole said he's paying your bill. And I know better than to argue with a Conway."

Sierra knew her mouth was open. Composing herself she said, "All right. I'll deal with Cole later. At least let me pay the tips for all your workers."

"Sorry. Cole's one step ahead of you." Mary Lou chuckled. "He insisted that the tips be included. And I know better—"

"—than to argue with a Conway," Sierra finished for her. With a shake of her head she said softly, "I'm very grateful, Mary Lou. You made this so much fun for all of us."

"It was my pleasure. And believe me, Cole Conway will see that I'm well paid for my service. By the way…" She turned and picked up four glittery bags, each bearing the name of the salon and filled to the brim with soaps and lotions and body washes. "These are included in our spa package."

The four were speechless as, with hugs and calls of thanks, they walked out of the salon and loaded their packages in the truck before driving down the street to Flora's Diner.

"I can't believe my eyes." Flora peered at them from the pass-through before walking over to greet them, wiping her hands on a towel. "Phoebe Hogan. Ela. I can't remember the last time I saw the two of you together in town. What's the occasion?"

"Girls' day out," Cheyenne said with a laugh. "Look." She lifted Phoebe's arm, then Ela's, and the two women wiggled their fingers to show off their neatly trimmed nails and soft, scented hands.

"Now I've seen it all." Flora's daughter, Dora, laughed. "You all smell so good, like a perfume factory. Are you sure somebody isn't getting married?"

"Nobody that we know of." Phoebe's laughter rang through the air as she looked pointedly at Sierra. "But after a day like this, nothing would surprise me."

Sierra actually blushed under her scrutiny. "We don't need a special occasion to treat the two hardest-working women I've ever known to a day of pampering."

At Sierra's words, both Phoebe and Ela flushed with pleasure.

When Cheyenne picked up a menu, Flora called out, "Don't even bother with that. In honor of this day, I'm making all of you my special. Dora, serve the ladies their drinks and salads while I slice up some of my slow-roasted beef."

A short time later the four women fell silent as they sipped tea and coffee and nibbled tender roast beef served over a nest of buttered noodles that melted in their mouths. Afterward, before they could say a word, Dora placed four plates in front of them, holding moist pound cake drizzled with powdered sugar and cinnamon, and topped with a dollop of whipped cream.

By the time Josh and Quinn drove the truck, laden with supplies from Homer's Grain and Seed, to the door of the diner, the four women floated out, their arms around each others' waists, their eyes crinkled with laughter, giggling like schoolgirls.

Josh took one look at Phoebe's pretty curls and Ela's fancy crown atop her head, and turned to Sierra. "Where are Phoebe and Ela, and who are these imposters?"

The two women couldn't seem to stop giggling.

Quinn caught Phoebe's hand. "Is that nail polish?"

"It is." Phoebe wiggled her fingers. "And you ought to see my pretty pink toes."

Quinn pulled Cheyenne close for a quick kiss. "You've corrupted them, woman."

"It's all Sierra's fault," Cheyenne said. "She's corrupted all of us. We've decided today that it's so much fun being girls, we're going to make this an annual affair."

The four women climbed into their truck and were

still laughing as they drove away, with Josh and Quinn following.

When they arrived back at the ranch, Cole and Big Jim were talking quietly in the kitchen. Seeing the women, they set aside their longnecks.

"Well?" Cole studied Phoebe's eyes, the soft, pretty curls that danced around her cheeks. Cheeks glowing with color. "How was your day?"

"It was...heavenly." She turned to Sierra and Cheyenne, and hugged each of them. "I can't remember when I've had so much fun."

"I'm glad." Sierra hugged her back. "I can't remember a better day, either. And we all have Cole to thank. Mary Lou wouldn't let me pay, because she said she didn't dare refuse Cole Conway." She lay a hand on his arm. "Thank you, Cole. That was so sweet and generous of you."

"It was my pleasure, honey." He looked beyond her to Phoebe, who was glowing with happiness. "I can't think of anyone who deserves it more than the four of you."

Sierra turned to Ela, who was standing quietly.

Suddenly the old woman opened her arms and enveloped Sierra in a bear hug.

When they stepped apart, Ela's eyes were dancing. "Thanks to you, I feel pretty."

"You're beautiful," Sierra said softly.

"And you are"—Ela lay a hand on Sierra's cheek—"a very special, generous soul."

Big Jim cleared his throat. "Cole and I were just going to take our beer in the other room. We started a fire, and there's coffee for anyone who wants it."

As the others made their way to the great room, Josh

paused in the doorway to see the dreamy look on Sierra's face.

He drew her close and brushed her cheek with a kiss. "Ela's right, you know. That was a very fine thing you did today. But I'm not surprised. You don't know how to be ordinary, Sierra. You've brought something to my family that is as rare and special as you."

As they joined the others, where Ela and Phoebe were eagerly recounting every minute of their day, Sierra hugged his words to her heart.

For now, for this one day, she'd helped make two women very happy. It was the least she could do after all they'd done for her. And the joy she could see in their faces was all the thanks she needed.

The four women were still floating on a cloud the following morning.

As they were nearing the end of breakfast, Sierra's cell phone rang. She excused herself and pushed away from the table to answer it.

After listening to the voice on the other end, her voice sounded a bit breathless. "You're sure? You're absolutely certain? Oh, thank you. Thank you."

A moment later she turned to the others with a blazing smile that revealed the depth of her relief. "That was Chief Fletcher. Ever since I filed the documents, he's been keeping an eye on Sebastian's comings and goings. When Sebastian left Paintbrush yesterday to drive to Jackson Hole, the chief asked the state police to follow up."

Cole interrupted. "So that's why the chief said you were free to come into Paintbrush and go wherever you pleased."

"Exactly." Sierra continued without a pause. "And just now Chief Fletcher got a call from the state police that a passenger identified as Sebastian Delray boarded a flight out of Jackson Hole, bound for California, with his final destination listed as Paris."

The others were up and out of their chairs as they gathered around her.

"Finally." Cheyenne hugged her fiercely. "It looks like Sebastian has given up and is heading home. Your nightmare is finally over."

"That's really great news, sweetheart." Big Jim gave a growl of pleasure as he squeezed her shoulder. "If it's true."

She shrugged. "I only know what the police chief told me. But I don't think he would have called me until the state police had thoroughly checked it out."

"I agree with you." Cole kissed her cheek. "Now you can relax and get to really experience life on our ranch, without that dark cloud hanging over your head." He turned to Josh, who stood back, allowing the others to have their moment with her. "Want to take Sierra up in the plane and give her a bird's-eye view of the Devil's Wilderness, son?"

Josh merely smiled. "I have a better idea." He turned to Sierra. "Didn't you say you wished you could hike to the high country and experience another snowstorm?"

At his mention of hiking, her eyes went wide with pleasure.

Seeing it, Josh said, "You'll see nearly as much of the land as you could from our plane. We can take a truck to the foothills and climb from there. If you're in a mood to spend a couple of days up there, we could take along a tent."

"Oh, Josh, could we?" Her voice, all soft and dreamy, betrayed the depth of her emotion.

"I don't see why not, now that your stalker is gone." He glanced at his father. "You sure you can spare me?"

Cole grinned. "Roundup's over, son. We've got everything covered here."

Phoebe spoke up. "If you're planning on hiking and camping out overnight, give us some time, and Ela and I will pack some food."

"Thanks, Phoebe." Josh gave her a kiss on the cheek before catching Sierra's hand. "Come on. We'd better check our supplies."

While the two hurried away to their rooms, the rest of the family gathered around talking about their good fortune.

Big Jim picked up the phone and called Chief Fletcher to suggest that he alert the authorities in California, just to be on the safe side.

The chief's voice boomed over the line, loud enough for all of them to hear. "I'm already ahead of you on that, Big Jim. I want proof that the scumbag isn't trying to con us. I'm having him watched until he's actually aboard a plane headed for Paris. I don't want him sneaking off somewhere between here and there, and coming back to cause trouble."

"Thanks, Everett. I should have known you'd think of everything." Big Jim's smile revealed his sense of relief.

An hour later, as Josh and Sierra hauled their supplies out the door, the family gathered on the back porch to see them off.

Josh hefted his backpack and shot a questioning look at Phoebe and Ela. "There are only two of us heading to the high country, not an army."

The two women laughed before Phoebe explained. "You always come home from a climb practically starving."

"I come home hungry for some good home cooking. That's not the same as starving."

"All the same," Ela said. "You need to think about stopping often to feed Sierra."

"From the weight of all this food, we'll have to stop every fifteen minutes just to lighten the load."

That had the others grinning as they gathered around the truck to slap Josh's shoulder or shake his hand, while they kissed Sierra's cheek and hugged her good-bye.

"Watch out for bears getting ready to hibernate," Big Jim cautioned.

"They'd better watch out for us." Josh stowed his rifle and ammunition in the truck.

"Don't forget the hungry wolves," Quinn deadpanned.

His wife smacked his shoulder. "Now you're just trying to scare Sierra." She looked over. "Quinn knows that the wolves would rather go a mile out of their way to avoid humans than follow their scent just to eat them."

He shrugged. "There's always a first time. You said yourself that Sierra is as sweet as candy."

Cheyenne merely laughed and rolled her eyes. "I'd worry more about those snow clouds than wolves."

Sierra glanced toward the distant hills, where low clouds hovered. "Oh, I hope it snows. I'd love to watch it from the high country."

"Be careful what you ask for, sweetheart. You won't just watch it." Big Jim gave her a hug. "You'll be smack in the middle of it. I just hope you don't have to dig your way out."

"We'll be fine." Josh walked to the passenger side of the truck and held the door for Sierra.

Both were wearing comfortable hoodies in the brisk autumn air, with warmer parkas and gloves stowed in their backpacks. As the family called out their good-byes, Josh turned on the ignition and they started out across the field, headed toward the high country in the distance.

CHAPTER NINETEEN

———◆◆◆———

This is as far as I can drive." Josh parked the truck in the shelter of a grove of evergreens. "Ready to start hiking?"

Sierra's smile was radiant. "More than ready. I can't wait."

After retrieving their backpacks from the bed of the truck, they started out on foot. At first the terrain was a gentle uphill climb, and they made good progress, stopping for a lazy lunch beside a swollen stream.

"Snow runoff," Josh announced as they watched the water foam and bubble before tumbling over rocks and fallen logs that clogged the waterway.

Sierra was busy snapping photographs. "Do you get flooding in springtime?"

He shook his head. "It gets absorbed into the ground long before it reaches our land. But all that runoff keeps the soil fertile."

They packed up and headed out at a good clip until they came to a series of steeper hills.

Josh noticed with growing admiration that no matter how challenging the climb became, Sierra managed to keep up with him.

He thought back to the heavy pack she'd managed without complaint. This time, he was carrying the extra load, with all the food Phoebe and Ela had prepared, as well as a tent they would use when the weather got rough.

He pointed to a rock shelf. "Let's stop up there and make camp for the night."

They climbed to the spot and dropped their backpacks before stepping out onto the smooth rock shelf to look around.

"Oh, Josh." Sierra touched a hand to his arm. "This takes my breath away."

"Yeah." Josh's voice was hushed, as though standing in a grand cathedral. "That's the same reaction I have every time I come here."

"Do you come here often?"

Josh nodded. "It's my special place. I call this my thinking place."

He settled down on the outcropping of rock, leaning his back against a giant boulder warmed by the sun.

Sierra settled herself beside him.

He drew his knee up and wrapped his arms around it. "I started coming here after my mother disappeared."

"Alone?"

"Yeah."

"But you were just a kid. What did your father and Big Jim think about that? Wasn't it dangerous for you to climb alone?"

"They didn't know about it at first. By the time they found out about it, there was no stopping me. So they just warned me to be careful."

"Isn't that what every parent says? Are you telling me you listened?"

He shot her a grin. "Not always. But I guess I've just been lucky. This old mountain has been good to me. So far it's never let me down."

She fell silent as she gazed out at the breathtaking vista of rolling hillsides, sparkling streams meandering between giant boulders, and green verdant meadows dotted with bright golden cottonwoods.

She leaned her arms on her drawn-up knees. "You're so lucky to have all this beauty to look at whenever you choose."

"Yeah. I love it." He turned to her. "That's why Big Jim gave it to me."

"Gave . . ." She looked puzzled. "This is yours?"

He nodded. "Big Jim wanted each of us to have part of the ranch that we could call our own. There was never a question which part of it I loved the most."

"And it's yours? Just like that?"

"Just like that."

She gave a long, deep sigh. "I can't even imagine getting such a gift." She turned to him. "What will you do with it?"

He touched a hand to her hair, studying the way it looked in the light of early evening. "Someday, when I'm ready, I'll build a home here. And I'll do what I've always done. Come up here to think, to unwind, to plan the next step in my life."

He leaned close and brushed his mouth over hers.

The rush of heat was so intense, he moved back to stare into her eyes.

Seeing the way she was watching him, he moved in and kissed her again. And though he thought he was ready, the quick sexual jolt managed to catch him by surprise.

Maybe it would always be this way, he thought, as he dragged her into his arms and kissed her until they were both sighing with need. This mind-numbing need. This breathless anticipation.

With their breaths hitching and their fingers fumbling in haste, they undressed each other, eager to taste, to touch, to possess.

It seemed that each time he thought the fire had burned itself out, it was only simmering and waiting for the next strong wind to coax it back to flame.

Maybe, he thought, as his fingers found her hot and wet and eager, she'd bewitched him, and he would never have enough of her.

And then all thought fled as he lost himself in the wild, sweet taste of her, and gave himself up to a pleasure unlike any he'd ever known.

They'd slipped into their jackets for warmth, though even that simple movement had been an effort.

Sierra managed to lift a hand to Josh's cheek. Her body felt limp and languid, as though she were caught in a dream. A wonderful, magical dream that she didn't want to end.

In a soft, languid voice she said, "You promised me dinner."

"I thought that's what we just had."

She laughed. "That was the appetizer. But you still have to feed me."

He kissed the tip of her nose. "You're turning into a very needy woman."

"Yes, I am. And now that we've...christened your thinking place, I need to restore my energy. Unless, of course, you don't care about an encore."

"An encore? I like the way you think." He sat up and reached for the backpack with mock-hurried movements. "Not to worry, my love. Your wish is my command." He opened a plastic container and handed her a crispy fried chicken leg.

"Um. Heavenly." She nibbled while he opened a bottle of water and took a long drink before handing it to her.

She sipped and passed it back to him. "What else did Phoebe and Ela fix?"

He arched a brow. "You want more? I figured after the chicken, we'd go for the encore."

That had her laughing. "Not so fast, cowboy. Show me the food."

"Let's see. There's cold pasta with vegetables. There's sliced roast beef, turkey breast, some sort of corn relish." He unwrapped several squares of corn bread and handed one to her. "We have strawberry preserves or some kind of jelly." He dipped a finger into it. "Apple."

"Um. Apple jelly, please."

He spread some on her corn bread and helped himself to a chicken leg.

She turned to him. "Why does everything taste so much better along the trail?"

"Because we've worked up an appetite?"

"Wrong answer." Her eyes crinkled with laughter. "Because there's something magical about this place."

"Oh." He looked down into her eyes and thought he'd happily drown in their depths. "Well, I've always known that. But now that you're here with me, the magic is even stronger."

They sat with their backs against the sun-warmed rock and ate their fill as they watched the land below them begin to darken with mist and shadows. And as the sun slowly began to fade below the horizon, they came together once more.

Bathed in the pink and mauve and purple glow of a spectacular sunset, they moved together in a rhythm as old as time.

And as silence stole over the land, they climbed into a single bedroll, laughing like children at Christmas, unwrapping their very own treasure trove of wonderful presents.

Josh and Sierra awoke to a distinct chill in the air and snuggled closer for warmth.

Josh pointed to the clouds, which were hanging so low they hid the peaks of the Tetons. "Snow's coming in. Think we ought to just huddle in our bedroll all day?"

"And miss the show?" Sierra tossed aside the covers and stretched. "I can't wait."

"That's what you say now." Josh grinned. "Let's see how excited you are about snow when you're up to your waist in it."

"Bring it on." Sierra opened her arms wide to the morning.

While Josh made coffee in the instant cooker, Sierra

walked to the very edge of the rock shelf, snapping photos of the fiery countryside before it became blanketed in white.

She turned to him with a wide smile. "Oh, just look at this. It's so beautiful, it's hard to believe that it's real."

"Maybe that's what people will say when they look at your pictures in a gallery someday. 'That place can't be real. She just used Hollywood props.'"

Her laughter rang on the cold, crisp air. "That's not at all what they'll say. They'll say, 'How in the world did that genius ever find such a fabulous place?' And then in the next breath they'll declare, 'We have to go there and see all that beauty for ourselves.' And then, guess what?"

"What?" He found himself loving her enthusiasm. It was thoroughly contagious.

"The Devil's Wilderness will become a famous tourist attraction, and your beautiful countryside will be overrun with all-terrain vehicles and snack shops and souvenir kiosks."

"When that happens, I predict that the Conway family will relocate to a new frontier." He handed her a steaming cup of coffee. "But until those snack shops arrive, we'll have to make do with this." He indicated two plates heaped with hard-boiled eggs and thick slices of ham, which Phoebe had tucked into their food bundles.

"Um. Heavenly." Sierra spread strawberry preserves on her corn bread and stretched out beside him, with her back to a boulder worn smooth over thousands of years.

She ran her hand over the ridges of the boulder. "Look at all the elements that went into making this. Quartz. Silver. And maybe even bits of gold and uranium and coal."

"Want to carve it up and see how many minerals we can find?"

She gave a firm shake of her head. "It would be a shame to disturb something so big and so old."

"Are you telling me you even have a soft spot in your heart for rocks?"

She shrugged. "Rocks have a place in our world, too."

He tousled her hair and couldn't help laughing. "Next you'll be telling me that rocks are people, too."

"How can you be certain they aren't? Not people from our planet, of course. But extraterrestrials."

"Just as long as they don't decide to take us back to their planets."

While they ate, they watched the lazy flight of an eagle edging closer and closer until they could almost reach out and touch the tips of its wings.

Sierra sucked in a breath at her close encounter with something so beautiful. She sat perfectly still as she picked up her camera, watched through her viewfinder, and silently clicked off picture after picture, fearful that the magnificent bird might be frightened off.

With no warning the eagle veered and dipped out of sight. Moments later they heard the screech of a wounded animal, and watched the bird lift a rabbit caught firmly in its talons high in the air.

"I bet he's taking breakfast back to the little woman," Josh said, as she captured the moment on film.

"Uh-huh." Sierra gave a short laugh. "I say she's bringing home the bacon to her lazy mate."

"Lazy? Careful, little lady. Up here in high country, those are fighting words. If the big guy's still home in the nest, more than likely it's not because he's lazy. It's probably because she wore him out all night with her loving."

Laughing, Sierra turned to him. "How about you, cowboy? Worn out yet?"

"Don't you worry, little missy. I've got plenty of moves left."

"I'll just bet you do."

He draped an arm around her shoulder, drew her close, and pressed a kiss to her cheek. "Maybe we'll make camp early tonight and I'll show you a few of them."

"Maybe I'll let you."

The two of them couldn't keep straight faces as they continued to watch the steady parade of wildlife and finish their meal.

Deer stepped out from the cover of the trees to pass by them as though they didn't even exist. Birds landed on the branches directly over their heads and helped themselves to berries. When Josh held out a handful of corn bread crumbs, one bird actually landed on his hand and helped himself before flying off.

Sierra was clearly enchanted as she snapped photos of everything. "I can't believe what I just saw. Did that bird actually eat out of your hand?"

"I guess he was hungry. Besides, up this high, they rarely see people. They're too innocent to be afraid."

Just then he pointed to a spot high overhead. Sierra followed his direction and caught sight of several bighorn sheep peering at them from behind a wall of boulders. Without a word she shot half a dozen pictures before the elusive creatures disappeared from view.

"Oh, Josh." Sierra shook her head, as though unable to believe all that she was experiencing. "I know that you told me this was your playground. I'm sure after a lifetime here, all of this seems so normal to you. But to me, this is a feast of sight and sound and color that I'll never forget."

She draped the cord of her camera around her neck, ready to snap off photos in the blink of an eye, lest her subjects disappear as silently as they'd arrived.

Despite the chill in the air, they kept their parkas in their backpacks, preferring the ease and comfort of hooded sweatshirts and comfortable denims as they packed up their supplies and resumed hiking.

Often, after a climb of an hour or more, they would remove their hoodies, tying the sleeves around their waists, dressed only in T-shirts to bare their arms to the bright autumn sunlight. Though the air had grown considerably colder, the bright sun and the exertion of their climb had them comfortably sweating.

In late afternoon Josh felt a vibration beneath his feet. At once he paused and pointed to a trail that led from the mountain peaks to a fiery meadow below. "Quick. Look at that."

Following his direction, Sierra stared in fascination at the sight of thousands of elk moving toward the lower elevations.

For long moments she could only stare in rapt silence. "I never dreamed I'd see something so majestic."

Then, letting out a long, slow breath, she lifted her camera and dropped to her knees on a low outcropping of rock, where she began recording the scene.

She glanced over at Josh. "My knees are vibrating so hard, I can actually feel them running."

"Yeah." Josh moved close beside her, staring in rapt attention at the sight. "Ela used to tell us to listen with our bodies, and not just our ears, and we'd hear the thundering herds long before they came into view."

Sierra thought about the old woman's words as she continued to capture the migration.

Using her various lenses, she was able to zoom in close enough to record their breath pluming in the frosty air, and to capture the amazing grace of the animals as they moved in perfect rhythm, as wave after wave of elk continued their downward trek.

More than an hour passed while she remained riveted to the spot, snapping pictures, and occasionally sighing at the sheer beauty of the panoramic scene unfolding before her very eyes.

While she lost herself in her work, Josh used the time to set up camp and prepare their dinner.

Soon the air was filled with a wonderful fragrance, and it reminded Sierra that except for an occasional drink and a quick snack along the trail, she hadn't eaten anything substantial since their long, lazy breakfast.

She lowered her camera and turned to Josh, who held out a cup of coffee.

"Umm, thanks." She breathed in the fragrance before drinking.

"Did you get enough pictures?"

She laughed. "More than enough. I've never seen anything like that before. It was..." Her laughter turned into a frown as a wave of unexpected emotions washed over her. She had to swallow the lump in her throat threatening to choke her. "I've used the word *breathtaking* so many times since coming here. I hope it doesn't sound trite. But that was just the most amazing thing to watch. I doubt any photo can do it justice."

He touched a hand to her cheek. "If there's a way to capture the majesty of what we just saw, I have no doubt you managed it."

She looked surprised and pleased. "Thank you. You're not just saying that to flatter me, are you?"

"Hmm." He tucked a stray strand of her hair behind her ear. "Are you easily flattered?"

"Of course I am. At least when it comes to my work."

"And you'll want to find a way to properly thank me, I suppose?"

She couldn't hold back the laughter. "Now you're feeling too sure of yourself, cowboy."

He shrugged. "Can't blame a guy for trying."

"You'll have to do better than that." She breathed in the wonderful aroma of beef simmering in mushroom gravy in the portable cooker. "But I may be persuaded to give you a proper thank-you if you feed me."

"I always thought that was the way to a guy's heart."

"You got it all wrong. I'm one woman who's a sucker for a guy who can cook."

"Now that I know your secret weakness..." Josh pulled the clean handkerchief from his pocket and draped it over his arm like a waiter. "Right this way, ma'am. Your table is ready. Chef Josh Conway has prepared a magnificent meal just for you."

He led her to the shelter of a cave formed by several overhanging rocks, where he'd laid out their sleeping bags side by side.

By the time she'd stowed her camera, he was sitting beside her, with two plates of corn bread smothered in mushroom gravy, slices of rare roast beef, chunks of perfectly browned potato, and green beans.

"Oh, Josh." After one bite, Sierra fell silent as she devoured her meal.

When at last she sat back, replete, content, she experienced a surge of such happiness, she wondered that her poor heart didn't burst clear through her chest. "I don't think I've ever enjoyed a more perfect day. An eagle, close enough to look into his eyes. Bighorn sheep. Deer close enough to touch. Birds eating right over our heads, and one brave enough to eat out of your hand. And now, this amazing herd of elk." She lifted her hand to indicate the autumn countryside spread out below them. "Not to mention the most glorious red and gold and orange foliage. I feel like I've landed in paradise."

"Yeah. I know the feeling." He took the empty plate from her hand and set it aside with his before turning to her with a dangerous smile. "I've been lost in paradise ever since I met you."

She shot him a quick grin. "Aw, shucks, cowboy. You're just saying that to soften me up for the conquest."

"You got that right." He arched an eyebrow. "Is it working?"

"I'll let you know when I've had a sample of how you operate."

He touched a finger to her lips and traced their outline. "I thought tonight I'd go for a slow and gentle seduction. Maybe just a tease of a kiss..." He softly pressed his mouth to hers and pulled back to look into her eyes, which had gone wide with pleasure. "And then a touch."

He brushed the back of his hand over her cheek, sliding around her jaw, then lower to her neck.

When his hand slid lower, to move seductively across her shoulder, she shivered and stopped it.

At his look she said, "Too slow, cowboy. Too cool. I'm sorry, but after the memorable day we've had, my blood is pumping way too fast for this. I need hot. And I need it now."

"Your wish..."

He dragged her roughly into his arms and covered her mouth in a kiss so searing it robbed her of breath.

They took each other in a firestorm of passion as wild and primitive as the land around them.

CHAPTER TWENTY

———◆◆◆———

Sebastian filled his lungs with the crisp, frigid air sweeping across the summit, and he felt the hum of anticipation. Everything was going according to plan. Not that he'd expected anything less. These small-town people with their small-town attitudes were so easy to fool.

He'd been skiing with his parents since he was old enough to walk. Their chalet in Gstaad, Switzerland, had been his playground. He'd spent many a weekend on the slopes with everyone from Hollywood starlets to royalty. He knew his way around groomed ski trails and rugged mountain paths where only the experts dared to ski. He and a group of friends had even been dropped by helicopter on a desolate stretch of the Alps, where they'd skied down expanses of snow-covered mountain never before seen by man. The adrenaline-pumping experience had left him high for days.

He lifted the binoculars and allowed his gaze to sweep across the frozen wilderness.

It was easy to spot the figures moving across one of the lower ranges. Theirs were the only tracks in the pristine snow cover.

His patience had paid off. From afar he'd watched and waited until he'd spotted the truck heading into the high country. He'd witnessed with a sense of smug satisfaction as Sierra and her rancher had unloaded their gear and had begun the climb.

To avoid leaving a trail, he'd taken a circuitous route, so that he wasn't visible to them or to anyone in the town who could report his presence to the police chief.

It would seem that the slut had wasted no time slipping away with her cowboy now that she thought the threat of danger had passed.

She was making this so easy.

These puny American mountains were little challenge to a man of his worldly experiences.

To his way of thinking, a local rancher would be easily overpowered. And when he had finished what he had come here to do, Sierra would pay.

He could already taste the heady sweetness of victory.

"You warm enough?" Josh draped his parka around Sierra's shoulders before retrieving two cups of coffee from the portable cooker.

"Thanks." She drew the edges of the coat together. "It's getting colder."

He returned to her side and handed her a cup.

They sat in silence on the rock shelf, watching the amazing change of colors in the sky as the sun began to set behind a bank of dark clouds.

Sierra felt the brush of something wet and cold on her

cheek. Looking up, she stuck out her tongue and tried to catch the snowflakes as they drifted past.

"Look." She held out a hand in wonder as several fat flakes landed in her palm. "It's snowing. Josh, it's snowing."

"Yeah. I see that." He couldn't help grinning at her excitement.

"It's"—she looked up into the darkening sky to watch the curtain of snow that fell—"so amazing."

"Didn't we just see all this in the mountains a week ago?"

"That was then, on the public slopes. I had my mind on other things, like capturing a storm in photos…" She ducked her head, still ashamed about having kept her troubles with Sebastian a secret from him. "And doing some heavy thinking. But this…" She shook her head, sending her hair dancing around her shoulders. "This is falling on our special trip on our mountain."

Josh felt a small, quick thrill at her use of the word *our*. Though he didn't want to probe too deeply, it meant more to him than anything else she could have said. "Admit it. You're falling for this place, aren't you?"

She didn't look at him. She was too busy trying to catch snowflakes. But something in the change in his voice snagged her attention.

She lowered her hand and turned to him. "I didn't say that."

"You don't have to. It's there in your eyes. In your voice."

She could feel him watching her closely. Too closely. So she turned her head and made a determined effort to keep her tone level. "It's a pretty place."

"There are plenty of pretty places. Admit it. This place is unique."

"I said it was pretty enough."

"That's like saying you're a pretty enough woman. That doesn't come anywhere near to describing your amazing qualities and your even more amazing spirit. And that doesn't explain why I have feelings for you."

"Stop." She set aside her coffee and covered her ears with her hands. "I told you, Josh. We're two adults. We're having a really grand time. Don't spoil it with all those empty, meaningless, juvenile words that guys like to use."

He took a long, deep drink of his coffee while he regarded her. Then he set the cup aside and shot her a dangerous smile. "Who said you get to set the rules?"

His hand shot out and he dragged her into his arms. Against her throat he growled, "I think that high-and-mighty little speech of yours calls for some very adult games. How about a little mindless sex? Or am I sounding way too juvenile?"

His hands were on her as his greedy mouth took hers.

This was something she could handle. Something she craved. No false promises. No pretty, empty words.

With a purr of pleasure she wrapped herself around him, hungry for all that he had to offer.

And as the snow fell and the darkness gathered around them, they lost themselves in the silken web of desire.

"Do you really think we need to set up the tent?" Sierra asked, as Josh unzipped the backpack.

"Something tells me that you wouldn't like to wake up buried in snow."

Her eyes widened. "You think it'll snow that much?"

"Probably all night. And maybe all day tomorrow. Have you taken a look at those clouds?"

Sierra was surprised to note that the snow-laden clouds now hovered directly overhead. The falling snow was no longer a gauzy curtain, but had now become a swirling, blinding blizzard.

She clapped her hands together. "I can't wait to see what these hills will look like by morning."

"Believe me, they'll look a whole lot better from inside a snug, dry tent." He set about assembling their campsite inside the shelter of the small cave, which gave them double protection.

Sierra helped him finish setting up. While Josh adjusted the small heater, she began moving their supplies inside. In no time they were warm enough to remove their parkas and stretch out on their bedrolls.

As Josh began to close the tent entrance, Sierra put a hand over his. "Do you mind leaving the flap open? Just until I'm ready to sleep? I want to watch the snow."

For the longest time they sat together, watching the snowflakes drifting past the entrance to the cave, until the ground outside their sheltered haven was no longer visible beneath all that white.

"Why do you love the snow so much?" Josh watched her as she stared transfixed at the scene unfolding before them.

She shrugged. "I've never really thought about it. I suppose because I didn't get to see much of it in England. Oh, there was snow. But it would fall and dust the grounds of our boarding school, and the next day it was melted. I have some vague memories of snowfalls from my childhood. Those deep, whipped-cream drifts that were such fun to jump in, while my father held my hand. There seemed to be a lot of snow at our Christmas reunions. I was always so happy then, just to be with both my parents. Whatever differences they had, they were able to put them aside for a few days while we felt like a family."

She turned pensive. "But it was all just an illusion. When the holidays were over, we'd go our separate ways. My mother with her latest guy, and my father with his latest love. Sometimes I wouldn't hear from them again for months."

"Is that when you stopped believing?"

His question had her turning toward him. "Believing in what?"

"In love."

"Oh. That." She dismissed it with a toss of her head. "My father said it's like a snowstorm. All soft and pretty for a while. But then it melts away, and all that's left is a puddle that dries up until there's no sign it was ever there."

She stifled a yawn. "I guess I've watched all the snow I can tonight. I just hope it's still here in the morning."

"Trust me." Josh watched as she secured the tent entrance before dropping down beside him. He gathered her close to whisper against her temple, "It'll still be here for you to enjoy."

Weary from the climb, and sated from their earlier lovemaking, they lay wrapped in each other's arms as they drifted into sleep.

Josh listened to the soft, easy breathing of the woman beside him and lay watching her as his mind drifted back to her first night at the ranch. He'd thought at the time that she was a beautiful, carefree butterfly who had escaped her unusual childhood unscathed. Now he knew better. Though she hid her wounds beneath a cheerful façade, there was painful scar tissue.

She had a real issue with trust. Obviously the ones she'd loved the most had let her down too many times. Now she was convinced that the only way to protect her heart was to lower her expectations.

What must it be like growing up without anyone to confide in? He thought about his own childhood. Despite the terrible loss of his mother, he'd always had his father, his grandfather, and, later, Phoebe to turn to. And throughout the years, they had never let him down.

Sierra had been completely alone. Through a troubling childhood, throughout the terrible teen years, she'd been forced to trust only her own instincts. Whatever mistakes she'd made along the way, there had been no one around to share the burden.

No wonder she was so strong. So resilient.

No wonder she was convinced that no man could ever be true to his word. In her young life, no man ever had. All she knew was abandonment.

It was another reason why he wanted to hold her. To comfort her. To keep her safe.

Sierra awoke to an eerie stillness. When she opened her eyes, she was surprised by the light flooding into their tent.

She glanced at Josh, who lay beside her, his hands beneath his head, his gaze fixed on her.

"How long have you been awake?"

He smiled and reached for her, drawing her close. "Just long enough to watch you while you slept."

She wrapped her arms around him and gave him a

slow, delicious kiss that had all his nerve endings humming with need.

Suddenly she pushed free of his arms to sit up. "What's that strange glow?"

His smile was quick and mysterious. "What was it you were wishing for when you fell asleep?"

"Oh." She unzipped the flap and stared at the scene outside their tent. "Look, Josh. Snow. Tons and tons of glorious snow."

"Yeah."

He lay back and watched as she sprang up and lifted her arms wide, trying to take it all in.

"Look at these hills. Aren't they a picture?"

"Not nearly as pretty as the one I'm looking it."

"Oh, you." With a laugh she snatched up her camera and began snapping off pictures of the pristine snow stretching as far as the eye could see. "Look at it." She motioned toward the trails, now covered completely, and the mounds of snow that topped every tree, shrub, and rock. "Come on. We have to walk in it."

"Why?"

"Because there isn't a single footprint in it yet. No bird tracks. No rabbit prints. No deer or fox or elk. We'll be the first creatures in the universe to leave our prints in this brand-new snowfall."

She lowered her camera and began pulling on her hiking gear.

"Wouldn't you like some breakfast before you venture out into the cold?"

"How can you think about eating at a time like this?" She slipped her arms into her parka. "I don't want to waste a minute."

"What about our camp? Do you want me to pack it up, or would you rather spend the day hiking and return here?"

She paused to give it some thought. "Why don't we leave our gear here, and hike to the next peak before turning back? Then maybe we could spend tonight here again before deciding whether to hike some more or head down."

He shrugged. "That makes things easy. I'll just secure our gear so we don't return to find some hungry bears enjoying all our good food."

A short time later, as he joined Sierra outside the tent, with a pocketful of dried beef and some corn bread tucked in his pocket, he shot a last, hungry look at the portable cooker and thought about the breakfast he'd planned.

There was always tomorrow, he consoled himself.

"Come on." Sierra was already sprinting ahead. "Last one to the top of that peak fixes supper tonight."

Josh led the way up the trail and caught Sierra's hand as he helped her over a snow-covered log.

"You getting tired yet?"

"Not at all. Oh." She pressed a finger to his lips and pointed toward the herd of deer feeding from the low-hanging branches of a stand of evergreens.

With a smile she snapped off several pictures before one of the deer alerted the others to their presence. Within minutes the entire herd had blended silently into the surrounding woods, leaving only their deep prints in the snow to show that they'd been there.

Sierra took aim and captured the prints in several more quick shots.

"Why do you want pictures of deer tracks?"

At Josh's question she turned. "I can see this in my mind. First I'll show the prints leading to the woods, and then some pictures of the herd, and then another photo of the prints leading away. I think I'll label the entire set of photos 'Guests on the Mountain.'"

He could see it exactly as she described it, and nodded in approval. "You have a gift, Sierra. A clear vision."

She felt such a warm glow of pleasure at his words. "Do you really think so?"

"I do." He brushed a strand of hair from her cheek. "And when your agent sees these, he'll have no trouble getting a gallery to showcase that talent."

"Oh, Josh. From your lips . . ."

As she continued moving out ahead of him, he felt a sudden tingling at the base of his skull. As though someone were watching.

He turned and scanned the frozen landscape.

Except for their footprints in the snow, there wasn't a single sign of another human.

Footprints.

This snowfall had made them as transparent and vulnerable as if they were holding up flashing neon signs. Anyone interested in tracking them needed only to follow their trail in the snow.

Still, if someone were tracking them, there would be other footprints in the snow.

And who would be tracking them?

Josh struggled to shake off the feeling of dread that had taken over his mood. It didn't make any sense. After all, weren't they free of any worry? Everett Fletcher had assured them that Sebastian Delray was thousands of miles away from here.

Still, the feeling persisted as he followed Sierra higher into the hills.

Over the years, whether climbing a mountain in search of a lost hiker, or charting a trail of his own, Josh had come to rely on his mental agility as much as his physical prowess. Early in life, he'd learned to follow his instincts. And right now, all of his instincts were telling him that there was some unseen danger lurking. If not human, it could very well be animal. There were countless animals in these parts that could pose a threat to unsuspecting hikers.

Up ahead, Sierra's laughter rang out on the clear, crisp air.

Her mood was as light as his was dark.

Despite his misgivings, he vowed to do or say nothing that would spoil her obvious joy.

But, he reminded himself, as long as this feeling persisted, he intended to remain alert and vigilant.

He found himself wishing he hadn't left the rifle back at their campsite.

CHAPTER TWENTY-ONE

———◆◆◆———

Cole stepped from the barn and into the blinding blizzard. The same storm that had blanketed the mountains had now descended to rage around their ranchland, the snow piling up faster than the crew could remove it. The only thing to do now was to handle indoor chores until the storm passed and they could begin the cleanup.

He walked into the mudroom and hung his wide-brimmed hat and parka on pegs by the door before prying off his dung-spattered boots and hosing them down. Then he rolled up his sleeves, moved to the big sink, and began scrubbing. He snatched up a towel and dried before tossing it into a basket.

He was just walking into the kitchen where the rest of the family had gathered for lunch, when his cell phone rang.

He flipped it open. "Cole Conway."

"Cole. Everett Fletcher."

Cole noted the gruff tone that indicated this was a business call, not a personal one. "Hey, Chief. What's up?"

"Just got a call from the state boys. As I explained to Big Jim, I'd asked them to track Sebastian Delray."

"Right." Cole pulled out his chair and settled himself at the table as Phoebe and Ela began serving up platters of beef stew and crusty rolls still warm from the oven.

After a morning round of chores, Cole's stomach was grumbling. He switched his phone to speaker and set it on the table to free his hands before reaching for a platter and filling his plate.

The chief's voice could be heard clearly by everyone around the table.

"Chalk it up to my years of dealing with bad guys. When Delray showed up at my office after I contacted his lawyer in Paris, he played it very cool. He was all stiff and formal and polite, but I could see the fire in his eyes when I presented him with Ms. Moore's restraining order. He reminded me of a guy just itching for a down-and-dirty fight. I had a hard time accepting the fact that he would meekly head home without the opportunity to face her and unload all that fury and frustration."

"Yeah. I had a hard time swallowing it, too. It seemed almost too easy. But you said the state police saw him leave."

"Yeah. That's why I asked them to track him for the complete flight. Since there was a scheduled change of planes in San Francisco, I wanted to be sure he didn't pull a fast one there, so the state boys alerted the California guys."

"And...?" Cole prompted.

"The passenger continued on to Paris."

"That's good to kno—"

"But my gut was correct. It wasn't Delray."

Cole's head came up sharply.

The movements of the rest of the family seemed to freeze in midair. Even Ela, pouring coffee, sloshed some over the rim of the cup before setting the carafe down with a clatter.

"What's that supposed to mean, Everett?" Big Jim's voice rolled around the room like a thunderclap.

They heard the chief suck in a deep breath before saying, "When the authorities in Paris checked the identification of the passenger claiming to be Sebastian Delray, they discovered it was one of the wranglers from the Brady ranch. Vic Bremmer's a tall, good-looking guy with black hair, going gray at the temples. He claims he was approached by a stranger in the saloon who offered him five thousand dollars to use the stranger's ID to fly to Paris. The guy said he was playing a joke on a buddy. All the wrangler had to do was land in Paris, call a number, and say, 'I've landed.' Then he could either stick around and see the sights of the city, or fly back home and bank the money. Either way, the wrangler figured it was too good to pass up, so he agreed. When the authorities checked the number he was given, it turned out to be Delray's cell phone here in this country. It was probably his cue that his little plan had worked, and the wrangler had landed in Paris."

Big Jim broke in to ask curtly, "Where is Delray now, Everett?"

Another long, deep sigh. "That's the million-dollar question. He hasn't been spotted since pretending to leave for that flight to Paris. His cell phone isn't sending out a signal. I figure he discarded it as soon as he got the call. But now that we know about his little scheme, it's just a matter of time before we find him. In the meantime, as long as Ms. Moore stays there with all of you, I can breathe easy knowing that she's safe while I do my job."

Cole's tone was as weary as the police chief's. "Sierra isn't here, Chief. Neither is Josh."

Everett Fletcher's voice sharpened. "Where are they?"

"Somewhere on the mountain. They left right after they heard that Delray was gone."

The chief swore. "Okay. I'll call Josh right away to warn him. As soon as they get their hides back to your place, see that they don't leave until this matter is resolved."

"Have you looked outside your window, Everett?" Cole pushed aside his chair and walked to the windows, staring bleakly at the clouds hiding the mountain peaks in the distance. "In case you haven't noticed, we're in the middle of a blizzard."

"I know. I know. I'll call you right back."

After the chief rang off, the family members pushed aside their plates, their meal forgotten.

Just as they began to voice their concerns, Cole's cell phone rang again.

He glanced at the number before saying, "It's Everett." He turned on the speaker, and the chief's voice filled the room.

"No signal. That means they've climbed too high, or it may be because of the storm. Whatever the reason, I believe they're in great danger. And the worst part is, if we aren't able to make contact with them to warn them about Delray, they won't even know they're in danger."

"We'll keep trying on this end." Cole glanced around at his family, whose faces reflected the seriousness of the suddenly grave situation. "We won't be able to take up the plane until this storm passes. How about the state police helicopters?"

"They'll be grounded as long as the snow continues. But you can be assured that as soon as the weather clears, they'll be up and searching. In the meantime, I'll alert the rangers." He paused a beat before saying, "Josh has faced plenty of dangerous situations in the past, Cole. He's smart and strong and cautious, and he knows those mountains better than anyone."

"I know that." Cole's voice lowered with emotion. "But it seems to me that Sebastian Delray has put a lot of planning into this. It doesn't sound like just a guy who wants to take back his woman. It sounds like this has become something bigger."

"I agree." The police chief's voice thickened. "This has become a game of revenge. And since Delray has already crossed a line, he doesn't care how many more laws are broken. I'd bet all my money on the fact that he's playing for keeps."

"There has to be something we can do." Jake was nervously pacing.

"Look out the window." Quinn stood watching the snow. "Until that storm blows over, we wouldn't get past the barn."

Phoebe and Ela, needing to be busy, silently cleared the table and began tidying the kitchen. Phoebe scrubbed the table, the stovetop, the counters, viciously rubbing at every little spot. Old Ela was on her hands and knees, erasing any marks on her already spotless floor. It had always been their way of coping with stress. Big Jim headed for the back door.

Cole swung around. "Where're you going?"

"Out to the barn. I need some thinking time."

"Don't you even think about trying any heroics." Cole's voice was rough with emotion.

Big Jim opened his mouth, but no words came out. Then, thinking better of it, he swung away and slammed out of the house. Minutes later he could be seen, bent nearly double against the swirling snow, heading toward the barn.

Cheyenne stood beside Quinn, her hand squeezing his, her gaze fixed on the snow falling on the mountain peaks in the distance.

So close, and yet so far.

It was the thought that tantalized all of them, and had terror constricting their hearts.

"Oh, Josh." Sierra stepped out of a wooded area and came to an abrupt halt. She was standing on a promontory that overlooked the land below, which was shrouded in snow.

As Josh stepped up beside her she finished snapping off several shots before turning to clutch his arm. "It's so beautiful."

He chuckled and forced himself to put aside the nagging little worry that had plagued him throughout their climb. "Do you know that you've said that at least a thousand times today?"

"Have I?" She joined his laughter. "But just look at it. Have you ever seen anything more beautiful than this?"

He stared around at the land, wearing a blanket of hazy white. Then he lifted a hand to her face and brushed away the snowflakes that frosted her lashes. "I've looked down from this very spot a hundred times or more. In July, when everything shimmered in blistering heat, and in February, when the land seemed touched by the hand of some mad scientist that had frozen everything in place. And I have to admit, I've never seen it look lovelier. So take a bow, Ms. Moore. You have to be the reason why everything seems so awesome." He framed her face with his hands and kissed her. "It's because you're so awesome."

He took the kiss deeper, letting himself sink into all that sweetness.

She sighed and wrapped her arms around his neck. "You're not bad yourself, cowboy."

"Not bad?" He lifted his head. "Lady, if we were back at camp, I'd show you just how good I am."

She dragged his head down for another kiss. Against his mouth she whispered, "Who says we need camp?"

He gave a growl of laughter and began nibbling his way across her chin and down her throat.

The wind picked up, sending a spray of snow into their faces. With a knowing smile he led her into the shelter of a stand of evergreens and, cushioning their bodies with his parka, they gave into a passion as raw and primitive as their surroundings.

Josh lifted a hand to Sierra's cheek. "I love the way you make love with me."

"And I love—"

A movement distracted her and she looked beyond him before whispering, "Look."

He turned to see a doe and her yearling stepping into the shelter of the trees.

For long moments the two deer merely stared at the humans. Then, as silently as they had appeared, they walked away and faded into the surrounding woods.

Sierra's voice was a hushed whisper. "Wasn't that magical?"

"Yeah."

"I think it's a sign of some sort."

Josh touched a finger to her lips. "A sign?"

"You know." Sierra's voice remained hushed. "As though the gods are smiling down on us." She turned to him. "Maybe I'm really a mythical goddess who was sent on a mission from some mystical kingdom to find the perfect man."

He couldn't help laughing. "And that doe and her fawn are really mythical creatures telling you that you're wasting your time with some Wyoming cowboy, when you ought to be out there in the big world looking for Mr. Perfect?"

She joined in his laughter. "Maybe. Or maybe they're here to tell me that I've already found him."

"Now, that's the ending to the story that I really like." He sat up and reached for his parka, wrapping it around her for warmth. "Right now, Mr. Perfect says the mythical goddess had better get some clothes on, or she's apt to get so cold she turns to stone. That wouldn't be a very good ending to your fairy tale."

Their laughter rang on the air as they fumbled with their clothes.

As Sierra reached for her parka, she paused to pick up a heart-shaped rock the size of her palm that had been buried beneath the fir branches. "Josh, look. Look at the shape of this." She held it out to him. "The mythical goddess has just found her heart. And she is presenting it to her very own Mr. Perfect."

He made a great show of accepting it. "Mr. Perfect thanks you." With a smile he tucked it into the breast pocket of his parka. "I'll keep it forever next to my heart as a reminder of this momentous occasion."

"See that you do. If you should ever remove it, you'd be removing my heart as well."

As they started to leave the shelter of the trees, Josh drew her back for another long, slow kiss.

"Umm." Her voice was a purr of pure pleasure. "That was nice."

He smiled down at her. "I just figured, since I don't have a magical heart-shaped rock to give you in return, I'd leave you with a kiss to remember me by. In case the gods decide to haul your magical hide back to your heavenly kingdom while my back is turned."

"Good thinking, cowboy. That way, if I ever get another chance at earth, I'll be tempted to look you up."

He caught her hand and pointed to a herd of deer that had just stepped out into the clearing. "Better get a photo of your heavenly angels."

He was smiling as he watched her frame the shot and continue photographing until the herd spotted them and moved silently into the surrounding woods.

He loved watching her work. She poured herself into it the same way she poured herself into their lovemaking. With her complete attention.

He'd had his share of women, both friends and lovers. But he'd never known a woman like Sierra, who was so generous with her love and so attentive to even the smallest details.

Like the stone heart. He touched a hand to his chest and could feel it there, already warmed by his body heat, its presence reminding him of her vivid imagination, no doubt fueled by a love of magic and mythical tales.

There was a sweetness, a goodness to this woman that touched his heart in a way that no one else ever had.

She'd made this hike to the place he considered his own special part of the mountain, a trip that he would remember forever.

No matter where her life, her career, took her in the future, he would always be able to return to this place and feel her here. And when he looked around at the beauty that surrounded him here, he would be seeing it through her eyes.

She made everything brighter, and better, and magical. And though he could no more hold her here than he could hold captive a beautiful butterfly, he knew that when she left him and moved on with her life, his grief would be deep.

And his loss unbearable.

CHAPTER TWENTY-TWO

———◆◆◆———

O h, Josh." Sierra looped her arm through his as they approached camp. "This has been such a perfect climb. I wish we could just stay up here on the mountain forever."

When she looked up at him, he bent to kiss the tip of her nose. "You know what they say? Be careful what you wish for. It just might come true."

"What would be so wrong about living here on top of your mountain?"

"Well, for one thing, you might get a little lonesome for company."

"You don't think you'd be enough to fill my days and nights?"

"Your nights definitely." He shot her a dangerous grin that sent an arrow straight through her heart. "But during the day, while I was off hunting and gathering like our ancestors, what would you be doing?"

"Cooking what you hunt, and storing what you gather."

"Sounds very domesticated, Ms. Moore. But as I seem to recall, that's the very thing you don't believe in."

"I never said any such thing." She paused to put her hands on her hips. "I just don't believe in marriage."

"Oh. I see. It's those pesky vows."

"Not the vows. It's what leads up to them. All those little white lies about loving only one person, and being faithful to that person until death. Why do so many people say them when they don't really mean them?"

"Yeah. I can see where that'd be a problem. All those dirty little lies."

She heard the thread of laughter in his voice and slapped his arm. "Why should I expect anything different from you? You are, after all, a man. And when it comes to love, men lie."

"Why, those lowdown, dirty rotten scoundrels."

She couldn't help laughing. "All right. So it sounds funny when you say it like that. But you know what I mean."

"I do indeed, Ms. Moore. You, being of sound mind and completely noble of spirit, will permit no lies to be spoken about love, life, and forever after. Even in the heat of passion."

"Exactly. Now…" As they stepped into camp, she turned toward the tent, sheltered in the cave. "I'm going to stash this camera and see what I can fix for our supper."

"Spoken like a good little cavewoman."

Josh watched as Sierra unzipped the tent flap and stepped inside. As she did, he felt the hairs on the back of his neck rise.

It was back. The feeling that someone was watching.

Taking care not to telegraph his fear, he intentionally

dropped a glove. As he knelt in the snow to retrieve it, he took that moment to glance around.

There were no footprints in the snow. But the snow wasn't smooth. Instead it was rough, as though it had been swept by... Josh glanced at an evergreen bough lying nearby. Had it fallen there, or had it been used to sweep the snow clean of prints before being dropped?

Though he could see nothing else out of the ordinary, he couldn't shake the feeling of being watched.

As quietly as possible, he stepped inside the tent.

"Did you notice if anything had been disturbed?"

"Hmm?" She turned. "Odd that you mention it. I was just thinking that my bedroll didn't look the way I'd left it."

His tone sharpened. "In what way? Is anything missing?"

She looked over at him. "I don't know, but I can check." She began unrolling her sleeping bag. "I don't see anything different. It was just a bit messy."

"You're sure?" He stepped closer.

His quiet, matter-of-fact tone had her arching a brow. "What's wrong, Josh?"

"I'm not sure yet. But I have a feeling..."

"Ah. Now isn't this perfect?" The crisp, slightly accented voice had them both looking over toward the entrance of their tent at the same moment. "I've been waiting for you, Sierra, my love."

Though Josh had never seen this man before, he knew his identity at once. He was exactly as Sierra had described Sebastian to the police chief. Tall, lean, handsome, with jet-black hair set off by a distinct patch of silver at each temple. He was dressed all in black. Black skier's pants tucked into black boots. A black turtleneck beneath a black ski jacket.

In his hand was a small black pistol.

It was aimed directly at Josh's heart.

For the space of several seconds, Sierra couldn't speak over the knot of terror that was threatening to choke her. "How did you get here, Sebastian? You were supposed to be in France."

"As you can see, I decided to stay here."

"Why?"

"I'll tell you why." He smiled then. A cool, chilling smile that never reached his eyes, which were as cold as the snow-covered countryside. "I originally came here to let you know that although you've been a naughty girl, Sierra, my love, I forgive you."

"You know I hate that term. I'm not your love. As for your forgiveness, I never asked for it. I don't want it. I want you to leave me alone."

"I'm afraid I can't do that."

"You were ordered not to come near me."

"Ordered? Be careful, Sierra." His smile faded. "You don't want to anger me."

She took a step back. "I don't. I don't want to hurt you either, Sebastian. I just want you to leave now. Before you do something"—she couldn't take her gaze from the pistol in his hand—"you'll regret."

"Ah." His smile returned. "You want to save me from myself. How very noble." When she remained silent, he said, "When I met you, you were nothing but a hungry little photographer, dreaming of being discovered as a great new American talent. What did I promise you?"

When she didn't answer, his voice rose in anger. "I promised to use my considerable influence to make you a star whose photographs would sell for thousands of euros. And you thanked me by leaving." His voice chilled as he spoke. "Leaving without even the decency of telling me to my face. Instead, you had your friend deliver your message after you'd fled like a thief in the night."

"I didn't want to see you again. You frightened me."

"And you disappointed me, Sierra, my love. I told you in my note that I'd forgiven you. You abandoned your rental car rather than let me near. I sent you diamonds, and you thanked me by signing a legal document that forbade me from coming near you."

He turned to Josh. "I'm about to do you a huge favor."

Josh had used these moments to gauge the distance between himself and Sebastian. His rifle wasn't within reach, and the span between them was too great to leap. He would have to keep this man talking until he could find a way to distract him and disarm him.

He decided his best bet was to jab at Sebastian's pride.

"The only favor you can do is to leave as quickly as you arrived. Otherwise, you may not like the outcome."

Sebastian waved his weapon. "In case you haven't noticed, I'm the one holding the gun."

"And that's the only reason you're still standing. If you'd like to lower your weapon, and face me man to man, I'd be happy to test your skill with your fists."

"Why would I resort to such brutality when a gunshot is so much quicker and cleaner?" Sebastian turned to Sierra. "You see, Sierra, my love, the man only cares about his own life. He cares this much"—he snapped his fingers—"for you."

He smiled at Josh. "Not that I blame you. Sierra and I are alike. We have an appetite for all that is new and exciting. Isn't that so, Sierra, my love?"

She lowered her head, refusing to look at him, hoping her silence would reach him the way her words had failed to.

He ignored her and directed his words at Josh. "You see? She can't deny the truth. I have no doubt you've slept with her. What man could refuse? Look at her."

When Josh pinned him with a narrowed look, he waved the pistol. "I said look at her. No man in his right mind could see her and not want her. She's a rare beauty, isn't she? But when the excitement wears off, as it must, she will come crawling back to me." He reached out with the pistol, using it to tip up her face so that she was forced to look at him. "And that is why I'm here. I won't ask you to beg or crawl, Sierra, my love. I'm a tolerant, forgiving man. I've come to take you back where you belong. With me."

"I belong to no one but myself." Her voice was choked with terror. "You don't own me. I won't go anywhere with you."

"Oh, you'll go. If you refuse"—his chilling smile remained as he added—"your lover's body won't be found until the summer, after the snow has melted."

Sierra paled by degrees. She had to swallow twice before she managed to say, "If I go with you willingly, will you let Josh live?"

"Josh. Ah." He drew out the sound. "I believe I heard something in your voice just now when you said his name aloud. He means that much to you?"

Sierra's heart was thundering so loudly in her chest, in her ears, at her temples, she feared he could surely hear it.

"He means"—she managed to snap her fingers just the way he had—"nothing to me. But it doesn't seem right for a man to give up his life for a . . . one-night stand."

"You admit you slept with him?"

Trapped. By her own words.

Sierra prayed that her voice wouldn't tremble and betray her lie. "You have to know that it didn't mean a thing."

"Of course. Sex. Your weapon of choice. You use it on all men but me, apparently. With me, you merely teased and toyed, and then withheld the one thing I wanted." Sebastian smiled. "But no more. Give me your hand, Sierra, my love."

"Don't do it." Josh's voice was low with warning. "Don't let him get hold of you."

Sierra shook her head. "You don't understand."

"I do. Once he has hold of you, he'll never let go. You can't do this, Sierra."

"I have to. If I don't—"

Josh cut her off. "I know why you think you have to, but you're wrong."

When Josh reached for her, Sebastian's hand holding the gun shot out in a wide arc, catching Josh on the temple, sending him staggering to his knees.

Sierra cried out his name and bent to catch him, but as he struggled to clear his vision, Sebastian grasped Sierra's hand and dragged her close.

His hand was hot, making her even more aware of how cold she felt. Cold and lifeless. And already dead.

Sebastian backed toward the tent entrance, taking Sierra with him.

She was trembling so violently, she wondered how long her legs would continue to support her weight. But, for Josh's sake, she knew she had to keep Sebastian's focus on her.

"You hurt the wrong person. It's me you want."

"It's you I have. You see? That wasn't so difficult, was it?" Sebastian squeezed her hand so hard she cringed. "I said, that wasn't so difficult, was it?"

She lifted her chin, determined to get through this. "No."

"Say good-bye to your lover."

"Where are we going?"

His smile grew. "Didn't I tell you? I'm taking you home."

"But how can we possibly leave this mountain in a blizzard? And even if we could, his family will see us when we cross their property. They'll stop you."

"You'd be amazed at what enough money can buy. I have my magic carpet awaiting my signal. Soon enough we'll be far from here, where nobody will ever again come between us, Sierra, my love."

For the first time she allowed herself to look at Josh. Despite the trickle of blood that oozed from the cut at his temple, she was desperate to memorize every curve of his mouth, every line of his brow. More than anything in this world she wished she could fling herself into his arms and feel safe.

Safe.

Tears sprang to her eyes, and she blinked them away. She dared not cry now. She didn't want to do anything to further anger this madman and drive him to do something even more violent.

She had once denied that violence. She'd tried to convince herself that Sebastian couldn't possibly be as dangerous as Chief Everett Fletcher had warned.

What a fool she'd been, to think she was safe from it. Safety, she thought with sudden clarity, was just another illusion.

She would never be safe as long as Sebastian held all the power. But the only thing she could do now was do her best to protect Josh.

He drew her close before dipping his hand into his pocket. When he lifted it, he was holding something as he wrapped an arm around her shoulders. "You're shivering. Afraid, Sierra, my love?"

She gritted her teeth at the hated endearment and struggled to pull herself together. She dared not let him sense her fear and weakness. "Of course not. It's the cold."

"Soon you will know nothing but the warmth of my body."

He looked over at Josh, who had struggled to his feet and began moving toward them. "Stop right there, or die where you stand."

As Josh halted in his tracks, Sebastian laughed as he lifted the pistol and took aim.

Sierra let out a cry of horror. "You said you'd let him live. I'm only coming with you so you'll keep your promise."

"And that's why he must die. Now that you've admitted sleeping with him, sharing with him what should have been mine alone, I can't allow him to live."

"But he didn't know—"

"You never should have left me, Sierra, my love. That was an unforgivable sin."

"Please, Sebastian. I'm sorry—"

"Too late for apologies. Did you think I would just walk away from such humiliation?"

"I didn't realize—"

"Silence. You must pay for your sins. And since I have other plans for you, your lover must pay the price with his life."

"But you promised—"

"I promise you this. You will never again leave me, Sierra, my love. No other man will have you. You will please me until I tire of you. And when I decide…" His voice turned to ice. "When I decide that I've had enough of you, I will cast you aside with the same callous disregard you gave to me. Now…" He took aim at Josh. "Say good-bye to your lover."

"No!"

Josh made a valiant effort to leap the distance that separated them, just as Sebastian pulled the trigger.

There was a tremendous explosion of sound that had Sierra watching in horrified fascination as Josh was knocked backward from the force of the bullet and lay sprawled on the ground, still as death.

When Sierra tried to fling herself on him, she was restrained in an iron grasp.

That image of Josh, so still and lifeless, was the last thing Sierra saw before Sebastian jabbed a needle into her arm.

She heard a voice screaming in her head. A voice unlike any she'd ever heard. The voice of a wild creature fighting for its life.

And then the voice was silenced and her world went black.

CHAPTER TWENTY-THREE

———◆◆◆———

Cole walked into the mudroom to find his two sons sorting through their hiking supplies.

"What's going on here?"

Quinn barely spared his father a glance. "Jake and I are heading out to the mountain."

"In this blizzard? Are you both crazy?"

As if to emphasize his words, a gust of wind tossed a spray of snow against the windowpane with such force, it sounded like bullets hitting the glass.

Jake fastened his boots. "We've been hiking these mountains since we were kids, Pa. We know what we're doing."

"For all you know, Josh and Sierra could be heading home right now."

"Or they could be facing a madman's wrath." Quinn calmly checked the ammunition in his pouch before adding it to his cache of supplies.

Cheyenne came rushing into the room, carrying a parka and her hiking gear. "You're not going without me."

Quinn lay a hand on her arm. "I already told you—"

"And I'm telling you that if you and Jake are going, I'm going with you. I won't be left behind, Quinn."

He saw the tight line of his bride's mouth, the slight flaring of her nostrils, and knew he was defeated. "Okay. But we don't have a clue what we're heading into."

"Whatever it is, I'm facing it with you."

Phoebe stepped into the room carrying several wrapped parcels. "Protein for the trail." She handed them to Cheyenne. "See that you take time to eat."

"We will." Cheyenne hugged her. "I know you're worried sick."

"We all are." Phoebe stood beside Cole as the three young people pulled on caps and goggles before heading for the door.

"Stop by the barn and say good-bye to Big Jim," Cole called as they trooped out. "He's out there raging like a bull."

"Right." Jake paused and returned to hug his father. "We'll do everything in our power to bring them home safely."

"I know you will." Cole sighed. "As soon as the weather clears, Big Jim and I will be in the air."

"We'll watch for you. As we track, we'll leave you some signs in the snow."

"We'll watch for them." Cole stood in the doorway as they made their way through the knee-deep drifts to the barn.

When he turned, Phoebe touched a hand to his arm, and she could feel the tension vibrating through him.

"I know how hard it has to be, staying behind while they go after Josh. But hold on to this thought, Cole. You've faced hard times in the past."

He nodded. "We all have."

Phoebe thought about the loss of her young husband, and the strange disappearance of Cole's Seraphine, leaving him to raise his three sons alone. And then she was reminded of the six graves on the hill behind the barn. "We've all faced painful losses, but nobody more than Big Jim."

"Yeah." Cole lifted a hand to her face, as though seeking her strength, before he abruptly turned away and shoved his hands deep into his pockets to stare out the window at the snow-covered mountain peaks in the distance.

After watching the rigid line of his back for several long moments, Phoebe returned to the kitchen, determined to remain as busy as possible, in order to hold her demons at bay.

Everyone was barely hanging on by a thread.

Sierra awoke and struggled to sit up. As she did, the world began spinning madly and she had to fight a wave of nausea. For several long minutes she forced herself to remain very still while she breathed in and out, in and out, until the nausea passed.

Whatever Sebastian had put in that syringe, it had affected her body in ways she couldn't understand. She seemed to have no control over her movements.

She lifted her hands, only to see them shaking violently. Her legs felt as weak as jelly. All she could do was lie there, helpless.

She was reminded of Josh, so still and lifeless, and of the ultimate price he'd paid. A low moan escaped her lips. At once she fell deathly silent, sucking in a breath and praying that Sebastian hadn't overheard her.

She looked around furtively. She appeared to be alone for the moment, deep inside a small cave. The only light came from the entrance, but it was so far away, she could only catch a glimpse of sunlight sparkling on snow.

How long had she been unconscious? The fact that it wasn't yet dark outside gave her hope that it only had been a short time. It would have been an effort for Sebastian to carry her dead weight through the snowdrifts on these narrow mountain passes. Surely she couldn't be too far from the cave and tent she'd shared with Josh.

Josh. The thought of him lying dead was a knife through her heart. If only she could have taken the bullet in his place.

Josh Conway was the finest man she'd ever known. A kind, honorable, decent man who'd never once taken advantage of her. And what hurt the most was the fact that he'd died believing that she didn't care.

Hadn't she tried everything possible not to care about him? She'd done everything she could to convince herself that he was like all the rest of the men who'd ever been in and out of her life. Men who took selfishly and gave nothing. But at every turn Josh had proven her wrong.

And now, without ever knowing how she felt about him, he had given his life trying to save hers.

The thought had her heart breaking. Her eyes filled and she struggled to blink back the tears.

A shadow appeared at the entrance to the cave, blocking out the sunlight. She reflexively cringed when Sebastian ducked and stepped inside.

"Ah, Sierra, my love." That cool, cultured voice sounded smugly pleased with himself. "You're awake. Good. I was beginning to wonder if I'd given you too much of that sedative."

"I wish you had. I'd rather be dead than be here with you."

"Well. Feeling feisty, are we?" He chuckled. "Good. That's the way I like my women."

"I'm not your woman. I told you that when I left Paris, and again when you followed me here to Wyoming and I was forced to sign that restraining order. I'm not your woman, Sebastian, and I never will be, no matter what you do to me."

He crossed the distance between them and yanked her painfully to her feet. His fingers tangled in her hair, forcing her head back until his face was inches from hers.

When she cried out, he gave her an evil smile. "Oh, dear. Did I hurt you?"

When she said nothing, he yanked harder, until she sucked in a breath at the pain. Still, she refused to let him know how much he was hurting her.

There was no smile on his face now. He had the look of a monster. "You don't even know what pain is yet, Sierra, my love. But I promise you, once we're free of this hellish place, you shall."

He gave her a rough backward shove. Her useless legs folded beneath her and, unable to break her fall, she sprawled on the ground, hitting her head hard as she did.

She lay very still, until the stars stopped dancing in front of her eyes.

When she opened them, Sebastian was standing over her, holding the syringe. When she tried to back away, he merely laughed. "I may prefer a wildcat in my bed, but right now I need you as docile as a kitten."

He plunged the needle into her arm and turned away to stride to the entrance of the cave. "I left a message in the snow for my...chauffeur." He chuckled at his little joke. "Now I won't have to worry about what you're doing while I keep watch until my magic carpet arrives. Once we're airborne and away from this filthy place, the authorities won't be able to touch me. Or to save you."

Josh lay perfectly still, wondering at the pressure on his chest. As though he'd been struck by a flying elephant. In fact, the elephant was still there, crushing him.

Or was it a boulder flung by a giant?

Every breath was an effort. The simple act of lifting his arm was so painful, he let it drop like a stone to his side while he lay very still, taking quick, shallow breaths.

He tried lifting his arm a second time and felt the quick, sharp stab of pain that left him gasping.

Unwilling to be defeated, he lifted his hand again and sucked in a breath at the pain. Then, bracing himself, he lifted his entire arm until his body was on fire.

This was a good sign. At least, if he could feel pain, he wasn't dead. He was very much alive. And hurting like hell.

And then all the vivid details of that scene with Sebastian came rushing back to him so clearly he forced himself to sit up.

Pain radiated through his entire body and he let out a moan of pain and rage.

Sebastian had shot him. At fairly close range.

Why then was he still alive?

He reached into his parka and probed for a wound. There was none. Just that painful heaviness in his chest, as though he'd been beaten senseless. And then he felt the edge of the stone in his breast pocket.

He took it out and stared at the heart-shaped rock that now bore the undeniable imprint of the bullet that had struck. Though the rock had cracks radiating from the point of impact, it hadn't shattered, but was still intact.

He experienced a moment of absolute wonder. His life had been spared by a stone. A silly, sentimental stone that Sierra had insisted was heaven-sent.

Sierra.

His own heart sank as the realization dawned.

Besides the gun pointed at him, he'd seen something else. Something shiny in Sebastian's other hand. A syringe.

Of course. A man like that would have planned every detail. Sebastian would have made sure that Sierra was rendered helpless, so that she was now completely under his control.

Josh had to push aside the wave of fear for Sierra and concentrate on the rules of survival that he'd always adhered to. He was a first responder. He knew what had to be done.

He lay breathing hard, sweat beading his forehead as he forced himself to act.

He plucked his cell phone from his pocket and turned it on. Though it flashed a no-signal warning, he left it turned on, knowing that even the slightest signal could be tracked by experts.

Just that slight movement had his head swimming, and he had to wait until the dizziness passed.

Despite the trauma his body had suffered, his thought process was now clear. He knew what he had to do, and was determined to see it through.

He rummaged through his backpack until he located all that he needed. He loaded bullets into his rifle and put the rest of the ammunition in a small pouch, which he tied around his neck, where it would be easy to reach. He zipped his parka and fastened his boots. Then, using his rifle as a crutch, he managed to get to his feet. Swaying slightly, he stepped from the tent and looked around in the fading light.

There was only one set of deep footprints leading away from camp. The thought came to him instantly. With Sierra sedated, Sebastian would have had to carry her.

Sebastian appeared to be a man who had gone to great pains to plan this carefully. Carrying an unconscious woman uphill in deep snowdrifts would be a challenge. Even though Sebastian had the build of an athlete, Josh had a hunch that his campsite couldn't be far.

He tried not to let his hopes get too high as he began following the deep footprints. It would be dark soon. Maybe, if he was lucky, he'd spot Sebastian's campfire. If not, he would wait, and watch, and listen.

The fact that Sebastian hadn't returned to finish him off told Josh that the gunman thought him already dead. That gave him a distinct advantage.

He was forced to move slowly, so as to conserve as much strength as possible for a confrontation.

The thought of Sierra in the hands of Sebastian gave him the impetus to keep moving when every fiber of his being was screaming for rest.

Though his body was a mass of pain, he had no intention of stopping until Sierra was safe.

CHAPTER TWENTY-FOUR

—◆—

I'm worried sick about Josh, Clemmy." Big Jim stood with his hand on the tombstone, speaking softly to his wife, as though she were right beside him. "That boy and I have always had a special bond. I swear, sometimes I can feel his pain before he even knows he's hurting. And right now, I sense big trouble. It's that madman who's been stalking Sierra. If he should find them in this snowstorm, they'd be caught completely unaware. And we know our Josh. He won't think twice about his own life when it comes to saving someone else's."

The old man lowered his voice. "Stay close to him, Clemmy, until Cole and I can be there with him."

Quinn, Cheyenne, and Jake found Big Jim out behind the barn, standing inside the circle of grave markers. From the amount of snow already piling up on his wide-brimmed hat and parka, they knew he'd been out there for some time, talking over his worries with Clementine.

He looked up when they drew near.

Quinn lay a hand on his grandfather's snowy sleeve. "We're heading up the mountain, Big Jim."

He didn't argue or try to discourage them. As though anticipating their plan, he merely nodded. "I'd do the same if I were your age."

Jake was startled by his grandfather's admission. It was the first time he could recall Big Jim conceding anything to his age. "I told Pa we'd leave a trail carved in the snow, showing you which way we'd gone."

"That's good." The old man lifted his head to study the curtain of snow. "As soon as this stops, Cole and I will be airborne."

"It can't come soon enough." Quinn hugged his grandfather. "We'll keep our cell phones on, hoping the authorities can track our signals. I know Josh will do the same."

Cheyenne hugged the old man, then stepped aside to allow Jake to say his good-bye.

He grabbed his grandfather in a bear hug. Against his cheek he said gruffly, "I know you're worried. We all are. But it's going to be fine, Big Jim."

"I know, boyo." The big man took a step back and studied his two grandsons. "I know you'll do all you can to find your brother. Stay safe."

They saluted him and turned away, heading into the blinding snow.

When Jake turned back for a last look at his grandfather, the old man was standing, head bent, hand on the tombstone, his mouth moving in quiet conversation with his Clemmy.

. . .

Because of his years spent tracking wolf packs, Quinn took the lead as they headed into the foothills, looking for anything that might point to where Josh and Sierra had made camp.

Cheyenne and Jake followed his lead, keeping their voices low as they picked their way through drifts, some of them waist-high.

"A lot more snow up here than down in the lower ranges," Jake muttered.

"Yeah. But have you noticed that the higher we get, the less snow is still falling?"

At Quinn's remark, the other two lifted their faces to the sky.

"You're right. The snowstorm is blowing over us." Cheyenne breathed a sigh of relief. "Maybe we'll find some tracks we can follow."

Quinn shrugged. "I'm sure any trail that Josh and Sierra left was covered over by a fresh snowfall hours ago. But if they venture out now, we'll be able to follow any fresh tracks."

He paused and studied a bit of thread snagged on the low-hanging branch of a fir growing along the trail. "I can't say if this is fresh, but it's definitely from Josh's parka."

Cheyenne touched a finger to the thread. "But how do you know if it was left here today, or months ago?"

Quinn frowned. "I can't say. I'll need a lot more to go on than this."

As they climbed higher, they felt the sting of cold, frosty air on their faces.

Winter was coming early to the Tetons. At least that

was what they blamed for the chill that had settled around their hearts.

Several hours later Big Jim poked his head in the utility barn, which they used as a hangar for their plane. After scraping snow from the runway, he'd parked the plow in the vehicle barn.

"The storm's just about blown itself out. I've cleared the runway. I say it's time to take to the air."

Cole looked up from his final check of the single-engine Cessna. He'd been there for the past hour, working off his frustration. "Then let's get going. I've got it fueled and ready."

While Big Jim rolled open the double doors to allow the plane to exit, Cole climbed aboard.

A short time later, when father and son were seated side by side at the controls, the plane rolled down the runway and they were airborne.

Cole tuned to the state police frequency to announce their location and intended destination. Then, leaving the frequency open so they could receive any important information sent by the authorities, they headed due north, keeping their attention focused on the frozen landscape below.

A short time later Big Jim pointed. "There's a giant arrow down there stomped into the snow. It has to be from Quinn and Jake."

Cole nodded and turned the plane in the direction of the arrow.

Some distance away they spotted a second arrow, and Cole made a slight adjustment, in order to follow the trail. He pointed to the dim ribbon of pink light on the horizon. "It'll be dark soon."

Big Jim kept his tone bland, to mask his frustration. "We've got maybe another hour."

"Maybe." Cole frowned.

Sometimes an hour could feel like an eternity. But right now, while they fought desperately to outwit a dangerous stalker, an hour felt like mere grains of sand sifting too quickly through an hourglass.

The thought that Sebastian Delray might have already located Josh and Sierra was too painful to consider. And so Cole held on to the thought that Delray was, like him, flying blind, with no idea where to begin to look for his prey.

It was the only way Cole Conway could keep his sanity.

Josh knelt on a snow-covered rock shelf and surveyed the pristine landscape spread out below him.

He would give Sebastian this. The man had been clever. Clever enough to follow a swollen stream to cover his tracks.

Josh had followed the trail to the stream, then, with no trace of movement on either side, had been forced to make a choice. First he had hiked to the lower elevations, hoping to find some tracks. Finding none, he'd backtracked to the stream and was now on the higher elevation. But so far, he'd found no sign of any footprints in the snow.

The climb had greatly taxed his strength, and he could feel himself beginning to fade. Not a good thing, when he was well aware that he would need his wits about him whenever he managed to encounter the armed madman.

He continued to hope that Sebastian would become careless, thinking he would be able to carry out his plan without interference.

Josh pressed his forehead to the cold metal of his rifle and struggled to think. He prided himself on knowing every trail, every pass, every cave in these hills. And yet, so far he'd found no trace of Sierra and Sebastian, though he'd explored most of the larger caves in the area.

If the two were in plain sight, he would have spotted them by now. He was convinced that they were hidden in one of the many caves in this area. But which one? There were hundreds of small indentations in the rock-strewn area that could conceal two people.

He got to his feet and was about to turn away when something below caught his eye. Creeping carefully to the very edge of the rock, he peered down.

Below him was a flat plateau called Wolf River Plateau. Though most of it was hidden from this vantage point, he could make out what appeared to be a series of straight lines and squares.

At first they didn't make any sense.

And then the thought struck.

Letters.

Someone had carved giant letters in the snow.

He needed to climb higher, away from all this rock, in order to get a clearer view.

Though every step caused fresh pain, he managed to make his way higher up the mountain until he came to a spot overlooking the plateau. He peered down.

Reading backward and upside down, he finally realized what the letters spelled:

LANDING AREA

Josh's heart leaped to his throat. Of course. Delray must have an accomplice. A pilot who could fly a copter and land it on the plateau.

He swore as he turned away. He'd made a very wrong choice and had climbed too high. It would take him half an hour to make his way to the plateau marked as a landing area.

As he started his descent, he held to one thought. Unless he made it in time, Sierra was lost to him.

Sierra struggled her way up through layers of darkness. The sedative had left her vision muddled, and that in turn left her dizzy and viciously nauseous.

The slightest movement made it worse.

The one thing she could see through the clouds of confusion was the fading light just beyond the entrance to the cave. Despite her fuzzy brain, she clung to the fact that somewhere out there was freedom. She knew instinctively that if she remained in here, Sebastian would soon take her away with him. And once he escaped this place, she would never be free of him.

She had to let the world know that he'd killed Josh.

Josh dead.

The thought left her numb with shock and pain, and for a moment she curled into a ball, fighting a depth of despair that rolled over her in waves.

Before the tears could start she shook her head, as though to deny the pain in her heart. If she gave up now, Sebastian would win. She couldn't let him get away with what he'd done. She had witnessed his crime. She would do whatever it took, pay whatever price necessary, to avenge Josh's death.

She saw, through the mist of sedative that still clouded her vision, a shadowy image step into the entrance to the cave, blocking the light.

A ripple of sheer terror crawled along her spine.

Sebastian was back.

She didn't know where he kept going when he left her alone, but he had said something about a message for his chauffeur.

She prayed that his driver hadn't appeared yet.

As he walked closer, she steeled herself. This time, she had to be ready for him. She wouldn't react, no matter what he did to her. She had to convince him that she was still unconscious, so that he wouldn't administer any more of the hated sedative.

"Sierra, my love."

She heard his voice above her and remained as still as a statue.

"Are you playing with me?" He kicked her with the toe of his boot.

She fought to keep her breathing slow and easy. There must be no hint that she was alert.

"Sierra." His voice was closer now, and she knew that he was kneeling over her.

His rough hands caught her shoulder, shaking her so hard she had to grit her teeth to keep from reacting to his touch.

"So."

She felt his hand at her throat, and for a moment she felt a rush of panic. Would her accelerated pulse rate give her away?

To distract him she moaned slightly, but kept her eyes closed.

"Open your eyes, you lying whore, or I'll blow you away right now."

She felt something icy cold pressed to her temple and knew instinctively that it was the muzzle of his pistol.

She knew she was risking her life by defying him, but she dared not open her eyes now.

She couldn't breathe as she waited for the explosion that would end her life.

The minutes ticked by interminably, and then, without warning, she heard his footfall as he made his way to the cave entrance. In the distance she could hear the sound of a helicopter.

She'd convinced him that she was still unconscious. Almost dizzy with relief, she waited a full minute or more before daring to open her eyes. When she did, she could see that she was alone.

When she tried to stand, her legs were trembling so violently, she knew they wouldn't support her. On her hands and knees she crawled across the floor of the cave to the entrance. Once there she breathed deeply before using the side of the cave to pull herself slowly to her feet. For a moment she feared that she would collapse in a heap. Instead, moving cautiously, she took a step and then another until she was standing outside the cave.

She stood there, breathing in the frigid air.

The sound of the helicopter was much closer now, as though hovering somewhere just out of sight beyond these peaks.

Was this what Sebastian was waiting for? Could this be his magic carpet?

She had to run. Now, while there was still time.

She was about to take a downward route when she

caught sight of the helicopter coming into view just over a ridge. On a plateau just below stood Sebastian, waving his arms at the pilot of the aircraft.

There was no time left. If Sebastian found her here when he returned, all was lost.

Without giving a thought to where she would go or how she would survive, she plunged into the snow and began clawing her way upward. At times crawling, at other times struggling to her feet, she used the branches of trees for support as she made her way unerringly into the cover of a line of trees and, hopefully, away from the clear and present danger.

CHAPTER TWENTY-FIVE

Quinn, Cheyenne, and Jake looked up at the sound of the helicopter.

"State police?" Jake shielded his eyes, hoping to see the familiar markings.

"Definitely not the state guys." Quinn studied the aircraft. "I haven't seen it around here before." He glanced at his brother. "You think Pa asked for help?"

Jake watched as the helicopter hovered above Wolf River Plateau. "I've got a bad feeling about this. What if this is part of Delray's plan? It would be an easy way to hit and run."

As soon as the words were out of his brother's mouth, Quinn nodded. "Of course. Eliminate Josh, grab Sierra, and get clean away before the authorities know where to look for him." He swore. "Come on. We have to get up there and stop him before he succeeds in getting away with it."

The three of them attacked the slopes with a renewed vengeance.

As the Cessna circled, Big Jim swiveled his head when something caught his eye. "Wait a minute."

Cole looked over at his father. "What is it? What'd you see?"

"I don't know. Head back to the other side of that peak again."

Cole made an adjustment and the plane circled back.

Big Jim strained to see anything out of the ordinary.

At last he pointed. "There. Letters." A moment later he swore. "Landing area. Hell, that can't be a message from Quinn and Jake. We couldn't land on that little spot unless we were—"

"—flying a helicopter." Cole pointed to the small aircraft just coming into view from the other side of the mountain peaks.

He lifted the speaker, tuned to the state police frequency. "Everett. Is that you approaching Wind River Plateau?"

After several seconds of static Everett Fletcher's voice broke through. "I can barely hear you, Cole. I'm with the state boys. We're airborne, but nowhere near the plateau. We're just on our way to join you in the hunt for Delray."

"Then I guess that copter we're watching means trouble for us. He's not on our frequency. I'm afraid you're a little late to the dance, Chief. There's a private helicopter preparing to land on the Wolf River Plateau. That could very well be where Josh and Sierra Moore are camped."

The chief muttered an oath. "Does that bastard Delray think he can violate our laws and then skip out without paying the price?" He could be heard speaking to the pilot before adding, "Hang on. We should be there within the hour."

Cole turned to his father. "I'm betting that Delray will be aboard that aircraft and halfway to hell before Everett and the state boys can even get close."

"Then I guess it's up to us to change Delray's plans."

Cole scanned the rugged landscape below. "This is no whirlybird, Big Jim. It would take a miracle to put this down on that postage-stamp piece of land."

"I don't see that we have a choice."

Cole stared around, hoping desperately to find a more hospitable area nearby to serve as a landing strip.

Seeing none he muttered, "Okay. We'll prepare for a crash landing. And pray for a miracle."

Josh stumbled down another slope, half-running, half-sliding as he lost his footing on the snow-slick trail. Whatever pain he'd suffered from the close-range gunshot was forgotten in his haste to reach the plateau. Nothing mattered now except reaching Sierra in time.

He tripped over a log buried under a mound of snow and fell forward, sliding headlong until he came to a sudden stop at the base of a tree.

The impact ripped the rifle from his grasp and it slid past him another hundred feet or more before it came to stop against a pile of snow-covered rocks.

Josh lifted his face from the snow and swore in frustration. This deadly situation had made him careless and clumsy at a time when he couldn't afford a single misstep.

He crawled forward until his fingers closed around the barrel of his rifle.

Just as he sat up, he caught the rustle of movement in a stand of trees and whirled, taking aim.

The spidery branches of a fir parted, revealing a sight that rendered him speechless.

Sierra was weaving like a drunk, using the flimsy branches to remain upright. And though her eyes were open, she didn't appear able to really see him.

"Sierra?"

At the sound of his voice she cried out and dropped to her knees.

"Oh, God, Sierra." He stumbled forward and wrapped his arms around her.

"Josh?" She lifted a hand to his face and struggled to focus. What she saw was a blur of dark, piercing eyes staring into hers.

Josh's wonderful, beautiful eyes.

She clutched his hand. "How can this be? I saw Sebastian kill you."

Almost reverently she traced the outline of his face, and then his mouth. There was no denying that mouth. Hadn't she kissed it a hundred times or more? "Oh, Josh. Tell me I'm not dreaming. It really is you. You're not dead."

"I'm alive, Sierra. Don't waste your time worrying about me. I'm more worried about you." He could see that her pupils were dilated and her speech slurred. "How did you escape Sebastian?"

"He drugged me. I'm still"—she struggled to put her thoughts into words—"weak and groggy. But when he went to signal the helicopter, I knew it was my only chance to escape."

"He'll come after you. You were bound to leave a

trail in the snow." Josh caught her hand. "We have to get away."

"You have to go without me. I'll just hold you back. I can barely stand."

"It doesn't matter. I'll carry you."

She touched a hand to his face, wishing she could bring him into clearer focus. "Listen to me, Josh. He'll kill you if he finds you with me."

"He's already tried that once."

"But you can't take the chance—"

"We don't have time to argue." He slung the rifle over his shoulder before lifting her in his arms. "Hold on, baby."

She wrapped her arms around his neck and buried her face against his shoulder as he made a desperate dash into the nearby woods.

Quinn figured he knew the Wolf River Plateau better than most hikers. This had been one of his favorite spots to sit and watch his pack when he'd first started tracking wolves.

"There's a shortcut up ahead. I've used it a hundred times or more." He led the way through a dense evergreen forest.

Jake and Cheyenne followed his lead with absolute trust.

Though they couldn't see the sky through the canopy of foliage, they were aware of the sound of whirling blades growing louder as they climbed. When they broke free on the far side of the forest, they could see the helicopter start to drop toward the landing area, before it suddenly veered off, changed course, and lifted into the air.

"I wonder what…?" Quinn halted in midsentence when he looked up to see the family's Cessna coming in low and fast from the opposite direction. "Sweet heaven. They'll never make it. It's impossible."

He swore and grabbed Cheyenne's hand so hard she winced before clapping a hand over her mouth to keep from crying out in horror.

Beside them, Jake stared transfixed at the sight of the aircraft barreling down on the plateau. "Not enough runway. They'll slam off the edge and crash on the rocks below."

It was like watching a train wreck. Though they all feared the outcome, they couldn't look away.

The small plane touched down, bounced once, twice, and began skidding sideways across the icy surface. Just as it slid toward the very edge of the plateau and looked as though it would continue on into the abyss beyond, it jerked to a shuddering halt, as though anchored by an invisible tether.

Moments later, as Quinn, Cheyenne, and Jake raced toward the aircraft, the doors opened, and Cole and Big Jim stepped out.

For a moment there was complete silence, as they tried to process the fact that they'd just accomplished the impossible.

"That was"—Cheyenne swallowed back the knot of fear that had nearly choked her—"simply incredible."

"Yeah." Cole shot a look of astonishment at his father, and the two men grinned foolishly. "It wasn't half bad, if I say so myself."

"Not bad?" It was Jake who brought them all down to earth as he slapped his father on the back and said, "You'd better thank Grandma Clementine for that miracle. You two couldn't have pulled that off by yourselves."

"Yeah." Quinn exchanged a knowing grin with his younger brother. "That's what I call flying by the seat of your pants. Admit it, Pa," he teased. "Did you close your eyes like a girl when you touched down?"

"I raised a couple of smart alecks. Trust me. I knew what I was doing every minute of that landing. I was in complete control."

"And pigs fly," Quinn said with a laugh.

Cole shrugged off their remarks. "There'll be time to enjoy your little jokes later. Right now, let's find Josh and Sierra before that helicopter finds another spot to land."

Josh carried Sierra into thick brush. He looked around carefully before depositing her on the ground.

"This is the safest spot I can think of to keep you hidden." He knelt beside her. "I'm going to leave you here and head back to find Delray."

"No." She caught his hand and held on to it with both of hers. "Don't go looking for him, Josh. You know he'll do everything in his power to see that you're dead. And this time, he won't trust a single bullet."

"I'm well aware of that. But I have to stop him, Sierra."

"Then I'm going with you." She scooped up a handful of snow and began wiping it over her face in a desperate effort to shock her senses and become more alert.

Josh lay a hand over hers to still her frantic movements. "Listen to me, Sierra. The sedative will wear off gradually. In the meantime, as long as you stay hidden in here, you're safe."

"I don't want to be safe if you're in danger."

"But don't you see? One of us has to survive, to testify to what Sebastian did here. Once he sees that I'm still alive, he'll realize that he has to eliminate me in order to get away with everything else. And once he follows me, you'll be free to make your escape."

Sierra felt tears spring to her eyes, and she struggled in vain to blink them back. "I can't bear it if you leave me."

Seeing her tears, Josh wiped them with his thumbs before brushing his mouth over hers.

If only, he thought, they had more time. But he had to move quickly if he hoped to save her from the fate this monster had in store for her.

"I don't want to leave you, either. But if we stay together, it will give Delray the perfect opportunity to carry out his plan. By separating, we'll force him to choose which one to follow. I'm willing to bet that he'll want to assure himself that I'm dead before he comes looking for you. Especially since he knows you're still under the influence of the sedative. He believes you're the easier mark."

She began to weep softly, knowing that he was right but wanting with all her heart to keep him with her.

"There's one more thing." Josh kissed her again, as gently as a snowflake. "If you hear gunshots, you have to run in the opposite direction as quickly as you can. No hesitating. No turning back."

"Josh..."

He took up his rifle and got to his feet.

They both heard the sound of evergreen branches rustling as though caught in a stiff breeze. Before either of them could react, a tall figure stepped into the clearing.

"Well, now. Conway. I wasn't expecting to see you." Sebastian's brow shot up at the sight of Josh.

The sound of that accented voice scraped over nerves already stretched to the breaking point.

"I would have sworn that I'd put that bullet straight through your heart."

Josh stood facing him, his eyes as dark and dangerous as the ones staring him down. "Looks like you missed."

Sebastian lifted his pistol and took aim. "Trust me. I'm an excellent shot. And I have no intention of missing a second time."

CHAPTER TWENTY-SIX

Big Jim stared around at the snow-covered terrain. "Has anybody spotted any sign of life out there?"

"We just got here," Quinn explained. "I think we ought to fan out and start searching. But first we need to arrange a signal in case we locate them."

"Right." Cole paused when his cell phone rang.

Reaching into his pocket he withdrew it and said, "Everett. Where are you guys?"

He listened, then relayed the chief's words to the others. "The state troopers have picked up a cell phone signal that had previously been blocked by the storm. They're currently tracking it, but until they narrow down the exact location, they can give us the general vicinity."

He listened again, then nodded before signing off. "Thanks, Everett. Get back to us with the information as soon as you can. In the meantime, we'll start climbing toward the last place you identified. You'll see my Cessna on the Wolf River Plateau."

The others heard the chief's exclamation, and saw Cole break into a smile. "Yeah, that's what I said. It was a tight fit, but I landed that son of a"—he glanced at Cheyenne and finished lamely—"landed on the plateau. I'd say somebody upstairs was looking out for us."

He tucked his phone in his breast pocket and turned to the others. "The state boys will hone in on that signal, but for now we're climbing to that tree line up there. We're not certain who's up there, but it's our best hope." He hefted his rifle to his shoulder. "One shot means one of them has been found. Two shots means both Josh and Sierra have been found."

"And what if we hear three shots?" Quinn asked.

"Then we start running toward it full speed ahead, 'cause it can only mean trouble."

Without a word they fell into step and began the upward hike.

Josh faced Sebastian's gun without flinching.

Sebastian's face was contorted with wild-eyed fury. It was obvious that things weren't going the way he'd planned, and now that his carefully arranged abduction was falling apart, he was becoming enraged and desperate.

That, Josh thought, could be a blessing or a curse. Sebastian could simply kill them quickly. Or, with any luck, he could become careless.

Josh intended to watch for any crack in this man's cool façade, which could give him the opportunity to take him down.

Sebastian waved his pistol. "Drop your weapon."

For a fraction of a second Josh's finger hovered on the trigger, and he briefly considered a shoot-out before discarding the idea. Not because he was afraid he could lose, but because Sierra would be caught in the cross fire. His only thought now was protecting her.

Keeping his eyes steady on Sebastian, he allowed the weapon to drop to his feet.

Sebastian vented his pent-up fury on the object of his obsession, the woman who lay in the snow. "You dared to defy me yet again? For that, Sierra, my love, you'll pay dearly."

"What will you do?" She struggled to focus her blurred vision. "Kill me twice?"

At her bold sarcasm, Sebastian swore and started toward her, propelled by a blinding rage as he brought his booted foot back backward, determined to deliver a painful blow.

Using that momentary distraction, Josh launched himself against Sebastian, taking him down.

The pistol fell from Sebastian's hand as Josh brought his fist into Sebastian's midsection, causing him to wheeze out a breath before landing a blow to Josh's jaw.

Josh shook his head to clear the stars, then smashed a fist into Sebastian's nose, sending up a fountain of blood.

Enraged, Sebastian reared back and kicked Josh so hard he fell backward into a snowbank. Before he could clear his head Sebastian was on him like a vicious dog, pummeling him with his fists.

Josh knew he had to end this soon, before his strength ebbed, and all the effort he and Sierra had put into escaping would be for nothing.

Sebastian reared back, ready to deliver a killing blow

when there was a thud, and he suddenly seemed to stiffen before falling forward.

Josh scrambled out of the way as Sebastian slumped into the snow and lay perfectly still. When Josh looked beyond the unconscious figure, he saw Sierra standing over him.

"What did you...?"

She lifted his rifle, which she'd used as a club. "I just grabbed the first thing I could find and hoped I hit my mark. I'm not even sure what I hit."

"His head, from the looks of him." Josh's smile was radiant as he studied her pale face. "Good girl. Thank heaven. My sweet, brave Sier—"

He was reaching for the rifle just as a shot rang out. He felt his arm drop to his side, while blood spurted like a fountain and flowed down the sleeve of his parka.

Only then did he feel the pain radiating from the bullet that had rendered his arm useless.

He and Sierra were stunned to see Sebastian on his knees in the snow. In his hand was his pistol. On his face was a look of black, blinding rage.

"Just a little reminder that I'm still in charge, and I'm a crack shot. I missed your heart on purpose this time. I've decided that I'm going to enjoy killing you a little bit at a time. All for my pleasure, of course."

Sebastian made a bow toward Sierra as he got slowly to his feet. "And also because I know hurting him will add considerably to your pain, Sierra, my love."

He took deliberate aim and shot Josh in the leg.

As if in slow motion Josh felt his leg fail him just before he dropped to the ground.

Sebastian stood over him with a chilling smile. "Now

that's more like it. I believe I'm going to enjoy this a great deal more than I'd expected."

With a cry Sierra started crawling toward Sebastian, determined to stop him.

He calmly lifted the pistol. "Every time you defy me, I'll make your lover pay with more pain."

He was pleased to see that his words had the desired effect. His threat had Sierra slumping weakly into the snow.

Sebastian took aim again, this time at Josh's mid-section. "I should warn you. This will result in a fatal loss of blood, but it will happen slowly, so that long before you die, you'll be begging me to end your life and put you out of your misery. I'll only comply, of course, if Sierra is willing to beg." He shot a quick glance at Sierra. "What do you think, Sierra, my—"

His words died on his lips when he saw her leaning weakly against the trunk of a tree, holding Josh's rifle aimed directly at him.

He threw back his head and laughed at the sight. "How pathetic. Do you really believe, when you're too weak to even stand, and still blind from the sedative, that you can manage to shoot that thing and actually hit any-thing?"

Her teeth were chattering so hard, she could barely get the words out. "Put down your pistol, Sebastian, or I'll have no choice."

He laughed harder and turned, taking aim once more at Josh. "Remember that you brought this on yourself. Say good-bye to your cowboy, Sierra, my love."

A single shot rang out, which seemed to echo and reecho across the hills.

· · ·

Cole's head came up sharply. "Dear God. That was a third shot."

At the first shot he'd started toward the thicket, with Big Jim close behind. Now they were both racing as fast as their legs could carry them.

Quinn, Cheyenne, and Jake, who had heard the first two shots and had changed direction, came barreling into the forest from the opposite side.

Directly overhead they could hear the drone of a helicopter, and prayed it wasn't Sebastian's associate. As it descended, the whirling blades flattened the trees and sent snow flying everywhere, nearly blinding them.

As quickly as it landed, Chief Everett Fletcher and several state police officers were swarming from the helicopter and racing toward the thicket.

When they arrived at the clearing, they found blood splattered across the ground, its crimson stain against the stark-white snow causing their hearts to plummet.

Josh was lying in a pool of blood, with Sierra kneeling beside him. Not far away Sebastian lay still, as blood slowly spilled from the front of his parka.

"Josh." It was the only word Cole could manage as he dropped to his knees beside his son and felt for a pulse.

Finding it, he sat back on his heels and said to the others, "He's alive."

There was a collective sigh at his words.

"He's been shot." Sierra barely looked up as she continued tearing her shirt into strips to use as a tourniquet.

She'd removed her parka in order to get to her shirt. Now, in her haste to bind his wounds, she wasn't even aware that she was shivering uncontrollably in the snow, clad only in her bra.

Cheyenne was the first to collect her wits. Seeing Sierra's apparent confusion, she caught the young woman's hands and eased her into her parka before zipping it up. "Here, honey. You're freezing."

"I am?"

The others merely gaped at her, aware that she was in a state of shock, but unable to stop her almost manic behavior.

Josh managed a grin. "Isn't she . . . something?"

Cole clapped a hand on his son's shoulder. "Yes, she is. And so are you." He nodded a head toward Sebastian's still body. "I'm glad you shot the bastard."

"Not . . . me." Josh could feel himself slipping in and out, and wanted to make his family understand. "Sierra . . . did it."

"Did what?" Jake dropped down beside Cole, before casting a startled glance at Sierra.

"He's confused." Cole squeezed Josh's hand. "Don't try to talk now, son. Just lie here and wait for the medics."

"Not confused." Josh found the effort to speak almost more than he could handle. His mouth was refusing to work properly. But his adrenaline was pumping, and he had a need to explain. "Sierra . . . shot . . . Sebastian."

Sierra seemed dazed as she looked over at Josh. "He's in a lot of pain." She looked around wildly. "He needs a doctor. He needs a tourniquet on those wounds. He needs something for pain. Someone get him a doctor. I can't bear to see him suffering."

"The medic's here." The police chief quickly took

charge, motioning for one of the state officers to fetch a gurney, while another checked Josh's vitals.

"Got some nasty gunshot wounds," the medic said tersely. "Losing a lot of blood. But it appears to be nothing fatal."

After giving a thumbs-up, the medic moved to Sebastian's body, feeling for a pulse. Moments later the officer shook his head, declaring Sebastian dead.

Chief Fletcher drew in a breath. "Considering the circumstances, we need to evacuate this crime scene and transport everyone to Paintbrush. Josh needs to be treated at the clinic." He studied Sierra, whose pupils were still dilated. "As does Ms. Moore."

"I'm fine." Her words were slightly slurred. "All I care about is getting someone to help Josh."

"I'm sure Doc Walton will take care of those bullet wounds and give him plenty of good drugs," the chief said dryly. "Then, after everyone's been taken care of and feeling calm and collected, I'll get the information I need to fill out the proper documentation."

He spoke briefly with the state police, who would remain on-scene and tag all the evidence, before he turned to Cole. "Let's head to the police copter."

Cole shook his head. "Big Jim and I will fly ourselves out."

"Not now." Everett glanced skyward. "The day's fading. Not a good time to try and take that plane off a plateau with no runway space. You may have had yourself a miracle once, but we're not tempting fate by trying it again. You're coming with us. We'll retrieve your plane tomorrow."

Big Jim slapped his son on the back. "The chief's right.

Let's leave the driving to someone else, Cole. Besides, we need to be with Josh at the clinic."

The others nodded in agreement.

Defeated, Cole agreed.

The police chief continued giving orders until everyone was herded aboard the police helicopter.

With a whirr of blades that had snow flying about them wildly, they were soon airborne and heading back to civilization.

After a lifetime practicing medicine in Wyoming, like her father before her, Dr. April Walton had seen it all. Ranch accidents that stole limbs, saloon brawls that left men and even women bloodied and bruised, and gunshot wounds that punctured organs and robbed strong, healthy bodies of the ability to do the simplest things.

She had the cool, professional demeanor of a healer, and the stern voice of a mother superior.

She needed both while treating one of the Conways. She'd come to expect a circus of chaos whenever the entire family congregated at her clinic, and this time was no exception.

An emergency vehicle transported most of the family from the small airport just outside of town to her clinic, where they trooped in and circled the bed in the small examining room. Phoebe and Ela, having been notified by cell phone, arrived with a screech of tires and squeal of brakes in one of the ranch trucks and raced inside to join them. Both of the women took one look at Josh, bloody and bruised, and promptly burst into tears.

Between the tears and the voices, each one shouting louder than the next, and all of them vying to be heard, it was impossible to maintain any sort of professional decorum.

Dr. Walton's voice roared above the din. "You will all wait in the other room. This is a hospital, and you will behave accordingly."

"I'm his father." Cole crossed his arms over his chest, ready to dig in.

"I'm his grandfather." Big Jim did the same, looking ready to spar with anyone who dared argue with him.

"I'm the oldest brother, and I'm not leaving until you tell me how bad it is, Doc." Quinn planted himself next to the bed.

"I'm..."

Before Jake could say another word Dr. Walton silenced him with a look. To the entire group she said sternly, "And I'm the physician in charge, and I say you will all leave the room this minute, or I'll ring for the police chief to have all of you thrown out and the doors barred."

As they fell silent and began filing out, Josh caught Sierra's hand and held her fast. His grasp was surprisingly strong for someone who'd just been shot.

"She stays," he said through gritted teeth.

The doctor was about to argue when she saw the set of his jaw. With a grim nod, she relented.

When they were alone, Dr. Walton began her examination. "You weren't satisfied with one gunshot, is that it?" The doctor's strong fingers probed Josh's arm, his leg, checking entrance wounds, exit wounds, and vital organs.

Through it all, Sierra remained beside the bed, her two hands gripping Josh's hand until it went numb.

"Are you in pain?" Sierra whispered.

"I don't mind the pain as long as you stay close."

When the doctor was finished, she rang for her assistant. As soon as a sedative had been administered, they began the long and painful task of removing the bullets, cleaning up a river of blood, and stitching the wounds.

Afterward, Dr. Walton examined Sierra. Finding her fit, except for the last dregs of anesthesia still in her system, she said gently, "Josh will be asleep for several hours now. I think you should go home with his family and get some rest."

Sierra shook her head. "I don't want him to wake up alone. I have to stay—I have to—"

"Honey, you look dead on your feet..." But as she saw determination flash in Sierra's eyes, Dr. Walton relented and took pity on her. "Okay. You have to promise me that you'll both get some rest, though." She pointed to a reclining chair across the room and instructed her assistant to move it over.

When the chair had been drawn up beside Josh's bed, she helped Sierra to lie down before covering her with a warm blanket.

Sierra rolled to her side and caught Josh's hand in hers. She was asleep before the doctor and her assistant slipped from the room.

The doctor smiled before squaring her shoulders. Now to face the noisy Conway family and tell them the patient would be as good as new in no time.

She couldn't wait for all of them to leave and head back to their ranch so she could have some peace.

CHAPTER TWENTY-SEVEN

T hey're coming." Ela had been peering through the windows for the past hour, waiting to see the ranch truck bearing Josh home from town.

Dr. Walton had ordered Sierra back to the ranch the previous day, as soon as she'd assured herself that all the sedative was out of the young woman's system.

Josh, however, had been ordered to spend an extra day in the clinic, since it was the only way the doctor could guarantee that he wouldn't resume ranch chores too soon. As it was, she'd felt the need to send him home with written orders to rest for at least forty-eight hours before lifting anything heavier than a saddle.

Quinn and Jake had driven into town, leaving the rest of them to find ways to fill the hours until they returned with Josh.

The women had been cooking and cleaning up a storm, while Cole and Big Jim finished up their ranch chores.

Though Sierra had offered to work alongside the others, they'd insisted that she rest. She'd slipped away to her room nearly an hour ago.

"Nerves," Phoebe had said. "She's as jumpy as a housecat when a storm's brewing."

"She misses Josh," Cheyenne said. "I saw her staring out the window half a dozen times. Just staring, as though she were taking pictures in her mind."

Old Ela nodded. "I saw that, too. But she looked sad, as though the pictures were not happy ones."

"Seeing Josh ought to be just what she needs." Spying the truck coming up the drive, Cheyenne dried her hands on a towel and shouted for Sierra.

The family spilled down the porch and out to the truck, where the women hugged Josh and the men slapped him on his back before leading him inside.

Sierra stood framed in the doorway, a hand at her throat as she drank in the sight of Josh, in need of a shave, still bearing the bruises and sporting a sling for his arm. Her eyes swam with tears, and she couldn't seem to find her voice.

Josh stepped closer and, because his family was watching, merely touched a hand to her cheek.

"How're you doing?"

She swallowed, struggling to find her voice. "I'm okay. How about you?"

"I feel a whole lot better now, just seeing you."

He lifted his head to breathe in the wonderful fragrance of Ela's corn bread and Phoebe's fried chicken, the meal he'd requested while still recovering at the clinic in Paintbrush.

"Smells like heaven," he said.

"And you look like hell." Jake held out a chair and Josh dropped into it, grateful to get off his feet.

"I can't believe how weak I feel. I'm not used to it, and I have to say I can't wait to get stronger. Doc Walton said I'll be feeling like myself by tomorrow."

"Of course you will, son." Cole parked himself at the table and sat back, content to simply stare at his family, now that they were all together again.

"I hope you're hungry," Phoebe said, as she and Ela began passing platters of chicken and mashed potatoes, garden vegetables, and corn bread.

"Now this is what I've missed." Josh filled his plate and handed the platter to Sierra, who helped herself to very little before passing it on to Jake and the others.

Josh glanced at her plate. "That wouldn't feed a bird."

"I'm not hungry." She shrugged and looked away, her face unusually pale.

While they ate, the family asked dozens of questions, determined to fill in the gaps of misinformation about what had really transpired on the mountain.

"Sierra told us that you were shot earlier, at close range, and survived. How is that possible?" Cheyenne gazed at Josh across the table.

"A direct shot to the chest. Sebastian figured I was dead." He closed his eyes for a moment at the wonderful taste of Phoebe's gravy and potatoes, before turning to Sierra. "I guess you thought I was gone, too."

She nodded, but couldn't manage to speak over the lump in her throat. Every time she thought about Josh nearly dying, the pain was almost more than she could bear.

Quinn studied his brother. "Okay, Superman. How did you manage to survive?"

Josh reached into his breast pocket and held up the heart-shaped rock that hadn't left his possession since the incident. "Sierra found this earlier. I had it inside my parka, and it deflected the bullet."

"Let me see." Jake took it from his hand and held it up for everyone's inspection. "You can actually see the indentation where the bullet struck, and all the little cracks radiating out from it."

"Yeah." Josh smiled at Sierra. "Talk about having an angel on my side."

Cole looked impressed. "I think that's more of a miracle than my landing on Wolf River Plateau."

Phoebe touched a hand to his shoulder. "They were both miracles, if you ask me."

"I won't argue with that." After the stone had been passed around the table, Josh tucked it back into his breast pocket.

Quinn turned to his grandfather. "Are the authorities finished with their investigation?"

Big Jim nodded. "Pretty much. Everett told us that they located the helicopter pilot, who claimed to know nothing about Sebastian's trouble with the law. He'd been paid a fortune to pick up two climbers, husband and wife, on the mountain and transport them to Canada. According to him, Sebastian had claimed that his wife had fallen ill during their hike and asked him to file a flight plan with the Canadian authorities, and had assured him that they would both present valid passports. The state police found forged passports in Sebastian's pocket using phony names for both himself and Sierra, and located a private jet that had been commissioned to take them to France. It would seem that Sebastian had laid out some pretty elaborate plans. Everett thinks he might have pulled it off if he'd made it over the border."

"There's something else," Big Jim said.

The others turned to him.

"It seems Sebastian Delray has a history of stalking women. His last victim was the daughter of an Italian billionaire, who vowed to destroy the Delray name and empire if he ever came near the girl again. The chief thinks that Delray went a little berserk when he learned from his lawyer that Sierra had filed legal documents naming him. His family had threatened to disinherit him if he brought further shame to their name."

Cole's voice was low with anger. "Maybe, instead of disinheriting him, they should have used their money to hire a watchdog to keep him from hurting another helpless woman."

Josh closed a hand over Sierra's. "Helpless? If you'd had a chance to watch this little female fight for her life, you'd never think of the word *helpless* again." He shook his head. "You were amazing."

"You were both amazing." Cole looked down at his empty plate, then over at Phoebe. "Did I spot a johnny-cake on the counter?"

"You did." Her smile was radiant. "And Ela's sweet vanilla sauce to pour over it."

He touched a hand to his chest. "Be still, my heart."

Phoebe merely smiled at him. "I'm sure the doctor wouldn't object if you had a tiny slice, since we're having a celebration."

"Hey, bro, you ought to get yourself shot up more often," Jake muttered, as he watched Phoebe cut the cake and begin passing it around. "I wouldn't mind having this kind of meal every day."

"You'd soon be fat and lazy, and then what would happen to all those girls in town who practically faint every time you walk by?"

At Quinn's comments, the others roared with laughter.

"I'm sure I could find a pleasant way to work off these calories." Jake took a bite of cake and closed his eyes. "Oh yeah. Definitely worth having you get shot at."

"Gee, thanks. As long as you're not the one being shot."

"You got that right." Jake winked at Cheyenne across the table, who was thoroughly enjoying the jokes.

"Well, boyo." Big Jim sat back and sipped strong, hot coffee. "I'm glad this ended well, but I have to say I think I'm getting too old for all this drama. I hope from now on you'll stick to rescuing others, while keeping yourself away from danger."

Josh grinned at his grandfather. "I'll do my best, Big Jim. Though I have to say that rescuing pretty women—"

He turned to where Sierra had been seated, hoping to take her hand, only to find the chair empty.

Before he could ask where she'd gone, he saw his family's attention focused on the doorway leading from the great room.

He turned to see Sierra carrying her gear.

He shoved back his chair. "What's this?"

"It's time I headed out." She studiously avoided looking at him. "I've had a lot of time to think while you were recovering. It's all I did, in fact. But I wanted to wait until I was sure you were going to be all right."

Those around the table had gone ominously silent.

Josh wasn't aware of anyone except Sierra.

"So..." He snapped his fingers. "Just like that, you're leaving?"

"I should think you'd be relieved. Have you forgotten? I'm the guest who came for a night. I seem to have over-stayed my welcome."

He started across the room and she shrank back, raising her hands palms up as though to hold him back. "Please, let me just say what's on my mind." She looked at the others. "I never meant to bring all this danger to your doorstep. I want you all to know how sorry I am."

They all started protesting at once.

"That's crazy..."

"You can't be serious..."

"Somebody make her understand..."

She raised her hands again, silencing their protests. "While I was at the clinic I heard from my agent. Several galleries are interested in showing my roundup photos. In fact, my agent says he'll take all the Western photo-graphs I can send him. So..." She stared at a spot over Josh's shoulder. "It's time I got back to concentrating on my career, so that you can do the same."

Josh backed up and looked as though he'd just taken a blow to the chest. "Well." His face was pale. Pale and angry. "Congratulations. I know it's what you'd been hop-ing for. That's...great news. I guess now you really will be married to your career."

She glanced around with a look of desperation. "I know it's another inconvenience, but I wonder if one of you would mind driving me to town?"

While the others remained adamantly silent, Big Jim's

voice boomed out, startling everyone. "I'll take care of it, sweetheart."

Jaws dropped. Eyes rounded.

He kept his tone conversational. "But while I'm finishing my cake, I think, Josh, you ought to take Sierra up the hill to say good-bye to Clemmy." He turned his gaze on Sierra. "I hope you don't mind, but it's a bit of a tradition in our family."

Sierra was already shaking her head. "I don't think—"

He ignored her and turned to his grandson. "Go ahead now. Take her up the hill and let her say a final good-bye."

"Tradition?" Josh looked at his grandfather.

"You heard me, boyo."

Josh nodded woodenly and looked over to where Sierra stood, pale and trembling, in the doorway. Without a word he moved to the door leading to the mudroom and held it open.

For the space of several moments she merely stared at it before lifting her head and following him from the room.

In the mudroom he paused and pulled on his parka, easing it around the sling. Then he opened the outer door and waited while she slipped into her parka and swept past him, before closing it firmly.

In the silence that followed, everyone turned to stare at Big Jim as if he had lost his mind.

"You're going to drive her...?" Cole's words died when Big Jim lifted a hand.

"I thought I'd buy Josh a little time. You could see in his face that Sierra's decision caught him by surprise. And I could see in her face that she'd shed a lot of tears over this. I figure they can both use a little time to sort things out, away from all of us. That hill's the perfect place for them to talk about what they need to do going forward."

"What they're about to do is go their separate ways," Jake said. "You heard Sierra. She has a career to think about. And I can't see Josh traipsing around the world just because he's crazy in love with her."

Big Jim smiled at his youngest grandson. "Sometimes the most impossible situations can have the simplest solutions. Trust me, boyo. After bringing them home safely when it looked like they didn't have a chance, you don't think my Clemmy will let them go wrong now, do you?"

Without a word the family rushed to the window to watch as Josh and Sierra, standing as far apart as possible, climbed the hill behind the barn.

CHAPTER TWENTY-EIGHT

————◆◆◆————

It was one of those rare autumn days, with the sun warm enough to burn off most of the snow that had fallen during the latest storm. A cluster of black crows swarmed around a patch of sunflowers growing out behind the barn. Horses grazing in the pasture looked up as the two figures walked along the fence, before returning their attention to the tufts of grass.

Josh and Sierra climbed to the very top of the hill and paused at the five headstones circling the larger grave marker. Just as his grandfather always did, Josh paused to touch a hand to the cool marble, tracing a finger around the letters that formed Clementine's name.

Despite the turmoil within, Sierra couldn't help but feel a tug at her heart at the sight of all those headstones and the peacefulness of the place. "Does Big Jim ever talk about how it felt to lose all the people he loved?"

"Not often. But he's fond of saying that every day, even

though his heart was broken, he knew he had to get up and keep going."

Sierra shook her head. "I can't imagine that kind of pain."

"I can."

At his words she lifted her head to study him. He looked as sad, as solemn as she felt. She wished she could offer him some comfort, but she had none left to give. Though her own heart was breaking, she knew what she had to do.

"I hope someday you'll understand why I'm leaving, Josh."

"I understand. You have a career to focus on now. A very successful career, if your agent is to be believed."

She hung her head. "I won't apologize for having a career that matters to me."

"Don't ever apologize for it. You deserve whatever success you achieve. You're good at what you do."

She swallowed. "I know now what I didn't know before coming here. I'm good at what I do when the subjects of my photos matter. You and your family matter to me, Josh. And that's why I have to leave. I've thought this through very carefully. The longer I stay here, the deeper my guilt will grow."

"Guilt? What for?"

"For knowing the pain I caused all of you by bringing Sebastian here."

"You didn't bring him. The choice was his. He was the one stalking you."

"Those are just words. The truth is, you nearly died because of me."

"I would have gladly died to save you."

She hissed in a breath. "Don't you think I know that? That's why I have to go."

"That doesn't make any sense. I thought this was about your career."

She shrugged. "Before I met you, photography was the most important thing in my life. But now..." Seeing the bleak look in his eyes she softened her tone. "Look, Josh. I've never met anyone like you before. You and your family are all the things that I didn't think really existed in this world. Whoever heard of three generations living and working together, and actually liking one another?"

"And you're leaving because of my family?"

She sighed. "How can I make you understand? I learned early in life how to be alone. And I was fine with it. How could I possibly miss what I'd never had? But now, seeing all of you..." She took in a deep breath, and decided to lay it all on the line. "I was a cynic long before my teens. Love was a joke. Family was a burden. Sebastian was right, you know. I dated him because I thought he might be able to further my career. That's what my friends urged me to do. I saw nothing wrong with it, until I saw the ugly side of him. And to be honest, I...I think I accepted your invitation to stay at the ranch because I was tired of running and I wanted a haven. I never thought about your safety—or your family's, either."

"Do you really believe that?"

She stood with her arms crossed firmly over her chest, as though holding herself together by a thread. "Yes, I do. But I made the mistake of getting to know you and your family, and you are all so real. There isn't a phony one in the bunch. You're all so...good. And I'm..." She shrugged.

"Ah."

At that word she looked up and found him smiling. "What's that supposed to mean?"

He nodded slowly. "I'm starting to figure it out. You've decided that the mistakes you made in the past have made you somehow unworthy of a good life."

"I didn't say that."

"You implied as much." His smile grew. "Sierra, I know that life dealt you an...interesting hand. Your parents wouldn't stay together, even for your sake. And that's made you unwilling to trust. I get it. So let's get some things out of the way. I *wanted* you to come here and stay with us. You weren't using me or my family—I offered. *We* offered. And I don't care what you did before. I'm not interested in how many guys you knew, or why you chose them, what phony lines they used, how you used them or they used you. What I'm trying to tell you is this. Maybe I didn't get to be your first, but all I care about is being your last."

She opened her mouth, then, unable to find any words, closed it.

Steeling himself, he took her hand and looked at it, so small inside his palm. Despite the warmth of the sun, it was cold. The merest touch of her caused the most amazing feelings inside him.

"You've made it plain that you really believe a man will say whatever it takes to get you into his bed. I don't know how to make you understand this. I don't know just when it happened, Sierra. But what I am sure of is this: I love you. What's more, I need you in my life. I want us to grow old together. Here on the land I love." Before she could speak he stopped her. "I respect the fact that you have a career. I hope you can be wildly successful. I wouldn't think of standing in your way. You can go on exotic photo shoots anywhere you please. Show your work in galleries around the world. But at the end of the day I want to be the guy standing beside you while you climb the ladder of success. I want to be free to say all those mushy things a guy says to the woman he loves. And here's the bottom line: Even though I know you don't believe in such things, I want it all. The ring. The vows. The promise of forever."

She was silent for so long, he wondered that his heart could keep on beating. He knew, by the look on her face, that he'd gone too far. Asked too much of her.

When she finally spoke, her voice was hushed, as though each word was something so new, so amazing, she could hardly believe what she was saying.

"I never thought I could trust anyone the way I trust you, Josh. Not because of the way you were up there"— she motioned with her head toward the mountain looming in the distance—"but because of the way you've accepted me every day, just the way I am. I think this thing that happened between us is so big, so earth-shattering, that I've been terrified of it and running for my life. I mean, we're talking the L word."

"It's called love. Why can't you just say it?"

Instead of speaking, she swallowed. Hard.

He stared into her eyes, feeling his heart stop. He could sense that she was about to shatter his poor heart, and there wasn't a thing he could do to stop her.

At last she smiled, and he felt some of the chill around his heart begin to thaw.

"Yeah. Love." She stopped and lifted her face to the sky, as though the word was something she'd just invented. "Love. Oh. My. Gosh. I love you, Josh Conway. I really do. I love you so much. I know it isn't possible, but it's true. I love you and that whole big wonderful family of yours. And I don't care if it's the corniest thing in the world, but if you're serious about wanting me, I intend to latch on to this love with both hands and just hold on for dear life."

"You mean it? You're not afraid of it now?"

"On the one hand, I'm terrified. But on the other..." Her voice lowered. "As long as you're with me, I don't think I'll ever be afraid of anything again."

He gathered her close and lowered his head to brush her trembling lips with his. "Sierra, there's nothing you could have said that would have made me happier. And you're sure now? You're willing to go through the whole ring-and-vows thing?"

"The whole thing. Bring it on. Ring, vows, minister, and forever after. I might even break down and buy a white gown, though I doubt I'll go that far."

She sighed and returned his kiss before throwing herself into his arms and wrapping herself around him. "I'm sure my parents will be very disappointed. But hey, they've had a chance to chase their dreams. Now it's my turn."

"Yeah. Our turn." He was nearly staggered by the feelings that poured through him. Relief. Gratitude that his grandfather had sent them up here to clear the air. And then, as the thought struck, he found himself laughing. "That sneaky old man. He knew the deck was stacked."

Sierra lifted her head. "What are you talking about?"

"Big Jim. That old softie sent us up here knowing his Clementine would see to it that two lovers got their happy ending."

At his words Sierra leaned over to touch a hand to the tombstone. "Thank you, Clemmy."

She looked up at Josh. "I suppose now we'd better get back and let Big Jim know that his strategy worked."

"Not on your life." Josh chuckled and took her hand before leading her toward the barn. "We'll tell him after he's cooled his heels a while." He drew her close and pressed a kiss to her temple. "But first, I'd like to have a romantic moment with my girl."

My girl.

At those simple, old-fashioned words, her heart soared.

Tears welled up in her eyes and she realized she was beginning to like all the mushy sentiments.

"Leave it to a cowboy to want to seal the bargain in the hay." She laughed, a clear, sweet sound that rang in the sunny air. "I guess, with all this love floating around, we'd better not waste a single minute."

Epilogue

Big Jim trudged up the hill behind the barns, his arms laden with masses of white mums, which he added to the tall urns already filled with evergreen boughs. He noted idly that Phoebe had already been here to tie big white satin bows to either end of the stone bench that faced the headstones of Clementine and her five sons.

The old man eased himself down on the bench and removed his wide-brimmed hat, twirling it around and around in his hands as he squinted into the sun reflecting off the marble headstone.

"You did good, Clemmy, just like I knew you would. We're adding another pretty woman to our family today. She's a real scrapper, and not at all what you'd call a domestic type, but she's good for our Josh, and they're wild about each other. I've never seen him looking happier."

He glanced over to watch as Cole and his three sons stepped from the back porch and started toward him. The heavenly aroma of roast chicken and corn bread drifted on the air.

Phoebe and Ela had been working all morning. He'd had a peek at the wedding cake before he'd walked outside. It was actually a series of cupcakes arranged on a huge platter to resemble the peaks of mountains, with a bride and groom dressed in hiking gear at the very top.

Sierra and Cheyenne had spent the morning in Paintbrush getting pampered, and were now closeted in the guest room, and giggles could be heard rippling from the upper windows every few minutes. The two had become closer than sisters.

Josh, clad in a denim jacket, walked between Quinn and Jake, who were carrying a bottle of good Irish whiskey and five crystal tumblers, as well as a box of finest cigars.

Cole stepped up beside his father and watched as Quinn began handing around glasses, before filling them.

Big Jim lifted his glass in the air. "If life's a crapshoot, boyo, you've tossed a hell of a winning hand."

"Thanks, Big Jim." Josh couldn't help grinning as he gave a nod toward the headstone. "But I can't take all the credit. There's my ace in the hole."

The others laughed as Big Jim nodded. "Leave it to my Clemmy to get the job done right."

"It was a brilliant move, Dad." Cole slapped his father on the back before tipping up his glass and drinking.

Then he offered a second toast. "Here's to Sierra, the latest addition to our family. You've made a good choice, Josh. I have a hunch that you and your beautiful free spirit are going to make a great team."

"Thanks, Pa."

They sipped while Quinn passed around a box of fine cigars. These they puffed in silence, until Jake proposed yet another toast.

"Here's to my two big brothers. I love them even though they got all weak and mushy when they got bitten by the L word. May some sort of rare immunity save me from the same fate until this plague is wiped from the land."

They were all laughing as they touched glasses and drank. Then, as they contentedly smoked their cigars and indulged in the last of the whiskey, they watched as Reverend Cornell stepped from his car and started toward them.

Cheyenne watched as Sierra stood by the window, speaking softly into the phone. When she disconnected and turned, Cheyenne studied her carefully, looking for traces of tears. She could see none.

"You okay?"

"I'm fine." Sierra drew in a breath. "I was hoping my folks would be more excited about this. But I guess, in a way, I expected them to find an excuse to avoid something they never experienced and don't believe in." She couldn't help laughing. "I'm sure I've disappointed them terribly, and they're wondering where they went wrong."

Cheyenne felt a wave of relief that her new best friend could find the humor in the situation.

"Wait until you give them a grandchild someday. That ought to really rock their world."

Sierra roared with laughter. "I like that idea."

"Rocking their world?"

"Giving them a grandchild someday. But for now..." She grabbed up a large manila envelope. "Come on. Let's find Phoebe and Ela."

Sierra and Cheyenne descended the stairs and found the two older women preparing to head outside.

"Oh. Look at you." Phoebe put a hand to her mouth to stifle her little gasp of pleasure. "Don't you look beautiful."

"Thanks to you." Sierra paused and twirled, to give them the full effect of the simple white gown with handkerchief points that fell to her ankles. "This wouldn't have been possible without you, Phoebe. You know I had no intention of buying a wedding gown. I can't believe you'd be willing to loan me yours."

"I don't know why I kept it all these years. Just sentimental, I guess. And when you said you were going to be married in denims, I just couldn't help myself." She touched a hand to Sierra's tiny waist. "It's hard to believe I was ever this slender in my youth."

"I bet it would still fit," Sierra said.

She turned to Ela before touching a hand to the feather that adorned her long hair. "And this is perfect, since I didn't want to wear a veil."

"The eagle feather suits you." The old woman studied her critically before smiling. "Eagles fly higher than most birds. So do you and Josh. This is a symbol of your flight together."

Sierra felt her eyes fill. "I wanted to give you both something special on my wedding day."

Phoebe chuckled. "The bride is supposed to get gifts, not give them."

Sierra removed the contents of the envelope and handed each of them an enlarged photograph, showing the four women giggling together in the Paintbrush salon, showing off their freshly oiled and pampered hands and feet.

"Oh, look at us." Phoebe turned to Ela with a laugh. "I'll never forget that day as long as I live. It was such fun."

"So was this." Sierra handed them a second photo of Phoebe and Ela standing proudly on the front porch, surrounded by their men. Big Jim and Cole on either side of them, with Quinn, Josh, and Jake behind them. The women looked flushed and happy, the men proud and content.

"I took it the day of the roundup, as Cole was thanking all the wranglers for their hard work."

"Oh, Sierra." Phoebe hugged her. "These are perfect. I'll treasure them."

Old Ela brushed away a tear before saying gruffly, "It's a good likeness."

"I want you to know how much I treasure both of you. You're the mother and grandmother I'd always wished for."

Then, before she embarrassed herself by giving in to the tears that threatened, she linked her arms with theirs and said, "Come on."

With a laugh Cheyenne joined them. "I say it's time we made this girl a legal member of the family."

Josh was laughing with his brothers at something Jake had said when he caught sight of Sierra approaching, surrounded by the flutter of ladies' skirts.

He handed Jake the tumbler of whiskey and moved forward just as the women stepped aside.

Sierra was all he could see. For several long moments all he could do was stare. When he found his voice, he managed to say, "I thought we agreed to keep it simple."

She looked down at the slim column of white silk, swirling around the white satin sandals. "Oh, this old thing?"

She sighed. "Phoebe talked me into trying on her wedding gown. Once I saw it, I knew I had to wear it."

"It's perfect." He touched a hand to her cheek. "You're perfect."

She felt the heat of his touch all the way to her toes. "Will you tell me that in ten years?"

"I intend to tell you that in fifty years."

She closed her eyes and gave a long, deep sigh. "I intend to hold you to that, cowboy."

Josh caught her hand and leaned close to whisper, "Did you pack your hiking gear?"

She nodded. "Did you tell anyone where we're going on our honeymoon?"

"Are you kidding? If the word got around, I'd probably get a call from the ranger station asking me to find some crazy hiker while I was up there."

She touched a hand to his cheek. "One crazy hiker is all you can handle, cowboy."

"Don't I know it?" He paused to draw her close for a long, slow kiss. "Now let's go speak those vows before you get cold feet."

"No cold feet. I'm not afraid of tradition anymore."

"That's good to hear. Baby, I intend to spend the rest of my life making you glad you didn't walk away."

"I'm already glad. Oh, Josh, I love you so much."

Sierra paused to look at the people who had gathered to celebrate. Cole and Phoebe stood beside Big Jim and Ela. Josh's brothers, standing on one side of the preacher, would now be her brothers. And Cheyenne, standing on the other side of the minister, would be the sister she'd always wanted.

Despite their differences, they accepted her as she

was. And actually loved her. Wasn't that amazing? And wasn't that what family did?

Family.

The very thought brought tears to her eyes.

They were now her family, and she was theirs.

Big Jim stepped forward and offered his arm. In an aside he whispered, "Join the preacher, boyo. I'd like the privilege of giving away the bride." He turned to Sierra. "I hope you don't mind?"

"Mind? Oh, Big Jim." She squeezed Josh's hand as he turned away to walk toward the preacher, and then she leaned close to press a kiss on the old man's cheek. "I can't think of anyone else I'd like right here beside me. I hope you'll always be here for me."

"Count on it, sweetheart." As she placed her hand on his arm, he stood a bit taller and closed a hand over hers before proceeding toward the preacher and Josh.

Cole, standing between Phoebe and Ela, was absolutely beaming as Sierra and Josh spoke their vows.

Along with the traditional promises to love and cherish, they surprised the family by adding their own words to the ceremony.

Josh took Sierra's hands in his and said solemnly, "Since I was a boy, the mountain has always been my refuge. But when I went to the mountain to rescue a lost hiker, I never dreamed I'd be the one rescued. Sierra, you saved my life. I give you my solemn vow. As long as these mountains stand, I will love you. And when I leave this life, like the mountains, my love will continue on for all time."

Sierra blinked back tears as she looked into his eyes and said, "I didn't even know I was lost until you found me. I didn't know what real love was until I saw it here, alive in this place. And so I promise you, wherever you go, I'll be right there beside you. I'll be your hiking partner. I'll be your life partner. I want to spend the rest of my life right here with you."

To the cheers of the family, they sealed their vows with a kiss.

Josh looked over at Big Jim, who had long ago encouraged him to follow his heart.

Who would have thought that finding a lost hiker in a frozen wilderness could lead to this—the greatest adventure of his life?

The youngest and wildest of the Conway brothers, Jake swears he'll never settle down—until he meets a beautiful veterinarian who sparks desire in him hotter than a prairie fire.

———◆———

Please turn this page
for a preview of

Jake

Available in February 2013

CHAPTER ONE

Paintbrush, Wyoming
Present Day

Thanks, Jake." The grizzled rancher pumped Jake Conway's hand hard enough to have him wincing. "Figured old Scout here had seen his last sunset. I tried every home remedy I could think of." The old man grinned. "Hated having to give in and pay a vet. You know how it is."

Jake nodded in understanding. Every rancher in these parts knew how to birth a calf, treat a lame horse, and cure the hundred and one things that could go wrong with ranch animals. A veterinarian was called only in extreme situations, or when an animal had to be put down and its owner couldn't bear to do the deed.

"Looks like I'd better start calling you Doc." The old rancher winked at his teenage granddaughter, who was practically swooning over the handsome young veterinarian as though he were a Greek god. Not that he was surprised. The women in his household all sighed over the youngest son of Cole Conway. Word in the tiny town of Paintbrush was that Jake Conway had the same effect on every female there from sixteen to sixty. It had been that way since Jake was twelve or thirteen, and still trailing his older brothers around town, wearing a sweaty T-shirt, dusty denims, and one of his grandfather's cast-off frayed, wide-brimmed cowboy hats. As he'd matured, he'd grown into a tall, muscled cowboy, whose rugged good looks were enhanced by a spill of curly black hair always in need of a trim, and devilish blue eyes that sparkled with unmistakable humor. A big part of his charm was that good-natured, rogue smile. Women just gravitated to him like bees to honey.

"I guess what I've heard around town is the truth. You're some kind of miracle worker."

"Not me. I've got miracle drugs." Jake smiled and patted his pocket before tucking away the syringe and vial. "Just doing my job, Will."

"The way I see it, thanks to that fancy vet school in Michigan, you're doing it even better'n old Doc Hunger did. And that's saying something."

Jake couldn't hide his pleasure at the compliment. It meant the world to him that the ranchers accepted him without question. Not an easy task when they still thought of the youngest Conway son as a lightweight compared with his father, grandfather, and two older brothers.

At his truck, the two men shook hands again before Jake climbed inside and started toward home.

As he drove along the dusty road, he played back his phone messages. One was from Phoebe, their housekeeper, reminding him that Ela was baking her famous corn bread to go with the ham she put in the oven and he'd better not be late.

His mouth watered as he played the second message,

this one from his brother Quinn, reminding him of dinner Saturday night as a surprise for his wife's birthday, and that if Cheyenne had so much as an inkling of what was planned, he'd know it was all Jake's fault for having a big mouth.

Jake was still grinning as the third message began. A woman's breathy voice, sounding either stressed or annoyed.

"This is Meg Stanford. I'm at my father's ranch to dispose of his estate, and there's a colt out in the barn that appears to be lame. I'm not sure there's anything you can do for it, but I'd like you to…" The voice paused for so long, Jake thought the call may have been interrupted. But then the message continued: "…do whatever it is you do with animals that are beyond help."

Unsure of what he'd heard, he played the message a second time before making a sharp U-turn and heading toward the Stanford ranch.

As he drew near, it occurred to Jake that though Porter Stanford had been his family's nearest neighbor, he'd never before set foot on the property. He and his brothers had been warned when they were just boys that they were to stay clear of the rancher, whose volatile temper was well-known around these parts.

In the town of Paintbrush gossip spread quicker than a prairie fire, and the juicy tales about Porter Stanford before his sudden death days ago had all been negative. Folks around these parts just shook their heads over his hair-trigger temper, the hellish life his two ex-wives had endured at his hands, all of which they'd been eager to share with anyone who would listen, and the fact that his third wife had been young enough to be his granddaughter. She'd died two years ago of a brain hemorrhage, leaving Porter with a young son.

Jake wondered about the woman claiming to be Porter's daughter. He could vaguely recall hearing about a wild child who matched her father in looks and temperament. But that was years ago, before Porter's very public first divorce, when she and her mother, Virginia, had taken themselves off to parts unknown.

Jake turned his truck onto the lane that led to the rustic ranch house. Nestled on a bluff, the house overlooked some of the richest grazing land in the territory. Now in early spring, the land was just turning green and was dotted with buds of Indian paintbrush and towering cottonwood. No wonder Porter Stanford had thought of himself as a king and all of Wyoming as his fiefdom. Maybe, Jake thought with sudden insight, that was another reason why Stanford had a particular dislike of the Conway family. Not only were they his nearest neighbors, but they owned all the land around him, leaving him unable to expand his kingdom.

Jake followed the curving driveway to the back door of the house and stepped out of his truck. A sleek candy-apple-red rental car was parked beside the porch.

He climbed the wide porch steps and knocked.

A sexy female voice called, "Come in."

He stepped into a kitchen offering a spectacular view of the Tetons in the distance. Finding no one there, he stepped through the open doorway into a massive great room, where a woman was just walking toward him, carrying a cardboard box that was bigger than she.

"Hello." Though he couldn't see the face, the view

from the waist down was enticing. A tiny waist and long, long legs encased in narrow denims.

"Oh. Hello. If you want to take a look at the farm implements, you may as well start tagging the things out in the second barn."

"You're planning an auction?"

She peered around the box. "Aren't you from the auction house?"

"No. Sorry. I'm the vet. Here. Let me help you." He took the box from her hands. "Where do you want this?"

"The kitchen table will be fine." She led the way and Jake followed.

As he set down the box, he shot her a grin. "What've you got in there? A safe?"

She sighed. "Sorry. I should have warned you. I found several locked metal boxes in an upstairs room and thought I'd bring them down before opening them." She offered her hand. "I'm Meg Stanford."

Jake accepted her handshake and took the moment to study her. She had her father's fiery hair, pinned back into a ponytail, and green eyes the color of prairie grass.

"Jake Conway." He was fascinated by her lips. Soft, pursed lips that, though bare of makeup, were absolutely enticing. "I'm sorry about your loss."

"Thank you." She spoke the words in a flat, unemotional tone. "You said you're the vet. I was expecting Dr. Hunger."

"He retired. His service directs his calls to me."

"I see." She nodded toward the door. "I'll take you to the barn."

Jake trailed behind her, enjoying the view of her trim backside in the shiny, new denims. They were so crisp they looked as though they'd just come off a store rack, as did the cotton shirt buttoned clear to her throat and tucked precisely into the waistband.

He glanced at her feet. Even the sneakers were brand-new, though they wouldn't remain that way once she stepped into the barn.

"Where are you from?"

She paused, her hand on the barn door. "Washington."

"As in Spokane?"

She smiled. "As in D.C."

"You're a long way from home. What do you do there?"

"I'm a lawyer."

His smile deepened. "That explains the new duds. I'd never mistake you for a rancher."

That brought a smile, transforming her face from pretty to gorgeous. "My usual wardrobe runs to tailored suits and heels. I figured I'd need something more practical for the week I'll be here."

"A week?"

She nodded. "My vacation time. I hadn't expected to spend it quite this way. I haven't been back to this place since I was a kid. I honestly never expected to see it again."

She lowered her voice. "As you can imagine, I've forgotten more than I can remember about ranch animals. The colt has a pronounced limp. I thought I'd ask a vet to take a look and advise me as to the best way to... deal with it." Her voice lowered to a near-whisper, as though sharing state secrets. "If you have to euthanize the colt, I'd appreciate it if you would offer to take it with you, rather than do it here. There's the boy..." When she faltered, Jake waited until she composed herself. "My father's sudden death wasn't my only surprise. I've learned that I have a half brother. I'm not sure of his birth-day, but I'm guessing he's about seven. I suspect that he was alone here when our father had his heart attack. That may be why he doesn't speak...at least not to me. But he seems really attached to the colt. That's why"—she stared at the ground—"I'd rather not add to the boy's suffering."

"All right." Jake nodded toward the door. "Let's have a look."

She opened the barn door and led the way to a stall. As Jake's eyes adjusted to the gloom, he could see the colt lying in the straw, its head cradled in the lap of a blond, shaggy-haired boy in dirty denims and an even dirtier T-shirt.

Meg's tone was cautious. "Cory, this is Dr. Conway. I asked him to take a look at your colt."

"Hey, Cory." Jake knelt beside the boy and ran a hand gently over the colt's forelock. "Does your horse have a name?"

The boy merely stared at him.

"Can your horse stand?"

Cory shuffled out from under the horse's head and got to his feet before tugging gently on the animal's mane.

The colt scrambled to its feet.

Jake pointed toward the door. "Would you mind leading him outside?"

Without a word the boy led the horse out into the sunshine, with Jake and Meg following.

The animal's limp, Jake noted, was pronounced, as Meg had said.

He watched as the boy led the colt in a wide circle. When they were close, Jake ran a hand along the animal's neck. "He's a real beauty."

The faintest flicker of a smile touched the boy's eyes before he looked away.

"Has he always had this limp, or is it a recent injury?"

The boy shrugged.

Jake decided to try again. "Was he born with this problem, Cory?"

The boy shook his head.

"So, this happened recently?"

"Yeah." The boy sighed, as though the weight of the world rested on his shoulders.

"Okay. It's a start." Relieved that the boy could speak, Jake glanced toward Meg, who seemed equally relieved.

Jake bent to the animal's leg and began gently probing. When he touched one particular spot, the colt flattened its ears and sidestepped.

"Tender. Did your horse take a fall?"

"No." The boy shook his head.

"Was he hit by something?"

The boy shrugged his thin shoulders.

"Maybe by a stone thrown by a truck?"

Seeing that the boy didn't intend to reply, he added, "Maybe he was attacked by a flying saucer?"

That had Cory smiling before he ducked his head.

Jake glanced at Meg, who stood with her arms crossed, her foot tapping impatiently.

"All right. Let's try something else. Walk him again, Cory."

As the boy did so, Jake moved along beside the colt and probed not only the leg but also the animal's underbelly as he took each step.

When he straightened, Meg asked in a low voice, "Will you be able to take him with you?"

Jake shrugged. "I'd like to try treating him here."

"Treating? I thought—" She looked at Cory, then away before whispering, "I thought real vets shot a horse when it was lame."

"I guess that was the treatment of choice back when women didn't have the vote, and ranchers chewed tobacco and played poker in the town saloon. Nowadays, ma'am," he added in his best drawl, "you wouldn't believe the miracle drugs we have. Aspirin, penicillin. Why there are even drugs with great big names that a hick like me can't pronounce. But they do the job."

She had a rich, throaty laugh. "I guess I deserved that. All right, Dr. Conway. I'll leave you to your patient. I have work to do in the house."

When she walked away, Jake watched until she'd climbed the steps. Turning, he saw the boy staring at him.

He winked. "You've got a pretty sister, Cory."

The boy hung his head and absently patted the colt.

Jake touched a hand to the boy's shoulder. "I'm sorry about the loss of your dad."

Cory glanced up at him. There was an eager, almost hungry look in his eyes. "Did you know him?"

Jake shook his head. "Not really. I knew who he was, and saw him in town a time or two, but other than that, he was a stranger. I guess he kept to himself a lot."

The eager look in the boy's eyes was gone in the instant before he looked away. "Yeah."

After a pronounced silence, Jake sighed. "While you take this little guy back to the stall, I'll get my bag of tricks."

He walked away and retrieved his supplies from his truck.

When he returned, he took his time, examining the colt while trying to find ways to engage the boy in conversation.

"How old are you, Cory?"

"Seven." His gaze followed every movement of Jake's fingers as he touched and probed the colt's leg.

"That would make you a second grader?"

The boy shrugged. "Don't go to school."

"Yeah. I never did either, when I was your age. Too far to town." He looked over. "So, you're homeschooled. Did your dad teach you?"

Another shrug. "Now that I can read, I get the lessons out of books and do my class assignments online."

"Who checks your homework?"

"I scan it in and send it to the teacher assigned to me."

"Did anybody live here on the ranch with you and your dad?"

"Yancy. But he doesn't live here. He stays in the bunkhouse."

Jake heard the warmth in the boy's tone and nodded. He'd heard that Yancy Jessup had taken over some of the ranch duties after Porter's young wife died. Yancy was one of the last of a dying breed. A cowboy with no desire to own his own spread. An old man who preferred living in a bunkhouse with other cowboys. A drifter who loved tending other rancher's herds, until the itch to move on became too great. Yancy Jessup had worked ranches all over Montana and Wyoming, and his work was universally praised. Nobody had ever had a bad word to say about him.

"I suppose Yancy's up in the hills with the herd?"

"Yeah."

"Does he know about your dad?"

The boy looked stricken, and Jake realized that the cowboy had no idea that his boss had passed away.

Jake pulled out his cell phone. "Give me his number, and I'll see that your sister calls him as soon as I'm finished here."

As Cory spoke the numbers, Jake programmed them into his phone. "I'd call Yancy myself, but I think this call should come from a family member." He looked over. "Do you have a cell phone?"

Cory nodded.

"Good. While I'm thinking about it, why don't I give you my number? That way, if you need me, just call."

He spoke the numbers and watched as Cory punched them into his phone. "Now give me yours." Jake added the numbers to his phone as Cory said them aloud.

For the next hour, while Cory soothed the colt, Jake applied ointment and wrapped the injured leg. When he was finished, he closed his bag and got to his feet.

"That's the best I can do for now. I'll look in on him tomorrow and see if he's improving."

The boy kept an arm around the colt's neck. "His name is Shadow."

Jake paused. "That's a good name. And you're a good friend to Shadow, Cory. I can see that he trusts you. Now I'd better report to your sister." He offered his hand. "Thanks for your help."

The boy looked surprised before giving him an awkward handshake.

With a thoughtful look Jake turned and made his way from the barn.

It was plain that the boy was feeling scared and confused. And he was probably in a lot of pain. And why not? In a matter of days he'd lost his father, gained a sister who was a stranger to him, and had to watch his colt going lame. It must seem as though his whole world had toppled. To make matters worse, his future would be decided by a woman who apparently couldn't wait to get away from here and back to the life she'd left behind. The fact that she'd already contacted an auction firm attested to that fact.

But Cory Stanford wasn't the only person in pain. His sister was, too. She may have spent her childhood on this ranch, but after so many years away she had become a stranger in a strange land. That city woman looked as out of place as a designer dress at a rodeo.

A week. Did she actually believe she could dispose of a ranch, a herd, and an entire way of life in the time it took to vacation at some tropical beach?

Jake paused on the porch and watched through the screen door as Meg struggled to pry open a metal box with a rusty screwdriver. Several other metal boxes, empty and misshapen from being forced, littered the floor around her feet.

Taking a deep breath, he knocked and stepped inside.

"Would you like a hand with that?"

Meg's head came up sharply. "Sorry. You startled me. I'd appreciate any help you can give." She handed him the screwdriver. "There are probably dozens of tools around here, if I knew where to look."

Jake nodded toward the door. "Probably the equipment barn, up the hill. That's the usual place to store tools."

"Of course. I'll check it out later." She gathered up a

pile of papers and documents, clutching them to her chest. "It looks as though lately my father's filing system was a lot like his life—careless. When I was a kid, he never would have dreamed of just throwing things into boxes with no apparent rhyme or reason."

"Maybe, as you sort through them, you'll discover some sort of order to them."

"Not likely." She deposited the papers on the kitchen counter before returning to stand beside him as he pried open the metal box. Once the lid was forced open, a haphazard stack of papers spilled out, littering the table-top.

"See what I mean?" She eyed the papers before turning to Jake. "What have you decided about the colt?"

"There's a small wound with swelling and redness that suggests infection. I've given him an antibiotic and wrapped the wound. I'll look in on him tomorrow and see if there's any improvement. If there is, I'll continue the treatment. If not, I'll try something else."

"I'm glad you got Cory to speak to you. From his reaction to me, I was really afraid he might be deaf and mute."

"He hadn't spoken at all?"

"Not to me. But he opened up to you right away."

Jake gave her one of his roguish smiles. "All part of my charm. Kids and animals just can't resist me."

She glanced at his ring finger. "I see that you can't make the same claim about women."

Seeing the direction of her gaze he chuckled. "It's been tough, but so far I've managed to resist their advances." He winked. "I keep a club in my truck, just in case I run into a really aggressive female who won't take no for an answer."

He was rewarded with her deep, throaty chuckle, which transformed her from pretty to absolutely gorgeous.

"Thanks for my laugh of the day. I needed it." She crossed her arms over her chest and tapped a nervous foot. "I'm at a loss as to what to do about Cory. And I get the distinct impression that he isn't about to give me any help at all."

"He'll come around. You've already learned that he can talk."

"To you."

Jake nodded. "Love and fear are pretty compelling motivators."

"Love and fear?"

"He loves that colt. Add to that the fact that he's lost his mother and father. I'm betting he's convinced that all the really important things in his life are going to be taken away from him."

"I'm his half sister, not his enemy."

"He doesn't know that. He knows only that another adult has come along to determine his fate."

"I hadn't thought of that." She frowned. "I guess I've been so busy dealing with my own feelings, I was overlooking all the things he must be going through."

"Does he have any family other than you? Grandparents? Aunts?"

Meg's lips turned into a pretty pout before she chewed her lower lip. "I can try asking him now that I know he can speak. So far I've found no documentation of any other family. That's why I'm so desperate to find all my father's legal documents. I have a frightened little boy, a sprawling ranch, and who knows how many debts I might encounter, and I don't have a clue what to do with any of them."

"I hate to add to your burden." Jake saw the way her eyes narrowed slightly. "Cory tells me that there's a wrangler up in the hills with your father's herd. His name is Yancy Jessup. A good man. Folks around here will tell you that he's someone you can trust. But right now, he doesn't even know that your father has passed away." He handed over his cell phone. "Cory gave me Yancy's number. I think you'd better give him a call."

She plucked a cell phone from her pocket and deftly added Yancy's name and number before extending her hand. "I'll call him. Thank you. I appreciate your help."

"You're welcome." Jake accepted her handshake, while keeping his gaze steady on hers.

She'd probably intended it to be a purely businesslike handshake, but it had become something else entirely. At least for Jake.

Was she feeling that same searing pulse of heat that he was? Or the icy fingers along her spine?

He couldn't help smiling at the startled look that came into her eyes before she removed her hand from his and stared pointedly at the floor.

It would seem that she and Cory shared another family trait. Neither of them was very good at hiding their feelings.

With a last look at her bowed head Jake turned away.

With his hand on the door he paused. "My family's ranch is just over those hills. We're your nearest neighbor."

She shot him a startled look. "The Conway ranch? Of course. Jake Conway. I was a little distracted when you introduced yourself."

His smile grew. "I gave my cell phone number to Cory. So if you need anything, just call."

As he made his way to his truck, he glanced toward the barn and felt a wave of sympathy for the boy caught up in all of this. He knew what it was to lose a parent at a very young age, and he could clearly recall the pain and confusion of those early days as he'd struggled with grief and fear of the unknown, and an unreasonable sense of loss and emptiness that had never gone away.

As his truck ate up the miles to his home, Jake decided that he would make the Stanford ranch his first stop in the morning. Not just to soothe a frightened little boy's fears, he realized, but also to indulge himself with another glimpse of the boy's gorgeous, pouty-lipped sister.

The thought of tasting those lips ought to be enough to fuel his dreams all through the night.

As the oldest of the Conway brothers, Quinn's only concern is protecting his family and their land. But when beautiful Cheyenne O'Brien's ranch is plagued by a series of "accidents," Quinn will risk his heart—and his very life—to keep her safe…

Please turn this page for a preview of

Quinn

Available now

CHAPTER THREE

———◆———

Quinn framed the wolf in his long-range viewfinder and snapped off a couple of quick photos. The male's coat, thick and shaggy, was matted with snow from the blizzard that had been raging now for three days.

After Quinn had left the ranch and returned to the mountain, it had taken considerable skill to locate the pack, despite the homing device implanted in the male. Cut off from their den by the storm and with the alpha female about to give birth, the pack had hunkered down in the shelter of some rocks near the top of a nearby hill. Since there'd been no sighting of the female, Quinn was fairly certain there would be a litter of pups before morning. That would create a problem for the leader of the pack, whose hunting ground had been narrowed considerably by the unexpected spring snowstorm. The alpha male would have to provide food and shelter for his pack, and all would have to wait out the storm before returning to their den.

Quinn saw the male's attention fixed on something in the distance. Using his binoculars, Quinn studied the terrain. When he spied a small herd of deer nearly hidden in a stand of trees, he understood what had snagged the wolf's interest.

The springtime blizzard had caught all of nature by surprise, it would seem. As Quinn watched, a doe dropped her newborn into the snow and began licking it clean of afterbirth.

Sadly, the doe and her fawn, in such a vulnerable state, would be the perfect mark for a hungry pack of wolves desperate for food during their own confinement.

The male wolf took up a predator position, dropping low as he crept slowly up the hill until he reached the very peak. For a moment he remained as still as a statue, gazing into the distance.

Quinn watched, transfixed. Even though he knew this would end in the bloody death of a helpless newborn fawn, he also knew that it would mean the difference between life and death for the pack of wolves unable to go forward until their own newborns were strong enough to travel. Their strength, their survival, depended upon sustenance. The female, too weak at the moment to hunt, would trust her leader to provide fresh meat while she nursed her young.

Quinn felt again the familiar thrill as he saw the alpha male rise up and begin to run full speed across the rim of the hill. The raw power, the fierce determination of this animal, never failed to touch a chord deep inside him.

The wolf dipped below the rim of the hill and was lost from sight.

Quinn experienced a rush of annoyance. He wanted to record the kill for his journal. But something had caused the wolf to veer off-course at the last moment. Snatching up his camera, Quinn was on his feet, racing up the hill, half-blinded by the curtain of snow that stung his face like shrapnel.

He was halfway up the hill when he heard the unmistakable sound of a rifle shot echo and reecho across the hills. It reverberated in his chest like a thunderous pulse.

Heart pounding, he ran full speed the rest of the distance.

When he came to the spot where the male had fallen, Quinn stared at the crimson snow, the beautiful body now silent and still, and felt a mingling of pain and rage rising up inside, clogging his throat, tightening a band around his heart until he had to struggle for each breath.

How dare anyone end such a magnificent life. Why?

He studied the prints left in the snow made by a single horse.

Far off in the distance, barely visible through the falling snow, was a tiny beam of light.

An isolated ranch house, it would seem.

Clouds scudded across the rising moon, leaving the countryside in near darkness.

Quinn knew that he needed to return to his campsite soon and settle in for the night or risk freezing. But he was determined to confront the rancher who had just robbed Quinn's pack of its leader. A cruel act that had not only left the vulnerable female and her newborn pups without a guardian but had also cut short the scholarly research that had consumed the past five years of Quinn's life.

With a heavy heart he turned away, knowing that by morning scavengers would have swept the area clean of any trace of carnage. It was the way of nature.

Even if he were so inclined, there wasn't time to dispose of the wolf's body. Quinn needed to follow the tracks in the snow before the storm obliterated them completely. Already the surrounding countryside had fallen under the mantle of darkness.

He returned to his campsite and began to pack up his meager supplies. As he did so, anger rose up like bile, burning the back of his throat and eyes.

All attempts at scholarly disinterest were swept away in a tide of fury at the loss of the wolf Quinn had come to love.

He could no longer hide behind a professional wall of anonymity.

This was personal.

He needed, for his own satisfaction, to confront the rancher who had snuffed out the life of the creature that had consumed every minute of every day of his life for the past five years.

As he shouldered his supplies and began the trek in the darkness, he found his thoughts turning to his father. There was no comparison between this despicable act and the horrible trauma Cole had suffered at losing Seraphine. Still, the loss was so deeply felt that it connected Quinn to Cole Conway in a way that nothing else ever had.

Was this how Cole had felt when he'd faced the greatest loss of his life? Had he been swamped with this helpless, hopeless sense that everything that he'd worked for had just been swept away by some cruel whim of fate?

Cole had been, in those early days, inconsolable. A man so grief stricken, even the love for his children and his father, Big Jim, hadn't been able to lift him out of the depths of hell. Cole's only coping mechanism had been to throw himself into every hard, physically demanding chore he could find around the ranch, many of which would have broken a less determined man.

Right this minute, Quinn would welcome any challenge that would lift him out of his own private hell.

Quinn moved through the waist-high drifts, keeping the light of the distant ranch house always in his sight.

Someone would answer for this vicious deed.

Someone would pay.

As Quinn drew close enough to peer through the falling snow, he could make out the sprawling ranch house and, some distance away, the first of several barns and outbuildings.

He was turning toward the house when he caught the glint of light in the barn. Pausing just outside the open door, he watched the rancher forking hay into a stall, where a horse stomped, blowing and snorting, as though winding down from a hard ride. The snow that coated the rancher's parka and wide-brimmed hat was further proof that he'd just retreated from the blizzard that raged beyond these walls.

Quinn stepped inside, holding his rifle loosely at his side. It wasn't his intention to threaten the rancher, merely to confront him. But right this minute, Quinn relished the thought of a good knock-down, drag-out fight. For one tiny instant he was that helpless boy again, confronting the rancher Porter Stanford as he'd gloated over the needless deaths of a wolf and her pups. Then Quinn snapped back to the present, though the thought of that long-ago scene had his voice lowering to a growl.

"I'm tracking a wolf-hating rancher. Looks like I found him."

The figure whirled.

Quinn continued to keep his rifle pointed at the ground, though his finger tightened reflexively on the trigger when he caught the glint of metal as the rancher lifted the pitchfork in a menacing gesture.

"Who the hell do you think you are?"

Quinn blinked. The voice didn't match the image he'd had of a tough Wyoming rancher. It was obviously female. Soft. Throaty. Breathless, as though she'd been running hard.

"My name is Quinn Conway. My spread's about fifty miles east of here. And you'd be . . . ?"

"Don't act coy with me. You know who I am. You're trespassing on my land. I'll give you one minute to turn tail and leave, or you'll answer to this."

Quinn realized that, though her left hand continued to hold the pitchfork aloft, her right hand had dipped into the pocket of her parka and she was holding a very small, very shiny pistol aimed at his chest.

He lifted a hand, palm up. "I didn't come here to hurt you."

"Oh, sure. That's why you burst into my barn holding a rifle?"

"I'm here to get some answers."

"Sorry. I'm fresh out." She tossed aside the pitchfork and in one quick motion pocketed the pistol and grabbed a rifle leaning against the wall. Taking careful aim, she hissed, "Now get, whoever you are. And tell Deke I have no intention of changing my mind. If he thinks he can send some bully—"

Quinn reacted so quickly she didn't have time to blink. He kicked aside her rifle, sending it flying into the air. Before it landed in the hay, he'd leaped at her, taking her down and pinning her arms and legs with such force beneath him that she was helpless to move anything except her head.

She let loose with a stream of oaths that would have withered a seasoned cowboy. That merely reinforced Quinn's determination to pin her down until her fury ran its course.

In the process, his own anger seemed to intensify. He'd come here to confront a cold-blooded wolf killer. What he'd found was a crazy woman.

"Let me up." Teeth clenched, she bucked and shuddered with impotent rage.

"Not until…" His breath was coming hard and fast and he found himself having to use every ounce of his strength to keep her pinned. In the process, he became aware of the soft curves beneath the parka, and the fresh, clean evergreen scent of her hair and clothes. "…you agree to give me some answers."

"Go to hell."

Damn her. He wanted to end this tussle, but she wasn't going to make it easy for him. And the longer he lay on top of her, the more aware he became of the woman and less of the enemy he'd come here to confront. "You're not going to cooperate?"

When she made no response, he dug in, using his size and weight to intimidate. "You shot a wolf out there on the trail. I want to know why."

"A wolf?" She stopped fighting him.

He absorbed a small measure of relief that she seemed to be relenting.

She was clearly out of breath. "What business is this of yours?"

"That wolf is my business."

He saw her eyes go wide. "This is really about the wolf?"

"What did you think it was about?"

He saw the way she was studying him beneath half-lowered lashes and realized how he must look, hair wild and tangled, his face heavily bearded from his days on the trail.

He decided to take a calculated risk. Moving quickly, he got to his feet and held out a hand.

Ignoring his offer of help, she rolled aside and got her bearings before turning to face him.

Her hand went to the pocket where she'd stowed her pistol but didn't dip inside, remaining instead where he could see it.

"Let's start over." He fought to keep the anger from his voice. "My name is Quinn Conway. I study the life cycle of wolves. I was tracking my pack when the alpha male was shot. I followed the shooter here. Now I want to know why a rancher would kill a wolf that was only hunting food for his pack."

When she held her silence, he arched a brow. "It's your turn to introduce yourself and say... 'My name is... I shot the wolf because...'"

"My name isn't important, but the wolf is. It was threatening my herd. That's what wolves do. And what smart ranchers do is shoot them before they can rip open a helpless calf."

"My wolf was stalking a herd of deer."

"Your wolf?" She eyed him suspiciously. "I didn't realize he was a pet."

"He isn't. Wasn't," Quinn corrected. "He was, in fact, the object of years of scholarly research."

"Uh-huh." She shot him a look guaranteed to freeze a man's heart at a hundred paces. "I wouldn't know anything about scholarly research, but common sense told me he was about to take out one of my calves. And I got him before he could get to my herd. Now if you don't mind..." She turned away.

Before she could reach for her rifle Quinn caught her arm. "I don't believe you. I saw the herd of deer."

She yanked herself free of his grasp. "I don't give a damn what you believe. I know what I saw."

"Prove it."

Her head came up sharply. "I don't have to prove anything to you."

"You already have. The fact that you're a liar."

Her eyes narrowed on him. "Look. I don't care what you call me. I know what I saw."

But even as she spoke, he could see the wheels turning as she cast a glance at the snow swirling in the darkness just beyond the barn. Neither of them was eager to face the blizzard. But neither of them was willing to concede that fact.

She took in a breath. "You can saddle up the mare over there."

Without another word she turned away and began saddling the big roan stallion she'd been tending.

Quinn crossed to the other stall and began saddling the spotted mare.

When both horses were saddled and ready, Quinn and the woman moved out single file, into the stinging snow and darkness of night.

Each of them was carrying a rifle.

Neither of them was willing to give an inch until this trek was over.

In Quinn's mind, it would end with this crazy woman admitting her mistake and apologizing for the wrong she'd done. Not that it would make anything right. The wolf would still be dead and his pack left without a leader. But for Quinn this was all about justice.

Once again he flashed back to that incident in his boyhood. He hadn't been able to do anything about that female wolf and her pups. But things were different now. This time, he would have the satisfaction of knowing he'd done all he could to persuade at least one angry rancher to give the wolves of this world a fighting chance to survive.

THE DISH

Where authors give you the inside scoop!

♥ ♥ ♥ ♥ ♥ ♥ ♥ ♥ ♥ ♥ ♥ ♥ ♥ ♥ ♥ ♥ ♥

From the desk of R.C. Ryan

Dear Reader,

When my daughter-in-law Patty came home from her first hike of the Grand Canyon, she was high on the beauty and majesty of the mountains for months. Since then, it has become her annual pilgrimage—one that fuels her dreams, and feeds my writer's imagination. I've wanted to create a character with the same passion for the mountains that Patty has for a long time, someone who experiences the same awe, freedom, and peace that she does just by being in eyesight of them. And with JOSH, I think I finally have.

Josh Conway, the hero of the second book in my Wyoming Sky series, is truly a hero in every sense of the word. He's a man who rescues people who've lost their way on the mountain he loves in all kinds of weather. There's just something about a guy who would risk his own safety, his very life, to help others, that is so appealing to me. To add to Josh's appeal, he's a hard-working rancher and a sexy cowboy—an irresistible combination. Not to mention that he loves a challenge.

Enter Sierra Moore. Sierra is a photographer who comes to the Grand Tetons in Wyoming to shoot photographs of a storm. At least that's what she'll admit to. But there's a mystery behind that beautiful smile. She's come to the mountains to disappear for a while, and being rescued—even if it is by a ruggedly handsome cowboy—is the last thing she needs or wants.

But when danger rears its ugly head, and Sierra's life is threatened, she and Josh must call on every bit of strength and courage they possess in order to survive. Yet an even greater test of their strength will be the courage to commit to a lifetime together.

I hope you enjoy JOSH!

R. C. Ryan

RyanLangan.com

♥ ♥ ♥ ♥ ♥ ♥ ♥ ♥ ♥ ♥ ♥ ♥ ♥ ♥

From the desk of Anna Campbell

Dear Reader,

Wow! I'm so excited that my first historical romance with Grand Central Publishing has hit the shelves (and the e-waves!). I hope you enjoy reading SEVEN NIGHTS IN A ROGUE'S BED as much as I enjoyed writing it. Not only is this my first book for GCP, but it's also the first book in my very first series, the Sons of Sin. Perhaps I should smash a bottle of champagne over my copy of SEVEN NIGHTS to launch it in appropriate style.

Hmm, having second thoughts here. Much better, I've decided, to read the book and drink the champagne!

Do you like fairy-tale romance? I love stories based on Cinderella or Sleeping Beauty or some other mythical hero or heroine. SEVEN NIGHTS IN A ROGUE'S BED is a dyed-in-the-wool Beauty and the Beast retelling. To me, this is the ultimate romantic fairy tale. The hero starts out as a monster, but when he falls in love, the fragments of goodness in his tortured soul multiply until he becomes a gallant prince (or, in this case, a viscount, but who's counting?). Beauty and the Beast is at heart about the transformative power of true love—what more powerful theme for a romance writer to explore?

Jonas Merrick, the Beast in SEVEN NIGHTS IN A ROGUE'S BED, is a scarred recluse who has learned through hard and painful experience to mistrust a hostile world. When the book opens, he's a rogue indeed. But meeting our heroine conspires to turn him into a genuine, if at first reluctant, hero worthy of his blissfully happy ending.

Another thing I love about Beauty and the Beast is that the heroine is more proactive than some other mythological girls. For a start, she stays awake throughout! Like Beauty, Sidonie Forsythe places herself in the Beast's power to save someone she loves, her reckless older sister, Roberta. Sidonie's dread when she meets brooding, enigmatic Jonas Merrick swiftly turns to fascination—but even as they fall in love, Sidonie's secret threatens to destroy Jonas and any chance of happiness for this Regency Beauty and the Beast.

I adore high-stakes stories where I wonder if the lovers can ever overcome what seem to be insurmountable barriers between them. In SEVEN NIGHTS IN A ROGUE'S BED, Jonas and Sidonie have to triumph over the bitter legacy of the past and conquer present dangers to achieve their happily-ever-after. Definitely major learning curves for our hero and heroine!

This story is a journey from darkness to light, and it allowed me to play with so many classic romance themes.

Redemption. A touch of the gothic. The steadfast, courageous heroine. The dark, tormented hero. The clash of two powerful personalities as they resist overwhelming passion. Secrets and revelations. Self-sacrifice and risk. Revenge and justice. You know, all the big stuff!

If you'd like to find out more about SEVEN NIGHTS IN A ROGUE'S BED and the Sons of Sin series, please visit my website: www.annacampbell.info. And in the meantime, happy reading!

Best wishes,

Anna Campbell

♥ ♥ ♥ ♥ ♥ ♥ ♥ ♥ ♥ ♥ ♥ ♥ ♥ ♥ ♥

From the desk of Katie Lane

Dear Reader,

One of my favorite things to do during the holidays is to read *The Night Before Christmas*. So I thought it would be fun to tell you about my new romance, HUNK FOR THE HOLIDAYS, by making up my own version of the classic.

> 'Twas four days before Christmas, and our heroine, Cassie,
> Is ready for her office party, looking red hot and sassy.
> When what to her wondering eyes should she see
> But the escort she hired standing next to her tree?
> His eyes how they twinkle, his dimples so cute,
> He has a smile that melts, a great body to boot.

There's only one problem: James is as controlling as Cass,
But she forgives him this flaw, when she gets a good look
    at his ass.
He goes straight to work at seducing his date,
And by the end of the evening, Cass is ready to mate.
Not to ruin the story, all I will say,
Is that James will be smiling when Cass gets her way.
Mixed in with their romance will be plenty of reason
For you to enjoy the fun of the season.
Caroling, shopping, and holiday baking,
A humorous great-aunt and her attempts at match making.
A perfect book to cozy up with all the way through December,
HUNK FOR THE HOLIDAYS will be out in September.
For now I will end by wishing you peace, love, and laughter.
And, of course, the best gift of all ... a happily-ever-after!

Katie Jane

♥ ♥ ♥ ♥ ♥ ♥ ♥ ♥ ♥ ♥ ♥ ♥ ♥ ♥

From the desk of Hope Ramsay

Dear Reader,

I love Christmas, but I have to say that trying to write a
holiday-themed book in the middle of a long, hot summer
is not exactly easy. It was hard to stay in the holiday
mood when my nonwriting time was spent weeding my
perennials border, watching baseball, and working on my
golf short game.

So how does an author get herself into the holiday mood in the middle of July?

She hauls out her iPod and plays Christmas music from sunup to sundown.

My husband was ready to strangle me, but all that Christmas music did the trick. And in the end, it was just one song that helped me find my holiday spirit.

The song is "The Longest Night," written by singer-songwriter Peter Mayer, a song that isn't quite a Christmas song. It's about the winter solstice. The lyrics are all about hope, even in the darkest hour. In the punchline, the songwriter gives a tiny nod to the meaning of Christmas when he says, "Maybe light itself is born in the longest night."

When I finished LAST CHANCE CHRISTMAS, I realized that this theme of light and dark runs through it like a river. My heroine is a war photographer, who literally sees the world as a battle between light and dark. When she arrives in Last Chance, she's troubled and alone, and the darkness is about to overwhelm her.

But of course, that doesn't last long after she meets Stone Rhodes, the chief of police and a man who is about as Grinch-like as they come. But as the saying goes, sometimes the only way to get yourself out of a funk is to help someone else. And when Stone does that, he manages to spark a very hot and bright light in the dead of winter.

I hope you love reading Stone and Lark's story as much as I did writing it.

Y'all have a blessed holiday, now, you hear?

Hope Ramsay

Find out more about Forever Romance!

Visit us at
www.hachettebookgroup.com/publishing_forever.aspx

Find us on Facebook
http://www.facebook.com/ForeverRomance

Follow us on Twitter
http://twitter.com/ForeverRomance

NEW AND UPCOMING TITLES

Each month we feature our new titles
and reader favorites.

CONTESTS AND GIVEAWAYS

We give away galleys, autographed copies,
and all kinds of exclusive items.

AUTHOR INFO

You'll find bios, articles, and links to personal websites
for all your favorite authors—and so much more.

GET SOCIAL

Connect with your favorite authors, editors, and
other Forever fans, and share what's important to you.

THE BUZZ

Sign up for our monthly romance newsletter,
and be the first to read all about it.